GORDON KEITH

BOOKS BY
THOMAS NELSON PAGE

IN OLE VIRGINIA. Marse Chan, and other Stories.

Cameo Edition. With an etching by W. L. Sheppard.

Illustrated Edition. With 24 full-page illustrations by A. B. Frost, Howard Pyle, W. T. Smedley, C. S. Reinhart, A. Castaigne, and B. West Clinedinst.

RED ROCK. A Chronicle of Reconstruction. Illustrated by B. West Clinedinst.

THE OLD GENTLEMAN OF THE BLACK STOCK. With 8 full-page colored illustrations by H. C. Christy.

SANTA CLAUS'S PARTNER. With 8 full-page colored illustrations by W. Glackens.

ON NEWFOUND RIVER: A STORY.

PASTIME STORIES. Illustrated by A. B. Frost.

THE BURIAL OF THE GUNS.

ELSKET, AND OTHER STORIES.

SOCIAL LIFE IN OLD VIRGINIA BEFORE THE WAR. Illustrated.

THE OLD SOUTH. Essays Social and Political.

"BEFO' DE WAR." Echoes of Negro Dialect. By A. C. Gordon and Thomas Nelson Page.

A CAPTURED SANTA CLAUS. With 4 full-page colored illustrations by W. L. Jacobs.

TWO LITTLE CONFEDERATES. Illustrated.

AMONG THE CAMPS, or Young People's Stories of the War. Illustrated.

TO
A GRANDDAUGHTER
OF ONE LOIS HUNTINGTON

CONTENTS

CONTENTS

ILLUSTRATIONS

GORDON KEITH

GORDON KEITH

CHAPTER I

INTRODUCTORY

GORDON KEITH'S PATRIMONY

GORDON KEITH was the son of a gentleman. And this fact, like the cat the honest miller left to his youngest son, was his only patrimony. As in that case also, it stood to the possessor in the place of a good many other things. It helped him over many rough places. He carried it with him as a devoted Romanist wears a sacred scapulary next to the heart.

His father, General McDowell Keith of "Elphinstone," was a gentleman of the old kind, a type so old-fashioned that it is hardly accepted these days as having existed. He knew the Past and lived in it; the Present he did not understand, and the Future he did not know. In his latter days, when his son was growing up, after war had swept like a vast inundation over the land, burying almost everything it had not borne away, General Keith still survived, unchanged, unmoved, unmarred, an antique memorial of the life of which he was a relic. His one standard was that of a gentleman.

This idea was what the son inherited from the father along with some other old-fashioned things which he did not know the value of at first, but which he came to understand as he grew older.

3

When in after times, in the swift rush of life in a great city, amid other scenes and new manners, Gordon Keith looked back to the old life on the Keith plantation, it appeared to him as if he had lived then in another world.

Elphinstone was, indeed, a world to itself: a long, rambling house, set on a hill, with white-pillared verandahs, closed on the side toward the evening sun by green Venetian blinds, and on the other side looking away through the lawn trees over wide fields, brown with fallow, or green with cattle-dotted pasture-land and waving grain, to the dark rim of woods beyond. To the westward "the Ridge" made a straight, horizontal line, except on clear days, when the mountains still farther away showed a tenderer blue scalloped across the sky.

A stranger passing through the country prior to the war would have heard much of Elphinstone, the Keith plantation, but he would have seen from the main road (which, except in summer, was intolerably bad) only long stretches of rolling fields well tilled, and far beyond them a grove on a high hill, where the mansion rested in proud seclusion amid its immemorial oaks and elms, with what appeared to be a small hamlet lying about its feet. Had he turned in at the big-gate and driven a mile or so, he would have found that Elphinstone was really a world to itself, almost as much cut off from the outer world as the home of the Keiths had been in the old country. A number of little blacks would have opened the gates for him; several boys would have run to take his horse, and he would have found a legion of servants about the house. He would have found that the hamlet was composed of extensive stables and barns, with shops and houses, within which mechanics were plying their trades with the ring of hammers, the clack of looms, and the hum of spinning-wheels—all for the plantation; whilst on a lower hill farther to the rear were the servants' quarters laid out in streets, filled with children.

Had the visitor asked for shelter, he would have received,

whatever his condition, a hospitality as gracious as if he had been the highest in the land; he would have found culture with philosophy and wealth with content, and he would have come away charmed with the graciousness of his entertainment. And yet, if from any other country or region than the South, he would have departed with a feeling of mystification, as though he had been drifting in a counter-current and had discovered a part of the world sheltered and to some extent secluded from the general movement and progress of life.

This plantation, then, was Gordon's world. The woods that rimmed it were his horizon, as they had been that of the Keiths for generations; more or less they always affected his horizon. His father appeared to the boy to govern the world; he governed the most important part of it—the plantation—without ever raising his voice. His word had the convincing quality of a law of nature. The quiet tones of his voice were irresistible. The calm face, lighting up at times with the flash of his gray eyes, was always commanding: he looked so like the big picture in the library of a tall, straight man, booted and spurred, and partly in armor, with a steel hat over his long curling hair, and a grave face that looked as if the sun were on it. It was no wonder, thought the boy, that he was given a sword by the State when he came back from the Mexican War; no wonder that the Governor had appointed him Senator, a position he declined because of his wife's ill health. Gordon's wonder was that his father was not made President or Commander-in-Chief of the army. It no more occurred to him that any one could withstand his father than that the great oak-trees in front of the house, which it took his outstretched arms six times to girdle, could fall.

Yet it came to pass that within a few years an invading army marched through the plantation, camped on the lawn, and cut down the trees; and Gordon Keith, whilst yet a boy, came to see Elphinstone in the hands of strangers, and his father and himself thrown out on the world.

5

His mother died while Gordon was still a child. Until then she had not appeared remarkable to the boy: she was like the atmosphere, the sunshine, and the blue, arching sky, all-pervading and existing as a matter of course. Yet, as her son remembered her in after life, she was the centre of everything, never idle, never hurried; every one and everything revolved about her and received her light and warmth. She was the refuge in every trouble, and her smile was enchanting. It was only after that last time, when the little boy stood by his mother's bedside awed and weeping silently in the shadow of the great darkness that was settling upon them, that he knew how absolutely she had been the centre and breath of his life. His father was kneeling beside the bed, with a face as white as his mother's, and a look of such mingled agony and resignation that Gordon never forgot it. As, because of his father's teaching, the son in later life tried to be just to every man, so, for his mother's sake, he remembered to be kind to every woman.

In the great upheaval that came just before the war, Major Keith stood for the Union, but was defeated. When his State seceded, he raised a regiment in the congressional district which he had represented for one or two terms. As his duties took him from home much of the time, he sent Gordon to the school of the noted Dr. Grammer, a man of active mind and also active arm, named by his boys, from the latter quality, "Old Hickory."

Gordon, like some older men, hoped for war with all his soul. A great-grandfather an officer of the line in the Revolution, a grandfather in the navy of 1812, and his father a major in the Mexican War, with a gold-hilted sword presented him by the State, gave him a fair pedigree, and he looked forward to being a great general himself. He would be Julius Cæsar or Alexander the Great at least. It was his preference for a career, unless being a mountain stage-driver was. He had seen one or two such beings in the mountains when he accompanied his father once on

6

a canvass that he was making for Congress, enthroned like Jove, in clouds of oil-coats and leather, mighty in power and speech; and since then his dreams had been blessed at times with lumbering coaches and clanking teams.

One day Gordon was sent for to come home. When he came down-stairs next morning his father was standing in the drawing-room, dressed in full uniform, though it was not near as showy as Gordon had expected it to be, or as dozens of uniforms the boy had seen the day before about the railway-stations on his journey home, gorgeous with gold lace. He was conscious, however, that some change had taken place, and a resemblance to the man-in-armor in the picture over the library mantel suddenly struck the boy. There was the high look, the same light in the eyes, the same gravity about the mouth; and when his father, after taking leave of the servants, rode away in his gray uniform, on his bay horse "Chevalier," with his sword by his side, to join his men at the county-seat, and let Gordon accompany him for the first few miles, the boy felt as though he had suddenly been transported to a world of which he had read, and were riding behind a knight of old. Ah! if there were only a few Roundheads formed at the big-gate, how they would scatter them!

About the third year of the war, Mr. Keith, now a brigadier-general, having been so badly wounded that it was supposed he could never again be fit for service in the field, was sent abroad by his government to represent it in England in a semi-confidential, semi-diplomatic position. He had been abroad before—quite an unusual occurrence at that time.

General Keith could not bring himself to leave his boy behind him and have the ocean between them, so he took Gordon with him.

After a perilous night in running the blockade, when they were fired on and escaped only by sending up rockets and passing as one of the blockading squadron, General Keith and Gordon transferred at Nassau to their steamer. The vessel touched at Halifax, and among the passengers taken on there were an American lady, Mrs. Wickersham of New York, and her son Ferdy Wickersham, a handsome, black-eyed boy a year or two older than Gordon. As the two lads were the only passengers aboard of about their age, they soon became as friendly as any other young animals would have become, and everything went on balmily until a quarrel arose over a game which they were playing on the lower deck. As General Keith had told Gordon that he must be very discreet while on board and not get into any trouble, the row might have ended in words had not the sympathy of the sailors been with Gordon. This angered the other boy in the dispute, and he called Gordon a liar. This, according to Gordon's code, was a cause of war. He slapped Ferdy in the mouth, and the next second they were at it hammer-and-tongs. So long as they were on their feet, Ferdy, who knew something of boxing, had much the best of it and punished Gordon severely, until the latter, diving into him, seized him.

In wrestling Ferdy was no match for him, for Gordon had wrestled with every boy on the plantation, and after a short scuffle he lifted Ferdy and flung him flat on his back on the deck, jarring the wind out of him. Ferdy refused to make up and went off crying to his mother, who from that time filled the ship with her abuse of Gordon.

The victory of the younger boy gave him great prestige among the sailors, and Mike Doherty, the bully of the forecastle, gave him boxing lessons during all the rest of the voyage, teaching him the mystery of the "side swing" and the "left-hand upper-cut," which Mike said was "as good as a belaying-pin."

"With a good, smooth tongue for the girlls and a good upper-cut for thim as treads on your toes, you are aall right," said Mr. Doherty; "you're rigged for ivery braize. But, boy, remember to be quick with both, and don't forgit who taaught you."

Thus, it was that, while Gordon Keith was still a boy of about twelve or thirteen, instead of being on the old plantation rimmed by the great woods, where his life had hitherto been spent, except during the brief period when he had been at Dr. Grammer's school, he found himself one summer in a little watering-place on the shores of an English lake as blue as a china plate, set amid ranges of high green hills, on which nestled pretty white or brown villas surrounded by gardens and parks.

The water was a new element for Gordon. The home of the Keiths was in the high country back from the great watercourses, and Gordon had never had a pair of oars in his hands, nor did he know how to swim; but he meant to learn. The sight of the boats rowed about by boys of his own age filled him with envy. And one of them, when he first caught sight of it, inspired him with a stronger feeling than envy. It was painted white and was gay with blue and red stripes around the gunwale. In it sat two boys. One, who sat in the stern, was about Gordon's age; the other, a little larger than Gordon, was rowing and used the oars like an adept. In the bow was a flag, and Gordon was staring at it, when it came to him with a rush that it was a "Yankee" flag. He was conscious for half a moment that he took some pride in the superiority of the oarsman over the boys in the other boats. His next thought was that he had a little Confederate flag in his trunk. He had brought it from home among his other treasures. He would show his colors and not let the Yankee boys have all of the honors. So away he put as hard as his legs could carry him. When he got back to the waterside he hired a boat from among those lying tied at the stairs, and soon had his little flag rigged up, when, taking his seat, he picked up the oars and pushed off. It was rather more difficult than it had looked. The oars would not go together. However, after a little he was able to move slowly, and was quite elated at his success when he found himself out on the lake. Just then he heard a shout:

"Take down that flag!"

Gordon wished to turn his boat and look around, but could not do so. However, one of the oars came out of the water, and as the boat veered a little he saw the boys in the white boat with the Union flag bearing down on him.

The oarsman was rowing with strong, swift strokes even while he looked over his shoulder, and the boat was shooting along as straight as an arrow, with the clear water curling about its prow. Gordon wished for a moment that he had not been so daring, but the next second his fighting blood was up, as the other boy called imperiously:

"Strike that flag!"

Gordon could see his face now, for he was almost on him. It was round and sunburnt, and the eyes were blue and clear and flashing with excitement. His companion, who was cheering him on, was Ferdy Wickersham.

"Strike that flag, I say," called the oarsman.

"I won't. Who are you? Strike your own flag."

"I am Norman Wentworth. That's who I am, and if you don't take that flag down I will take it down for you, you little nigger-driving rebel."

Gordon Keith was not a boy to neglect the amenities of the occasion.

"Come and try it then, will you, you nigger-stealing Yankees!" he called. "I will fight both of you." And he settled himself for defence.

"Well, I will," cried his assailant. "Drop the tiller, Ferdy, and sit tight. I will fight fair." Then to Gordon again: "I have given you fair warning, and I will have that flag or sink you."

Gordon's answer was to drop one oar as useless, seize the other, and steadying himself as well as he could, raise it aloft as a weapon.

"I will kill you if you try it," he said between clinched teeth.

However, the boy rowing the other boat was not to be

10

frightened. He gave a vigorous stroke of his oars that sent his boat straight into the side of Gordon's boat.

The shock of the two boats coming together pitched Gordon to his knees, and came near flinging him into the water; but he was up again in a second, and raising his oar, dealt a vicious blow with it, not at the boy in the boat, but at the flag in the bow of the boat. The unsteadiness of his footing, however, caused him to miss his aim, and he only splintered his oar into fragments.

"Hit him with the oar, Norman," called the boy in the stern. "Knock him out of the boat."

The other boy made no answer, but with a quick turn of his wrist twisted his boat out of its direct course and sent it skimming off to one side. Then dropping one oar, he caught up the other with both hands, and with a rapid, dexterous swing swept a cataract of water in Gordon's face, drenching him, blinding him, and filling his eyes, mouth, and ears with the unexpected deluge. Gordon gasped and sputtered, and before he could recover from this unlooked-for flank movement, another turn of the wrist brought the attacking boat sharp across his bow, and, with a shout of triumph, Norman wrenched the defiant flag out of its socket.

Gordon had no time for thought. He had time only to act. With a cry, half of rage, half of defiance, he sprang up on the point of the bow of his boat, and with outstretched arms launched himself at the bow of the other, where the captor had flung the flag, to use both oars. His boat slipped from under his feet, and he fell short, but caught the gunwale of the other, and dragged himself up to it. He held just long enough to clutch both flags, and the next second, with a faint cheer, he rolled off and sank with a splash in the water.

Norman Wentworth had risen, and with blazing eyes, his oar uplifted, was scrambling toward the bow to repel the boarder, when the latter disappeared. Norman gazed at the spot with staring eyes. The next second he took in what was happening, and, with an exclamation of horror,

11

he suddenly dived overboard. When he came to the top, he was pulling the other boy up with him.

Though Norman was a good swimmer, there was a moment of extreme danger; for, half unconscious, Gordon pulled him under once. But fortunately Norman kept his head, and with a supreme effort breaking the drowning boy's hold, he drew him to the top once more. Fortunately for both, a man seeing the trouble had brought his boat to the spot, and, just as Norman rose to the surface with his burden, he reached out and, seizing him, dragged both him and the now unconscious Gordon aboard his boat.

It was some days before Gordon was able to sit up, and meanwhile he learned that his assailant and rescuer had been every day to make inquiry about him, and his father, Mr. Wentworth, had written to Gordon's father and expressed his concern at the accident.

"It is a strange fate," he wrote, "that should after all these years have arrayed us against each other thus, and have brought our boys face to face in a foreign land. I hear that your boy behaved with the courage which I knew your son would show."

General Keith, in turn, expressed his gratitude for the promptness and efficiency with which the other's son had apprehended the danger and met it.

"My son owes his life to him," he said. "As to the flag, it was the fortune of war," and he thought the incident did credit to both combatants. He "only wished," he said, "that in every fight over a flag there were the same ability to restore to life those who defended it."

Gordon, however, could not participate in this philosophic view of his father's. He had lost his flag; he had been defeated in the battle. And he owed his life to his victorious enemy.

He was but a boy, and his defeat was gall and wormwood to him. It was but very little sweetened by the knowledge that his victor had come to ask after him.

He was lying in bed one afternoon, lonely and homesick

12

and sad. His father was away, and no one had been in to him for, perhaps, an hour. The shrill voices of children and the shouts of boys floated in at the open window from somewhere afar off. He was not able to join them. It depressed him, and he began to pine for the old plantation— a habit that followed him through life in the hours of depression.

Suddenly there was a murmur of voices outside the room, and after a few moments the door softly opened, and a lady put her head in and looked at him. She was a stranger and was dressed in a travelling-suit. Gordon gazed at her without moving or uttering a sound. She came in and closed the door gently behind her, and then walked softly over to the side of the bed and looked down at him with kind eyes. She was not exactly pretty, but to Gordon she appeared beautiful, and he knew that she was a friend. Suddenly she dropped down on her knees beside him and put her arm over him caressingly.

"I am Norman's mother," she said, "and I have come to look after you and to take you home with me if they will let me have you." She stooped over and kissed him.

The boy put up his pinched face and kissed her.

"I will go," he said in his weak voice.

She kissed him again, and smiled down at him with moist eyes, and talked to him in tender tones, stroking his hair and telling him of Norman's sorrow for the trouble, of her own unhappiness, and of her regret that the doctors would not let him be moved. When she left, it was with a promise that she would come back again and see him ; and Gordon knew that he had a friend in England of his own kind, and a truth somehow had slipped into his heart which set at odds many opinions which he had thought principles. He had never thought to feel kindly toward a Yankee.

When Gordon was able to be out again, his father wished him to go and thank his former foe who had rescued him. But it was too hard an ordeal for the boy to face.

13

Even the memory of Mrs. Wentworth could not reconcile him to this.

"You don't know how hard it is, father," he said, with that assurance with which boyhood always draws a line between itself and the rest of the world. "Did you ever have to ask pardon of one who had fought you?"

General Keith's face wore a singular expression. Suddenly he felt a curious sensation in a spot in his right side, and he was standing in a dewy glade in a piece of woodland on a Spring morning, looking at a slim, serious young man standing very straight and still a few paces off, with a pistol gripped in his hand, and, queerly enough, his name, too, was Norman Wentworth. But he was not thinking of him. He was thinking of a tall girl with calm blue eyes, whom he had walked with the day before, and who had sent him away dazed and half maddened. Then some one a little to one side spoke a few words and began to count, "One, two—" There was a simultaneous report of two pistols, two little puffs of smoke, and when the smoke had cleared away, the other man with the pistol was sinking slowly to the ground, and he himself was tottering into the arms of the man nearest him.

He came back to the present with a gasp.

"My son," he said gravely, "I once was called on and failed. I have regretted it all my life, though happily the consequences were not as fatal as I had at one time apprehended. If every generation did not improve on the follies and weaknesses of those that have gone before, there would be no advance in the world. I want you to be wiser and stronger than I."

Gordon's chance of revenge came sooner than he expected. Not long after he got out of doors again he was on his way down to the lake, where he was learning to swim, when a number of boys whom he passed began to hoot at him. In their midst was Ferdy Wickersham, the boy who had crossed the ocean with him. He was setting the others on. The cry that came to Gordon was: "Nig-

14

ger-driver! Nigger-driver!" Sometimes Fortune, Chance, or whatever may be the deity of fortuitous occurrence, places our weapons right to hand. What would David have done had there not been a stony brook between him and Goliath that day? Just as Gordon with burning face turned to defy his deriders, a pile of small stones lay at his feet. It looked like Providence. He could not row a boat, but he could fling a stone like young David. In a moment he was sending stones up the hill with such rapidity that the group above him were thrown into confusion.

Then Gordon fell into an error of more noted generals. Seizing a supply of missiles, he charged straight up the hill. Though the group had broken at the sudden assault, by the time he reached the hill-top they had rallied, and while he was out of ammunition they made a charge on him. Wheeling, he went down the hill like the wind, while his pursuers broke after him with shouts of triumph. As he reached the stone-pile he turned and made a stand, which brought them to a momentary stop. Just then a shout arose below him. Gordon turned to see rushing up the hill toward him Norman Wentworth. He was picking up stones as he ran. Gordon heard him call out something, but he did not wait for his words. Here was his arch-enemy, his conqueror, and here, at least, he was his equal. Without wasting further time with those above him, Gordon sprang toward his new assailant, and steadying himself, hurled his heaviest stone. Fortunately, Norman Wentworth had been reared in the country and knew how to dodge as well as to throw a stone, or his days might have ended then and there.

"Hold on! don't throw!" he shouted; "I am coming to help you," and, without waiting, he sent a stone far over Gordon's head at the party on the height above. Gordon, who was poising himself for another shot, paused amazed in the midst of his aim, open-mouthed and wide-eyed.

"Come on," cried Norman. "You and I together can lick them. I know the way, and we will get above them." So saying, he dashed down a side alley, Gordon close at his heels, and, by making a turn, they came out a few minutes later on the hill above their enemies, who were rejoicing in their easy victory, and, catching them unprepared, routed them and scattered them in an instant.

Ferdy Wickersham, finding himself defeated, promptly surrendered and offered to enlist on their side. Norman, however, had no idea of letting him off so easy.

"I am going to take you prisoner, but not until I have given you a good kicking. You know better than to take sides against an American."

"He is a rebel," said Ferdy.

"He is an American," said Norman. And he forthwith proceeded to make good his word, and to do it in such honest style that Ferdy, after first taking it as a joke, got angry and ran away howling.

Gordon was doubtful as to the wisdom of this severity.

"He will tell," he said.

"Let him," said Norman, contemptuously. "He knows what he will get if he does. I was at school with him last year, and I am going to school with him again. I will teach him to fight with any one else against an American !"

This episode made the two boys closer allies than they would have been in a year of peace.

General Keith, finding his mission fruitless, asked leave to return home immediately, so that Gordon saw little more of his former foe and new ally.

A few days before their departure, Gordon, passing along a road, came on a group of three persons, two children and a French governess with much-frizzled hair, very black eyes, and a small waist. One of the children was a very little girl, richly dressed in a white frock with a blue sash that almost covered it, with big brown eyes and yellow ringlets ; the other child was a ragged girl several years older, with tangled hair, gray eyes, and the ruddy, chubby cheeks so often seen in children of her class. The governess was in a state of great excitement, and was talking French so fast that it was a wonder any tongue could utter the words. The little girl of the fine frock and brown eyes was clutching to her bosom with a defiant air a large doll which the governess was trying to get from her, while the other child stood by, looking first toward one of them and then toward the other, with an expression divided between timidity and eagerness. A big picture of a ballet-dancer with a gay frock and red shoes in a flaring advertisement on a sign-board had something to do with the trouble. Now the girl drew nearer to the other child and danced a few steps, holding out her hand ; now she cast a look over her shoulder down the hill, as if to see that her retreat were not cut off.

"*Mais, c'est à moi*—it's *my* doll. I *will* have it," insisted the little girl, backing away and holding it firmly ; at which the governess began again almost tearing her hair in her desperation, though she ended by giving it a pat to see that it was all right.

The approach of Gordon drew her attention to him.

"Oh," she exclaimed in desperation, "*c'est épouvantable* —it ees terr-e-ble ! Dese young ladie weel give de doll to dat meeseerable creature !"

"She is not a 'meeseerable creature' !" insisted the little girl, mocking her, her brown eyes flashing. "She danced for me, and I will give it to her—I like her."

"Oh, *ciel !* What shall I do ! Madame weel abuse me— weel keel me !"

"Mamma will not mind ; it is *my* doll. Aunt Abby gave it to me. I can get a plenty more, and I *will* give it to her," insisted the little girl again. Then suddenly, gaining more courage, she turned quickly, and, before the governess could stop her, thrust the doll into the other child's arms.

"Here, you *shall* have it."

The governess, with a cry of rage, made a spring for the child, but too late : the grimy little hands had clutched the doll, and turning without a word of thanks, the little creature sped down the road like a frightened animal, her ragged frock fluttering behind her.

"Why, she did not say 'Thank you'!" exclaimed the child, in a disappointed tone, looking ruefully after the retreating figure.

The governess broke out on her vehemently in French, very comically mingling her upbraidings of her charge, her abuse of the little girl, and her apprehension of "Madame."

"Never mind; she does not know any better," said Gordon.

The child's face brightened at this friendly encouragement.

"She is a nasty little creature! You shall not play with her," cried the governess, angrily.

"She is not nasty! I like her, and I will play with her," declared the child, defiantly.

"What is your name?" asked the boy, much amused by such sturdiness in so small a tot.

"Lois Huntington. What is your name?" She looked up at him with her big brown eyes.

"Gordon Keith."

"How do you do, Gordon Keith?" She held out her hand.

"How do you do, Lois Huntington?"

She shook hands with him solemnly.

A day or two later, as Gordon was passing through one of the streets in the lower part of the village, he came upon a hurdy-gurdy playing a livelier tune than most of them usually gave. A crowd of children had gathered in the street. Among them was a little barelegged girl who, inspired by the music, was dancing and keeping perfect time as she tripped back and forth, pirouetted and swayed on the tips of her bare toes, flirting her little ragged frock, and kicking with quite the air of a ballet-dancer. She divided the honors with the dismal Savoyard, who ground away at his organ, and she brought a flicker of admiration into his bronzed and grimy face, for he played for her the same tune over and over, encouraging her with nods and bravas. She was enjoying her triumph quite as much as any prima donna who ever tripped it on a more ambitious stage.

Gordon recognized in the little dancer the tangled-haired child who had run away with the little girl's doll a few days before.

CHAPTER II

GENERAL KEITH BECOMES AN OVERSEER

WHEN the war closed, though it was not recognized at first, the old civilization of the South passed away. Fragments of the structure that had once risen so fair and imposing still stood for a time, even after the foundations were undermined : a bastion here, a tower there ; but in time they followed the general overthrow, and crumbled gradually to their fall, leaving only ruins and decay.

For a time it was hoped that the dilapidation might be repaired and the old life be lived again. General Keith, like many others, though broken and wasted in body, undertook to rebuild with borrowed money, but with disastrous results. The conditions were all against him.

Three or four years' effort to repair his fallen fortunes only plunged him deeper in debt. General Keith, like most of his neighbors and friends, found himself facing the fact that he was hopelessly insolvent. As soon as he saw he could not pay his debts he stopped spending and notified his creditors.

"I see nothing ahead of me," he wrote, "but greater ruin. I am like a horse in a quicksand : every effort I make but sinks me deeper."

Some of his neighbors took the benefit of the bankrupt-law which was passed to give relief. General Keith was urged to do likewise, but he declined.

"Though I cannot pay my debts," he said, "the least I

can do is to acknowledge that I owe them. I am unwilling to appear, even for a short time, to be denying what I know to be a fact."

He gave up everything that he owned, reserving nothing that would bring in money.

When Elphinstone was sold, it brought less than the debts on it. The old plate, with the Keith coat-of-arms on it, from which generations of guests had been served, and which old Richard, the butler, had saved during the war, went for its weight in silver. The library had been pillaged until little of it remained. The old Keith pictures, some of them by the best artists, which had been boxed and stored elsewhere until after the war, now went to the purchaser of the place for less than the price of their frames. Among them was the portrait of the man in the steel coat and hat, who had the General's face.

What General Keith felt during this transition no one, perhaps, ever knew; certainly his son did not know it, and did not dream of it until later in life.

It was, however, not only in the South that fortunes were lost by the war. As vast as was the increase of riches at the North among those who stayed at home, it did not extend to those who took the field. Among these was a young officer named Huntington, from Brookford, a little town on the sunny slope that stretches eastwardly from the Alleghanies to the Delaware. Captain Huntington, having entered the army on the outbreak of the war, like Colonel Keith rose to the rank of general, and, like General Keith, received a wound that incapacitated him for service. His wife was a Southern woman, and had died abroad, just at the close of the war, leaving him a little girl, who was the idol of his heart. He was interested in the South, and came South to try and recuperate from the effects of his wound and of exposure during the war.

The handsomest place in the neighborhood of Elphinstone was "Rosedale," the family-seat of the Berkeleys. Mr. Berkeley had been killed in the war, and the plantation went, like Elphinstone and most of the other old estates, for debt. And General Huntington purchased it.

As soon as General Keith heard of his arrival in the neighborhood, he called on him and invited him to stay at his house until Rosedale should be refurnished and made comfortable again. The two gentlemen soon became great friends, and though many of the neighbors looked askance at the Federal officer and grumbled at his possessing the old family-seat of the Berkeleys, the urbanity and real kindness of the dignified, soldierly young officer soon made his way easier and won him respect if not friendship. When a man had been a general at the age of twenty-six, it meant that he was a man, and when General Keith pronounced that he was a gentleman, it meant that he was a gentleman. Thus reasoned the neighbors.

His only child was a pretty little girl of five or six years, with great brown eyes, yellow curls, and a rosebud face that dimpled adorably when she laughed. When Gordon saw her he recognized her instantly as the tot who had given her doll to the little dancer two years before. Her eyes could not be mistaken. She used to drive about in the tiniest of village carts, drawn by the most Liliputian of ponies, and Gordon used to call her "Cindy,"—short for Cinderella,—which amused and pleased her. She in turn called him her sweetheart; tyrannized over him, and finally declared that she was going to marry him.

"Why, you are not going to have a rebel for a sweetheart?" said her father.

"Yes, I am. I am going to make him Union," she declared gravely.

"Well, that is a good way. I fancy that is about the best system of Reconstruction that has yet been tried."

He told the story to General Keith, who rode over very soon afterwards to see the child, and thenceforth called her his fairy daughter.

One day she had a tiff with Gordon, and she announced to him that she was not going to kiss him any more.

"Oh, yes, you are," said he, teasing her.

"I am not." Her eyes flashed. And although he often teased her afterwards, and used to draw a circle on his cheek which, he said, was her especial reservation, she kept her word, even in spite of the temptation which he held out to her to take her to ride if she would relent.

One Spring General Huntington's cough suddenly increased, and he began to go downhill so rapidly as to cause much uneasiness to his friends. General Keith urged him to go up to a little place on the side of the mountains which had been quite a health-resort before the war.

"Ridgely is one of the most salubrious places I know for such trouble as yours. And Dr. Theophilus Balsam is one of the best doctors in the State. He was my regimental surgeon during the war. He is a Northern man who came South before the war. I think he had an unfortunate love-affair."

"There is no place for such trouble as mine," said the younger man, gravely. "That bullet went a little too deep." Still, he went to Ridgely.

Under the charge of Dr. Balsam the young officer for a time revived, and for a year or two appeared on the way to recovery. Then suddenly his old trouble returned, and he went down as if shot. The name Huntington had strong association for the old physician ; for it was a Huntington that Lois Brooke, the younger sister of Abigail Brooke, his old sweetheart, had married, and Abigail Brooke's refusal to marry him had sent him South. The Doctor discovered early in his acquaintance with the young officer that he was Abigail Brooke's nephew. He, however, made no reference to his former relation to his patient's people.

Division bitterer than that war in which he had fought lay between them, the division that had embittered his life and made him an exile from his people. But the little girl with her great, serious eyes became the old physician's idol and tyrant, and how he worked over her father!

23

Even in those last hours when the end had unexpectedly appeared, and General Huntington was making his last arrangements with the same courage which had made him a noted officer when hardly more than a boy, the Doctor kept his counsel almost to the end.

"How long have I to live, Doctor?" panted the dying man, when he rallied somewhat from the attack that had struck him down.

"Not very long."

"Then I wish you to send for General Keith. I wish him to take my child to my aunt, Miss Abigail Brooke."

"I will attend to it," said the Doctor.

"So long as she lives she will take care of her. But she is now an old woman, and when she dies, God knows what will become of her."

"I will look after her as long as I live," said the Doctor.

"Thank you, Doctor." There was a pause. "She is a saint." His mind had gone back to his early life. To this Dr. Balsam made no reply. "She has had a sad life. She was crossed in love; but instead of souring, it sweetened her."

"I was the man," said the Doctor, quietly. "I will look after your child."

"You were! I never knew his name. She never married."

He gave a few directions, and presently said : "My little girl? I wish to see her. It cannot hurt me?"

"No, it will not hurt you," said the Doctor, quietly.

The child was brought, and the dying man's eyes lit up as they rested on her pink face and brown eyes filled with a vague wonder.

"You must remember papa."

She stood on tiptoe and, leaning over, kissed him.

"And you must go to Aunt Abby when I have gone."

"I will take Gordon Keith with me," said the child.

The ghost of a smile flickered about the dying man's eyes. Then came a fit of coughing, and when it had passed, his head, after a few gasps, sank back.

GENERAL KEITH BECOMES AN OVERSEER

At a word from the Doctor, an attendant took the child out of the room.

That evening the old Doctor saw that the little girl was put to bed, and that night he sat up alone with the body. There were many others to relieve him, but he declined them and kept his vigil alone.

What memories were with him; what thoughts attended him through those lonely hours, who can tell!

General Keith went immediately to Ridgely on hearing of General Huntington's death. He took Gordon with him, thinking that he would help to comfort the little orphaned girl. The boy had no idea how well he was to know the watering-place in after years. The child fell to his care and clung to him, finally going to sleep in his arms. While the arrangements were being made, they moved for a day or two over to Squire Rawson's, the leading man of the Ridge region, where the squire's granddaughter, a fresh-faced girl of ten or twelve years, took care of the little orphan and kept her interested.

The burial, in accordance with a wish expressed by General Huntington, took place in a corner of the little burying-ground at Ridgely, which lay on a sunny knoll overlooking the long slope to the northeastward. The child walked after the bier, holding fast to Gordon's hand, while Dr. Balsam and General Keith walked after them.

As soon as General Keith could hear from Miss Brooke he took the child to her; but to the last Lois said that she wanted Gordon to come with her.

Soon afterwards it appeared that General Huntington's property had nearly all gone. His plantation was sold.

Several times Lois wrote Gordon quaint little letters scrawled in a childish hand, asking about the calves and pigeons and chickens that had been her friends. But after a while the letters ceased to come.

When Elphinstone was sold, the purchaser was a certain Mr. Aaron Wickersham of New York, the father of Ferdy Wickersham, with whom Gordon had had the rock-battle.

25

Mr. Wickersham was a stout and good-humored man of fifty, with a head like a billiard-ball, and a face that was both shrewd and kindly. He had, during the war, made a fortune out of contracts, and was now preparing to increase it in the South, where the mountain region, filled with coal and iron, lay virgin for the first comer with sufficient courage and astuteness to take it. He found the new legislature of the State an instrument well fitted to his hands. It could be manipulated.

The Wickershams had lately moved into a large new house on Fifth Avenue, where Fashion was climbing the hill toward the Park in the effort to get above Murray Hill, and possibly to look down upon the substantial and somewhat prosaic mansions below, whose doors it had sometimes been found difficult to enter. Mrs. Wickersham was from Brookford, the same town from which the Huntingtons came, and, when a young and handsome girl, having social ambitions, had married Aaron Wickersham when he was but a clerk in the banking-house of Wentworth & Son. And, be it said, she had aided him materially in advancing his fortunes. She was a handsome woman, and her social ambitions had grown. Ferdy was her only child, and was the joy and pride of her heart. Her ambition centred in him. He should be the leader of the town, as she felt his beauty and his smartness entitled him to be. It was with this aim that she induced her husband to build the fine new house on the avenue. She knew the value of a large and handsome mansion in a fashionable quarter. Aaron Wickersham knew little of fashion; but he knew the power of money, and he had absolute confidence in his wife's ability. He would furnish the means and leave the rest to her. The house was built and furnished by contract, and Mrs. Wickersham took pride in the fact that it was much finer than the Wentworth mansion on Washington Square, and more expensive than the house of the Yorkes, which was one of the big houses on the avenue, and had been the talk of the town when it was built ten years before. Will Stirling, one of the wags, said that it was a good thing that Mr. Wickersham did not take the contract for himself.

Mr. Wickersham, having spent a considerable sum in planning and preparing his Southern enterprise, and having obtained a charter from the legislature of the State that gave him power to do almost anything he wished, suddenly found himself balked by the fact that the people in the mountain region which he wished to reach with his road were so bitterly opposed to any such innovation that it jeopardized his entire scheme. From the richest man in that section, an old cattle-dealer and lumberman named Rawson, to Tim Gilsey, who drove the stage from Eden to Gumbolt Gap, they were all opposed to any "new-fangled" notions, and they regarded everything that came from carpet-baggers as "robbery and corruption."

He learned that "the most influential man down there" was General Keith, and that his place was for sale.

"I can reach him," said Mr. Wickersham, with a gleam in his eye. "I will have a rope around his neck that will lead him." So he bought the place.

Fortunately, perhaps, for Mr. Wickersham, he hinted something of his intentions to his counsel, a shrewd old lawyer of the State, who thought that he could arrange the matter better than Mr. Wickersham could.

"You don't know how to deal with these old fellows," he said.

"I know men," said Mr. Wickersham, "and I know that when I have a hold on a man—"

"You don't know General Keith," said Mr. Bagge. The glint in his eye impressed the other and he yielded.

So Mr. Wickersham bought the Keith plantation and left it to Greene Bagge, Esq., to manage the business. Mr. Bagge wrote General Keith a diplomatic letter eulogistic of the South and of Mr. Wickersham's interest in it, and invited the General to remain on the place for the present as its manager.

27

General Keith sat for some time over that letter, his face as grave as it had ever been in battle. What swept before his mental vision who shall know? The history of two hundred years bound the Keiths to Elphinstone. They had carved it from the forest and had held it against the Indian. From there they had gone to the highest office of the State. Love, marriage, death—all the sanctities of life —were bound up with it. He talked it over with Gordon.

Gordon's face fell.

"Why, father, you will be nothing but an overseer."

General Keith smiled. Gordon remembered long afterwards, with shame for his speech, how wistful that smile was.

"Yes; I shall be something more than that. I shall be, at least, a faithful one. I wish I could be as successful a one."

He wrote saying that, as he had failed for himself, he did not see how he could succeed for another. But upon receiving a very flattering reassurance, he accepted the offer. Thus, the General remained as an employé on the estate which had been renowned for generations as the home of the Keiths. And as agent for the new owner he farmed the place with far greater energy and success than he had ever shown on his own account. It was a bitter cup for Gordon to have his father act as an "overseer"; but if it contained any bitterness for General Keith, he never gave the least evidence of it, nor betrayed his feeling by the slightest sign.

When Mr. Wickersham visited his new estate he admitted that Mr. Bagge knew better than he how to deal with General Keith.

When he was met at the station by a tall, gray-haired gentleman who looked like something between a general and a churchwarden, he was inclined to be shy; but when the gentleman grasped his hand, and with a voice of unmistakable sincerity said he had driven out himself to meet him, to welcome him among them, he felt at home.

GENERAL KEITH BECOMES AN OVERSEER

"It is gentlemen like yourself to whom we must look for the preservation of our civilization," said General Keith, and introduced him personally to every man he met as, "the gentleman who has bought my old place—not a 'carpet-bagger,' but a gentleman interested in the development of our country, sir."

Mr. Wickersham, in fact, was treated with a distinction to which he had been a stranger during his former visits South. He liked it. He felt quite like a Southern gentleman, and with one or two Northerners whom he met held himself a little distantly.

Once or twice the new owner of Elphinstone came down with parties of friends—"to look at the country." They were interested in developing it, and had been getting sundry acts passed by the legislature with this in view. (General Keith's nose always took a slight elevation when the legislature was mentioned.) General Keith entertained the visitors precisely as he had done when he was the master, and Mr. Wickersham and his guests treated him, in the main, as if he were still the master. General Keith sat at the foot of the table opposite Mr. Wickersham, and directed the servants, who still called him "Master," and obeyed him as such.

Mr. Wickersham conceived a great regard for General Keith, not unmingled with a certain contempt for his inability to avail himself of the new conditions. "Fine old fellow," he said to his friends. "No more business-sense than a child. If he had he would go in with us and make money for himself instead of telling us how to make it." He did not know that General Keith would not have "gone in" with him in the plan he had carried through that legislature to save his life. But he honored the old fellow all the more. He had stood up for the General against Mrs. Wickersham, who hated all Keiths on Ferdy's account. The old General, who was as oblivious of this as a child, was always sending Mrs. Wickersham his regards.

"Perhaps, she might like to come down and see the

place?" he suggested. "It is not what it used to be, but we can make her comfortable." His glance as it swept about him was full of affection.

Mr. Wickersham said he feared that Mrs. Wickersham's health would not permit her to come South.

"This is the very region for her," said the General. "There is a fine health-resort in the mountains, a short distance from us. I have been there, and it is in charge of an old friend of mine, Dr. Balsam, one of the best doctors in the State. He was my regimental surgeon. I can recommend him. Bring her down, and let us see what we can do for her."

Mr. Wickersham thanked him with a smile. Time had been when Mrs. Wickersham had been content with small health-resorts. But that time was past. He did not tell General Keith that Mrs. Wickersham, remembering the fight between her son and Gordon, had consented to his buying the place from a not very noble motive, and vowed that she would never set her foot on it so long as a Keith remained there. He only assured the General that he would convey his invitation.

Mr. Wickersham's real interest, however, lay in the mountains to the westward. And General Keith gave him some valuable hints as to the deposits lying in the Ridge and the mountains beyond the Ridge.

"I will give you letters to the leading men in that region," he said. "The two most influential men up there are Dr. Balsam and Squire Rawson. They have, like Abraham and Lot, about divided up the country."

Mr. Wickersham's eyes glistened. He thanked him, and said that he might call on him.

Once there came near being a clash between Mr. Wickersham and General Keith. When Mr. Wickersham mentioned that he had invited a number of members of the legislature—"gentlemen interested in the development of the resources of the State"—to meet him, the General's face changed. There was a little tilting of the nose and a slight quivering of the nostrils. A moment later he spoke.

"I will have everything in readiness for your—f—for your guests; but I must ask you to excuse me from meeting them."

Mr. Wickersham turned to him in blank amazement. "Why, General?"

The expression on the old gentleman's face answered him. He knew that at a word he should lose his agent, and he had use for him. He had plans that were far-reaching, and the General could be of great service to him.

When the statesmen arrived, everything on the place was in order; they were duly met at the station, and were welcomed at the house by the owner. Everything for their entertainment was prepared. Even the fresh mint was in the tankard on the old sideboard. Only the one who had made these preparations was absent.

Just before the vehicles were to return from the railway, General Keith walked into the room where Mr. Wickersham was lounging. He was booted and spurred for riding.

"Everything is in order for your guests, sir. Richard will see that they are looked after. These are the keys. Richard knows them all, and is entirely reliable. I will ask you to excuse me till—for a day or two."

Mr. Wickersham had been revolving in his mind what he should say to the old gentleman. He had about decided to speak very plainly to him on the folly of such narrowness. Something, however, in the General's air again deterred him: a thinning of the nostril; an unwonted firmness of the mouth. A sudden increase in the resemblance to the man-in-armor over the mantel struck him—a mingled pride and gravity. It removed him a hundred years from the present.

The keen-eyed capitalist liked the General, and in a way honored him greatly. His old-fashioned ideas entertained

31

him. So what he said was said kindly. He regretted that the General could not stay; he "would have liked him to know his friends."

"They are not such bad fellows, after all. Why, one of them is a preacher," he said jocularly as he walked to the door, "and a very bright fellow. J. Quincy Plume is regarded as a man of great ability."

"Yes, sir; I have heard of him. His doctrine is from the 'Wicked Bible'; he omits the 'not.' Good morning." And General Keith bowed himself out.

When the guests arrived, Mr. Wickersham admitted to himself that they were a strange lot of "assorted statesmen." He was rather relieved that the General had not remained. When he looked about the table that evening, after the juleps were handed around and the champagne had followed, he was still more glad. The set of old Richard's head and the tilt of his nose were enough to face. An old and pampered hound in the presence of a pack of puppies could not have been more disdainful.

The preacher he had mentioned, Mr. J. Quincy Plume, was one of the youngest members of the party and one of the most striking—certainly one of the most convivial and least abashed. Mr. Plume had, to use his own expression, "plucked a feather from many wings, and bathed his glistening pinions in the iridescent light of many orbs." He had been "something of a doctor"; then had become a preacher —to quote him again, "not exactly of the gospel as it was understood by mossbacked theologians, of 'a creed outworn,'" but rather the "gospel of the new dispensation, of the new brotherhood—the gospel of liberty, equality, fraternity." Now he had found his true vocation, that of statesmanship, where he could practise what he had preached; could "bask in the light of the effulgent sun of progress, and, shod with the sandals of Mercury, soar into a higher empyrean than he had yet attained." All of which, being translated, meant that Mr. Plume, having failed in several professions, was bent now on elevating

32

himself by the votes of the ignorant followers whom he was cajoling into taking him as a leader.

Mr. Wickersham had had some dealing with him and had found him capable and ready for any job. When he had been in the house an hour Mr. Wickersham was delighted with him, and mentally decided to secure him for his agent. When he had been there a day Mr. Wickersham mentally questioned whether he had not better drop him out of his schemes altogether.

One curious thing was that each guest secretly warned him against all the others.

The prices were much higher than Mr. Wickersham had expected. But they were subject to scaling.

"Well, Richard, what do you think of the gentlemen?" asked Mr. Wickersham of the old servant, much amused at his disdain.

"What gent'mens?"

"Why, our guests." He used the possessive that the General used.

"Does you call dem 'gent'mens'?" demanded the old servant, fixing his eyes on him.

"Well, no; I don't think I do—all of them."

"Nor, suh; dee ain't gent'mens; dee's scalawags!" said Richard, with contempt. "I been livin' heah 'bout sixty years, I reckon, an' I never seen nobody like dem eat at de table an' sleep in de beds in dis house befo'."

When the statesmen were gone and General Keith had returned, old Richard gave Mr. Wickersham an exhibition of the manner in which a gentleman should be treated.

CHAPTER III

THE ENGINEER AND THE SQUIRE

MARIUS amid the ruins of Carthage is not an inspiring figure to us while we are young; it is Marius riding up the Via Sacra at the head of his resounding legions that then dazzles us. But as we grow older we see how much greater he was when, seated amid the ruins, he sent his scornful message to Rome. So, Gordon Keith, when a boy, thought being a gentleman a very easy and commonplace thing. He had known gentlemen all his life—had been bred among them. It was only later on, after he got out into the world, that he saw how fine and noble that old man was, sitting unmoved amid the wreck not only of his life and fortunes, but of his world.

General Keith was unable to raise even the small sum necessary to send the boy to college, but among the débris of the old home still remained the relics of a once choice library, and General Keith became himself his son's instructor. It was a very irregular system of study, but the boy, without knowing it, was browsing in those pastures that remain ever fresh and green. There was nothing that related to science in any form.

"I know no more of science, sir, than an Indian," the General used to say. "The only sciences I ever thought I knew were politics and war, and I have failed in both."

He knew very little of the world—at least, of the modern world. Once, at table, Gordon was wishing that they had money.

34

THE ENGINEER AND THE SQUIRE

"My son," said his father, quietly, "there are some things that gentlemen never discuss at table. Money is one of them." Such were his old-fashioned views.

It was fortunate for his son, then, that there came to the neighborhood about this time a small engineering party, sent down by Mr. Wickersham to make a preliminary survey for a railroad line up into the Ridge country above General Keith's home. The young engineer, Mr. Grinnell Rhodes, brought a letter to General Keith from Mr. Wickersham. He had sent his son down with the young man, and he asked that the General would look after him a little and would render Mr. Rhodes any assistance in his power. The tall young engineer, with his clear eyes, pleasant voice, and quick ways, immediately ingratiated himself with both General Keith and Gordon. The sight of the instruments and, much more, the appearance of the young "chief," his knowledge of the world, and his dazzling authority as, clad in corduroy and buttoned in high yellow gaiters, he day after day strode forth with his little party and ran his lines, sending with a wave of his hand his rodmen to right or left across deep ravines and over eminences, awakened new ambitions in Gordon Keith's soul. The talk of building great bridges, of spanning mighty chasms, and of tunnelling mountains inspired the boy. What was Newton making his calculations from which to deduce his fundamental laws, or Galileo watching the stars from his Florentine tower? This young captain was Archimedes and Euclid, Newton and Galileo, all in one. He made them live.

It was a new world for Gordon. He suddenly awoke.

Both the engineer and Gordon could well have spared one of the engineer's assistants. Ferdy Wickersham had fulfilled the promise of his boyhood, and would have been very handsome but for an expression about the dark eyes which raised a question. He was popular with girls, but made few friends among men, and he and Mr. Rhodes had already clashed. Rhodes gave some order which Ferdy refused to obey. Rhodes turned on him a cold blue eye. "What did you say?"

"I guess this is my father's party; he's paying the freight, and I guess I am his son."

"I guess it's my party, and you'll do what I say or go home," said Mr. Rhodes, coldly. "Your father has no 'son' in this party. I have a rodman. Unless you are sick, you do your part of the work."

Ferdy submitted for reasons of his own; but his eyes lowered, and he did not forget Mr. Rhodes.

The two youngsters soon fell out. Ferdy began to give orders about the place, quite as if he were the master. The General cautioned Gordon not to mind what he said. "He has been spoiled a little; but don't mind him. An only child is at a great disadvantage." He spoke as if Gordon were one of a dozen children.

But Ferdy Wickersham misunderstood the other's concession. He resented the growing intimacy between Rhodes and Gordon. He had discovered that Gordon was most sensitive about the old plantation, and he used his knowledge. And when Mr. Rhodes interposed it only gave the sport of teasing Gordon a new point.

One morning, when the three were together, Ferdy began, what he probably meant for banter, to laugh at Gordon for bragging about his plantation.

"You ought to have heard him, Mr. Rhodes, how he used to blow about it."

"I did not blow about it," said Gordon, flushing.

Rhodes, without looking up, moved in his seat uneasily. "Ferdy, shut up—you bother me. I am working."

But Ferdy did not heed either this warning or the look on Gordon's face. His game had now a double zest: he could sting Gordon and worry Rhodes.

"I don't see why my old man was such a fool as to want such a dinged lonesome old place for, anyhow," he said, with a little laugh. "I am going to give it away when I get it."

Gordon's face whitened and flamed again, and his eyes began to snap.

"Then it's the only thing you ever would give away," said Mr. Rhodes, pointedly, without raising his eyes from his work.

Gordon took heart. "Why did you come down here if you feel that way about it?"

"Because my old man offered me five thousand if I'd come. You didn't think I'd come to this blanked old place for nothin', did you? Not much, sonny."

"Not if he knew you," said Mr. Rhodes, looking across at him. "If he knew you, he'd know you never did anything for nothing, Ferdy."

Ferdy flushed. "I guess I do it about as often as you do. I guess you struck my governor for a pretty big pile."

Mr. Rhodes's face hardened, and he fixed his eyes on him. "If I do, I work for it honestly. I don't make an agreement to work, and then play 'old soldier' on him."

"I guess you would if you didn't have to work."

"Well, I wouldn't," said Mr. Rhodes, firmly, "and I don't want to hear any more about it. If you won't work, then I want you to let me work."

Ferdy growled something under his breath about guessing that Mr. Rhodes was "working to get Miss Harriet Creamer and her pile"; but if Mr. Rhodes heard him he took no notice of it, and Ferdy turned back to the boy.

Meantime, Gordon had been calculating. Five thousand dollars! Why, it was a fortune! It would have relieved his father, and maybe have saved the place. In his amazement he almost forgot his anger with the boy who could speak of such a sum so lightly.

Ferdy gave him a keen glance. "What are you so huffy about, Keith?" he demanded. "I don't see that it's anything to you what I say about the place. You don't own it. I guess a man has a right to say what he chooses of his own."

Gordon wheeled on him with blazing eyes, then turned

around and walked abruptly away. He could scarcely keep back his tears. The other boy watched him nonchalantly, and then turned to Mr. Rhodes, who was glowering over his papers. "I'll take him down a point or two. He's always blowing about his blamed old place as if he still owned it. He's worse than the old man, who is always blowing about 'before the war' and his grandfather and his old pictures. I can buy better ancestors on Broadway for twenty dollars."

Mr. Rhodes gathered up his papers and rose to his feet.

"You could not make yourself as good a descendant for a million," he said, fastening his eye grimly on Ferdy.

"Oh, couldn't I? Well, I guess I could. I guess I am about as good as he is, or you either."

"Well, you can leave me out of the case," said Mr. Rhodes, sharply. "I will tell you that you are not as good as he, for he would never have said to you what you have said to him if your positions had been reversed."

"I don't understand you."

"I don't expect you do," said Mr. Rhodes. He stalked away. "I can't stand that boy. He makes me sick," he said to himself. "If I hadn't promised his governor to make him stick, I would shake him."

Ferdy was still smarting under Mr. Rhodes's biting sarcasm when the three came together again. He meant to be even with Rhodes, and he watched his opportunity.

Rhodes was a connection of the Wentworths, and had been helped at college by Norman's father, which Ferdy knew. One of the handsomest girls in their set, Miss Louise Caldwell, was a cousin of Rhodes, and Norman was in love with her. Ferdy, who could never see any one succeeding without wishing to supplant him, had of late begun to fancy himself in love with her also, but Mr. Rhodes, he knew, was Norman's friend. He also knew that Norman was Mr. Rhodes's friend in a little affair which Mr. Rhodes was having with one of the leading belles of the town, Miss Harriet Creamer, the daughter of Nicholas Creamer of Creamer, Crustback & Company.

Ferdy had received that day a letter from his mother which stated that Louise Caldwell's mother was making a set at Norman for her daughter. Ferdy's jealousy was set on edge, and he now began to talk about Norman. Rhodes sniffed at the sneering mention of his name, and Gordon, whose face still wore a surly look, pricked up his ears.

"You need not always be cracking Norman up," said Wickersham to Rhodes. "You would not be if I were to tell you what I know about him. He is no better than anybody else."

"Oh, he is better than some, Ferdy," said Mr. Rhodes.

Gordon gave an appreciative grunt which drew Ferdy's eyes on him.

"You think so too, Keith, I suppose?" he said. "Well, you needn't. You need not be claiming to be such a friend of his. He is not so much of a friend of yours, I can tell you. I have heard him say as many mean things about you as any one."

It was Gordon's opportunity. He had been waiting for one.

"I don't believe it. I believe it's a lie," he declared, his face whitening as he gathered himself together. His eyes, which had been burning, had suddenly begun to blaze.

Mr. Rhodes looked up. He said nothing, but his eyes began to sparkle.

"You're a liar yourself," retorted Wickersham, turning red.

Gordon reached for him. "Take it back!" At the same moment Rhodes sprang and caught him, but not quite in time. The tip of Gordon's fingers as he slapped at Ferdy just reached the latter's cheek and left a red mark there.

"Take it back," he said again between his teeth as Rhodes flung his arm around him.

For answer Ferdy landed a straight blow in his face, making his nose bleed and his head ring.

"Take that!"

Gordon struggled to get free, but in vain. Rhodes with

one arm swept Wickersham back. With the other he
held Gordon in an iron grip. "Keep off, or I will let him
go," he said.

The boy ceased writhing, and looked up into the young
man's face. "You had just as well let me go. I am going
to whip him. He has told a lie on my friend, who saved
my life. And he's hit me. Let me go." He began to
whimper.

"Now, look here, boys," said Rhodes; "you have got
to stop right here and make up. I won't have this
fighting."

"Let him go. I can whip him," said Ferdy, squaring
himself, and adding an epithet.

Gordon was standing quite still. "I am going to fight
him," he said, "and whip him. If he whips me, I am going
to fight him again until I do whip him."

Mr. Rhodes's face wore a puzzled expression. He looked
down at the sturdy face with its steady eyes, tightly
gripped mouth, and chin which had suddenly grown
squarer.

"If I let you go will you promise not to fight?"

"I will promise not to fight him here if he will come out
behind the barn," said Gordon. "But if he don't, I'm
going to fight him here. I am going to fight him and I am
going to whip him."

Mr. Rhodes considered. "If I go out there with you
and let you have two rounds, will you make up and agree
never to refer to the subject again?"

"Yes," said Wickersham.

"If I whip him," said Gordon.

"Come along with me. I will let you two boys try each
other's mettle for two rounds, but, remember, you have got
to stop when I call time."

So they came to a secluded spot, where the two boys took
off their coats.

"Come, you fellows had better make up now," said Mr.
Rhodes, standing above them good-humored and kindly.

THE ENGINEER AND THE SQUIRE

"I don't see what we are fighting about," said Ferdy.

"Take back what you said about Norman," demanded Gordon.

"There is nothing to take back," declared Ferdy.

"Then take that!" said Gordon, stepping forward and tapping him in the mouth with the back of his hand.

He had not expected the other boy to be so quick. Before he could put himself on guard, Ferdy had fired away, and catching him right in the eye, he sent him staggering back. He was up again in a second, however, and the next moment was at his opponent like a tiger. The rush was as unlooked for on Wickersham's part as Wickersham's blow had been by Gordon, and after a moment the lessons of Mike Doherty began to tell, and Gordon was ducking his head and dodging Wickersham's blows; and he began to drive him backward.

"By Jove! he knows his business," said Rhodes to himself.

Just then he showed that he knew his business, for, swinging out first with his right, he brought in the cut which was Mr. Doherty's *chef d'œuvre*, and catching Wickersham under the chin, he sent him flat on his back on the ground.

Mr. Rhodes called time and picked him up.

"Come, now, that's enough," he said.

Gordon wiped the blood from his face.

"He has got to take back what he said about Norman, or I have another round."

"You had better take it back, Ferdy. You began it," said the umpire.

"I didn't begin it. It's a lie!"

"You did," said Mr. Rhodes, coldly. He turned to Gordon. "You have one more round."

"I take it back," growled Ferdy.

Just then there was a step on the grass, and General Keith stood beside them. His face was very grave as he chided the boys for fighting; but there was a gleam in his eyes that showed Mr. Rhodes and possibly the two combatants that he was not wholly displeased. At his instance and Mr. Rhodes's, the two boys shook hands and promised not to open the matter again.

As Wickersham continued to shirk the work of rodman, Rhodes took Gordon in his party, instructed him in the use of the instruments, and inspired him with enthusiasm for the work, none the less eager because he contrasted him with Ferdy. Rhodes knew what General Keith's name was worth, and he thought his son being of his party would be no hindrance to him.

The trouble came when he proposed to the General to pay Gordon for his work.

"He is worth no salary at present, sir," said the General. "I shall be delighted to have him go with you, and your instruction will more than compensate us."

The matter was finally settled by Rhodes declining positively to take Gordon except on his own terms. He needed an axeman and would pay him as such. He could not take him at all unless he were under his authority.

Mr. Rhodes was not mistaken. General Keith's name was one to conjure with. Squire Rawson was the principal man in all the Ridge region, and he had, as Rhodes knew, put himself on record as unalterably opposed to a railroad. He was a large, heavy man, deep-chested and big-limbed, with grizzled hair and beard, a mouth closer drawn than might have been expected in one with his surroundings, and eyes that were small and deep-set, but very keen. His two-storied white house, with wings and portico, though not large, was more pretentious than most of those in the section, and his whitewashed buildings, nestled amid the fruit-trees on a green hill looking up the valley to the Gap, made quite a settlement. He was a man of considerable property and also of great influence, and in the Ridge region, as elsewhere, wealth is a basis of position and influence. The difference is one of degree. The evidences of wealth in the Ridge country were land and cattle, and these Squire Rawson had in abundance. He was esteemed the best judge of cattle in all that region.

Consistency is a jewel; but there are regions where Hospitality is reckoned before Consistency, and as soon as the old squire learned that General Keith's son was with the surveying party, even though it was, to use a common phrase, "comin' interferin'" with that country, he rode over to their camp and invited Gordon and his "friends" to be his guests as long as they should remain in that neighborhood.

"I don't want you to think, young man," he said to Rhodes, "that I'm goin' to agree to your dod-rotted road comin' through any land of mine, killin' my cattle; but I'll give you a bed and somethin' to eat."

Rhodes felt that he had gained a victory; Gordon was doubtful.

Though the squire never failed to remind the young engineer that the latter was a Yankee, and as such the natural and necessary enemy of the South, he and Rhodes became great friends, and the squire's hospitable roof remained the headquarters of the engineering party much longer than there was any necessity for its being so.

The squire's family consisted of his wife, a kindly, bustling little old dame, who managed everything and everybody, including the squire, with a single exception. This was her granddaughter, Euphronia Tripper, a plump and fresh young girl with light hair, a fair skin, and bright eyes. The squire laid down the law to those about him, but Mrs. Rawson—"Elizy"—laid down the law for him. This the old fellow was ready enough to admit. Sometimes he had a comical gleam in his deep eyes when he turned them on his guests as he rose at her call of "Adam, I want you."

"Boys, learn to obey promptly," he said; "saves a sight o' trouble. It's better in the family 'n a melojeon. It's got to come sooner or later, and the sooner the better for you. The difference between me and most married men around here is that they lies about it, and I don't. I know I belongs to Eliza. She owns me, but then she treats me

43

well. I'm sort o' meek when she's around, but then I make up for it by bein' so durned independent when I'm away from home. Besides, it's a good deal better to be ordered about by somebody as keers for you than not to have anybody in the world as keers whether you come or stay."

Besides Mrs. Rawson, there were in the family a widowed daughter, Mrs. Tripper, a long, pale, thin woman, with sad eyes, who had once been pretty, and her daughter Euphronia, already referred to, who, in right of being very pretty, was the old squire's idol and was never thwarted in anything. She was, in consequence, a spoiled little damsel, self-willed, very vain, and as susceptible as a chameleon. The ease with which she could turn her family around her finger gave her a certain contempt for them. At first she was quite enamoured of the young engineer; but Mr. Rhodes was too busy to give any thought to a girl whom he regarded as a child, and she turned her glances on Gordon. Gordon also was impervious to her charms. He was by no means indifferent to girls; several little damsels who attended St. Martin's Church had at one time or another been his load-stars for a while; but he was an aristocrat at heart, and held himself infinitely above a girl like Miss Euphronia.

Ferdy Wickersham had no such motives for abstaining from a flirtation with the young girl as those which restrained Rhodes and Keith.

Euphronia had not at first taken much notice of him. She had been inclined to regard Ferdy Wickersham with some disfavor as a Yankee; but when the other two failed her, Wickersham fell heir to her blandishments. Her indifference to him had piqued him and awakened an interest which possibly he might not otherwise have felt. He had seen much of the world for a youngster, and could make a good show with what he knew. He could play on the piano, and though the aged instrument which the old countryman had got at second-hand for his granddaughter gave forth sounds which might have come from a tinkling cymbal, yet Ferdy played with a certain dash and could bring from it tunes which the girl thought very fine. The two soon began to be so much together that both Rhodes and Keith fell to rallying Ferdy as to his conquest. Ferdy accepted it with complacency.

"I think I shall stay here while you are working up in the mountains," he said to his chief as the time drew near for them to leave.

"You will do nothing of the kind. I promised to take you with me, and I will take you dead or alive."

A frown began on the youngster's face, but passed away quickly, and in its place came a look of covert complacency.

"I thought your father had offered you five thousand dollars if you would stick it out through the whole trip?" Keith said.

Ferdy shut one eye slowly and gazed at Gordon with the other.

"Sickness was barred. I'll tell the old man I've studied. He'd never drop on to the game. He is a soft old bird, anyway."

"Do you mean you are going to lie to him?" asked Gordon.

"Oh, you are sappy! All fellows lie to their governors," declared Ferdy, easily. "Why, I wouldn't have any fun at all if I did not lie. You stay with me a bit, my son, and I'll teach you a few useful things."

"Thank you. I have no doubt you are a capable teacher," sniffed Gordon; "but I think I won't trouble you."

That evening, as Keith was coming from his work, he took a cross-cut through the fields and orchard, and under an overshadowing tree he came on Ferdy and Euphronia. They were so deeply engaged that Keith hastily withdrew and, making a detour, passed around the orchard to the house.

At supper Mrs. Tripper casually inquired of her daughter where she had been, a remark which might have escaped Keith's observation had not Ferdy Wickersham answered it in some haste.

"She went after the cows," he said, with a quick look at her, "and I went fishing, but I did not catch anything."

"I thought, Phrony, I saw you in the orchard," said her mother.

Wickersham looked at her quickly again.

"No, she wasn't in the orchard," he said, "for I was there."

"No, I wasn't in the orchard this evening," said Euphronia. "I went after the cows." She looked down in her plate.

Keith ate the rest of his supper in silence. He could not tell on Ferdy; that would not be "square." He consulted his mentor, his chief, who simply laughed at him.

"Leave 'em alone," he counselled. "I guess she knew how to lie before he came. Ferdy has some sense. And we are going to leave for the mountains in a little while. I am only waiting to bring the old squire around."

Gordon shook his head.

"My father says you mistake his hospitality for yielding," he said. "You will never get him to consent to your plan."

Rhodes laughed.

"Oh, won't I! I have had these old countrymen to deal with before. Just give them time and show them the greenbacks. He will come around. Wait until I dangle the shekels before him."

But Mr. Rhodes found that in that provincial field there were some things stronger than shekels. And among these were prejudices. The more the young engineer talked, the more obstinate appeared the old countryman.

"I raise cattle," he said in final answer to all his eloquence.

46

"Raise cattle! You can make more by raising coal in one year than you can by raising cattle all your life. Why, you have the richest mineral country back here almost in the world," said the young diplomat, persuasively.

"And that's the reason I want to keep the railroads out," said the squire, puffing quietly. "I don't want the Yankees to come down and take it away from us."

Rhodes laughed. "I'd like to see any one take anything from you. They will develop it for you."

"I never seen anybody develop anything for another man, leastways a Yankee," said Squire Rawson, reflectively.

Just then Ferdy chipped in. He was tired of being left out.

"My father'll come down here and show you old mossbacks a thing or two," he laughed.

The old man turned his eyes on him slowly. Ferdy was not a favorite with him. For one thing, he played on the piano. But there were other reasons.

"Who is your father, son?" The squire drew a long whiff from his pipe.

"Aaron Wickersham of Wickersham & Company, who is setting up the chips for this railroad. We are going to run through here and make it one of the greatest lines of the country."

"Oh, you're *goin'* to run it! From the way you talked I thought maybe you *had* run it. Was a man named Aaron once thought he knew more 'bout runnin' a' expedition than his brother did. Ever heard what became of him?"

"No," said Ferdy.

"Well, he run some of 'em in the ground. He didn't have sense to know the difference between a calf and God."

Ferdy flushed.

"Well, my old man knows enough to run this railroad. He has run bigger things than this."

"If he knows as much as his son, he knows a lot. He ought to be able to run the world." And the squire turned back to Rhodes:

"What are you goin' to do, my son, when you've done all you say you're goin' to do for us? You will be too good to live among them Yankees; you will have to come back here, I reckon."

"No; I'm going to marry and settle down," said Rhodes, jestingly. "Maybe I'll come back here sometime just to receive your thanks for showing you how benighted you were before I came, and for the advice I gave you."

"He is trying to marry a rich woman," said Ferdy, at which Rhodes flushed a little.

The old man took no notice of the interruption.

"Well, you must," he said to Rhodes, his eyes resting on him benevolently. "You must come back sometime and see me. I love to hear a young man talk who knows it all. But you take my advice, my son; don't marry no rich man's daughter. They will always think they have done you a favor, and they will try to make you think so too, even if your wife don't do it. You take warnin' by me. When I married, I had just sixteen dollars and my wife she had seventeen, and I give you my word I have never heard the last of that one dollar from that day to this."

Rhodes laughed and said he would remember his advice.

"Sometimes I think," said the old man, "I have mistaken my callin'. I was built to give advice to other folks, and instid of that they have been givin' me advice all my life. It's in and about the only thing I ever had given me, except physic."

The night before the party left, Ferdy packed his kit with the rest; but the next morning he was sick in his bed. His pulse was not quick, but he complained of pains in every limb. Dr. Balsam came over to see him, but could find nothing serious the matter. He, however, advised Rhodes to leave him behind. So, Ferdy stayed at Squire

Rawson's all the time that the party was in the mountains. But he wrote his father that he was studying.

During the time that Rhodes's party was in the mountains Squire Rawson rode about with them examining lands, inspecting coal-beds, and adding much to the success of the undertaking.

He appeared to be interested mainly in hunting up cattle, and after he had introduced the engineers and secured the tardy consent of the landowners for them to make a survey, he would spend hours haggling over a few head of mountain cattle, or riding around through the mountains looking for others.

Many a farmer who met the first advances of the stranger with stony opposition yielded amicably enough after old Rawson had spent an hour or two looking at his "cattle," or had conversed with him and his weather-beaten wife about the "craps" and the "child'en."

"You are a miracle!" declared young Rhodes, with sincere admiration. "How do you manage it?"

The old countryman accepted the compliment with becoming modesty.

"Oh, no; ain't no miracle about it. All I know I learned at the Ridge College, and from an old uncle of mine, and in the war. He used to say, 'Adam, don't be a fool; learn the difference between cattle.' Now, before you come, I didn't know nothin' about all them fureign countries— they was sort of vague, like the New Jerusalem—or about coal. You've told me all about that. I had an idea that it was all made jest so,—jest as we find it,—as the Bible says 'twas; but you know a lot—more than Moses knowed, and he was 'skilled in all the learnin' of the Egyptians.' You haven't taken to cattle quite as kindly as I'd 'a' liked, but you know a lot about coal. Learn the difference between cattle, my son. There's a sight o' difference between 'em."

Rhodes declared that he would remember his advice, and the two parted with mutual esteem.

CHAPTER IV

TWO YOUNG MEN

THE young engineer, on his return to New York, made a report to his employer. He said that the mineral resources were simply enormous, and were lying in sight for any one to pick up who knew how to deal with the people to whom they belonged. They could be had almost for the asking. But he added this statement: that the legislative charters would hardly hold, and even if they did, it would take an army to maintain what they gave against the will of the people. He advised securing the services of Squire Rawson and a few other local magnates.

Mr. Wickersham frowned at this plain speaking, and dashed his pen through this part of the report. "I am much obliged to you for the report on the minerals. The rest of it is trash. You were not paid for your advice on that. When I want law I go to a lawyer."

Mr. Rhodes rose angrily.

"Well, you have for nothing an opinion that is worth more than that of every rascally politician that has sold you his opinion and himself, and you will find it out."

Mr. Wickersham did find it out. However much was published about it, the road was not built for years. The legislative charters, gotten through by Mr. J. Quincy Plume and his confrères, which were to turn that region into a modern Golconda, were swept away with the legislatures that created them, and new charters had to be obtained.

TWO YOUNG MEN

Squire Rawson, however, went on buying cattle and, report said, mineral rights, and Gordon Keith still followed doggedly the track along which Mr. Rhodes had passed, sure that sometime he should find him a great man, building bridges and cutting tunnels, commanding others and sending them to right or left with a swift wave of his arm as of old. Where before Gordon studied as a task, he now worked for ambition, and that key unlocked unknown treasures.

Mr. Rhodes fell in with Norman just after his interview with Mr. Wickersham. He was still feeling sore over Mr. Wickersham's treatment of his report. He had worked hard over it. He attributed it in part to Ferdy's complaint of him. He now gave Norman an account of his trip, and casually mentioned his meeting Gordon Keith.

"He's a good boy," he said, "a nice kid. He licked Ferdy—a very pretty little piece of work. Ferdy had both the weight and the reach on him."

"Licked Ferdy! It's an old grudge, I guess?" said Norman.

"No. They started in pretty good friends. It was about you."

"About me?" Norman's face took on new interest.

"Yes; Ferdy said something, and Keith took it up. He seems pretty fond of you. I think he had it in for Ferdy, for Ferdy had been bedevilling him about the place. You know old Wickersham owns it. Ferdy's strong point is not taste. So I think Gordon was feeling a bit sore, and when Ferdy lit into you, Keith slapped him."

Norman was all alert now.

"Well? Which licked?"

"Oh, that was all. Keith won at the end of the first round. He'd have been fighting now if he had not licked him."

The rest of the talk was of General Keith and of the hardship of his position.

"They are as poor as death," said Rhodes. He told of his surroundings.

51

When Norman got home, he went to his mother. Her eye lighted up as it rested on the alert, vigorous figure and fresh, manly, eager face. She knew he had something on his mind.

"Mother, I have a plan," he said. "You remember Gordon Keith, the boy whose boat I sank over in England—'Keith the rebel'?"

Mrs. Wentworth remembered well. She remembered an older fight than that, between a Keith and a Wentworth.

"Well, I have just heard of him. Rhodes—you remember Rhodes? Grinnell Rhodes? Used to be stroke, the greatest stroke ever was. Well, Rhodes has been down South and stayed at Keith's father's home. He says it's a beautiful old place, and now belongs to Mr. Wickersham, Ferdy's father, and the old gentleman, General Keith, who used to own it farms it for him. Think of that! It's as if father had to be a bookkeeper in the bank! Rhodes says he's a fine old fellow, and that Gordon is one of the best. He was down there running a railway line for Mr. Wickersham, and took Gordon with him. And he says he's the finest sort of a fellow, and wants to go to college dreadfully, but hasn't a cent nor any way to get anything. Rhodes says it's awful down there. They are so poor."

Mrs. Wentworth smiled. "Well?"

Norman blushed and stammered a little, as he often did when he was embarrassed.

"Well, you know I have some money of my own, and I thought if you don't mind it I'd like to lend him a little. I feel rather piggish just spending it right and left for nothing, when a fellow like that would give his eyes for the chance to go to college. Grinnell Rhodes says that he is ever so fond of me; that Ferdy was blowing once and said something against me, and Gordon jumped right into him—said I was a friend of his, and that Ferdy should not say anything against me in his presence. He knocked Ferdy down. I tell you, when a fellow is ready to fight for another years after he has seen him, he is a good friend."

Mrs. Wentworth's face showed that she too appreciated such a friend.

"How do you know he needs it, or would accept it if he did?"

"Why, Rhodes says we have no idea of the poverty down there. He says our poorest clerks are rich compared with those people. And I'll write him a letter and offer to lend it to him. I'll tell him it's mine."

Mrs. Wentworth went over and kissed the boy. The picture rose to her mind of a young man fresh from fields where he had won renown, honored by his State, with everything that wealth and rank could give, laying his honors at the feet of a poor young girl.

"All right, my son."

That night Norman sat down and wrote a letter.

A few days later than this, Gordon Keith received a letter with the post-mark "New York." Who was there in New York who could know him? Not his young engineer. He knew his hand. He was now abroad. As he read the letter he wondered yet more. It was from Norman Wentworth. He had met an old friend, he said, who had told him about Gordon and about his father's misfortunes. He himself, he said, was at college, and he found himself in a position to be able to help a friend. He did not know to what extent aid might be of service; but he had some means of his own, and he asked that Gordon would allow him to make him a loan of whatever might be necessary to relieve his father and himself.

When Gordon finished reading the letter there were tears in his eyes.

He laid the letter in his father's lap, and the old gentleman read it through slowly. He sat lost in reflection for a few moments and then handed the letter back to Gordon.

"Write to him and thank him, my son—thank him warmly for both of us. I will never forget his kindness. He is a gentleman."

53

This was all; but he too showed in his face that that far-off shaft of light had reached his heart and rested there.

The General afterwards meditated deeply as to the wisdom of this action. Just then, however, Providence seemed to come to his aid.

Old Adam Rawson, hearing that he was hard up, or moved by some kindly impulse, offered to make him a loan. He "happened to have," he wrote, " a little pile lying by that he didn't have any particular use for just then, and it had come to him that, maybe, the General might be able to use it to advantage. He didn't care anything about security or interest."

The General was perplexed. He did not need it himself, but he was glad to borrow enough to send Gordon to college for a year. He sent Gordon up to old Rawson's with a letter.

The old man read the letter and then looked Gordon over; he read it and looked him over again, much as if he were appraising a young steer.

"Well, I didn't say I'd lend it to you," he said; "but, maybe, I'll do it if 'twill help the General. Investin' in a young man is kind of hazardous; it's like puttin' your money in a harry-dick—you don't know what he's goin' to be. All you has to go on is the frame and your jedgment."

Fortunately for Keith, the old cattle-dealer had a good opinion of his "jedgment." He went on : "But I admit blood counts for somethin', and I'm half minded to adventure some on your blood."

Gordon laughed. He would be glad to be tried on any account, he said, and would certainly repay the money.

"Well, I b'lieve you will if you can," said the squire. "And that's more than I can say of everybody. I'll invest a leetle money in your future, and I want to say this to you, that your future will depend on whether you pay it back or not. I never seen a young man as didn't pay his debts come to any good in my life, and I never seen one as did as didn't. I've seen many a man 'd shoot you if you dared to question his honor, an' wouldn't pay you a dollar if he was lousy with 'em." He took out his wallet, and untying the strings carefully, began to count out the greenbacks.

"I have to carry a pretty good pile to buy calves with," he chuckled; "but I reckon you'll be a fair substitute for one or two. How much do you want?—I mean, how little can you git along with?"

Gordon told him the amount his father had suggested. It was not a great sum.

"That seems a heap of money to put in book-learnin'," said the old man, thoughtfully, his eyes fixed on Gordon. "My whole edication didn't cost twenty-five dollars. With all that learnin', you'd know enough to teach the Ridge College."

Gordon, who had figured it out, began to give his necessary expenses. When he had finished, the old man counted out his bills. Gordon said he would give him his note for it, and his father would indorse it. The other shook his head.

"No; I don't want any bond. I'll remember it and you'll remember it. I've known too many men think they'd paid a debt when they'd given their bond. I don't want you to think that. If you're goin' to pay me, you'll do it without a bond, and if you ain't, I ain't goin' to sue you; I'm jest goin' to think what a' o'nery cuss you are."

So Gordon returned home, and a few weeks later was delving deep into new mysteries.

Gordon's college life may be passed over. He worked well, for he felt that it was necessary to work.

Looking around when he left college, the only thing that appeared in sight for Gordon Keith was to teach school. To be sure, the business, "the universal refuge of educated indigents," as his father quoted with a smile, was already overcrowded. But Gordon heard of a school which up to this time had not been overwhelmed with applicants. There was a vacancy at the Ridge College. Finally poor Gunn, after holding out as long as he could, had laid down his arms, as all soldiers must do sooner or later, and Gordon applied for the position. The old squire remembered the straight, broad-shouldered boy with his father's eyes and also remembered the debt he owed him, and with the vision of a stern-faced man with eyes of flame riding quietly at the head of his men across a shell-ploughed field, he wrote to Gordon to come.

"If he's got half of his daddy in him he'll straighten 'em out," he said.

So, Gordon became a school-teacher.

"I know no better advice to give you," said General Keith to Gordon, on bidding him good-by, "than to tell you to govern yourself, and you will be able to govern them. 'He that is slow to anger is better than the mighty; and he that ruleth his spirit than he that taketh a city.' "

During the years in which Gordon Keith was striving to obtain an education as best he might, Ferdy Wickersham had gone to one of the first colleges of the land. It was the same college which Norman Wentworth was attending. Indeed, Norman's being there was the main reason that Ferdy was sent there. Mr. Wickersham wished his son to have the best advantages. Mrs. Wickersham desired this too, but she also had a further motive. She wished her son to eclipse Norman Wentworth. Both were young men of parts, and as both had unlimited means at their disposal, neither was obliged to study.

Norman Wentworth, however, had applied himself to secure one of the high class-honors, and as he was universally respected and very popular, he was regarded as certain to have it, until an unexpected claimant suddenly appeared as a rival.

Ferdy Wickersham never took the trouble to compete for anything until he discovered that some one else valued it. It was a trait he had inherited from his mother, who could never see any one possessing a thing without coveting it.

The young man was soon known at college as one of the leaders of the gay set. His luxuriously furnished rooms, his expensive suppers and his acquaintance with dancing-girls were talked about, and he soon had a reputation for being one of the wildest youngsters of his class.

"Your son will spend all the money you can make for him," said one of his friends to Mr. Wickersham.

"Well," said the father, "I hope he will have as much pleasure in spending it as I have had in making it, that's all."

He not only gave Ferdy all the money he suggested a need for, but he offered him large bonuses in case he should secure any of the honors he had heard of as the prizes of the collegiate work.

Mrs. Wickersham was very eager for him to win this particular prize. Apart from her natural ambition, she had a special reason. The firm of Norman Wentworth & Son was one of the oldest and best-known houses in the country. The home of Norman Wentworth was known to be one of the most elegant in the city, as it was the most exclusive, and both Mr. and Mrs. Wentworth were recognized as representatives of the old-time gentry. Mrs. Wickersham might have endured the praise of the elegance of the mansion. She had her own ideas as to house-furnishing, and the Wentworth mansion was furnished in a style too quiet and antiquated to suit her more modern tastes. If it was filled with old mahogany and hung with damask-satin, Mrs. Wickersham had carved walnut and gorgeous hangings. And as to those white marble busts, and those books that were everywhere, she much preferred her brilliant figures which she "had bought in Europe," and books were "a nuisance about a house." They ought to be kept in a library, as she kept hers— a carved-walnut case with glass doors.

The real cause of Mrs. Wickersham's dislike of Mrs. Wentworth lay deeper.

The elder lady had always been gracious to Mrs. Wickersham when they met, as she was gracious to every one, and when a very large entertainment was given by her, had invited Mrs. Wickersham to it. But Mrs. Wickersham felt that Mrs. Wentworth lived within a charmed circle. And Mrs. Wickersham was envious.

It must be said that Ferdy needed no instigation to supersede Norman in any way that did not require too much work. He and Norman were very good friends; certainly Norman thought so; but at bottom Ferdy was envious of Norman's position and prestige, and deep in his heart lurked a long-standing grudge against the older boy, to which was added of late a greater one. Norman and he fancied the same girl, and Louise Caldwell was beginning to favor Norman.

Ferdy announced to his father that the class-honor would be won if he would give him money enough, and the elder Wickersham, delighted, told him to draw on him for all the money he wanted. This Ferdy did promptly. He suddenly gave up running away from college, applied himself to cultivating the acquaintance of his fellow-students, spent his money lavishly in entertainments, and for a time it appeared that he might wrest the prize from Norman's grasp.

College boys, however, are a curious folk. The mind of youth is virtuous. It is later on in life that it becomes sordid. Ferdy wrote his father that he had the prize, and that Norman, his only rival, had given up the fight. Mrs. Wickersham openly boasted of her son's success and of her motive, and sent him money lavishly. Young Wickersham's ambition, however, like that of many another man, o'erleaped itself. Wickersham drew about him many companions, but they were mainly men of light weight, roisterers and loafers, whilst the better class of his fellow-students quickly awoke to a true realization of the case. A new element was being introduced into college politics. The recognition of danger was enough to set the best element in the college to meet it. At the moment when Ferdy Wickersham felt himself victor, and abandoned himself to fresh pleasures, a new and irresistible force unexpectedly arose which changed the fate of the day. Wickersham tried to stem the current, but in vain. It was a tidal wave. Ferdy Wickersham faced defeat, and he could not stand it. He suddenly abandoned college, and went off, it was said, with a coryphée. His father and mother did not know of it for some time after he had left.

Mr. Wickersham received the first intimation of it in the shape of a draft which came to him from some distant point. When Mrs. Wickersham learned of it, she fell into a consuming rage, and then took to her bed. The downfall of her hopes and of her ambition had come through the person she loved best on earth. Finally she became so ill that Mr. Wickersham telegraphed a peremptory order to his son to come home, and after a reasonable time the young man appeared.

His mother's joy at meeting him overshadowed everything else with her, and the prodigal was received by her with that forgiveness which is both the weakness and the strength of a mother's heart. The father, however, had been struck as deeply as the mother. His ambition, if of a different kind, had been quite as great as that of Mrs. Wickersham, and the hard-headed, keen-sighted man, who had spent his life fighting his way to the front, often with little consideration for the rights of others, felt that one of his motives and one of his rewards had perished together.

The interview that took place in his office between him and his son was one which left its visible stamp on the older man, and for a time appeared to have had an effect even on the younger, with all his insolence and impervious selfishness. When Aaron Wickersham unlocked his private door and allowed his son and heir to go out, the clerks in the outer office knew by the young man's face, quite as well as by the rumbles of thunder which had come through the fast-closed door, that the "old man" had been giving the young one a piece of his mind.

At first the younger man had been inclined to rebel; but for once in his life he found that he had passed the limit of license, and his father, whom he had rather despised as foolishly pliable, was unexpectedly his master. He laid before Ferdy, with a power which the latter could not but acknowledge, the selfishness and brutality of his conduct since he was a boy. He told him of his own earlier privations, of his labors, of his ambitions.

"I have worked my heart out," he said, "for your mother and for you. I have never known a moment of rest or of what you call 'fun.' I set it before me when your mother promised to marry me that I would make her as good as the first lady in the land—that is, in New York. She should have as big a house and as fine a carriage and as handsome frocks as any one of them—as old Mrs. Wentworth or old Mrs. Brooke of Brookford, who were the biggest people I ever knew. And I have spent my life for it. I have grown old before my time. I have gotten so that things have lost their taste to me; I have done things that I never dreamed I would do to accomplish it. I have lost the power to sleep working for it, and when you came I thought I would have my reward in you. I have not only never stinted you, but I have lavished money on you as if I was the richest man in New York. I wanted you to have advantages that I never had: as good as Norman Wentworth or any one else. I have given you things, and seen you throw them away, that I would have crawled on my knees from my old home to this office to get when I was a boy. And I thought you were going to be my pride and my stay and my reward. And you said you were doing it, and your mother and I had staked our hearts on you. And all the time you were running away and lying to me and to her, and not doing one honest lick of work."

The young man interrupted him. "That is not so," he said surlily.

His father pulled out a drawer and took from it a letter.

Spreading it open on his desk, he laid the palm of his open hand on it. "Not so? I have got the proof of it here." He looked at the young man with level eyes, eyes in which was such a cold gleam that Ferdy's gaze fell.

"I did not expect you to do it for *me*," Aaron Wickersham went on slowly, never taking his eyes from his son's face, "for I had discovered that you did not care a button for my wishes; but I did think you would do it for your mother. For she thought you were a god and worshipped you. She has been talking for ten years of the time when she would go to see you come out at the head of your class. She was going to Paris to get the clothes to wear if you won, and you—" His voice broke—"you won't even graduate! What will you think next summer when Mrs. Wentworth is there to see her son, and all the other men and women I know who have sons who graduate there, and your mother—?" The father's voice broke completely, and he looked away. Even Ferdy for a moment seemed grave and regretful. Then after a glance at his father he recovered his composure.

"I'm not to blame," he said surlily, "if she did. It was her fault."

Aaron Wickersham turned on him.

"Stop," he said in a quiet voice. "Not another word. One other word, and, by God! I'll box your head off your shoulders. Say what you please about me, but not one word against her. I will take you from college and put you to sweeping the floor of this office at twenty dollars a month, and make you live on your salary, too, or starve, if you say one other word."

Ferdy's face blanched at the implacable anger that blazed in his father's eyes, but even more at the coldness of the gleam. It made him shiver.

A little later young Wickersham entered his father's office, and though he was not much liked by the older clerks, it soon appeared that he had found a congenial occupation and one for which he had a natural gift. For the first time in his life he appeared inclined to work.

CHAPTER V

THE RIDGE COLLEGE

THE school over which Gordon had undertaken to preside was not a very advanced seminary of learning, and possibly the young teacher did not impart to his pupils a great deal of erudition.

His predecessors in the schoolmaster's chair had been, like their patrons, the product of a system hardly less conservative than that of the Locrians. Any one who proposed an innovation would have done so with a rope about his neck, and woe to him if it proved unsuccessful.

When Gordon reported first to the squire, the old man was manifestly pleased.

"Why, you've growed considerable. I didn't have no idea you'd be so big a man." He measured him with satisfaction. "You must be nigh as big as your pa."

"I'm broader across the shoulders, but not so tall," said the young man.

"He is a pretty tall man," said the squire, slowly, with the light of reflection in his eye. "You're a-goin' to try the Ridge College, are you?" He had a quizzical twinkle in his eye as it rested on the younger man's face.

"I'm going to try it." And Gordon's face lit up. "I don't know much, but I'll do the best I can."

His modesty pleased the other.

"You know more than Jake Dennison, I reckon, except about devilment. I was afred you mightn't be quite up to the place here; you was rather young when I seen you last." He measured him as he might have done a young bullock.

"Oh, I fancy I shall be," interrupted the young man, flushing at the suggestion.

"You've got to learn them Dennison boys, and them Dennison boys is pretty hard to learn anything. You will need all the grit you've got."

"Oh, I'll teach them," asserted Gordon, confidently.

The old man's eye rested on him.

"'Tain't *teachin'* I'm a-talkin' about. It's *learnin'* I'm tellin' you they need. You've got to learn 'em a good deal, or they'll learn you. Them Dennison boys is pretty slow at learnin'."

The young man intimated that he thought he was equal to it.

"Well, we'll see," grunted the old fellow, with something very like a twinkle in his deep eyes. "Not as they'll do you any harm without you undertake to interfere with them," he drawled. "But you're pretty young to manage 'em jest so; you ain't quite big enough either, and you're too big to git in through the cat-hole. And I allow that you don't stand no particular show after the first week or so of gittin' into the house any other way."

"I'll get in, though, and I won't go in through the cat-hole either. I'll promise you that, if you'll sustain me."

"Oh, I'll sustain you," drawled the squire. "I'll sustain you in anything you do, except to pizon 'em with *slow* pizon, and I ain't altogether sure that wouldn' be jest man-slaughter."

"All right." Keith's eyes snapped, and presently, as the older man's gaze rested on him, his snapped also.

So the compact was struck, and the trustee went on to give further information.

"Your hours will be as usual," said he: "from seven to two and fo' to six in summer, and half-past seven to two and three to five in winter, and you'll find all the books necessary in the book-chist. We had to have 'em locked up to keep 'em away from the rats and the dirt-daubers. Some of 'em's right smartly de-faced; but I reckon you'll git on with 'em all right."

"Well, those are pretty long hours," said Gordon. "Seems to me they had better be shortened. I shall—"

"Them's the usual hours," interrupted the old man, positively. "I've been trustee now for goin' on twenty-six year, an' th'ain't never been any change in 'em. An' I ain't see as they've ever been too long—leastways, I never see as the scholars ever learned too much in 'em. They ain't no longer than a man has to work in the field, and the work's easier."

Gordon looked at the old man keenly. It was his first battle, and it had come on at once, as his father had warned him. The struggle was bitter, if brief, but he conquered— conquered himself. The old countryman's face had hardened.

"If you want to give satisfaction you'd better try to learn them scholars an' not the trustees," he said dryly. "The Dennison boys is hard, but we're harder."

Gordon looked at him quickly. His eyes were resting on him, and had a little twinkle in them.

"We're a little like the old fellow 'at told the young preacher 'at he'd better stick to abusin' the sins of Esau and Jacob and David and Peter, an' let the sins o' that congregation alone."

"I'll try and give you satisfaction," said Keith.

The squire appeared pleased. His face relaxed and his tone changed.

"*You* won't have no trouble," he said good-humoredly. "Not if you're like your father. I told 'em you was his son, an' I'd be responsible for you."

Gordon Keith looked at him with softened eyes. A mention of his father always went to his heart.

"I'll try and give you satisfaction," he said earnestly. "Will you do me a favor?"

"Yes."

64

"Will you come over to the examination of the school when it opens, and then let me try the experiment of running it my way for, say, two months, and then come to another examination? Then if I do not satisfy you I'll do anything you say; I'll go back to the old way."

"Done," said the trustee, cordially. And so, Gordon Keith won another victory, and started the school under favorable auspices.

Adam Rawson asked him to come and live at his house. "You might give Phrony a few extra lessons to fit her for a bo'din'-school," he said. "I want her to have the best edvantages."

Keith soon ingratiated himself further with the old squire. He broke his young horses for him, drove his wagon, mended his vehicles, and was ready to turn his hand to anything that came up about the place.

As his confidence in the young man grew, the squire let Keith into a secret.

"You mind when you come up here with that young man from the North,—that engineer fellow,—what come a-runnin' of a railroad a-hellbulgin' through this country, and was a-goin' to carry off all the coal from the top of the Alleghanies spang down to Torment?" Keith remembered. "Well, he was right persuasive," continued the squire, "and I thought if all that money was a-goin' to be made and them railroads had to come, like he said, jest as certain as water runnin' down a hill, I might as well git some of it. I had a little slipe or two up there before, and havin' a little money from my cattle, lumber, and sich, I went in and bought a few slipes more, jest to kind of fill in like, and Phrony's growin' up, and I'm a-thinkin' it is about time to let the railroads come in; so, if you kin git your young man, let him know I've kind o' changed my mind."

Miss Euphronia Tripper had grown up into a plump and pretty country girl of fifteen or sixteen, whose rosy cheeks, flaxen hair, and blue eyes, as well as the fact that she was the only heiress of the old squire, who was one of the "best-fixed" men in all that "country," made her quite the belle of the region. She had already made a deep impression on both big Jake Dennison and his younger brother Dave. Dave was secretly in love with her, but Jake was openly so, a condition which he manifested by being as plainly and as hopelessly bound in her presence as a bear cub tangled in a net. For her benefit he would show feats of strength which might have done credit to a boy-Hercules; but let her turn on him the glow of her countenance, and he was a hopeless mass of perspiring idiocy.

Keith found her a somewhat difficult pupil to deal with. She was much more intent on making an impression on him than on progressing in her studies.

After the first shyness of her intercourse with the young teacher had worn off, she began for a while rather to make eyes at him, which if Keith ever dreamed of, he never gave the least sign of it. She, therefore, soon abandoned the useless campaign, and for a time held him in mingled awe and disdain.

The Ridge College was a simple log-building of a single room, with a small porch in front, built of hewn logs and plastered inside.

Gordon Keith, on entering on his new duties, found his position much easier than he had been led to expect.

Whether it was the novelty of the young teacher's quiet manner, clear eyes, broad shoulders, and assured bearing, or the idea of the examination with which he undertook to begin the session, he had a week of surprising quiet. The school filled day after day, and even the noted Dennison boys, from Jacob Dennison, the strapping six-foot senior, down to Dave, who was the youngest and smartest of the three, appeared duly every morning, and treated the young teacher with reasonable civility, if with somewhat insolent familiarity.

The day of the examination Squire Rawson attended,

solemn and pompous with a superfluity of white shirt-front.

Brief as was the examination, it revealed to Keith an astonishing state of ignorance of the simplest things. It was incredible to him that, with so many hours of so-called study, so little progress had been made. He stated this in plain language, and outlined his plan for shorter hours and closer application. A voice from the boys' side muttered that the owner did not see anything the matter with the old hours. They were good enough for them. Keith turned quickly:

"What is that?"

There was no answer.

"What is that, Dennison?" he demanded. "I thought I heard you speak."

"Wall, if you did, I warn't speakin' to you," said Jacob Dennison, surlily.

"Well, when you speak in school, address yourself to me," said Keith. He caught Euphronia Tripper's eyes on him.

"I mought an' I moughtn't," said Jacob, insolently.

"I propose to see that you do."

Jacob's reply was something between a grunt and a sneer, and the school rustled with a sound very much like applause.

Next morning, on his arrival at school, Keith found the door fastened on the inside. A titter from within revealed the fact that it was no accident, and the guffaw of derision that greeted his sharp command that the door should be opened immediately showed that the Dennison boys were up to their old tricks.

"Open the door, Jake Dennison, instantly!" he called.

The reply was sung through the keyhole:

" ' Ole Molly hyah, what you doin' dyah?
Settin' in de cordner, smokin' a ciggyah.' "

It was little Dave's voice, and was followed by a puff of tobacco smoke through the keyhole and a burst of laughter led by Phrony Tripper.

An axe was lying at the woodpile near by, and in two minutes the door was lying in splinters on the school-house floor, and Keith, with a white face and a dangerous tremble in his voice, was calling the amazed school to order. He heard the lessons through, and at noon, the hour he had named the day before, dismissed all the younger scholars. The Dennisons and one or two larger boys he ordered to remain. As the scholars filed out, there was a colloquy between Jacob Dennison and his younger brother Dave. Dave had the brains of the family, and he was whispering to Jake. Keith moved his chair and seated himself near the door. There was a brief muttered conversation among the Dennisons, and then Jake Dennison rose, put on his hat slowly, and, addressing the other boys, announced that he didn't know what they were going to do, but he was "a-gwine home and git ready to go and see the dance up at Gates's."

He swaggered toward the door, the others following in his wake.

Keith rose from his seat.

"Go back to your places." He spoke so quietly that his voice could scarcely be heard.

"Go nowhere! You go to h—l!" sneered the big leader, contemptuously. "'Tain't no use for you to try to stop me—I kin git away with two like you."

Perhaps, he could have done so, but Keith was too quick for him. He seized the split-bottomed chair from which he had risen, and whirling it high above his head, brought it crashing down on his assailant, laying him flat on the floor. Then, without a second's hesitation, he sprang toward the others.

"Into your seats instantly!" he shouted, as he raised once more the damaged, but still formidable, weapon. By an instinct the mutineers fell into the nearest seats, and

Keith turned back to his first opponent, who was just rising from the floor with a dazed look on his face. A few drops of blood were trickling down his forehead.

"If you don't go to your seat instantly, I'll dash your brains out," said Keith, looking him full in the eye. He still grasped the chair, and as he tightened his grip on it, the crestfallen bully sank down on the bench and broke into a whimper about a grown man hitting a boy with a chair.

Suddenly Keith, in the moment of victory, found himself attacked in the rear. One of the smaller boys, who had gone out with the rest, hearing the fight, had rushed back, and, just as Keith drove Jake Dennison to his seat, sprang on him like a little wild-cat. Turning, Keith seized and held him.

"What are you doing, Dave Dennison, confound you?" he demanded angrily.

"I'm one of 'em," blubbered the boy, trying to reach him with both fist and foot. "I don't let nobody hit my brother."

Keith found that he had more trouble in quelling Dave, the smallest member of the Dennison tribe, than in conquering the bigger brothers.

"Sit down and behave yourself," he said, shoving him into a seat and holding him there. "I'm not going to hit him again if he behaves himself."

Keith, having quieted Dave, looked to see that Jake was not much hurt. He took out his handkerchief.

"Take that and wipe your face with it," he said quietly, and taking from his desk his inkstand and some writing-paper, he seated himself on a bench near the door and began to write letters. It grew late, but the young teacher did not move. He wrote letter after letter. It began to grow dark; he simply lit the little lamp on his desk, and taking up a book, settled down to read; and when at last he rose and announced that the culprits might go home, the wheezy strains of the three instruments that composed the band at Gates's had long since died out, and Gordon Keith was undisputed master of Ridge College.

His letter to the trustees was delivered that morning, saying that if they would sustain his action he would do his best to make the school the best in that section; but if not, his resignation was in their hands.

"I guess he is the sort of medicine those youngsters need," said Dr. Balsam. "We'd better let it work."

"I reckon he can ride 'em," said Squire Rawson.

It was voted to sustain him.

The fact that a smooth-faced boy, not as heavy as Jake Dennison by twenty pounds, had "faced down" and quelled the Dennisons all three together, and kept Jake Dennison from going where he wanted to go, struck the humor of the trustees, and they stood by their teacher almost unanimously, and even voted to pay for a new door, which he had offered to pay for himself, as he said he might have to chop it down again. Not that there was not some hostility to him among those to whom his methods were too novel; but when he began to teach his pupils boxing, and showed that with his fists he was more than a match for Jake Dennison, the chief opposition to him died out; and before the year ended, Jake Dennison, putting into practice the art he had learned from his teacher, had thrashed Mr. William Bluffy, the cock of another walk high up across the Ridge, for ridiculing the "newfangled foolishness" of Ridge College, and speaking of its teacher as a "dom-fool furriner." Little Dave Dennison, of all those opposed to him, alone held out. He appeared to be proof against Keith's utmost efforts to be friends.

One day, however, Dave Dennison did not come to school. Keith learned that he had fallen from a tree and broken his leg—"gettin' hawks' eggs for Phrony," Keith's informant reported. Phrony was quite scornful about it, but a little perky as well.

"If a boy was such a fool as to go up a tree when he had been told it wouldn't hold him, she could not help it. She did not want the eggs, anyhow," she said disdainfully. This was all the reward that little Dave got for his devotion and courage.

That afternoon Keith went over the Ridge to see Dave.

The Dennison home was a small farm-house back of the Ridge, in what was known as a "cove," an opening in the angle between the mountains, where was a piece of level or partly level ground on the banks of one of the little mountain creeks. When Keith arrived he found Mrs. Dennison, a small, angular woman with sharp eyes, a thin nose, and thin lips, very stiff and suspicious. She had never forgiven Keith for his victory over her boys, and she looked now as if she would gladly have set the dogs on him instead of calling them off as she did when he strode up the path and the yelping pack dashed out at him.

She "didn' know how Dave was," she said glumly. "The Doctor said he was better. She couldn' see no change. Yes, he could go in, she s'posed, if he wanted to," she said ungraciously.

Keith entered. The boy was lying on a big bed, his head resting against the frame of the little opening which went for a window, through which he was peeping wistfully out at the outside world from which he was to be shut off for so many weary weeks. He returned Keith's greeting in the half-surly way in which he had always received his advances since the day of the row; but when Keith sat down on the bed and began to talk to him cheerily of his daring in climbing where no one else had ventured to go, he thawed out, and presently, when Keith drifted on to other stories of daring, he began to be interested, and after a time grew almost friendly.

He was afraid they might have to cut his leg off. His mother, who always took a gloomy view of things, had scared him by telling him she thought it might have to be done; but Keith was able to reassure him. The Doctor had told him that, while the fracture was very bad, the leg would be saved.

"If he had not been as hard as a lightwood knot, that fall would have mashed him up," said the Doctor. This compliment Keith repeated, and it evidently pleased Dave. The pale face relaxed into a smile. Keith told him stories of other boys who had had similar accidents and had turned them to good account—of Arkwright and Sir William Jones and Commodore Maury, all of whom had laid the foundation for their future fame when they were in bed with broken legs.

When Keith came away he left the boy comforted and cheered, and even the dismal woman at the door gave him a more civil parting than her greeting had been.

Many an afternoon during the boy's convalescence Keith went over the Ridge to see him, taking him story-books, and reading to him until he was strong enough to read himself. And when, weeks later, the lame boy was able to return to school, Keith had no firmer friend in all the Ridge region than Dave Dennison, and Dave had made a mental progress which, perhaps, he would not have made in as many months at school, for he had received an impulse to know and to be something more than he was. He would show Phrony who he was.

It was fine to Gordon to feel that he was earning his own living. He was already making his way in the world, and often from this first rung of the ladder the young teacher looked far up the shining steep to where Fame and Glory beckoned with their radiant hands. He would be known. He would build bridges that should eclipse Stevenson's. He would be like Warren Hastings, and buy back the home of his fathers and be a great gentleman.

The first pay that he received made him a capitalist. He had no idea before of the joy of wealth. He paid it to old Rawson.

"There is the first return for your investment," he said.

"I don' know about its bein' the first return," said the squire, slowly ; "but an investment ain't done till it's all returned." His keen eyes were on Keith's face.

"I know it," said Keith, laughing.

But for Dr. Balsam, Keith sometimes thought that he must have died that first winter, and, in fact, the young man did owe a great deal to the tall, slab-sided man, whose clothes hung on him so loosely that he appeared in the distance hardly more than a rack to support them. As he came nearer he was a simple old countryman with a deeply graved face and unkempt air. On nearer view still, you found the deep gray eyes both shrewd and kindly; the mouth under its gray moustache had fine lines, and at times a lurking smile, which yet had in it something grave.

To Dr. Balsam, Keith owed a great deal more than he himself knew at the time. For it is only by looking back that Youth can gauge the steps by which it has climbed.

CHAPTER VI

ALICE YORKE

IT is said that in Brazil a small stream which rises under a bank in a gentleman's garden, after flowing a little distance, encounters a rock and divides into two branches, one of which flows northward and empties into the Amazon, whilst the other, turning to the southward, pours its waters into the Rio del Plata. A very small obstruction caused the divergence and determined the course of those two streams. So it is in life.

One afternoon in the early Spring, Gordon Keith was walking home from school, his books under his arm, when, so to speak, he came on the stone that turned him from his smooth channel and shaped his course in life.

He was going to break a colt for Squire Rawson that afternoon, so he was hurrying; but ever as he strode along down the winding road, the witchery of the tender green leaves and the odors of Spring filled eyes and nostrils, and called to his spirit with that subtle voice which has stirred Youth since Youth's own Spring awoke amid the leafy trees. In its call were freedom, and the charm of wide spaces, and the unspoken challenge of Youth to the world, and haunting vague memories, and whisperings of unuttered love, and all that makes Youth Youth.

Presently Gordon became aware that a little ahead of him, under the arching boughs, were two children who were hunting for something in the road, and one of them was crying. At the same moment there turned the curve beyond them, coming toward him, a girl on horseback. He watched her with growing interest as she galloped toward him, for he saw that she was young and a stranger. Probably she was from "the Springs," as she was riding one of Gates's horses and was riding him hard.

The rider drew in her horse and stopped as she came up to the children. Keith heard her ask what was the matter with the little one, and the older child's reply that she was crying because she had lost her money. "She was goin' to buy candy with it at the store, but dropped it."

The girl sprang from her horse.

"Oh, you poor little thing! Come here, you dear little kitten. I'll give you some money. Won't you hold my horse? He won't hurt you." This to the elder child.

She threw herself on her knees in the road, as regardless of the dust as were the children, and drawing the sobbing child close to her, took her handkerchief from her pocket and gently wiped its little, dirty, smeared face, and began comforting it in soothing tones. Keith had come up and stood watching her with quickening breath. All he could see under her hat was an oval chin and the dainty curve of a pink cheek where it faded into snow, and at the back of a small head a knot of brown hair resting on the nape of a shapely neck. For the rest, she had a trim figure and wore new gloves which fitted perfectly. Keith mentally decided that she must be about sixteen or seventeen years old, and, from the glimpse he had caught of her, must be pretty. He became conscious suddenly that he had on his worst suit of clothes.

"Good evening," he said, raising his hand to his hat.

The girl glanced up just as the hat was lifted.

"How do you do?"

Their eyes met, and the color surged into Keith's face, and the hat came off with quite a flourish.

Why, she was beautiful! Her eyes were as blue as wet violets.

"I will help you hunt for it," he said half guilefully,

half kindly. "Where did she drop it?" He did not take his eyes from the picture of the slim figure on her knees.

"She has lost her money, poor little dear! She was on her way to the store to buy candy, and lost all her money."

At this fresh recital of her loss, the little, smeared face began to pucker again. But the girl cleared it with a kiss.

"There, don't cry. I will give you some. How much was it? A nickel! A whole nickel!" This with the sweetest smile. "Well, you shall have a quarter, and that's four nickels — I mean five."

"She is not strong on arithmetic," said Keith to himself. "She is like Phrony in that."

She began to feel about her skirt, and her face changed.

"Oh, I haven't a cent. I have left my purse at the hotel." This was to Keith.

"Let me give it to her." And he also began to feel in his pocket, but as he did so his countenance fell. He, too, had not a cent.

"I have left my purse at home, too," he said. "We shall have to do like the woman in the Bible, and sweep diligently till we find the money she lost."

"We are a pauper lot," said Alice Yorke, with a little laugh. Then, as she glanced into the child's big eyes that were beginning to be troubled again, she paused. The next second she drew a small bracelet from her wrist, and began to pull at a small gold charm. "Here, you shall have this; this is gold."

"Oh, don't do that," said Keith. "She wouldn't appreciate it, and it is a pity to spoil your bracelet."

She glanced up at him with a little flash in her blue eyes, as a vigorous twist broke the little gold piece from its chain.

"She shall have it. There, see how she is smiling. I have enjoyed it, and I am glad to have you have it. Now, you can get your candy. Now, kiss me."

Somehow, the phrase and the tone brought back to Keith a hill-top overlooking an English village, and a blue lake below, set like a mirror among the green hills. A little girl in white, with brown eyes, was handing a doll to another child even more grimy than this one. The reminiscence came to him like a picture thrown by a magic lantern.

The child, without taking her eyes from the tiny bit of metal, put up her little mouth, and the girl kissed her, only to have the kiss wiped off with the chubby, dirty little hand.

The next moment the two little ones started down the road, their heads close together over the bit of yellow gold. Then it was that Alice Yorke for the first time took a real look at Keith,—a look provoked by the casual glance she had had of him but a moment before,—and as she did so the color stole up into her cheeks, as she thought of the way in which she had just addressed him. But for his plain clothes he looked quite a gentleman. He had a really good figure ; straight, broad shoulders, and fine eyes.

" Can you tell me what time it is ? " she asked, falteringly. "I left my watch at the hotel."

" I haven't a watch ; but I think it must be about four o'clock—it was half-past three when I left school, by the school clock ; I am not sure it was just right."

"Thank you." She looked at her horse. "I must get back to the hotel. Can you— ? "

Keith forestalled her.

"May I help you up ? "

"Thanks. Do you know how to mount me ? "

"I think so," he said airily, and stepped up close to her, to lift her by the elbows to her saddle. She put out a foot clad in a very pretty, neat shoe. She evidently expected Keith to let her step into his hand. He knew of this mode of helping a lady up, but he had never tried it. And, though he stooped and held his hand as if quite accustomed to it, he was awkward about it, and did not lift her ; so she did not get up.

"I don't think you can do it that way," said the girl.

"I don't think so either," said Keith. "I must learn it.

But I know how to do it this way." He caught her by both elbows. "Now jump!"

Taken by surprise she gave a little spring, and he lifted her like a feather, and seated her in her saddle.

As she rode away, he stood aside and lifted his hat with an air that surprised her. Also, as she rode away, he remarked that she sat her horse very well and had a very straight, slim figure; but the picture of her kneeling in the dust, with her arm around the little sobbing child, was what he dwelt on.

Just as she disappeared, a redbird in its gorgeous uniform flitted dipping across the road, and, taking his place in a bush, began to sing imperiously for his mate.

"Ah, you lucky rascal," thought Keith, "you don't get caught by a pretty girl, in a ragged coat. You have your best clothes on every day."

Next second, as the bird's rich notes rang out, a deeper feeling came to him, and a wave of dissatisfaction with his life swept over him. He suddenly seemed lonelier than he had been. Then the picture of the girl on her knees came back to him, and his heart softened toward her. He determined to see her again. Perhaps, Dr. Balsam knew her?

As the young girl rode back to the hotel she had her reward in a pleasant sensation. She had done a good deed in helping to console a little child, and no kindness ever goes without this reward. Besides, she had met a young, strange man, a country boy, it was true, and very plainly dressed, but with the manner and tone of a gentleman, quite good-looking, and very strong. Strength, mere physical strength, appeals to all girls at certain ages, and Miss Alice Yorke's thoughts quite softened toward the stranger. Why, he as good as picked her up! He must be as strong as Norman Wentworth, who stroked his crew. She recalled with approval his good shoulders.

She would ask the old Doctor who he was. He was a

pleasant old man, and though her mother and Mrs. Nailor, another New York lady, did not like the idea of his being the only doctor at the Springs, he had been very nice to her. He had seen her sitting on the ground the day before and had given her his buggy-robe to sit on, saying, with a smile, "You must not sit on the wet ground, or you may fall into my hands."

"I might do worse," she had said. And he had looked at her with his deep eyes twinkling.

"Ah, you young minx! When do you begin flattering? And at what age do you let men off?"

When Miss Alice Yorke arrived at the hotel she found her mother and Mrs. Nailor engaged in an animated conversation on the porch.

The girl told of the little child she had found crying in the road, and gave a humorous account of the young countryman trying to put her on her horse.

"He was very good-looking, too," she declared gayly. "I think he must be studying for the ministry, like Mr. Rimmon, for he quoted the Bible."

Both Mrs. Yorke and Mrs. Nailor thought it rather improper for her to be riding alone on the public roads.

The next day Keith put on his best suit of clothes when he went to school, and that afternoon he walked home around the Ridge, as he had done the day before, thinking that possibly he might meet the girl again, but he was disappointed. The following afternoon he determined to go over to the Springs and see if she was still there and find out who she was. Accordingly, he left the main road, which ran around the base of the Ridge, and took a foot-path which led winding up through the woods over the Ridge. It was a path that Gordon often chose when he wanted to be alone. The way was steep and rocky, and was so little used that often he never met any one from the time he plunged into the woods until he emerged from them on the other side of the Ridge. In some places the pines were so thick that it was always twilight among them; in others they rose high and stately in the full majesty of primeval growth, keeping at a distance from each other, as though, like another growth, the higher they got the more distant they wished to hold all others. Trees have so much in common with men, it is no wonder that the ancients, who lived closer to both than we do nowadays, fabled that minds of men sometimes inhabited their trunks.

Gordon Keith was in a particularly gloomy frame of mind on this day. He had been trying to inspire in his pupils some conception of the poetry contained in history. He told them the story of Hannibal—his aim, his struggles, his conquest. As he told it the written record took life, and he marched and fought and lived with the great Carthaginian captain—lived for conquest.

"Beyond the Alps lies Italy." He had read the tale with lips that quivered with feeling, but as he looked up at his little audience, he met only listless eyes and dull faces. A big boy was preparing a pin to evoke from a smaller neighbor the attention he himself was withholding. The neighbor was Dave Dennison. Dave was of late actually trying to learn something. Dave was the only boy who was listening. A little girl with a lisp was trying in vain to divide her attention between the story and an imprisoned fly the boy next her was torturing, whilst Phrony was reading a novel on the sly. The others were all engaged in any other occupation than thinking of Hannibal or listening to the reader.

Gordon had shut the book in a fit of disappointment and disgust and dismissed the school, and now he was trying with very poor success to justify himself for his outbreak of impatience. His failure spoiled the pleasure he had anticipated in going to the Springs to find out who the Madonna of the Dust was.

At a spot high up on the rocky backbone, one could see for a long way between the great brownish-gray trunks, and Gordon turned out of the dim path to walk on the thick brown carpet of pine-needles. It was a favorite spot with

Gordon, and here he read Keats and Poe and other poets of melancholy, so dear to a young man's heart.

Beyond the pines at their eastern edge, a great crag jutted forth in a sort of shoulder, a vast flying-buttress that supported the pine-clad Ridge above—a mighty stone Atlas carrying the hills on its shoulder. From this rock one looked out eastward over the rolling country below to where, far beyond sloping hills covered with forest, it merged into a soft blue that faded away into the sky itself. In that misty space lay everything that Gordon Keith had known and loved in the past. Off there to the eastward was his old home, with its wide fields, its deep memories. There his forefathers had lived for generations and had been the leaders, making their name always the same with that of gentleman.

Farther away, beyond that dim line lay the great world, the world of which he had had as a boy a single glimpse and which he would yet conquer.

Keith had climbed to the crest of the Ridge and was making his way through the great pines to the point where the crag jutted out sheer and massive, overlooking the reaches of rolling country below, when he lifted his eyes, and just above him, half seated, half reclining against a ledge of rock, was the very girl he had seen two days before. Her eyes were closed, and her face was so white that the thought sprang into Keith's mind that she was dead, and his heart leaped into his throat. At the distance of a few yards he stopped and scanned her closely. She had on a riding-habit; her hat had fallen on her neck; her dark hair, loosened, lay about her throat, increasing the deep pallor of her face. Keith's pity changed into sorrow. Suddenly, as he leaned forward, his heart filled with a vague grief, she opened her eyes—as blue as he remembered them, but now misty and dull. She did not stir or speak, but gazed at him fixedly for a little space, and then the eyes closed again wearily, her head dropped over to the side, and she began to sink down.

Gordon sprang forward to keep her from rolling down

the bank. As he gently caught and eased her down on the soft carpeting of pine-needles, he observed how delicate her features were; the blue veins showed clearly on her temples and the side of her throat, and her face had that refinement that unconsciousness often gives.

Gordon knew that the best thing to do was to lower her head and unfasten her collar. As he loosened the collar, the whiteness of her throat struck him almost dazzlingly. Instinctively he took the little crumpled handkerchief that lay on the pine carpet beside her, and spread it over her throat reverently. He lifted her limp hand gently and felt her little wrist for her pulse.

Just then her eyelids quivered; her lips moved slightly, stopped, moved again with a faint sigh; and then her eyelids opened slowly, and again those blue eyes gazed up at him with a vague inquiry.

The next second she appeared to recover consciousness. She drew a long, deep breath, as though she were returning from some unknown deep, and a faint little color flickered in her cheek.

"Oh, it's you?" she said, recognizing him. "How do you do? I think I must have hurt myself when I fell. I tried to ride my horse down the bank, and he slipped and fell with me, and I do not remember much after that. He must have run away. I tried to walk, but—but I am better now. Could you catch my horse for me?"

Keith rose and followed the horse's track for some distance along the little path. When he returned, the girl was still seated against the rock.

"Did you see him?" she asked languidly, sitting up.

"I am afraid that he has gone home. He was galloping. I could tell from his tracks."

"I think I can walk. I must."

She tried to rise, but, with the pain caused by the effort, the blood sprang to her cheek for a second and then fled back to her heart, and she sank back, her teeth catching her lip sharply to keep down an expression of anguish.

"I must get back. If my horse should reach the hotel without me, my mother will be dreadfully alarmed. I promised her to be back by—"

Gordon did not hear what the hour was, for she turned away her face and began to cry quietly. She tried to brush the tears away with her fingers; but one or two slipped past and dropped on her dress. With face still averted, she began to feel about her dress for her handkerchief; but being unable to find it, she gave it up.

There was something about her crying so quietly that touched the young man very curiously. She seemed suddenly much younger, quite like a little girl, and he felt like kissing her to comfort her. He did the next thing.

"Don't cry," he said gently. "Here, take mine." He pressed his handkerchief on her. He blessed Heaven that it was uncrumpled.

Now there is something about one's lending another a handkerchief that goes far toward breaking down the barriers of conventionality and bridges years. Keith in a moment had come to feel a friendliness for the girl that he might not have felt in years, and he began to soothe her.

"I don't know what is the matter—with me," she said, as she dried her eyes. "I am not—usually so—weak and foolish. I was only afraid my mother would think something had happened to me—and she has not been very well." She made a brave effort to command herself, and sat up very straight. "There. Thank you very much." She handed him his handkerchief almost grimly. "Now I am all right. But I am afraid I cannot walk. I tried, but—. You will have to go and get me a carriage, if you please."

Keith rose and began to gather up his books and stuff them in his pockets.

"No carriage can get up here; the pines are too thick below, and there is no road; but I will carry you down to where a vehicle can come, and then get you one."

She took a glance at his spare figure. "You cannot carry

me; you are not strong enough. I want you to get me a carriage or a wagon, please. You can go to the hotel. We are stopping at the Springs."

By this time Gordon had forced the books into his pocket, and he squared himself before her.

"Now," he said, without heeding her protest; and leaning down, he slipped his arms under her and lifted her as tenderly and as easily as if she had been a little girl.

As he bore her along, the pain subsided, and she found opportunity to take a good look at his face. His profile was clean-cut; the mouth was pleasant and curved slightly upward, but, under the weight he was carrying, was so close shut as to bring out the chin boldly. The cheek-bones were rather high; the gray eyes were wide open and full of light. And as he advanced, walking with easy strides where the path was smooth, picking his way carefully where it was rough, the color rose under the deep tan of his cheeks.

She was the first to break the silence. She had been watching the rising color in his face, the dilation of his nostrils, and feeling the quickening rise and fall of his chest.

"Put me down now and rest; you are tired."

"I am not tired." He trudged on. He would show her that if he had not been able to mount her on her horse, at least it was not from lack of strength.

"Please put me down; it pains me," she said guilefully.

He stopped instantly, and selecting a clear place, seated her softly.

"I beg your pardon. I was a brute, thinking only of myself."

He seated himself near her, and stole a glance at her face. Their eyes met, and he looked away. He thought her quite beautiful.

To break the silence, she asked, a little tone of politeness coming into her voice: "May I inquire what your name is? I am Miss Yorke—Miss Alice Yorke," she added, intending to make him feel at ease.

"Gordon Keith is my name. Where are you from?"
His manner was again perfectly easy.

"From New York."

"I thought you were."

She fancied that a little change came over his face and
into his manner, and she resented it. She looked down
the hill. Without a word he rose and started to lift her
again. She made a gesture of dissent. But before she
could object further, he had lifted her again, and, with
steady eyes bent on the stony path, was picking his way
down the steep hill.

"I am dreadfully sorry," he said kindly, as she gave a
start over a little twinge. "It is the only way to get
down. No vehicle could get up here at present, unless it
were some kind of a flying chariot like Elijah's. It is
only a little farther now."

What a pleasant voice he had! Every atom of pride
and protection in his soul was enlisted.

When they reached the road, the young lady wanted Gordon to go off and procure a vehicle at the hotel. But he
said he could not leave her alone by the roadside ; he would
carry her on to a house only a little way around the bend.

"Why, I can carry a sack of salt," he said, with boyish
pride, standing before her very straight and looking down
on her with frank eyes.

Her eyes flashed in dudgeon over the comparison.

"A girl is very different from a sack of salt."

"Not always—Lot's wife, for instance. If you keep on
looking back, you don't know what may happen to you.
Come on."

Just then a vehicle rapidly driven was heard in the distance, and the next moment it appeared in sight.

"There comes mamma now," said the girl, waving to the
lady in it.

Mrs. Yorke sprang from the carriage as soon as it drew
up. She was a handsome woman of middle age and was richly
dressed. She was now in a panic of motherly solicitude.

"Oh, Alice, how you have frightened me!" she exclaimed. "You were due at the hotel two hours ago, and when your horse came without you! You will kill me!" She clapped her hands to her heart and panted. "You know my heart is weak!"

Alice protested her sorrow, and Keith put in a word for her, declaring that she had been dreadfully troubled lest the horse should frighten her.

"And well she might be," exclaimed Mrs. Yorke, giving him a bare glance and then turning back to her daughter. "Mrs. Nailor was the first who heard your horse had come home. She ran and told me. And, oh, I was so frightened! She was sure you were killed."

"You might be sure she would be the first to hear and tell you," said the girl. "Why, mamma, one always sprains one's knee when one's horse falls. That is part of the programme. This—gentleman happened to come along, and helped me down to the road, and we were just discussing whether I should go on farther when you came up. Mother, this is Mr. Keith."

Keith bowed. He was for some reason pleased that she did not say anything of the way in which he had brought her down the Ridge.

Mrs. Yorke turned and thanked him with graciousness, possibly with a little condescension. He was conscious that she gave him a sweeping glance, and was sorry his shoes were so old. But Mrs. Yorke took no further notice of him.

"Oh, what will your father say! You know he wanted us to go to California; but you would come South. After Mr. Wickersham told you of his place, nothing else would satisfy you."

"Oh, papa! You know I can settle him," said the girl.

Mrs. Yorke began to lament the wretchedness of a region where there was no doctor of reputation.

"There is a very fine surgeon in the village. Dr. Balsam is one of the best surgeons anywhere," said Keith.

"Oh, I know that old man. No doubt, he is good enough for little common ailments," said Mrs. Yorke, "but in a case like this! What does he know about surgery?" She turned back to her daughter. "I shall telegraph your father to send Dr. Pilbury down at once."

Keith flushed at her manner.

"A good many people have to trust their lives to him," he said coldly. "And he has had about as much surgical practice as most men. He was in the army."

The girl began again to belittle her injury.

It was nothing, absolutely nothing, she declared.

"And besides," she said, "I know the Doctor. I met him the other day. He is a dear old man." She ended by addressing Keith.

"One of the best," said Keith, warmly.

"Well, we must get you into the vehicle and take you home immediately," said her mother. "Can you help put my daughter into the carriage?" Mrs. Yorke looked at the driver, a stolid colored man, who was surly over having had to drive his horses so hard.

Before the man could answer, Gordon stepped forward, and, stooping, lifted the girl, and quietly put her up into the vehicle. She simply smiled and said, "Thank you," quite as if she were accustomed to being lifted into carriages by strange young men whom she had just met on the roadside.

Mrs. Yorke's eyes opened wide.

"How strong you must be!" she exclaimed, with a woman's admiration for physical strength.

Keith bowed, and, with a flush mounting to his cheeks, backed a little away.

"Oh, he has often lifted sacks of salt," said the girl, half turning her eyes on Keith with a gleam of satisfaction in them.

Mrs. Yorke looked at her in astonishment.

"Why, Alice!" she exclaimed reprovingly under her breath.

"He told me so himself," asserted the girl, defiantly.

"I may have to do so again," said Keith, dryly.

Mrs. Yorke's hand went toward the region of her pocket, but uncertainly; for she was not quite sure what he was. His face and air belied his shabby dress. A closer look than she had given him caused her to stop with a start.

"Mr.—ah—?" After trying to recall the name, she gave it up. "I am very much obliged to you for your kindness to my daughter," she began. "I do not know how I can compensate you; but if you will come to the hotel sometime to-morrow—any time—perhaps, there is something—? Can you come to the hotel to-morrow?" Her tone was condescending.

"Thank you," said Keith, quietly. "I am afraid I cannot go to the village to-morrow. I have already been more than compensated in being able to render a service to a lady. I have a school, and I make it a rule never to go anywhere except Friday evening or Saturday." He lifted his hat and backed away.

As they drove away the girl said, "Thank you" and "Good-by," very sweetly.

"Who is he, Alice? What is he?" asked her mother.

"I don't know. Mr. Keith. He is a gentleman."

As Gordon stood by the roadside and saw the carriage disappear in a haze of dust, he was oppressed with a curious sense of loneliness. The isolation of his position seemed to strike him all on a sudden. That stout, full-voiced woman, with her rich clothes, had interposed between him and the rest of his kind. She had treated him condescendingly. He would show her some day who he was. But her daughter! He went off into a revery.

He turned, and made his way slowly and musingly in the direction of his home.

A new force had suddenly come into his life, a new land had opened before him. One young girl had effected it. His school suddenly became a prison. His field was the world.

As he passed along, scarcely conscious of where he was, he met the very man of all others he would rather have met—Dr. Balsam. He instantly informed the Doctor of the accident, and suggested that he had better hurry on to the Springs.

"A pretty girl, with blue eyes and brown hair?" inquired the Doctor.

"Yes." The color stole into Gordon's cheeks.

"With a silly woman for a mother, who is always talking about her heart and pats you on the back?"

"I don't know. Yes, I think so."

"I know her. Is the limb broken?" he asked with interest.

"No, I do not think it is; but badly sprained. She fainted from the pain, I think."

"You say it occurred up on the Ridge?"

"Yes, near the big pines—at the summit."

"Why, how did she get down? There is no road." He was gazing up at the pine-clad spur above them.

"I helped her down." A little color flushed into his face.

"Ah! You supported her? She can walk on it?"

"Ur—no. I brought her down. I had to bring her. She could not walk—not a step."

"Oh! ah! I see. I'll hurry on and see how she is."

As he rode off he gave a grunt.

"Humph!" It might have meant any one of several things. Perhaps, what it did mean was that "Youth is the same the world over, and here is a chance for this boy to make a fool of himself, and he will probably do it, as I did." As the Doctor jogged on over the rocky road, his brow was knit in deep reflection; but his thoughts were far away among other pines on the Piscataqua. That boy's face had turned the dial back nearly forty years.

CHAPTER VII

MRS. YORKE FINDS A GENTLEMAN

WHEN Mrs. Yorke arrived at the hotel, Dr. Balsam was nowhere to be found. She was just sending off a messenger to despatch a telegram to the nearest city for a surgeon, when she saw the Doctor coming up the hill toward the hotel at a rapid pace.

He tied his horse, and, with his saddle-pockets over his arm, came striding up the walk. There was something reassuring in the quick, firm step with which he came toward her. She had not given him credit for so much energy.

Mrs. Yorke led the way toward her rooms, giving a somewhat highly colored description of the accident, the Doctor following without a word, taking off his gloves as he walked. They reached the door, and Mrs. Yorke flung it open with a flurry.

"Here he is at last, my poor child!" she exclaimed.

The sight of Alice lying on a lounge quite effaced Mrs. Yorke from the Doctor's mind. The next second he had taken the girl's hand, and holding it with a touch that would not have crumpled a butterfly's wings, he was taking a flitting gauge of her pulse. Mrs. Yorke continued to talk volubly, but the Doctor took no heed of her.

"A little rest with fixation, madam, is all that is neces·sary," he said quietly, at length, when he had made an examination. "But it must be rest, entire rest of limb and body—and mind," he added after a pause. "Will you ask

Mrs. Gates to send me a kettle of hot water as soon as possible?"

Mrs. Yorke had never been so completely ignored by any physician. She tossed her head, but she went to get the water.

"So my young man Keith found you and brought you down the Ridge?" said the Doctor presently to the girl.

"Yes; how do you know?" she asked, her blue eyes wide open with surprise.

"Never mind; I may tell you next time I come, if you get well quickly," he said smiling.

"Who is he?" she asked.

"He is the teacher of the school over the Ridge—what is known as the Ridge College," said the Doctor, with a smile.

Just at this moment Mrs. Yorke bustled in.

"Alice, I thought the Doctor said you were not to talk."

The Doctor's face wore an amused expression.

"Well, just one more question," said the girl to him. "How much does a sack of salt weigh?"

"About two hundred pounds. To be accurate,—"

"No wonder he said I was light," laughed the girl.

"Who is a young man named Keith—a school-boy, who lives about here?" inquired Mrs. Yorke, suddenly.

"The Keiths do not live about here," said the Doctor. "Gordon Keith, to whom you doubtless refer, is the son of General Keith, who lives in an adjoining county below the Ridge. His father was our minister during the war—"

At this moment the conversation was interrupted by the appearance of Mrs. Gates with the desired kettle of hot water, and the Doctor, stopping in the midst of his sentence, devoted all of his attention to his patient.

The confidence which he displayed and the deftness with which he worked impressed Mrs. Yorke so much that when he was through she said : "Doctor, I have been wondering how a man like you could be content to settle down in this mountain wilderness. I know many fashionable physicians in cities who could not have done for Alice a bit better than you have done—indeed, nothing like so well—with such simple appliances."

Dr. Balsam's eyes rested on her gravely. "Well, madam, we could not all be city doctors. These few sheep in the wilderness need a little shepherding when they get sick. You must reflect also that if we all went away there would be no one to look after the city people when they come to our mountain wilderness; they, at least, need good attendance."

By the time Gordon awoke next morning he had determined that he would see his new acquaintance again. He must see her; he would not allow her to go out of his life so; she should, at least, know who he was, and Mrs. Yorke should know, too.

That afternoon, impelled by some strange motive, he took the path over the Ridge again. It had been a long day and a wearing one. He had tried Hannibal once more; but his pupils cared less for Hannibal than for the bumble-bees droning in the window-frame. For some reason the dull routine of lessons had been duller than usual. The scholars had never been so stupid. Again and again the face that he had seen rest on his arm the day before came between him and his page, and when the eyes opened they were as blue as forget-me-nots. He would rouse himself with a start and plunge back bravely into the mysteries of physical geography or of compound fractions, only to find himself, at the first quiet moment, picking his way through the pines with that white face resting against his shoulder.

When school was out he declined the invitation of the boys to walk with them, and settled himself in his chair as though he meant to prepare the lessons for the next day. After a quarter of an hour, spent mostly in revery, he rose, put up his books, closed the door, and took the same path he had followed the day before. As he neared the spot where he had come on the girl, he almost expected to find her propped against the rock as he had found her the afternoon before. He was conscious of a distinct shock of loneliness that she was not there. The woods had never appeared so empty; the soughing of the pines had never sounded so dreary.

He threw himself down on the thick brown carpet. He had not felt so lonely in years. What was he! And what chance did he have! He was alone in the wilderness. He had been priding himself on being the superior of those around him, and that strange woman had treated him with condescension, when he had strained his heart out to get her daughter to the road safely and without pain.

His eyes rested on the level, pale line of the horizon far below him. Down there lay all he had ever known and loved. All was changed; his home belonged to an alien. He turned his face away. On the other side, the distant mountains lay a mighty rampart across the sky. He wondered if the Alps could be higher or more beautiful. A line he had been explaining the day before to his scholars recurred to him: "Beyond those mountains lies Italy."

Gradually it came to him that he was duller than his scholars. Those who were the true leaders of men surmounted difficulties. Others had crossed the mountains to find the Italy of their ambition. Why should not he? The thought strung him up sharply, and before he knew it he was standing upright, his face lifted to the sky, his nerves tense, his pulses beating, and his breath coming quickly. Beyond that blue rim lay the world. He would conquer and achieve honors and fame, and win back his old home, and build up again his fortune, and do honor to his name. He seized his books, and, with one more look at the heights beyond, turned and strode swiftly along the path.

It was, perhaps, fortunate that the day had been a dull one for both Mrs. Yorke and Alice. Alice had been confined to her lounge, and after the first anxiety was over Mrs. Yorke had been inclined to scold her for her carelessness and the fright she had given her. They had not agreed about a number of matters. Alice had been talking about her adventure until Mrs. Yorke had begun to criticise her rescuer as "a spindling country boy."

"He was strong enough to bring me down the mountain a mile in his arms," declared the girl. "He said it was half a mile, but I am sure it was a mile."

Mrs. Yorke was shocked, and charged Alice with being susceptible enough to like all men.

"All those who are strong and good-looking," protested Alice.

Their little difference had now been made up, and Alice, who had been sitting silent, with a look of serious reflection on her face, said :

"Mamma, why don't you invite him over to dinner?"

Mrs. Yorke gave an exclamation of surprise.

"Why, Alice, we know nothing about him."

But the girl was insistent.

"Why, mamma, I am sure he is a gentleman. Dr. Balsam said he was one of the best people about here, and his father was a clergyman. Besides, he is very interesting. His father was in the war ; I believe he was a general."

Mrs. Yorke pondered a moment, her pen in the air. Her thoughts flew to New York and her acquaintances there. Their view was her gauge.

"Well," she said doubtfully, "perhaps, later I will ; there is no one here whom we know except Mrs. Nailor. I have heard that the people are very interesting if you can get at them. I'll invite him first to luncheon Saturday, and see how he is."

It is, doubtless, just as well that none of us has the magic mirror which we used to read of in our childhood, which showed what any one we wished to know about was doing. It would, no doubt, cause many perplexities from which, in our ignorance, we are happily free. Had Gordon Keith known the terms on which he was invited to take a meal in the presence of Mrs. Yorke, he would have been incensed. He had been fuming about her condescension ever since he had met her; yet he no sooner received her polite note than he was in the best humor possible. He brushed up his well-worn clothes, treated himself to a new necktie, which he had been saving all the session, and just at the appointed hour presented himself with a face so alight with expectancy, and a manner which, while entirely modest, was so natural and easy, that Mrs. Yorke was astonished. She could scarcely credit the fact that this bright-eyed young man, with his fine nose, firm chin, and melodious voice, was the same with the dusty, hot-faced, dishevelled-looking country boy to whom she had thought of offering money for a kindness two days before.

When Keith first entered the room Alice Yorke was seated in a reclining-chair, enveloped in soft white, from which she gave him a smiling greeting. For years afterwards, whenever Gordon Keith thought of beauty it was of a girl smiling up at him out of a cloud of white. It was a charming visit for him, and he reproached himself for his hard thoughts about Mrs. Yorke. He aired all of his knowledge, and made such a favorable impression on the good lady that she became very friendly with him. He did not know that Mrs. Yorke's kindness to him was condescension, and her cordiality inspired as much by curiosity as courtesy.

"Dr. Balsam has been telling us about you, Mr. Keith," said Mrs. Yorke, with a bow which brought a pleased smile to the young man's face.

"He has? The Doctor has always been good to me. I am afraid he has a higher opinion of me than I deserve," he said, with a boy's pretended modesty, whilst his eyes strongly belied his words.

Mrs. Yorke assured him that such could not be the case.

"Don't you want to know what he said?" asked Miss Alice, with a bell-like laugh.

"Yes; what?" he smiled.

95

"He said if you undertook to carry a bag of salt down a mountain, or up it either, you would never rest until you got there."

Her eyes twinkled, and Gordon appeared half teased, though he was inwardly pleased.

Mrs. Yorke looked shocked.

"Oh, Alice, Dr. Balsam did not say that, for I heard him!" she exclaimed reprovingly. "Dr. Balsam was very complimentary to you, Mr. Keith," she explained seriously. "He said your people were among the best families about here." She meant to be gracious; but Gordon's face flushed in spite of himself. The condescension was too apparent.

"Your father was a pre—a—a—clergyman?" said Mrs. Yorke, who had started to say "preacher," but substituted the other word as more complimentary.

"My father a clergyman! No'm. He is good enough to be one; but he was a planter and a—a—soldier," said Gordon.

Mrs. Yorke looked at her daughter in some mystification. Could this be the wrong man?

"Why, he said he was a clergyman?" she insisted.

Gordon gazed at the girl in bewilderment.

"Yes; he said he was a minister," she replied to his unspoken inquiry.

Gordon broke into a laugh.

"Oh, he was a special envoy to England after he was wounded."

The announcement had a distinct effect upon Mrs. Yorke, who instantly became much more cordial to Gordon. She took a closer look at him than she had given herself the trouble to take before, and discovered, under the sunburn and worn clothes, something more than she had formerly observed. The young man's expression had changed. A reference to his father always sobered him and kindled a light in his eyes. It was the first time Mrs. Yorke had taken in what her daughter meant by calling him handsome.

"Why, he is quite distinguished-looking!" she thought to herself. And she reflected what a pity it was that so good-looking a young man should have been planted down there in that out-of-the-way pocket of the world, and thus lost to society. She did not know that the kindling eyes opposite her were burning with a resolve that not only Mrs. Yorke, but the world, should know him, and that she should recognize his superiority.

CHAPTER VIII

MR. KEITH'S IDEALS

AFTER this it was astonishing how many excuses Gordon could find for visiting the village. He was always wanting to consult a book in the Doctor's library, or get something, which, indeed, meant that he wanted to get a glimpse of a young girl with violet eyes and pink cheeks, stretched out in a lounging-chair, picturesquely reclining amid clouds of white pillows. Nearly always he carried with him a bunch of flowers from Mrs. Rawson's garden, which were to make patches of pink or red or yellow among Miss Alice's pillows, and bring a fresh light into her eyes. And sometimes he took a basket of cherries or strawberries for Mrs. Yorke. His friends, the Doctor and the Rawsons, began to rally him on his new interest in the Springs.

"I see you are takin' a few nubbins for the old cow," said Squire Rawson, one afternoon as Gordon started off, at which Gordon blushed as red as the cherries he was carrying. It was just what he had been doing.

"Well, that is the way to ketch the calf," said the old farmer, jovially ; "but I 'low the mammy is used to pretty high feedin'." He had seen Mrs. Yorke driving along in much richer attire than usually dazzled the eyes of the Ridge neighborhood, and had gauged her with a shrewd eye.

Miss Alice Yorke's sprain turned out to be less serious than had been expected. She herself had proved a much less refractory patient than her mother had ever known her.

It does not take two young people of opposite sexes long to overcome the formalities which convention has fixed among their seniors, especially when one of them has brought the other down a mountain-side in his arms.

Often, in a sheltered corner of the long verandah, Keith read to Alice on balmy afternoons, or in the moonlit evenings sauntered with her through the fields of their limited experience, and quoted snatches from his chosen favorites, poems that lived in his heart, and fancied her the "maid of the downward look and sidelong glance."

Thus, by the time Alice Yorke was able to move about again, she and Keith had already reached a footing where they had told each other a good deal of their past, and were finding the present very pleasant, and one of them, at least, was beginning, when he turned his eyes to the future, to catch the glimmer of a very rosy light.

It showed in his appearance, in his face, where a new expression of a more definite ambition and a higher resolution was beginning to take its place.

Dr. Balsam noted it, and when he met Gordon he began to have a quizzical light in his deep-gray eyes. He had, too, a tender tone in his voice when he addressed the girl. Perhaps, a vision came to him at times of another country lad, well-born like this one, and, like this one, poor, wandering on the New England hills with another young girl, primmer, perhaps, and less sophisticated than this little maiden, who had come from the westward to spend a brief holiday on the banks of the Piscataqua, and had come into his life never to depart—of his dreams and his hopes; of his struggles to achieve the education which would make him worthy of her; and then of the overthrow of all : of darkness and exile and wanderings.

When the Doctor sat on his porch of an evening, with his pipe, looking out over the sloping hills, sometimes his face grew almost melancholy. Had he not been intended for other things than this exile? Abigail Brooke had never married, he knew. What might have happened had he gone back? And when he next saw Alice Yorke there would be a softer tone in his voice, and he would talk a deeper and higher philosophy to her than she had ever heard, belittling the gaudy rewards of life, and instilling in her mind ideas of something loftier and better and finer than they. He even told her once something of the story of his life, and of the suffering and sorrow that had been visited upon the victims of a foolish pride and a selfish ambition. Though he did not confide to her that it was of himself he spoke, the girl's instinct instantly told her that it was his own experience that he related, and her interest was deeply excited.

"Did she ever marry, Doctor?" she asked eagerly. "Oh, I hope she did not. I might forgive her if she did not; but if she married I would never forgive her!"

The Doctor's eyes, as they rested on her eager face, had a kindly expression in them, and a look of amusement lurked there also.

"No; she never married," he said. "Nor did he."

"Oh, I am glad of that," she exclaimed; and then more softly added, "I know he did not."

Dr. Balsam gazed at her calmly. He did not pursue the subject further. He thought he had told his story in such a way as to convey the moral without disclosing that he spoke of himself. Yet she had discovered it instantly. He wondered if she had seen also the moral he intended to convey.

Alice Yorke was able to walk now, and many an afternoon Gordon Keith invited her to stroll with him on the mountain-side or up the Ridge, drawing her farther and farther as her strength returned.

The Spring is a dangerous season for a young man and a pretty girl to be thrown closely together for the first time, and the budding woods are a perilous pasture for their browsing thoughts. It was not without some insight that the ancient poets pictured dryads as inhabitants of the woods, and made the tinkling springs and rippling streams the abiding-places of their nymphs.

The Spring came with a burst of pink and green. The mountains took on delicate shades, and the trees blossomed into vast flowers, feathery and fine as lace.

An excursion in the budding woods has been dangerous ever since the day when Eve found a sinuous stranger lurking there in gay disguise, and was beguiled into tasting the tempting fruit he offered her. It might be an interesting inquiry to collect even the most notable instances of those who, wandering all innocent and joyous amid the bowers, have found the honey of poisonous flowers where they meant only innocence. But the reader will, perhaps, recall enough instances in a private and unrecorded history to fill the need of illustration. It suffices, then, to say that, each afternoon that Gordon Keith wandered with Alice Yorke through the leafy woods, he was straying farther in that perilous path where the sunlight always sifts down just ahead, but the end is veiled in mist, and where sometimes darkness falls.

These strolls had all the charm for him of discovery, for he was always finding in her some new trait, and every one was, he thought, an added charm, even to her unexpected alternations of ignorance and knowledge, her little feminine outbreaks of caprice. One afternoon they had strolled farther than usual, as far even as the high pines beyond which was the great rock looking to the northeastward. There she had asked him to help her up to the top of the rock, but he had refused. He told her that she had walked already too far, and he would not permit her to climb it.

"Not permit me! Well, I like that!" she said, with a flash of her blue eyes; and springing from her seat on the brown carpet, before he could interpose, she was climbing up the high rock as nimbly as if she were a boy.

He called to her to stop, but she took no heed. He began to entreat her, but she made no answer. He was in terror lest she might fall, and sprang after her to catch her; but up, up she climbed, with as steady a foot and as sure an eye as he could have shown himself, until she reached the top, when, looking down on him with dancing eyes, she kissed her hand in triumph and then turned away, her cheeks aglow. When he reached the top, she was standing on the very edge of the precipice, looking far over the long reach of sloping country to the blue line of the horizon. Keith almost gasped at her temerity. He pleaded with her not to be so venturesome.

"Please stand farther back, I beg you," he said as he reached her side.

"Now, that is better," she said, with a little nod to him, her blue eyes full of triumph, and she seated herself quietly on the rock.

Keith began to scold her, but she laughed at him.

He had done it often, she said, and what he could do she could do.

The beauty of the wide landscape sank into both their minds, and after a little they both took a graver tone.

"Tell me where your old home is," she said presently, after a long pause in which her face had grown thoughtful. "You told me once that you could see it from this rock."

Keith pointed to a spot on the far horizon. He did not know that it was to see this even more than to brave him that she had climbed to the top of the rock.

"Now tell me about it," she said. "Tell me all over what you have told me before." And Keith related all he could remember. Touched with her sympathy, he told it with more feeling than he had ever shown before. When he spoke of the loss of his home, of his mortification, and of his father's quiet dignity, she turned her face away to keep him from seeing the tears that were in her eyes.

"I can understand your feeling a little," she said presently; "but I did not know that any one could have so much feeling for a plantation. I suppose it is because it is in the country, with its trees and flowers and little streams.

We have had three houses since I can remember. The one that we have now on Fifth Avenue is four times as large —yes, six times as large—and a hundred times as fine as the one I can first remember, and yet, somehow, I always think, when I am sad or lonely, of the little white house with the tiny rooms in it, with their low ceilings and small windows, where I used to go when I was a very little girl to see my father's mother. Mamma does not care for it; she was brought up in the city ; but I think my father loves it just as I do. He always says he is going to buy it back, and I am going to make him do it."

"I am going to buy back mine some day," said Keith, very slowly.

She glanced at him. His eyes were fastened on the far-off horizon, and there was that in his face which she had never seen there before, and which made her admire him more than she had ever done.

"I hope you will," she said. She almost hated Ferdy Wickersham for having spoken of the place as Keith told her he had spoken.

When Keith reached home that evening he had a wholly new feeling for the girl with whom accident had so curiously thrown him. He was really in love with her. Hitherto he had allowed himself merely to drift with the pleasant tide that had been setting in throughout these last weeks. But the phases that she had shown that afternoon, her spirit, her courage, her capricious rebelliousness, and, above all, that glimpse into her heart which he had obtained as she sat on the rock overlooking the wide sweep where he had had his home, and where the civilization to which it belonged had had its home, had shown him a new creature, and he plunged into love. Life appeared suddenly to open wide her gates and flood him with her rosy light.

CHAPTER IX

MR. KEITH IS UNPRACTICAL, AND MRS. YORKE GIVES HIM GOOD ADVICE

THE strolls in the budding woods and the glimpses shown her of a spirit somewhat different from any she had known were beginning to have their influence on Alice. It flattered her and filled her with a certain content that the young school-teacher should like her so much; yet, knowing herself, it gave her a vague feeling that he was wanting in that quality of sound judgment which she recognized in some of her other admirers. It rather frightened her to feel that she was on a pedestal; and often he soared away from her with his poetry and his fancies, and she was afraid that he would discover it and think she was a hypocrite. Something that her mother had said remained in her mind.

"He knows so much, mamma," said Alice one day. "Why, he can quote whole pages of poetry."

"He is too romantic, my dear, to be practical," said Mrs. Yorke, who looked at the young men who approached her daughter with an eye as cool as a physician's glass. "He, perhaps, does know more about books than any boy of his age I am acquainted with; but poetry is a very poor thing to live on; and if he were practical he would not be teaching that wretched little school in the wilderness."

"But, mamma, he will rise. You don't know how ambitious he is, and what determination he has. They have lost everything. The place that Ferdy Wickersham told me about his father owning, with its old pictures and all that, was his old home. Old Mr. Keith, since he lost it, has been farming it for Mr. Wickersham. Think of that!"

"Just so," said Mrs. Yorke. "He inherits it. They are all unpractical. Your father began life poor; but he was practical, and he had the ability to succeed."

Alice's face softened. "Dear old dad!" she said; "I must write to him." Even as she thought of him she could not but reflect how absorption in business had prevented his obtaining the culture of which this young school-teacher had given her a glimpse, and had crushed, though it could not wholly quench, the kindliness which lived in his big heart.

Though Alice defended Keith, she felt in her heart there was some truth in her mother's estimate. He was too romantic. She soon had proof of it.

General Keith came up to the Ridge just then to see Gordon. At least, he gave this out as the reason for his visit, and Gordon did not know until afterwards that there was another reason for it—that he had been in correspondence for some time with Dr. Balsam. He was looking thin; but when Gordon spoke of it, he put it by with a smile.

"Oh, I am very well. We need not worry about my troubles. I have but two: that old wound, and Old Age; both are incurable."

Gordon was very pleased to have the opportunity to introduce his father to Mrs. Yorke and Miss Alice. As he scanned the thin, fine face with its expression of calm and its lines of fortitude, he felt that it was a good card to play. His resemblance to the man-in-armor that hung in the old dining-room had increased.

The General and Miss Alice promptly became great friends. He treated her with a certain distinction that pleased her. Mrs. Yorke, too, was both pleased and flattered by his gracious manner. She was, however, more critical toward him than her daughter was.

General Keith soon discovered Gordon's interest in the young girl. It was not difficult to discover, for every moment of his spare time was devoted to her in some way. The General observed them with a quiet smile in his eyes. Now and then, however, the smile died out as he heard Gordon expressing views which were somewhat new to him. One evening they were all seated on the verandah together, and Gordon began to speak of making a fortune as a high aim. He had heard Mrs. Yorke express the same sentiments a few days before.

"My son," said his father, gently, looking at him with grave eyes, "a fortune is a great blessing in the hands of the man who knows how to spend it. But riches considered as something to possess or to display is one of the most despicable and debasing of all the aims that men can have."

Mrs. Yorke's eyes opened wide and her face hardened a little. Gordon thought of the toil and patience it had cost him to make even his little salary, and wealth appeared to him just then a very desirable acquisition.

"Why, father," he said, "it opens the world to a man. It gives such great opportunities for everything; travel, knowledge, art, science, power, the respect and esteem of the world, are obtained by it."

Something like this Mrs. Yorke had said to him, meaning, kindly enough, to encourage him in its pursuit.

The old General smiled gravely.

"Opportunity for travel and the acquirement of knowledge wealth undoubtedly gives, but happily they are not dependent upon wealth, my son. The Columbuses of science, the Galileos, Newtons, Keplers; the great benefactors of the world, the great inventors, the great artists, the great poets, philosophers, and statesmen have few of them been rich."

"He appears to have lived in another world, mamma," said Alice when he had left. "He is an old dear. I never knew so unworldly a person."

Mrs. Yorke's chin tilted a little.

"Now, Alice, don't you be silly. He lives in another world now, and certainly, of all the men I know, none appears less fitted to cope with this world. The only real people to him appear to be those whom he has read of. He never tried wealth."

"He used to be rich—very rich. Don't you remember what that lady told you?"

"I don't believe it," said Mrs. Yorke, sententiously.

Alice knew that this closed the argument. When her mother in such cases said she did not believe a thing, it meant that the door of her mind was fast shut and no reason could get into it.

Mrs. Yorke could not but notice that some change had taken place in Alice of late. In a way she had undoubtedly improved. She was more serious, more thoughtful of Mrs. Yorke herself, less wilful. Yet it was not without some misgiving that Mrs. Yorke noted the change.

She suddenly had her eyes opened. Mrs. Nailor, one of her New York friends, performed this amiable office. She assigned the possible cause, though not directly—Mrs. Nailor rarely did things directly. She was a small, purring lady, with a tilt of the head, and an insinuating voice of singular clearness, with a question-mark in it. She was of a very good family, lived in a big house on Murray Hill, and had as large a circle of acquaintance as any one in New York. She prided herself on knowing everybody worth knowing, and everything about everybody. She was not lacking in amiability; she was, indeed, so amiable that she would slander almost any absent friend to please one who was present. She had a little grudge against Keith, for she had been struck from the first by his bright eyes and good manners; but Keith had been so much engrossed by his interest in Alice Yorke that he had been remiss in paying Mrs. Nailor that attention which she felt her position required. Mrs. Nailor now gave Mrs. Yorke a judicious hint.

"You have such a gift for knowing people?" she said to her, "and your daughter is so like you?" She showed her even teeth.

Mrs. Yorke was not quite sure what she meant, and she answered somewhat coldly that she was glad that Mrs. Nailor thought so. Mrs. Nailor soon indicated her meaning.

"The young schoolmaster—he is a schoolmaster in whom your daughter is interested, isn't he? Yes? He appears so well-read? He brought your daughter down the mountain the day her horse ran off with her? So romantic to make an acquaintance that way—I quite envy you? There is so little real romance these days! It is delightful to find it?" She sighed, and Mrs. Yorke thought of Daniel Nailor and his little bald head and round mouth. "Yes, I quite envy you—and your daughter. Who is he?"

Mrs. Yorke said he was of a very old and distinguished family. She gave him a pedigree that would have done honor to a Derby-winner.

"I am so glad," declared Mrs. Nailor. "I knew he must be, of course. I am sure you would never encourage such an intimacy unless he were?" She smiled herself off, leaving Mrs. Yorke fuming.

"That woman is always sticking pins into people," she said to herself. But this pin had stuck fast, and Mrs. Yorke was in quite a panic.

Mrs. Yorke determined to talk to Alice on the first occasion that offered itself; but she would not do it too abruptly. All that would be needed would be a hint judiciously given. For surely a girl of such sound sense as Alice, a girl brought up so wisely, could not for a moment think of acting so foolishly. And really Mrs. Yorke felt that she herself was very fond of this young man. She might do something for him—something that should be of use to him in after life. At first this plan took the form in her mind of getting her husband to give him a place; but she reflected that this would necessitate bringing him where his acquaintance with them might prove inconvenient. She would aid him in going to college for another year. This would be a delicate way to discharge the obligation under which his kindness had placed her.

Keith, meantime, was happily ignorant of the plot that was forming against him. The warm weather was coming, and he knew that before long Mrs. Yorke and Alice would be flitting northward. However, he would make his hay while the sun shone for him. So one afternoon Keith had borne Miss Alice off to his favorite haunt, the high rock in the Ridge woods. He was in unusual spirits; for he had escaped from Mrs. Nailor, who of late had appeared to be rather lying in wait for him. It was the spot he loved best; for the pines behind him seemed to shut out the rest of the world, and he felt that here he was in some sort nearer to having Alice for his own than anywhere else. It was here that he had caught that glimpse of her heart which he felt had revealed her to him.

This afternoon he was talking of love and of himself; for what young man who talks of love talks not of himself? She was dressed in white, and a single red rose that he had given her was stuck in her dress. He had been reading a poem to her. It contained a picture of the goddess of love, decked out for "worship without end." The book now lay at his side, and he was stretched at her feet.

"If I ever am in love," he said suddenly, "it will be with a girl who must fill full the measure of my dreams." He was looking away through the pine-trees to the sky far beyond; but the soft light in his face came not from that far-off tent of blue. He was thinking vaguely how much bluer than the sky were her eyes.

"Yes?" Her tone was tender.

"She must be a beauty, of course." He gazed at her with that in his eyes which said, as plainly as words could have said it, "You are beautiful."

But she was looking away, wondering to herself who it might be.

"I mean she must have what *I* call beauty," he added by way of explanation. "I don't count mere red and white beauty. Phrony Tripper has that." This was not without intention. Alice had spoken of Phrony's beauty one day when she saw her at the school.

"But she is very pretty," asserted the girl, "so fresh and such color!"

"Oh, pretty! yes; and color—a wine-sap apple has color. But I am speaking of real beauty, the beauty of the rose, the freshness that you cannot define, that holds fragrance, a something that you love, that you feel even more than you see."

She thought of a school friend of hers, Louise Caldwell, a tall, statuesque beauty, with whom another friend, Norman Wentworth, was in love, and she wondered if Keith would think her such a beauty as he described.

"She must be sweet," he went on, thinking to himself for her benefit. "I cannot define that either, but you know what I mean?"

She decided mentally that Louise Caldwell would not fill his measure.

"It is something that only some girls have in common with some flowers—violets, for instance."

"Oh, I don't care for sweet girls very much," she said, thinking of another schoolmate whom the girls used to call *eau sucré*.

"You do," he said positively. "I am not talking of that kind. It is womanliness and gentleness, fragrance, warmth, beauty, everything."

"Oh, yes. That kind?" she said acquiescingly. "Well, go on; you expect to find a good deal."

"I do," he said briefly, and sat up. "I expect to find the best."

She glanced at him with new interest. He was very good-looking when he was spirited. And his eyes now were full of light.

110

"Well, beauty and sweetness," she said ; "what else? I must know, for I may have to help you find her. There don't appear to be many around Ridgely, since you have declined to accept the only pretty girl I have seen."

"She must be good and true. She must know the truth as—" His eye fell at that instant on a humming-bird, a gleaming jewel of changing sapphire that, poised on half-invisible wings, floated in a bar of sunlight before a sprig of pink honeysuckle. "—As that bird knows the flowers where the honey lies."

"Where do you expect to find this paragon?"

As if in answer, the humming-bird suddenly caught sight of the red rose in her dress, and, darting to it, thrust its bill deep into the crimson heart of the flower. They both gave an exclamation of delighted wonder.

"I have found her," he said firmly, leaning a little toward her, with mantling cheeks and close-drawn lips, his glowing eyes on her face. "The bird has found her for me."

The bird darted away.

"Ah, it is gone ! What will you give her in return?" She turned to him and spoke half mockingly, wishing to get off such delicate ground.

He turned and gazed into her eyes.

" 'Worship without end.' " There was that in his face that made her change color. She looked away and began to think of her own ideal. She found that her idea of the man she loved had been of height of figure and breadth of shoulders, a handsome face and fashionable attire. She had pictured him as tall and straight, taller than this boy and larger every way, with a straight nose, brown eyes, and dark hair. But chiefly she had thought of the style of his clothes. She had fancied the neckties he should wear, and the pins that should be stuck in them. He must be brave, of course, a beautiful dancer, a fine tennis-player. She had once thought that black-eyed, handsome young Ferdy Wickersham was as near her ideal as any one else she knew. He led germans divinely. But he was selfish, and she had never admired him as much as another man, who

111

was less showy, but was, she knew, more of a man: Norman Wentworth, a bold swimmer, a good horseman, and a leader of their set. It suddenly occurred to her now how much more like this man Norman Wentworth was than Ferdy Wickersham, and following her thought of the two, she suddenly stepped up on a higher level and was conscious of a certain elation, much like that she had had the day she had climbed up before Gordon Keith on the outjutting rock and looked far down over the wide expanse of forest and field, to where his home had been.

She sat for a little while in deep reflection. Presently she said, quite gravely and a little shyly:

"You know, I am not a bit what you think I am. Why, you treat me as if I were a superior being. And I am not; I am a very matter-of-fact girl."

He interrupted her with a gesture of dissent, his eyes full of light.

"Nonsense! You don't know me, you don't know men, or you would know that any girl is the superior of the best man," he reiterated.

"You don't know girls," she retorted.

"I know one, at least," he said, with a smile that spoke his admiration.

"I am not sure that you do," she persisted, speaking slowly and very seriously. She was gazing at him in a curious, reflective way.

"The one I know is good enough for me." He leaned over and shyly took her hand and raised it to his lips, then released it. She did not resist him, but presently she said tentatively:

"I believe I had rather be treated as I am than as something I am not. I like you too much to want to deceive you, and I think you are deceived."

He, of course, protested that he was not deceived. He "knew perfectly well," he said. She was not convinced; but she let it go. She did not want to quarrel with him for admiring her.

That afternoon, when Alice came in, her manner was so different from what it had been of late that her mother could not but observe it. One moment she was distraite; the next she was impatient and even irritable; then this mood changed, and she was unusually gay; her cheeks glowed and her eyes sparkled; but even as she reflected, a change came, and she drifted away again into a brown study.

Next day, while Mrs. Yorke was still considering what to do, a card was handed her. It was a name written simply on one of the slips of paper that were kept on the hotel counter below. Keith of late had not been sending up his card; a servant simply announced his name. This, then, decided her. It was the most fortunate thing in the world that Alice had gone off and was out of the way. It gave Mrs. Yorke the very opportunity she desired. If, as she divined, the young man wished to talk to her about anything personal, she would speak kindly to him, but so plainly that he could never forget it. After all, it would be true kindness to him to do so. She had a virtuous feeling as she smoothed her hair before a mirror.

He was not in the sitting-room when she came down; so she sought for him on one of the long verandahs where they usually sat. He was seated at the far end, where he would be more or less secluded, and she marched down on him. He was evidently on the watch for her, and as soon as she appeared he rose from his seat. She had made up her mind very clearly what she would say to him; but as she approached him it was not so easy to say as she had fancied it. There was something in his bearing and expression that deterred her from using the rather condescending words she had formulated. His face was somewhat pale; his mouth was firmly set, throwing out the chin in a way to make it quite strong; his eyes were anxious, but steady; his form was very erect, and his shoulders were very square and straight. He appeared to her older than she had considered him. It would not do to

113

patronize this man. After greeting her, he handed her a chair solemnly, and the next moment plunged straight into his subject. It was so sudden that it almost took her breath away; and before she knew it he had, with the blood coming and going in his cheeks, declared his love for her daughter, and asked her permission to pay her his addresses. After the first gulp or two he had lost his embarrassment, and was speaking in a straightforward, manly way. The color had come rushing back into his face, and his eyes were filled with light. Mrs. Yorke felt that it was necessary to do something. So, though she felt some trepidation, she took heart and began to answer him. As she proceeded, her courage returned to her, and seeing that he was much disturbed, she became quite composed.

She regretted extremely, she said, that she had not foreseen this. It was all so unexpected to her that she was quite overwhelmed by it. She felt that this was a lie, and she was not sure that he did not know it. Of course, it was quite impossible that she could consent to anything like what he had proposed.

"Do you mean because she is from the North and I am from the South?" he asked earnestly.

"No; of course not. I have Southern blood myself. My grandmother was from the South." She smiled at his simplicity.

"Then why?"

This was embarrassing, but she must answer.

"Why, you — we — move in — quite different—spheres, and—ah, it's really not to be thought of, Mr. Keith," she said, half desperately.

He himself had thought of the different spheres in which they moved, but he had surmounted that difficulty. Though her father, as he had learned, had begun life as a store-boy, and her mother was not the most learned person in the world, Alice Yorke was a lady to her finger-tips, and in her own fine person was the incontestable proof of a strain of gentle blood somewhere. Those delicate features, fine hands, trim ankles, and silken hair told their own story.

So he came near saying, "That does not make any difference"; but he restrained himself. He said instead, "I do not know that I understand you."

It was very annoying to have to be so plain, but it was, Mrs. Yorke felt, quite necessary.

"Why, I mean that my daughter has always moved in the — the most — exclusive society; she has had the best advantages, and has a right to expect the best that can be given her."

"Do you mean that you think my family is not good enough for your daughter?"

There was a tone in his quiet voice that made her glance up at him, and a look on his face that made her answer quickly:

"Oh, no; not that, of course. I have no doubt your family is — indeed, I have heard it is — ur —. But my daughter has every right to expect the best that life can give. She has a right to expect— an — establishment."

"You mean money?" Keith asked, a little hoarsely.

"Why, not in the way in which you put it; but what money stands for — comforts, luxuries, position. Now, don't go and distress yourself about this. You are nothing but a silly boy. You fancy yourself in love with my daughter because she is the only pretty girl about here."

"She is not; but she is the prettiest I know," ejaculated Keith, bitterly.

"You think that, and so you fancy you are in love with her."

"It is no fancy; I am," asserted Keith, doggedly. "I would be in love with her if she were as ugly as—as she is beautiful."

"Oh, no, you wouldn't," declared Mrs. Yorke, coolly. "Now, the thing for you to do is to forget all about her, as she will in a short time forget all about you."

"I know she will, though I hope she will not," groaned the young man. "I shall never forget her—never."

His voice and manner showed such unfeigned anguish that the lady could not but feel real commiseration for him, especially as he appeared to be accepting her view of the case. She glanced at him almost kindly.

"Is there nothing I can do for you? I should like very much to do something—something to show my appreciation of what you have done for us to make our stay here less dreary than it would have been."

"Thank you. There is nothing," said Keith. "I am going to turn my attention now to—getting an establishment." He spoke half sarcastically, but Mrs. Yorke did not see it.

"That is right," she said warmly.

"It is not right," declared Keith, with sudden vehemence. "It is all wrong. I know it is all wrong."

"What the world thinks is right can't be all wrong." Mrs. Yorke spoke decisively.

"When are you going away?" the young man asked suddenly.

"In a few days." She spoke vaguely, but even as she spoke, she determined to leave next day.

"I thank you for all your kindness to me," said Keith, standing very straight and speaking rather hoarsely.

Mrs. Yorke's heart smote her. If it were not for her daughter's welfare she could have liked this boy and befriended him. A vision came to her from out of the dim past; a country boy with broad shoulders suddenly flashed before her; but she shut it off before it became clear. She spoke kindly to Keith, and held out her hand to him with more real sincerity than she had felt in a long time.

"You are a good boy," she said, "and I wish I could have answered you otherwise, but it would have been simple madness. You will some day know that it was kinder to you to make you look nakedly at facts."

"I suppose so," said Keith, politely. "But some day, Mrs. Yorke, you shall hear of me. If you do not, remember I shall be dead."

With this bit of tragedy he turned and left her, and Mrs. Yorke stood and watched him as he strode down the path, meaning, if he should turn, to wave him a friendly adieu, and also watching lest that which she had dreaded for a quarter of an hour might happen. It would be dreadful if her daughter should meet him now. He did not turn, however, and when at last he disappeared, Mrs. Yorke, with a sigh of relief, went up to her room and began to write rapidly.

CHAPTER X

MRS. YORKE CUTS THE KNOT

WHEN Alice Yorke came from her jaunt, she had on her face an expression of pleasant anticipation. She had been talking to Dr. Balsam, and he had said things about Gordon Keith that had made her cheeks tingle. "Of the best blood of two continents," he had said of him. "He has the stuff that has made England and America." The light of real romance was beginning to envelop her.

As she entered the hall she met Mrs. Nailor. Mrs. Nailor smiled at her knowingly, much as a cat, could she smile, might smile at a mouse.

"I think your mother is out on the far end of the verandah. I saw her there a little while ago talking with your friend, the young schoolmaster. What a nice young man he is? Quite uncommon, isn't he?"

Alice gave a little start. "The young schoolmaster" indeed!

"Yes, I suppose so. I don't know." She hated Mrs. Nailor with her quiet, cat-like manner and inquisitive ways. She now hated her more than ever, for she was conscious that she was blushing and that Mrs. Nailor observed it.

"Your mother is very interested in schools? Yes? I think that is nice in her? So few persons appreciate education?" Her air was absolute innocence.

"I don't know. I believe she is—interested in everything," faltered Alice. She wanted to add, "And so you appear to be also."

"So few persons care for education these days," pursued Mrs. Nailor, in a little chime. "And that young man is such a nice fellow? Has he a good school? I hear you were there? You are interested in schools, too?" She nodded like a little Japanese toy-baby.

"I am sure I don't know. Yes; I think he has. Why don't you go?" asked the girl at random.

"Oh, I have not been invited." Mrs. Nailor smiled amiably. "Perhaps, you will let me go with you some-time?"

Alice escaped, and ran up-stairs, though she was eager to go out on the porch. However, it would serve him right to punish him by staying away until she was sent for, and she could not go with Mrs. Nailor's cat-eyes on her.

She found her mother seated at a table writing busily. Mrs. Yorke only glanced up and said, "So you are back? Hope you had a pleasant time?" and went on writing.

Alice gazed at her with a startled look in her eyes. She had such a serious expression on her face.

"What are you doing?" She tried to speak as indifferently as she could.

"Writing to your father." The pen went on busily.

"What is the matter? Is papa ill? Has anything happened?"

"No; nothing has happened. I am writing to say we shall be home the last of the week."

"Going away!"

"Yes; don't you think we have been here long enough? We only expected to stay until the last of March, and here it is almost May."

"But what is the matter? Why have you made up your mind so suddenly? Mamma, you are so secret! I am sure something is the matter. Is papa not well?" She crossed over and stood by her mother.

Mrs. Yorke finished a word and paused a moment, with the end of her silver penholder against her teeth.

"Alice," she said reflectively, "I have something I want

to say to you, and I have a mind to say it now. I think I ought to speak to you very frankly."

"Well, for goodness' sake, do, mamma; for I'm dying to know what has happened." She seated herself on the side of a chair for support. Her face was almost white.

"Alice—"

"Yes, mamma." Her politeness was ominous.

"Alice, I have had a talk with that young man—"

Alice's face flushed suddenly.

"What young man?" she asked, as though the Ridge Springs were thronged with young men behind every bush.

"That young man—Mr. Keith," firmly.

"Oh!" said Alice. "With Mr. Keith? Yes, mamma?" Her color was changing quickly now.

"Yes, I have had a quite—a very extraordinary conversation with Mr. Keith." As Mrs. Yorke drifted again into reflection, Alice was compelled to ask:

"What about, mamma?"

"About you."

"About me? What about me?" Her face was belying her assumed innocence.

"Alice, I hope you are not going to behave foolishly. I cannot believe for a minute that you would—a girl brought up as you have been—so far forget yourself—would allow yourself to become interested in a perfectly unknown and ignorant and obscure young man."

"Why, mamma, he is not ignorant; he knows more than any one I ever saw,—why, he has read piles of books I never even heard of,—and his family is one of the best and oldest in this country. His grandfathers or great-grandfathers were both signers of the Decla—"

"I am not talking about that," interrupted Mrs. Yorke, hastily. "I must say you appear to have studied his family-tree pretty closely."

"Dr. Balsam told me," interjected Alice.

"Dr. Balsam had very little to talk of. I am talking of his being unknown."

"But I believe he will be known some day. You don't know how clever and ambitious he is. He told me—"

But Mrs. Yorke had no mind to let Alice dwell on what he had told her. He was too good an advocate.

"Stuff! I don't care what he told you! Alice, he is a perfectly unknown and untrained young—creature. All young men talk that way. He is perfectly gauche and boorish in his manner—"

"Why, mamma, he has beautiful manners!" exclaimed Alice "I heard a lady saying the other day he had the manners of a Chesterfield."

"Chester-nonsense!" exclaimed Mrs. Yorke.

"I think he has, too, mamma."

"I don't agree with you," declared Mrs. Yorke, energetically. "How would he appear in New York? Why, he wears great heavy shoes, and his neckties are something dreadful."

"His neckties are bad," admitted Alice, sadly.

Mrs. Yorke, having discovered a breach in her adversary's defences, like a good general directed her attack against it.

"He dresses horribly; he wears his hair like a—countryman; and his manners are as antiquated as his clothes. Think of him at the opera or at one of Mrs. Wentworth's receptions! He says 'madam' and 'sir' as if he were a servant."

"I got after him about that once," said the girl, reflectively. "I said that only servants said that."

"Well, what did he say?"

"Said that that proved that servants sometimes had better manners than their masters."

"Well, I must say, I think he was excessively rude!" asserted Mrs. Yorke, picking up her fan and beginning to fan rapidly.

"That's what I said; but he said he did not see how it could be rude to state a simple and impersonal fact in a perfectly respectful way."

Alice was warming up in defence and swept on.

"He said the new fashion was due to people who were not sure of their own position, and were afraid others might think them servile if they employed such terms."

"What does he know about fashion?"

"He says fashion is a temporary and shifting thing, sometimes caused by accident and sometimes made by tradesmen, but that good manners are the same to-day that they were hundreds of years ago, and that though the ways in which they are shown change, the basis is always the same, being kindness and gentility."

Mrs. Yorke gasped.

"Well, I must say, you seem to have learned your lesson!" she exclaimed.

Alice had been swept on by her memory not only of the words she was repeating, but of many conversations and interchanges of thought Gordon Keith and she had had during the past weeks, in which he had given her new ideas. She began now, in a rather low and unsteady voice, her hands tightly clasped, her eyes in her lap:

"Mamma, I believe I like him very much—better than I shall ever—"

"Nonsense, Alice! Now, I will not have any of this nonsense. I bring you down here for your health, and you take up with a perfectly obscure young countryman about whom you know nothing in the world, and—"

"I know all about him, mamma. I know he is a gentleman. His grandfather—"

"You know *nothing* about him," asserted Mrs. Yorke, rising. "You may be married to a man for years and know very little of him. How can you know about this boy? You will go back and forget all about him in a week."

"I shall never forget him, mamma," said Alice, in a low tone, thinking of the numerous promises she had made to the same effect within the past few days.

"Fiddlesticks! How often have you said that? A half-dozen times at least. There's Norman and Ferdy Wicker-sham and—"

"I have not forgotten them," said Alice, a little impressed by her mother's argument.

"Of course, you have not. I don't think it's right, Alice, for you to be so—susceptible and shallow. At least once every three months I have to go through this same thing. There's Ferdy Wickersham—handsome, elegant manners, very ri—with fine prospects every way, devoted to you for ever so long. I don't care for his mother, but his people are now received everywhere. Why—?"

"Mamma, I would not marry Ferdy Wickersham if he were the last man in—to save his life—not for ten millions of dollars. And he does not care for me."

"Why, he is perfectly devoted to you," insisted Mrs. Yorke.

"Ferdy Wickersham is not perfectly devoted to any one except himself—and never will be," asserted Alice, vehemently. "If he ever cared for any one it is Louise Caldwell."

Mrs. Yorke shifted her ground.

"There's Norman Wentworth? One of the best—"

"Ah! I don't love Norman. I never could. We are the best of friends, but I just like and respect him."

"Respect is a very safe ground to marry on," said Mrs. Yorke, decisively. "Some people do not have even that when they marry."

"Then I am sorry for them," said Miss Alice. "But when I marry, I want to love. I think it would be a crime to marry a man you did not love. God made us with a capacity to form ideals, and if we deliberately fall below them—"

Mrs. Yorke burst out laughing.

"Oh, stuff! That boy has filled your head with enough nonsense to last a lifetime. I would not be such a parrot. I want to finish my letter now."

Mrs. Yorke concluded her letter, and two mornings later

123

the Yorkes took the old two-horse stage that plied between the Springs and the little grimy railway-station, ten
miles away at the foot of the Ridge, and metaphorically
shook the dust of Ridgely from their feet, though, from their
appearance when they reached the railway, it, together
with much more, must have settled on their shoulders.

The road passed the little frame school-house, and as
the stage rattled by, the young school-teacher's face changed.
He stood up and looked out of the window with a curious
gaze in his burning eyes. Suddenly his face lit up : a little
head under a very pretty hat had nodded to him. He
bowed low, and went back to his seat with a new expression. That bow chained him for years. He almost forgave her high-headed mother.

Alice bore away with her a long and tragic letter which
she did not think it necessary to confide to her mother at
this time, in view of the fact that the writer declared that
in his present condition he felt bound to recognize her
mother's right to deny his request to see her ; but that he
meant to achieve such success that she would withdraw her
prohibition, and to return some day and lay at her feet
the highest honors life could give.

A woman who has discarded a man is, perhaps, nearer
loving him just afterwards than ever before. Certainly
Miss Alice Yorke thought more tenderly of Gordon Keith
when she found herself being borne away from him than
she had ever done during the weeks she had known him.

It is said that a broken heart is a most valuable possession for a young man. Perhaps, it was so to Keith.

The rest of the session dragged wearily for him. But
he worked like fury. He would succeed. He would rise.
He would show Mrs. Yorke who he was.

Mrs. Yorke, having reached home, began at once to lead
her daughter back to what she esteemed a healthier way of
thinking than she had fallen into. This opportunity came
in the shape of a college commencement with a consequent
boat-race, and all the gayeties that this entailed.

Mrs. Yorke was, in her way, devoted to her daughter, and had a definite and what she deemed an exalted ambition for her. This meant that she should be the best-dressed girl in society, should be a belle, and finally should make the most brilliant marriage of her set—to wit, the wealthiest marriage. She had dreamed at times of a marriage that should make her friends wild with envy—of a title, a high title. Alice had beauty, style, wealth, and vivacity; she would grace a coronet, and mamma would be "Madam, the Countess's mother." But mamma encountered an unexpected obstacle.

When Mrs. Yorke, building her air-castles, casually let fall her idea of a title for Alice, there was a sudden and unexpected storm from an unlooked-for quarter. Dennis Yorke, usually putty in his wife's hands, had two or three prejudices that were principles with him. As to these he was rock. His daughter was his idol.

For her, from the time she had opened her blue eyes on him and blinked at him vaguely, he had toiled and schemed until his hair had turned from brown to gray and then had disappeared from his round, strongly set head. For the love he bore her he had served longer than Jacob served for Rachel, and the time had not appeared long. The suggestion that the money he had striven for from youth to age should go to some reprobate foreigner, to pay his gambling-debts, nearly threw him into a convulsion. His ancestors had been driven from home to starve in the wilderness by such creatures. "Before any d—d foreign reprobate should have a dollar of his money he would endow a lunatic asylum with it." So Mrs. Yorke prudently refrained from pressing this subject any further at this time, and built her hopes on securing the next most advantageous alliance —a wealthy one. She preferred Norman Wentworth to any of the other young men, for he was not only rich, but the Wentworths were an old and established house, and Mrs. Wentworth was one of the old aristocrats of the State, whose word was law above that of even the wealthiest of the new leaders. To secure Norman Wentworth would be "almost as good as a title." An intimacy was sedulously cultivated with "dear Mrs. Wentworth," and Norman, the "dear boy," was often brought to the house.

Perversely, he and Alice did not take to each other in the way Mrs. Yorke had hoped. They simply became the best of friends, and Mrs. Yorke had the mortification of seeing a tall and statuesque schoolmate of Alice's capture Norman, while Alice appeared totally indifferent to him. What made it harder to bear was that Mrs. Caldwell, Louise Caldwell's mother, a widow with barely enough to live respectably on, was quietly walking off with the prize which Mrs. Yorke and a number of other mothers were striving to secure, and made no more of it than if it had been her right. It all came of her family connections. That was the way with those old families. They were so selfishly exclusive and so proud. They held themselves superior to every one else and appeared to despise wealth. Mrs. Yorke did not believe Mrs. Caldwell really did despise wealth, but she admitted that she made a very good show of doing it.

Mrs. Yorke, foreseeing her failure with Norman Wentworth, was fain to accept in his place Ferdy Wickersham, who, though certainly not Norman's equal in some respects, was his superior in others.

To be sure, Ferdy was said to be a somewhat reckless young fellow, and Mr. Yorke did not fancy him ; but Mrs. Yorke argued, "Boys will be boys, and you know, Mr. Yorke, you have told me you were none too good yourself." On this, Dennis Yorke growled that a man was "a fool ever to tell his wife anything of the kind, and that, at least, he never was in that young Wickersham's class."

All of which Mrs. Yorke put aside, and sacrificed herself unstintedly to achieve success for her daughter and compel her to forget the little episode of the young Southern schoolmaster, with his tragic air.

Ah, the dreams of the climbers ! How silly they are ! Golden clouds at the top, and just as they are reached, some little Jack comes along and chops down the bean-stalk, clouds and all.

So, Mrs. Yorke dreamed, and, a trifle anxious over Alice's persistent reference to the charms of Spring woods and a Southern climate, after a week or two of driving down-town and eager choosing of hats and wearying fitting of dresses, started off with the girl on the yacht of Mr. Lancaster, a wealthy, dignified, and cultivated friend of her husband's. He had always been fond of Alice, and now got up a yacht-party for her to see the boat-race.

Keith had thought that the time when he should leave the region where he had been immersed so long would be the happiest hour of his life. Yet, when the day came, he was conscious of a strange tugging at his heart. These people whom he was leaving, and for whom he had in his heart an opinion very like contempt on account of their ignorance and narrowness, appeared to him a wholly different folk. There was barely one of them but had been kind to him. Hard they might appear and petty; but they lived close together, and, break through the crust, one was sure to find a warm heart and often a soft one.

He began to understand Dr. Balsam's speech : "I have lived in several kinds of society, and I like the simplest best. One can get nearer to men here. I do not ask gratitude. I get affection."

Keith had given notice that the school would close on a certain day. The scholars always dropped off as summer came, to work in the crops; and the attendance of late had been slim. This last day he hardly expected to have half a dozen pupils. To his surprise, the school-house was filled.

Even Jake Dennison, who had been off in the mountains for some little time getting out timber, was on hand, large and good-humored, sitting beside Phrony Tripper in her pink ribbons, and fanning her hard enough to keep a mine fresh. A little later in the day quite a number of the fathers and mothers of the children arrived in their rickety vehicles. They had come to take leave of the young teacher. There were almost as many as were present at the school celebration. Keith was quite overcome, and when the hour arrived for closing the school, instead of, as he had expected, tying up the half-dozen books he kept in his desk, shaking hands with the dozen children eager to be turned loose in the delightful pasturage of summer holiday, turning the key in the lock, and plodding alone down the dusty road to Squire Rawson's, he now found the school-room full, not of school-children only, but of grown people as well. He had learned that they expected him to say something, and there was nothing for him to do but to make the effort. For an hour, as he sat during the last lessons,—which were in the nature of a review,—the pages before him had been mere blurred spaces of white, and he had been cogitating what he should say. Yet, when he rose, every idea that he had tried so faithfully to put into shape fled from his brain.

Dropping all the well-turned phrases which he had been trying to frame, he said simply that he had come there two years before with the conceit of a young man expecting to teach them a good deal, and that he went away feeling that he had taught very little, but that he had learned a great deal; he had learned that the kindest people in the world lived in that region; he should never forget their kindness and should always feel that his best friends were there. A few words more about his hopes for the school and his feeling for the people who had been so good to him, and he pronounced the school closed. To his surprise, at a wink from Squire Rawson, one of the other trustees, who had formerly been opposed to Keith, rose, and, addressing the assemblage, began to say things about him that pleased him as much as they astonished him.

He said that they, too, had begun with some doubt as to how things would work, as one "could never tell what a colt would do till he got the harness on him," but this colt had "turned out to be a pretty good horse." Mr. Keith, maybe, had taught more than he knew. He had taught some folks—this with a cut of his eye over toward where Jake Dennison sat big and brown in the placid content of a young giant, fanning Euphronia for life—he had "taught some folks that a door had to be right strong to keep out a teacher as knowed his business." Anyhow, they were satisfied with him, and the trustees had voted to employ him another year, but he had declined. He had " business " that would take him away. Some thought they knew that business. (At this there was a responsive titter throughout the major portion of the room, and Gordon Keith was furious with himself for finding that he suddenly turned hot and red.) He himself, the speaker said, didn't pretend to know anything about it, but he wanted to say that if Mr. Keith didn't find the business as profitable as he expected, the trustees had determined to hold the place open for him for one year, and had elected a successor temporarily to hold it in case he should want to come back.

At this there was a round of approval, as near general applause as that stolid folk ever indulged in.

Keith spent the next day in taking leave of his friends.

His last visit that evening was to Dr. Balsam. He had not been to the village often in the evening since Mrs. Yorke and her daughter had left the place. Now, as he passed up the walk, the summer moonlight was falling full on the white front of the little hotel. The slanting moonlight fell on the corner of the verandah where he had talked so often to Alice Yorke as she lay reclining on her lounge, and where he had had that last conversation with Mrs. Yorke, and Keith saw a young man leaning over some one enveloped in white, half reclining in an arm-chair. He wondered if the same talk were going on that had gone on there before that evening when Mrs. Yorke had made him look nakedly at Life.

When Keith stated his errand, the Doctor looked almost as grave as he could have done had one of his cherished patients refused to respond to his most careful treatment.

"One thing I want to say to you," he said presently. "You have been eating your heart out of late about something, and it is telling on you. Give it up. Give that girl up. You will have to sooner or later. They will prove too strong for you. Even if you do not, she will not suit you; you will not get the woman you are after. She is an attractive young girl, but she will not remain so. A few years in fashionable society will change her. It is the most corroding life on earth!" exclaimed the Doctor, bitterly. "Convention usurps the place of every principle, and becomes the only god. She must change. All is Vanity!" repeated the Doctor, almost in a revery, his eyes resting on Keith's face.

"Well," he said, with a sigh, "if you ever get knocked down and hurt badly, come back up here, and I will patch you up if I am living; and if not, come back anyhow. The place will heal you provided you don't take drugs. God bless you! Good-by." He walked with Keith to the outer edge of his little porch and shook hands with him again, and again said, "Good-by: God bless you!" When Keith turned at the foot of the hill and looked back, he was just reëntering his door, his spare, tall frame clearly outlined against the light within. Keith somehow felt as if he were turning his back on a landmark.

Just as Keith approached the gate on his return home, a figure rose up from a fence-corner and stood before him in the starlight.

"Good even'n', Mr. Keith." The voice was Dave Dennison's. Keith greeted him wonderingly. What on earth could have brought the boy out at that time of the night?

"Would you mind jest comin' down this a-way a little piece?"

Keith walked back a short distance. Dave was always mysterious when he had a communication to make. It was partly a sort of shyness and partly a survival of frontier craft.

Dave soon resolved Keith's doubt. "I hear you're a-goin' away and ain't comin' back no more?"

130

"How did you hear that—I mean, that I am not coming back again?" asked Keith.

"Well, you're a-sayin' good-by to everybody, same's if they were all a-goin' to die. Folks don't do that if they're a-comin' back." He leaned forward, and in the semi-darkness Keith was aware that he was scrutinizing his face.

"No, I do not expect to come back—to teach school again; but I hope to return some day to see my friends."

The boy straightened up.

"Well, I wants to go with you."

"You! Go with me?" Keith exclaimed. Then, for fear the boy might be wounded, he said: "Why, Dave, I don't even know where I am going. I have not the least idea in the world what I am going to do. I only know I am going away, and I am going to succeed."

"That's right. That's all right," agreed the boy. "You're a-goin' somewheres, and I want to go with you. You don't know where you're a-goin', but you're a-goin'. You know all them outlandish countries like you've been a-tellin' us about, and I don't know anything, but I want to know, and I'm a-goin' with you. Leastways, I'm a-goin', and I'm a-goin' with you if you'll let me."

Keith's reply was anything but reassuring. He gave good reasons against Dave's carrying out his plan; but his tone was kind, and the youngster took it for encouragement.

"I ain't much account, I know," he pleaded. "I ain't *any* account in the *worl'*," he corrected himself, so that there could be no mistake about the matter. "They say at home I used to be some account—some little account—before I took to books—before I *sorter* took to books," he corrected again shamefacedly; "but since then I ain't been no manner of account. But I think—I kinder think—I could be some account if I knowed a little and could go somewheres to be account."

Keith was listening earnestly, and the boy went on:

"When you told us that word about that man Hannibal tellin' his soldiers how everything lay t'other side the

131

mountains, I begin to see what you meant. I thought
before that I knowed a lot; then I found out how durned
little I did know, and since then I have tried to learn, and
I mean to learn; and that's the reason I want to go with
you. You know and I don't, and you're the only one as
ever made me want to know."

Keith was conscious of a flush of warm blood about his
heart. It was the first-fruit of his work.

The boy broke in on his pleasant revery.

"You'll let me go?" he asked. "'Cause I'm a-goin' certain sure. I ain't a-goin' to stay here in this country no
longer. See here." He pulled out an old bag and poked
it into Keith's hand. "I've got sixteen dollars and
twenty-three cents there. I made it, and while the other
boys were spendin' theirn, I saved mine. You can pour
it out and count it."

Keith said he would go and see his father about it the
next day.

This did not appear to satisfy Dave.

"I'm a-goin' whether he says so or not," he burst forth.
"I want to see the worl'. Don't nobody keer nothin' about
me, an' I want to git out."

"Oh, yes! Why, I care about you," said Keith.

To his surprise, the boy began to whimper.

"Thankee. I'm obliged to you. I—want to go away—
where Phrony ner nobody—ner anybody won't never see
me no more—any more."

The truth dawned on Keith. Little Dave, too, had his
troubles, his sorrows, his unrequited affections. Keith
warmed to the boy.

"Phrony is a lot older than you," he said consolingly.

"No, she ain't; we are just of an age; and if she was I
wouldn't keer. I'm goin' away."

Keith had to interpose his refusal to take him in such a
case. He said, however, that if he could obtain his father's
consent, as soon as he got settled he would send for him.
On the basis of this compromise the boy went home.

CHAPTER XI

GUMBOLT

WITH the savings of his two years of school-teaching Keith found that he had enough, by practising rigid economy, to give himself another year at college, and he practised rigid economy.

He worked under the spur of ambition to show Alice Yorke and those who surrounded her that he was not a mere country clod.

With his face set steadily in the direction where stood the luminous form of the young girl he had met and come to worship amid the blossoming woods, he studied to such good purpose that at the end of the session he had packed two years' work into one.

Keith had no very definite ideas, when he started out at the end of his college year, as to what he should do. He only knew that he had strong pinions, and that the world was before him. He wished to bury himself from observation until he should secure the success with which he would burst forth on an astonished world, overwhelm Mrs. Yorke, and capture Alice. His first intention had been to go to the far West; but on consideration he abandoned the idea.

Rumors were already abroad that in the great Appalachian mountain-range opportunity might be as golden as in that greater range on the other side of the continent.

Keith had a sentiment that he would rather succeed in the South than elsewhere.

"Only get rifles out and railroads in, and capital will come pouring after them," Rhodes had said. "Old Wickersham knows his business."

That was a good while ago, and at last the awakening had begun. Now that carpet-bagging was at an end, and affairs were once more settled in that section, the wealth of the country was again being talked of in the press.

The chief centre of the new life was a day's drive farther in the mountains than Eden, the little hamlet which Keith had visited once with Dr. Balsam when he attended an old stage-driver, Gilsey by name, and cut a bullet out of what he called his "off-leg." This was the veiled Golconda. To the original name of Humboldt the picturesque and humorous mountaineer had given the name of "Gumbolt."

This was where old Adam Rawson, stirred by the young engineer's prophecy, had taken time by the forelock and had bought up the mineral rights, and "gotten ahead" of Wickersham & Company.

Times and views change even in the Ridge region, and now, after years of delay, Wickersham & Company's railroad was about to be built. It had already reached Eden.

Keith, after a few days with his father, stopped at Ridgely to see his old friends. The Doctor looked him over with some disapproval.

"As gaunt as a greyhound," he muttered. "My patient not married yet, I suppose? Well, she will be. You'd better tear her out of your memory before she gets too firmly lodged there."

Keith boldly said he would take the chances.

When old Rawson saw him he, too, remarked on his thinness; but more encouragingly.

"Well, 'a lean dog for a long chase,'" he said.

"How are cattle?" inquired Keith.

The old fellow turned his eyes on him with a keen look.

"Cattle's tolerable. I been buyin' a considerable number up toward Gumbolt, where you're goin'. I may get you to look after 'em some day," he chuckled.

Gordon wrote to Dave Dennison that he was going to Gumbolt and would look out for him. A little later he learned that the boy had already gone there.

The means of reaching Gumbolt from Eden, the terminus of the railroad which Wickersham & Company were building, was still the stage, a survivor of the old-time mountain coach, which had outlasted all the manifold chances and changes of fortune.

Happily for Keith, he had been obliged, though it was raining, to take the outside seat by the driver, old Tim Gilsey, to whom he recalled himself, and by his coolness at "Hellstreak Hill," where the road climbed over the shoulder of the mountain along a sheer cliff, and suddenly dropped to the river below, a point where old Gilsey was wont to display his skill as a driver and try the nerves of passengers, he made the old man his friend for life.

When the stage began to ascend the next hill, the old driver actually unbent so far as to give an account of a "hold-up" that had occurred at that point not long before, "all along of the durned railroad them Yankees was bringin' into the country," to which he laid most of the evils of the time. "For when you run a stage you know who you got with you," declared Mr. Gilsey; "but when you run a railroad you dunno who you got."

"Well, tell me about the time you were held up."

"Didn't nobody hold me up," sniffed Mr. Gilsey. "If I had been goin' to stop I wouldn't 'a' started. It was a dom fool they put up here when I was down with rheumatiz. Since then they let me pick my substitute.

"Well," he said, as a few lights twinkled below them, "there she is. Some pretty tough characters there, too. But you ain't goin' to have no trouble with 'em. All you got to do is to put the curb on 'em onct."

As Keith looked about him in Gumbolt, the morning after his arrival, he found that his new home was only a rude mining-camp, raw and rugged; a few rows of frame houses, beginning to be supplanted by hasty brick structures, stretched up the hills on the sides of unpaved roads, dusty in dry weather and bottomless in wet. Yet it was, for its size, already one of the most cosmopolitan places in the country. Of course, the population was mainly American, and they were beginning to pour in—sharp-eyed men from the towns in black coats, and long-legged, quiet-looking and quiet-voiced mountaineers in rusty clothes, who hulked along in single file, silent and almost fugitive in the glare of daylight. Quiet they were and well-nigh stealthy, with something of the movement of other denizens of the forest, unless they were crossed and aroused, and then, like those other denizens, they were fierce almost beyond belief. A small cavil might make a great quarrel, and pistols would flash as quick as light.

The first visit that Keith received was from J. Quincy Plume, the editor of the *Gumbolt Whistle*. He had the honor of knowing his distinguished father, he said, and had once had the pleasure of being at his old home. He had seen Keith's name on the book, and had simply called to offer him any services he or his paper could render him. "There are so few gentlemen in this——hole," he explained, "that I feel that we should all stand together." Keith, knowing J. Quincy's history, inwardly smiled.

Mr. Plume had aged since he was the speaker of the carpet-bag legislature; his black hair had begun to be sprinkled with gray, and had receded yet farther back on his high forehead; his hazel eyes were a little bleared; and his full lips were less resolute than of old. He had evidently seen bad times since he was the facile agent of the Wickersham interests. He wore a black suit and a gay necktie which had once been gayer, a shabby silk hat, and patent-leather shoes somewhat broken.

His addiction to cards and drink had contributed to Mr. Plume's overthrow, and after a disappearance from public view for some time he had turned up just as Gumbolt began to be talked of, with a small sheet somewhat larger than a pocket-handkerchief, which, in prophetic tribute to

Gumbolt's future manufactures, he christened the *Gumbolt Whistle*.

Mr. Plume offered to introduce Keith to "the prettiest woman in Gumbolt," and, incidentally, to "the best cocktail" also. "Terpsichore is a nymph who practises the Terpsichorean art; indeed, I may say, presides over a number of the arts, for she has the best faro-bank in town, and the only bar where a gentleman can get a drink that will not poison a refined stomach. She is, I may say, the leader of Gumbolt society."

Keith shook his head; he had come to work, he declared.

"Oh, you need not decline; you will have to know Terpy. I am virtue itself; in fact, I am Joseph—nowadays. You know, I belong to the cloth?" Keith's expression indicated that he had heard this fact. "But even I have yielded to her charms—intellectual, I mean, of course."

Mr. Plume withdrew after having suggested to Keith to make him a small temporary loan, or, if more convenient, to lend him the use of his name on a little piece of bank-paper "to tide over an accidental and unexpected emergency," assuring Keith that he would certainly take it up within sixty days.

Unfortunately for Keith, Plume's cordiality had made so much impression on him that he was compliant enough to lend him the use of his name, and as neither at the expiration of sixty days, nor at any other time, did Mr. Plume ever find it convenient to take up his note, Keith found himself later under the necessity of paying it himself. This circumstance, it is due to Mr. Plume to say, he always deplored, and doubtless with sincerity.

Women were at a premium in Gumbolt, and Mr. Plume was not the only person who hymned the praises of "Terpsichoar," as she was mainly called. Keith could not help wondering what sort of a creature she was who kept a dance-house and a faro-bank, and yet was spoken of with unstinted admiration and something very like respect by the crowd that gathered in the "big room of the Windsor." She must be handsome, and possibly was a good dancer, but she was no doubt a wild, coarse creature, with painted cheeks and dyed hair. The mental picture he formed was not one to interfere with the picture he carried in his heart.

Next day, as he was making a purchase in a shop, a neat and trim-looking young woman, with a fresh complexion and a mouth full of white teeth, walked in, and in a pleasant voice said, "Good mornin', all." Keith did not associate her at all with Terpsichore, but he was surprised that old Tim Gilsey should not have known of her presence in town. He was still more surprised when, after having taken a long and perfectly unabashed look at him, with no more diffidence in it than if he had been a lump of ore she was inspecting, she said :

"You're the fellow that come to town night before last? Uncle Tim was tellin' me about you."

"Yes ; I got here night before last. Who is Uncle Tim?"

"Uncle Tim Gilsey."

She walked up and extended her hand to him with the most perfect friendliness, adding, with a laugh as natural as a child's :

"We'll have to be friends; Uncle Tim says you're a white man, and that's more than some he brings over the road these days are."

"Yes, I hope so. You are Mr. Gilsey's niece? I am glad to meet you."

The young woman burst out laughing.

"Lor', *no*. I ain't anybody's niece ; but he's my uncle— I've adopted *him*. I'm Terpy—Terpsichore ; run Terpsichore's Hall," she said by way of explanation, as if she thought he might not understand her allusion.

Keith's breath was almost taken away. Why, she was not at all like the picture he had formed of her. She was a neat, quiet-looking young woman, with a fine figure, slim and straight and supple, a melodious voice, and laughing gray eyes.

"You must come and see me. We're to have a blow-out to-night. Come around. I'll introduce you to the boys. I've got the finest ball-room in town—just finished —and three fiddles. We christen it to-night. Goin' to be the biggest thing ever was in Gumbolt."

Keith awoke from his daze.

"Thank you, but I am afraid I'll have to ask you to excuse me," he said.

"Why?" she inquired simply.

"Because I can't come. I am not much of a dancer."

She looked at him first with surprise and then with amusement.

"Are you a Methodist preacher?"

"No."

"Salvation?"

"No."

"I thought, maybe, you were like Tib Drummond, the Methodist, what's always a-preachin' ag'in' me." She turned to the storekeeper. "What do you think he says? He says he won't come and see me, and he ain't a preacher nor Salvation Army neither. But he will, won't he?"

"You bet," said the man, peeping up with a grin from behind a barrel. "If he don't, he'll be about the only one in town who don't."

"No," said Keith, pleasantly, but firmly. "I can't go."

"Oh, yes, you will," she laughed. "I'll expect you. By-by"; and she walked out of the store with a jaunty air, humming a song about the "iligint, bauld McIntyres."

The "blow-out" came off, and was honored with a column in the next issue of the *Whistle*—a column of reeking eulogy. But Keith did not attend, though he heard the wheezing of fiddles and the shouting and stamping of Terpsichore's guests deep into the night.

Keith was too much engrossed for the next few days in looking about him for work and getting himself as comfortably settled as possible to think of anything else.

If, however, he forgot the "only decent-looking woman

in Gumbolt," she did not forget him. The invitation of a sovereign is equivalent to a command the world over; and Terpsichore was as much the queen regnant of Gumbolt as Her Majesty, Victoria, was Queen of England, or of any other country in her wide realm. She was more; she was absolute. She could have had any one of a half-dozen men cut the throat of any other man in Gumbolt at her bidding.

The mistress of the "Dancing Academy" had not forgotten her boast. The institution over which she presided was popular enough almost to justify her wager. There were few men of Keith's age in Gumbolt who did not attend its sessions and pay their tribute over the green tables that stretched along the big, low room.

In fact, Miss Terpsichore was not of that class that forget either friends or foes; whatever she was she was frankly and outspokenly. Mr. Plume informed Keith that she was "down on him."

"She's got it in for you," he said. "Says she's goin' to drive you out of Gumbolt."

"Well, she will not," said Keith, with a flash in his eye.

"She is a good friend and a good foe," said the editor. "Better go and offer a pinch of incense to Diana. She is worth cultivating. You ought to see her dance."

Keith, however, had made his decision. A girl with eyes like dewy violets was his Diana, and to her his incense was offered.

A day or two later Keith was passing down the main street, when he saw the young woman crossing over at the corner ahead of him, stepping from one stone to another quite daintily. She was holding up her skirt, and showed a very neat pair of feet in perfectly fitting boots. At the crossing she stopped. As Keith passed her, he glanced at her, and caught her eye fastened on him. She did not look away at all, and Keith inclined his head in recognition of their former meeting.

"Good morning," she said.

"Then why don't you answer me?"

"Good morning." Keith lifted his hat and was passing on.

"Why haven't you been to see me?" she demanded.

Keith pretended not to hear.

"I thought I invited you to come and see me?"

Still, Keith did not answer, but he paused. His head was averted, and he was waiting until she ceased speaking to go on.

Suddenly, to his surprise, she bounded in front of him and squared her straight figure right before him.

"Did you hear what I said to you?" she demanded tempestuously.

"Yes."

"Then why don't you answer me?" Her gaze was fastened on his face. Her cheeks were flushed, her voice was imperative, and her eyes flashed.

"Because I didn't wish to do so," said Keith, calmly.

Suddenly she flamed out and poured at him a torrent of vigorous oaths. He was so taken by surprise that he forgot to do anything but wonder, and his calmness evidently daunted her.

"Don't you know that when a lady invites you to come to see her, you have to do it?"

"I have heard that," said Keith, beginning to look amused.

"You have? Do you mean to say I am not a lady?"

"Well, from your conversation, I might suppose you were a man," said Keith, half laughing.

"I will show you that I am man enough for you. Don't you know I am the boss of this town, and that when I tell you to do a thing you have to obey me?"

"No; I do not know that," said Keith. "You may be the boss of this town, but I don't have to obey you."

"Well, I will show you about it, and —— quick, too. See if I don't! I will run you out of this town, my young man."

"Oh, I don't think you will," said Keith, easily.

"Yes, I will, and quick enough, too. You look out for me."

"Good morning," said Keith, raising his hat.

The loudness of her tone and the vehemence of her manner had arrested several passers-by, who now stood looking on with interest.

"What's the matter, Terpy?" asked one of them. "What are you so peppery about? Bank busted?"

The young woman explained the matter with more fairness than Keith would have supposed.

"Oh, he is just a fool. Let him alone," said the man; whilst another added: "He'll come around, darlin'; don't you bother; and if he don't, I will."

"—— him! He's got to go. I won't let him now. You know when I say a thing it's got to be, and I mean to make him know it, too," asserted the young Amazon. "I'll have him driven out of town, and if there ain't any one here that's man enough to do it, I'll do it myself." This declaration she framed with an imprecation sufficiently strong if an oath could make it so.

That evening Tim Gilsey came in to see Keith. He looked rather grave.

"I am sorry you did not drop in, if it was for no more than to git supper," he said. "Terpy is a bad one to have against you. She's the kindest gal in the world; but she's got a temper, and when a gal's got a temper, she's worse'n a fractious leader."

"I don't want her against me; but I'll be hanged if I will be driven into going anywhere that I don't want to go," asserted Keith.

"No, I don't say as you should," said the old driver, his eye resting on Keith with a look that showed that he liked him none the less for his pluck. "But you've got to look out. This ain't back in the settlements, and there's a plenty around here as would cut your throat for a wink of Terpy's eye. They will give you a shake for it, and if you come out of that safe it will be all right. I'll see one or two of the boys and see that they don't let 'em double up on you. A horse can't do nothin' long if he has got a double load on him, no matter what he is."

Tim strolled out, and, though Keith did not know it for some time, he put in a word for him in one or two places which stood him in good stead afterwards.

The following day a stranger came up to Keith. He was a thin man between youth and middle age, with a long face and a deep voice, and light hair that stuck up on his head. His eyes were deep-set and clear; his mouth was grave and his chin strong. He wore a rusty black coat and short, dark trousers.

"Are you Mr. Keith?" His voice was deep and melancholy.

Keith bowed. He could not decide what the stranger was. The short trousers inclined him to the church.

"I am proud to know you, sir. I am Mr. Drummond, the Methodist preacher." He gripped Keith's hand.

Keith expressed the pleasure he had in meeting him.

"Yes, sir; I am proud to know you," repeated Mr. Drummond. "I hear you have come out on the right side, and have given a righteous reproof to that wretched dancing Jezebel who is trying to destroy the souls of the young men of this town."

Keith said that he was not aware that he had done anything of the kind. As to destroying the young men, he doubted if they could be injured by her—certainly not by dancing. In any event, he did not merit his praise.

Mr. Drummond shook his head. "Yes, sir. You are the first young man who has had the courage to withstand the wiles of that person. She is the most abandoned creature in this town; she beguiles the men so that I can make no impression on them. Even when I am holding my meetings, I can hear the strains of her fiddles and the shouts of the ribald followers that throng her den-of-Satan. I have tried to get her to leave, but she will not go."

Keith's reply was that he thought she had as much right there as any one, and he doubted if there were any way to meet the difficulty.

"I am sorry to hear you say that," said the preacher. "I shall break up her sink of iniquity if I have to hold a revival meeting at her very door and call down brimstone and fire upon her den of wickedness."

"If you felt so on the subject of dancing, why did you come here?" demanded Keith. "It seems to me that dancing is one of the least sins of Gumbolt."

The preacher looked at him almost pensively. "I thought it my duty. I have encountered ridicule and obloquy; but I do not mind them. I count them but dross. 'Wherever I have found the print of my Lord's shoe in the earth, there I have coveted to set my feet also.'"

Keith bowed. The speech of Mr. Valiant-for-Truth carried its cachet with it. The stiff, awkward figure had changed. The preacher's sincerity had lent him dignity, and his simple use of a simple tinker's words had suddenly uplifted him to a higher plane.

"Do not you think you might go about it in a less uncompromising spirit? You might succeed better and do more good," said Keith.

"No, sir; I will make no compromise with the devil—not even to succeed. Good-by. I am sorry to find you among the obdurate." As he shook hands, his jaw was set fast and his eye was burning. He strode off with the step of a soldier advancing in battle.

Keith had not long to wait to test old Gilsey's advice. He was sitting in the public room of the Windsor, a few evenings later, among the motley crew that thronged that popular resort, who were discoursing of many things, from J. Quincy Plume's last editorial on "The New Fanny Elssler," to the future of Gumbolt, when Mr. Plume himself entered. His appearance was the signal for some humor, for Mr. Plume had long passed the time when any one but himself took him seriously.

"Here comes somebody that can tell us the news," called some one. "Come in, J. Quincy, and tell us what you know."

"That would take too long," said Mr. Plume, as he edged himself toward the stove. "You will find all the news in the *Whistle* to-morrow."

Just then another new arrival, who had pushed his way in toward the stove, said: "I will tell you a piece of news: Bill Bluffy is back."

"Come back, has he?" observed one of the company. "Well, that is more interesting to J. Quincy than if the railroad had come. They are hated rivals. Since J. Quincy has taken to writing editorials on Terpy, Bill says there ain't no show for him. He threatened to kill Terp, I heard."

"Oh, I guess he has got more sense than that, drunk or sober. He had better stick to men; shootin' of women ain't popular in most parts, an' it ain't likely to get fashionable in Gumbolt, I reckon."

"He is huntin' for somebody," said the newcomer.

"I guess if he is going to get after all of Terpy's ardent admirers, he will have his hands pretty full," observed Mr. Plume—a sentiment which appeared to meet with general approval.

Just then the door opened a little roughly, and a man entered slowly whom Keith knew intuitively to be Mr. Bill Bluffy himself. He was a young, brown-bearded man, about Keith's size, but more stockily built; his flannel shirt was laced up in front, and had a full, broad collar turned over a red necktie with long ends. His slouch-hat was set on the back of his head. The gleaming butts of two pistols that peeped out of his waistband gave a touch of piquancy to his appearance. His black eyes were restless and sparkling with excitement. He wavered slightly in his gait, and his speech was just thick enough to confirm what his appearance suggested, and what he was careful to declare somewhat superfluously, that he was "on a —— of a spree."

145

"I am a-huntin' for a —— furriner 'at I promised to run out of town before to-morrow mornin'. Is he in here?" He tried to stand still, but finding this difficult, advanced.

A pause fell in the conversation around the stove. Two or three of the men, after a civil enough greeting, hitched themselves into a more comfortable posture in their chairs, and it was singular, though Keith did not recall it until afterwards, that each of them showed by the movement a pistol on his right hip.

After a general greeting, which in form was nearer akin to an eternal malediction than to anything else, Mr. Bluffy walked to the bar. Resting himself against it, he turned, and sweeping his eye over the assemblage, ordered every man in the room to walk up and take a drink with him, under penalties veiled in too terrific language to be wholly intelligible. The violence of his invitation was apparently not quite necessary, as every man in the room pulled back his chair promptly and moved toward the bar, leaving Keith alone by the stove. Mr. Bluffy had ordered drinks, when his casual glance fell on Keith standing quietly inside the circle of chairs on the other side of the stove. He pushed his way unsteadily through the men clustered at the bar.

"Why in the —— don't you come up and do what I tell you? Are you deaf?"

"No," said Keith, quietly; "but I'll get you to excuse me."

"Excuse ——! You aren't too good to drink with me, are you? If you think you are, I'll show you pretty—d quick you ain't."

Keith flushed.

"Drink with him," said two or three men in an undertone. "Or take a cigar," said one, in a friendly aside.

"Thank you, I won't drink," said Keith, yet more gravely, his face paling a little, "and I don't care for a cigar."

"Come on, Mr. Keith," called some one.

The name caught the young bully, and he faced Keith more directly.

"Keith?—Keith!" he repeated, fastening his eyes on him with a cold glitter in them. "So you're Mr. Keith, are you?"

"That is my name," said Keith, feeling his blood tingling.

"Well, you're the man I'm a-lookin' for. No, you won't drink with me, 'cause I won't let you, you —— —— ——! You are the —— —— that comes here insultin' a lady?"

"No; I am not," said Keith, keeping his eyes on him.

"You're a liar!" said Mr. Bluffy, adding his usual expletives. "And you're the man I've come back here a-huntin' for. I promised to drive you out of town to-night if I had to go to hell a-doin' it."

His white-handled pistol was out of his waistband with a movement so quick that he had it cocked and Keith was looking down the barrel before he took in what had been done. Quickness was Mr. Bluffy's strongest card, and he had played it often.

Keith's face paled slightly. He looked steadily over the pistol, not three feet from him, at the drunken creature beyond it. His nerves grew tense, and every muscle in his frame tightened. He saw the beginning of the grooves in the barrel of the pistol and the gray cones of the bullets at the side in the cylinder; he saw the cruel, black, drunken eyes of the young desperado. It was all in a flash. He had not a chance for his life. Yes, he had.

"Let up, Bill," said a voice, coaxingly, as one might to soothe a wild beast. "Don't—"

"Drop that pistol!" said another voice, which Keith recognized as Dave Dennison's.

The desperado half glanced at the latter as he shot a volley of oaths at him. That glance saved Keith. He ducked out of the line of aim and sprang upon his assailant at the same time, seizing the pistol as he went, and turning it up

147

just as Bluffy pulled the trigger. The ball went into the remote corner of the ceiling, and the desperado was carried off his feet by Keith's rush.

The only sounds heard in the room were the shuffling of the feet of the two wrestlers and the oaths of the enraged Bluffy. Keith had not uttered a word. He fought like a bulldog, without noise. His effort was, while he still gripped the pistol, to bring his two hands together behind his opponent's back. A sudden relaxation of the latter's grip as he made another desperate effort to release his pistol favored Keith, and, bringing his hands together, he lifted his antagonist from his feet, and by a dexterous twist whirled him over his shoulder and dashed him with all his might, full length flat on his back, upon the floor. It was an old trick learned in his boyish days and prac-tised on the Dennisons, and Gordon had by it ended many a contest, but never one more completely than this. A buzz of applause came from the bystanders, and more than one, with sudden friendliness, called to him to get Bluffy's pistol, which had fallen on the floor. But Keith had no need to do so, for just then a stoutly built young fellow snatched it up. It was Dave Dennison, who had come in just as the row began. He had been following up Bluffy. The desperado, however, was too much shaken to have used it immediately, and when, still stunned and breathless, he rose to his feet, the crowd was too much against him to have allowed him to renew the attack, even had he then desired it.

As for Keith, he found himself suddenly the object of universal attention, and he might, had he been able to dis-tribute himself, have slept in half the shacks in the camp.

The only remark Dave made on the event was char-acteristic:

"Don't let him git the drop on you again."

The next morning Keith found himself, in some sort, famous. "Tacklin' Bill Bluffy without a gun and cleanin' him up," as one of his new friends expressed it, was no mean feat, and Keith was not insensible to the applause it brought him. He would have enjoyed it more, perhaps, had not every man, without exception, who spoke of it given him the same advice Dave had given—to look out for Bluffy. To have to kill a man or be killed oneself is not the pleasantest introduction to one's new home; yet this appeared to Keith the dilemma in which he was placed, and as, if either had to die, he devoutly hoped it would not be himself, he stuck a pistol in his pocket and walked out the next morning with very much the same feeling he supposed he should have if he had been going to battle. He was ashamed to find himself much relieved when some one he met volunteered the information that Bluffy had left town by light that morning.

"Couldn't stand the racket. Terpy wouldn't even speak to him. But he'll come back. Jest as well tote your gun a little while, till somebody else kills him for you."

A few mornings later, as Keith was going down the street, he met again the "only decent-lookin' gal in Gumbolt." It was too late for him to turn off, for when he first caught sight of her he saw that she had seen him, and her head went up, and she turned her eyes away. He hoped to pass without appearing to know her; but just before they met, she cut her eye at him, and though his gaze was straight ahead, she said, "Good morning," and he touched his hat as he passed.

That afternoon he met her again. He was passing on as before, without looking at her, but she stopped him.

"Good afternoon." She spoke rather timidly, and the color that mounted to her face made her very handsome.

He returned the salutation coldly, and with an uneasy feeling that he was about to be made the object of another outpouring of her wrath. Her intention, however, was quite different.

"I don't want you to think I set that man on you; it was somebody else done it." The color came and went in her cheeks.

Keith bowed politely, but preserved silence.

"I was mad enough to do it, but I didn't, and them that says I done it lies." She flushed, but looked him straight in the face.

"Oh, that's all right," said Keith, civilly, starting to move on.

"I wish they would let me and my affairs alone," she began. "They're always a-talkin' about me, and I never done 'em no harm. First thing they know, I'll give 'em something to talk about."

The suppressed fire was beginning to blaze again, and Keith looked somewhat anxiously down the street, wishing he were anywhere except in that particular company. To relieve the tension, he said:

"I did not mean to be rude to you the other day. Good morning."

At the kind tone her face changed.

"I knew it. I was riled that mornin' about another thing—somethin' what happened the day before, about Bill," she explained. "Bill's bad enough when he's in liquor, and I'd have sent him off for good long ago if they had let him alone. But they're always a-peckin' and a-diggin' at him. They set him on drinkin' and fightin', and not one of 'em is man enough to stand up to him."

She gave a little whimper, and then, as if not trusting herself further, walked hastily away. Mr. Gilsey said to Gordon soon afterwards:

"Well, you've got one friend in Gumbolt as is a team by herself; you've captured Terp. She says you're the only man in Gumbolt as treats her like a lady."

Keith was both pleased and relieved.

A week or two after Keith had taken up his abode in Gumbolt, Mr. Gilsey was taken down with his old enemy, the rheumatism, and Keith went to visit him. He found him in great anxiety lest his removal from the box should hasten the arrival of the railway. He unexpectedly gave Keith evidence of the highest confidence he could have in any man. He asked if he would take the stage until he got well. Gordon readily assented.

So the next morning at daylight Keith found himself sitting in the boot, enveloped in old Tim's greatcoat, enthroned in that high seat toward which he had looked in his childhood-dreams.

It was hard work and more or less perilous work, but his experience as a boy on the plantation and at Squire Rawson's, when he had driven the four-horse wagon, stood him in good stead.

Old Tim's illness was more protracted than any one had contemplated, and, before the first winter was out, Gordon had a reputation as a stage-driver second only to old Gilsey himself.

Stage-driving, however, was not his only occupation, and before the next Spring had passed, Keith had become what Mr. Plume called "one of Gumbolt's rising young sons." His readiness to lend a hand to any one who needed a helper began to tell. Whether it was Mr. Gilsey trying to climb with his stiff joints to the boot of his stage, or Squire Rawson's cousin, Captain Turley, the sandy-whiskered, sandy-clothed surveyor, running his lines through the laurel bushes among the gray débris of the crumbled mountain-side; Mr. Quincy Plume trying to evolve new copy from a splitting head, or the shouting wagon-drivers thrashing their teams up the muddy street, he could and would help any one.

He was so popular that he was nominated to be the town constable, a tribute to his victory over Mr. Bluffy.

Terpy and he, too, had become friends, and though Keith stuck to his resolution not to visit her "establishment," few days went by that she did not pass him on the street or happen along where he was, and always with a half-abashed nod and a rising color.

CHAPTER XII

KEITH DECLINES AN OFFER

WITH the growth of Gumbolt, Mr. Wickersham and his friends awakened to the fact that Squire Rawson was not the simple cattle-dealer he appeared to be, but was a man to be reckoned with. He not only held a large amount of the most valuable property in the Gap, but had as yet proved wholly intractable about disposing of it. Accordingly, the agent of Wickersham & Company, Mr. Halbrook, came down to Gumbolt to look into the matter. He brought with him a stout, middle-aged Scotchman, named Matheson, with keen eyes and a red face, who was represented to be the man whom Wickersham & Company intended to make the superintendent of their mines as soon as they should be opened.

The railroad not having yet been completed more than a third of the way beyond Eden, Mr. Halbrook took the stage to Gumbolt.

Owing to something that Mr. Gilsey had let fall about Keith, Mr. Halbrook sent next day for Keith. He wanted him to do a small piece of surveying for him. With him was the stout Scotchman, Matheson.

The papers and plats were on a table in his room, and Keith was looking at them.

"How long would it take you to do it?" asked Mr. Halbrook. He was a short, alert-looking man, with black eyes and a decisive manner. He always appeared to be in a hurry.

Keith was so absorbed that he did not answer immediately, and the agent repeated the question with a little asperity in his tone.

"I say how long would it take you to run those lines?"

"I don't know," said Keith, doubtfully. "I see a part of the property lies on the mountain-side just above and next to Squire Rawson's lands. I could let you know to-morrow."

"To-morrow! You people down here always want to put things off. That is the reason you are so behind the rest of the world. The stage-driver, however, told me that you were different, and that is the reason I sent for you."

Keith straightened himself. "Dr. Chalmers said when some one praised him as better than other Scotchmen, 'I thank you, sir, for no compliment paid me at the expense of my countrymen.'" He half addressed himself to the Scotchman.

Matheson turned and looked him over, and as he did so his grim face softened a little.

"I know nothing about your doctors," said Mr. Halbrook; "what I want is to get this work done. Why can't you let me know to-day what it will cost? I have other things to do. I wish to leave to-morrow afternoon."

"Well," said Keith, with a little flush in his face, "I could guess at it to-day. I think it will take a very short time. I am familiar with a part of this property already, and—"

Mr. Halbrook was a man of quick intellect; moreover, he had many things on his mind just then. Among them he had to go and see what sort of a trade he could make with this Squire Rawson, who had somehow stumbled into the best piece of land in the Gap, and was now holding it in an obstinate and unreasonable way.

"Well, I don't want any guessing. I'll tell you what I will do. I will pay you so much for the job." He named a sum which was enough to make Keith open his eyes. It

153

was more than he had ever received for any one piece of work.

"It would be cheaper for you to pay me by the day," Keith began.

"Not much! I know the way you folks work down here. I have seen something of it. No day-work for me. I will pay you so many dollars for the job. What do you say? You can take it or leave it alone. If you do it well, I may have some more work for you." He had no intention of being offensive; he was only talking what he would have called "business"; but his tone was such that Keith answered him with a flash in his eye, his breath coming a little more quickly.

"Very well; I will take it."

Keith took the papers and went out. Within a few minutes he had found his notes of the former survey and secured his assistants. His next step was to go to Captain Turley and take him into partnership in the work, and within an hour he was out on the hills, verifying former lines and running such new lines as were necessary. Spurred on by the words of the newcomer even more than by the fee promised him, Keith worked with might and main, and sat up all night finishing the work. Next day he walked into the room where Mr. Halbrook sat, in the company's big new office at the head of the street. He had a roll of paper under his arm.

"Good morning, sir." His head was held rather high, and his voice had a new tone in it.

Mr. Wickersham's agent looked up, and his face clouded. He was not used to being addressed in so independent a tone.

"Good morning. I suppose you have come to tell me how long it will take you to finish the job that I gave you, or that the price I named is not high enough?"

"No," said Keith, "I have not. I have come to show you that my people down here do not always put things off till to-morrow. I have come to tell you that I have done the work. Here is your survey." He unrolled and spread out before Mr. Halbrook's astonished gaze the plat he had made. It was well done, the production of a draughtsman who knew the value of neatness and skill. The agent's eyes opened wide.

"Impossible! You could not have done it, or else you—"

"I have done it," said Keith, firmly. "It is correct."

"You had the plat before?" Mr. Halbrook's eyes were fastened on him keenly. He was feeling a little sore at what he considered having been outwitted by this youngster.

"I had run certain of the lines before," said Keith : "these, as I started to tell you yesterday. And now," he said, with a sudden change of manner, "I will make you the same proposal I made yesterday. You can pay me what you think the work is worth. I will not hold you to your bargain of yesterday."

The other sat back in his chair, and looked at him with a different expression on his face.

"You must have worked all night?" he said thoughtfully.

"I did," said Keith, "and so did my assistant, but that is nothing. I have often done that for less money. Many people sit up all night in Gumbolt," he added, with a smile.

"That old stage-driver said you were a worker." Mr. Halbrook's eyes were still on him. "Where are you from?"

"Born and bred in the South," said Keith.

"I owe you something of an apology for what I said yesterday. I shall have some more work for you, perhaps."

The agent, when he went back to the North, was as good as his word. He told his people that there was one man in Gumbolt who would do their work promptly.

"And he's straight," he said. "He says he is from the South ; but he is a new issue."

He further reported that old Rawson, the countryman who owned the land in the Gap, either owned or controlled the cream of the coal-beds there. "He either knows or has

been well advised by somebody who knows the value of all
the lands about there. And he has about blocked the game.
I think it's that young Keith, and I advise you to get hold
of Keith."

"Who is Keith? What Keith? What is his name?"
asked Mr. Wickersham.

"Gordon Keith."

Mr. Wickersham's face brightened. "Oh, that is all
right; we can get him. We might give him a place?"

Mr. Halbrook nodded.

Mr. Wickersham sat down and wrote a letter to Keith,
saying that he wished to see him in New York on a matter
of business which might possibly turn out to his advantage.
He also wrote a letter to General Keith, suggesting that
he might possibly be able to give his son employment, and
intimating that it was on account of his high regard for the
General.

That day Keith met Squire Rawson on the street. He
was dusty and travel-stained.

"I was jest comin' to see you," he said.

They returned to the little room which Keith called his
office, where the old fellow opened his saddle-bags and took
out a package of papers.

"They all thought I was a fool," he chuckled as he laid
out deed after deed. "While they was a-talkin' I was
a-ridin'. They thought I was buyin' cattle, and I was, but
for every cow I bought I got a calf in the shape of the mineral rights to a tract of land. I'd buy a cow and I'd offer
a man half as much again as she was worth if he'd sell me
the mineral rights at a fair price, and he'd do it. He never
had no use for 'em, an' I didn't know as I should either;
but that young engineer o' yourn talked so positive I
thought I might as well git 'em inside my pasture-fence."
He sat back and looked at Keith with quizzical complacency.

"Come a man to see me not long ago," he continued; "Mr.
Halbrook—black-eyed man, with a face white and hard

like a tombstone. I set up and talked to him nigh all night and filled him plumb full of old applejack. That man sized me up for a fool, an' I sized him up for a blamed smart Yankee. But I don't know as he got much the better of me."

Keith doubted it too.

"I think it was in and about the most vallyble applejack that I ever owned," continued the old landowner, after a pause. "You know, I don't mind Yankees as much as I used to—some of 'em. Of course, thar was Dr. Balsam ; he was a Yankee ; but I always thought he was somethin' out of the general run, like a piebald horse. That young engineer o' yourn that come to my house several years ago, he give me a new idea about 'em—an' about some other things, too. He was a very pleasant fellow, an' he knowed a good deal, too. It occurred to me 't maybe you might git hold of him, an' we might make somethin' out of these lands on our own account. Where is he now ? "

Keith explained that Mr. Rhodes was somewhere in Europe.

"Well, time enough. He'll come home sometime, an' them lands ain't liable to move away. Yes, I likes some Yankees now pretty well ; but, Lord ! I loves to git ahead of a Yankee ! They're so kind o' patronizin' to you. Well," he said, rising, "I thought I'd come up and talk to you about it. Some day I'll git you to look into matters a leetle for me."

The next day Keith received Mr. Wickersham's letter requesting him to come to New York. Keith's heart gave a bound.

The image of Alice Yorke flashed into his mind, as it always did when any good fortune came to him. Many a night, with drooping eyes and flagging energies, he had sat up and worked with renewed strength because she sat on the other side of the hot lamp.

It is true that communication between them had been but rare. Mrs. Yorke had objected to any correspondence, and he now began to see, though dimly, that her objection was natural. But from time to time, on anniversaries, he had sent her a book, generally a book of poems with marked passages in it, and had received in reply a friendly note from the young lady, over which he had pondered, and which he had always treasured and filed away with tender care.

Keith took the stage that night for Eden on his way to New York. As they drove through the pass in the moonlight he felt as if he were soaring into a new life. He was already crossing the mountains beyond which lay the Italy of his dreams.

He stopped on his way to see his father. The old gentleman's face glowed with pleasure as he looked at Gordon and found how he had developed. Life appeared to be reopening for him also in his son.

"I will give you a letter to an old friend of mine, John Templeton. He has a church in New York. But it is not one of the fashionable ones; for

> ' Unpractised he to fawn or seek for power
> By doctrines fashioned to the varying hour:
> Far other aims his heart had learned to prize,
> More skilled to raise the wretched than to rise.'

You will find him a safe adviser. You will call also and pay my respects to Mr. and Mrs. Wentworth."

On his way, owing to a break in the railroad, Keith had to change his train at a small town not far from New York. Among the passengers was an old lady, simply and quaintly dressed, who had taken the train somewhere near Philadelphia. She was travelling quite alone, and appeared to be much hampered by her bags and parcels. The sight of an old woman, like that of a little girl, always softened Keith's heart. Something always awoke in him that made him feel tender. When Keith first observed this old lady, the entire company was streaming along the platform in that haste which always marks the transfer of passengers from one train to another. No one appeared to notice her, and under the weight of her bags and bundles she was gradually dropping to the rear of the crowd. As Keith, bag in hand, swung past her with the rest, he instinctively turned and offered his services to help carry her parcels. She panted her thanks, but declined briefly, declaring that she should do very well.

"You may be doing very well," Keith said pleasantly, "but you will do better if you will let me help you."

"No, thank you." This time more firmly than before. "I am quite used to helping myself, and am not old enough for that yet. I prefer to carry my own baggage," she added with emphasis.

"It is not the question of age, I hope, that gives me the privilege of helping a lady," said Keith. He was already trying to relieve her of her largest bag and one or two bundles.

A keen glance from a pair of very bright eyes was shot at him.

"Well, I will let you take that side of that bag and this bundle—no; that one. Now, don't run away from me."

"No; I will promise not," said Keith, laughing; and relieved of that much of her burden, the old lady stepped out more briskly than she had been doing. When they finally reached a car, the seats were nearly all filled. There was one, however, beside a young woman at the far end, and this Keith offered to the old lady, who, as he stowed her baggage close about her, made him count the pieces carefully. Finding the tale correct, she thanked him with more cordiality than she had shown before, and Keith withdrew to secure a seat for himself. As, however, the car was full, he stood up in the rear of the coach, waiting until some passengers might alight at a way-station. The first seat that became vacant was one immediately behind the old lady, who had now fallen into a cheerful conversation with the young woman beside her.

"What do you do when strangers offer to take your bags?" Keith heard her asking as he seated himself.

"Why, I don't know; they don't often ask. I never let them do it," said the young woman, firmly.

"A wise rule, too. I have heard that that is the way nowadays that they rob women travelling alone. I had a young man insist on taking my bag back there; but I am very suspicious of these civil young men." She leaned over and counted her parcels again. Keith could not help laughing to himself. As she sat up she happened to glance around, and he caught her eye. He saw her clutch her companion and whisper to her, at which the latter glanced over her shoulder and gave him a look that was almost a stare. Then the two conferred together, while Keith chuckled with amusement. What they were saying, had Keith heard it, would have amused him still more than the other.

"There he is now, right behind us," whispered the old lady.

"Why, he doesn't look like a robber."

"They never do. I have heard they never do. They are the most dangerous kind. Of course, a robber who looked it would be arrested on sight."

"But he is very good-looking," insisted the younger woman, who had, in the meantime, taken a second glance at Keith, who pretended to be immersed in a book.

"Well, so much the worse. They are the very worst kind. Never trust a good-looking young stranger, my dear. They may be all right in romances, but never in life."

As her companion did not altogether appear to take this view, the old lady half turned presently, and taking a long look down the other side of the car, to disarm Keith of any suspicion that she might be looking at him, finally let her eyes rest on his face, quite accidentally, as it were. A moment later she was whispering to her companion.

"I am sure he is watching us. I am going to ask you to stick close beside me when we get to New York until I find a hackney-coach."

"Have you been to New York often?" asked the girl, smiling.

"I have been there twice in the last thirty years; but I spent several winters there when I was a young girl. I suppose it has changed a good deal in that time?"

The young lady also supposed that it had changed in that time, and wondered why Miss Brooke—the name the other had given—did not come to New York oftener.

"You see, it is such an undertaking to go now," said the old lady. "Everything goes with such a rush that it takes my breath away. Why, three trains a day each way pass near my home now. One of them actually rushes by in the most impetuous and disdainful way. When I was young we used to go to the station at least an hour before the train was due, and had time to take out our knitting and compose our thoughts; but now one has to be at the station just as promptly as if one were going to church, and if you don't get on the train almost before it has stopped, the dreadful thing is gone before you know it. I must say, it is very destructive to one's nerves."

Her companion laughed.

"I don't know what you will think when you get to New York."

"Think! I don't expect to think at all. I shall just shut my eyes and trust to Providence."

"Your friends will meet you there, I suppose?"

"I wrote them two weeks ago that I should be there to-day, and then my cousin wrote me to let her know the train, and I replied, telling her what train I expected to take. I would never have come if I had imagined we were going to have this trouble."

The girl reassured her by telling her that even if her friends did not meet her, she would put her in the way of reaching them safely. And in a little while they drew into the station.

Keith's first impression of New York was dazzling to him. The rush, the hurry, stirred him and filled him with a sense of power. He felt that here was the theatre of action for him.

The offices of Wickersham & Company were in one of the large buildings down-town. The whole floor was filled with pens and railed-off places, beyond which lay the private offices of the firm. Mr. Wickersham was "engaged," and Keith had to wait for an hour or two before he could secure an interiew with him. When at length he was admitted to Mr. Wickersham's inner office, he was received with some cordiality. His father was asked after, and a number of questions about Gumbolt were put to him. Then Mr. Wickersham came to the point. He had a high regard for his father, he said, and having heard that Gordon was living in Gumbolt, where they had some interests, it had occurred to him that he might possibly be able to give him a position. The salary would not be large at first, but if he showed himself capable it might lead to something better.

Keith was thrilled, and declared that what he most wanted was work and opportunity to show that he was able to work. Mr. Wickersham was sure of this, and informed him briefly that it was outdoor work that they had for him—"the clearing up of titles and securing of such lands as we may wish to obtain," he added.

This was satisfactory to Keith, and he said so.

Mr. Wickersham's shrewd eyes had a gleam of content in them.

"Of course, our interest will be your first consideration?" he said.

"Yes, sir; I should try and make it so."

"For instance," proceeded Mr. Wickersham, "there are certain lands lying near our lands, not of any special value; but still you can readily understand that as we are running a railroad through the mountains, and are expending large sums of money, it is better that we should control lands through which our line will pass."

Keith saw this perfectly. "Do you know the names of

162

any of the owners?" he inquired. "I am familiar with some of the lands about there."

Mr. Wickersham pondered. Keith was so ingenuous and eager that there could be no harm in coming to the point.

"Why, yes; there is a man named Rawson that has some lands or some sort of interest in lands that adjoin ours. It might be well for us to control those properties."

Keith's countenance fell.

"It happens that I know something of those lands."

"Yes? Well, you might possibly take those properties along with others?"

"I could certainly convey any proposition you wish to make to Mr. Rawson, and should be glad to do so," began Keith.

"We should expect you to use your best efforts to secure these and all other lands that we wish," interrupted Mr. Wickersham, speaking with sudden sharpness. "When we employ a man we expect him to give us all his services, and not to be half in our employ and half in that of the man we are fighting."

The change in his manner and tone was so great and so unexpected that Keith was amazed. He had never been spoken to before quite in this way. He, however, repressed his feeling.

"I should certainly render you the best service I could," he said; "but you would not expect me to say anything to Squire Rawson that I did not believe? He has talked with me about these lands, and he knows their value just as well as you do."

Mr. Wickersham looked at him with a cold light in his eyes, which suddenly recalled Ferdy to Keith.

"I don't think that you and I will suit each other, young man," he said.

Keith's face flushed; he rose. "I don't think we should, Mr. Wickersham. Good morning." And turning, he walked out of the room with his head very high.

As he passed out he saw Ferdy. He was giving some

163

directions to a clerk, and his tone was one that made Keith glad he was not under him.

"Haven't you any brains at all?" Keith heard him say.

"Yes, but I did not understand you."

"Then you are a fool," said the young man.

Just then Keith caught his eye and spoke to him. Ferdy only nodded "Hello!" and went on berating the clerk.

Keith walked about the streets for some time before he could soothe his ruffled feelings and regain his composure. How life had changed for him in the brief interval since he entered Mr. Wickersham's office! Then his heart beat high with hope; life was all brightness to him; Alice Yorke was already won. Now in this short space of time his hopes were all overthrown. Yet, his instinct told him that if he had to go through the interview again he would do just as he had done.

He felt that his chance of seeing Alice would not be so good early in the day as it would be later in the afternoon; so he determined to deliver first the letter which his father had given him to Dr. Templeton.

The old clergyman's church and rectory stood on an ancient street over toward the river, from which wealth and fashion had long fled. His parish, which had once taken in many of the well-to-do and some of the wealthy, now embraced within its confines a section which held only the poor. But, like an older and more noted divine, Dr. Templeton could say with truth that all the world was his parish; at least, all were his parishioners who were needy and desolate.

The rectory was an old-fashioned, substantial house, rusty with age, and worn by the stream of poverty that had flowed in and out for many years.

When Keith mounted the steps the door was opened by some one without waiting for him to ring the bell, and he found the passages and front room fairly filled with a number of persons whose appearance bespoke extreme poverty.

The Doctor was "out attending a meeting, but would be back soon," said the elderly woman who opened the door. "Would the gentleman wait?"

Just then the door opened and some one entered hastily. Keith was standing with his back to the door; but he knew by the movement of those before him, and the lighting up of their faces, that it was the Doctor himself, even before the maid said: "Here he is now."

He turned to find an old man of medium size, in a clerical dress quite brown with age and weather, but whose linen was spotless. His brow under his snow-white hair was lofty and calm; his eyes were clear and kindly; his mouth expressed both firmness and gentleness; his whole face was benignancy itself.

His eye rested for a moment on Keith as the servant indicated him, and then swept about the room; and with little more than a nod to Keith he passed him by and entered the waiting-room. Keith, though a little miffed at being ignored by him, had time to observe him as he talked to his other visitors in turn. He manifestly knew his business, and appeared to Keith, from the scraps of conversation he heard, to know theirs also. To some he gave encouragement; others he chided; but to all he gave sympathy, and as one after another went out their faces brightened.

When he was through with them he turned and approached Keith with his hands extended.

"You must pardon me for keeping you waiting so long; these poor people have nothing but their time, and I always try to teach them the value of it by not keeping them waiting."

"Certainly, sir," said Keith, warmed in the glow of his kindly heart. "I brought a letter of introduction to you from my father, General Keith."

The smile that this name brought forth made Keith the old man's friend for life.

"Oh! You are McDowell Keith's son. I am delighted to see you. Come back into my study and tell me all about your father."

When Keith left that study, quaint and old-fashioned as were it and its occupant, he felt as though he had been in a rarer atmosphere. He had not dreamed that such a man could be found in a great city. He seemed to have the heart of a boy, and Keith felt as if he had known him all his life. He asked Gordon to return and dine with him; but Gordon had a vision of sitting beside Alice Yorke at dinner that evening and declined.

CHAPTER XIII

KEITH IN NEW YORK

KEITH and Norman Wentworth had, from time to time, kept up a correspondence, and from Dr. Templeton's Keith went to call on Norman and his mother.

Norman, unfortunately, was now absent in the West on business, but Keith saw his mother.

The Wentworth mansion was one of the largest and most dignified houses on the fine old square—a big, double mansion. The door, with its large, fan-shaped transom and side-windows, reminded Keith somewhat of the hall door at Elphinstone, so that he had quite a feeling of old association as he tapped with the eagle knocker. The hall was not larger than at Elphinstone, but was more solemn, and Keith had never seen such palatial drawing-rooms. They stretched back in a long vista. The heavy mahogany furniture was covered with the richest brocades; the hangings were of heavy crimson damask. Even the walls were covered with rich crimson damask-satin. The floor was covered with rugs in the softest colors, into which, as Keith followed the solemn servant, his feet sank deep, giving him a strange feeling of luxuriousness. A number of fine pictures hung on the walls, and richly bound books lay on the shining tables amid pieces of rare bric-à-brac.

This was the impression received from the only glance he had time to give the room. The next moment a lady rose from behind a tea-table placed in a nook near a window at the far end of the spacious room. As Gordon turned toward her she came forward. She gave him a cordial hand-shake and gracious words of welcome that at once made Keith feel at home. Turning, she started to offer him a chair near her table; but Keith had instinctively gone behind her chair and was holding it for her.

"It is so long since I have had the chance," he said.

As she smiled up at him her face softened. It was a high-bred face, not always as gentle as it was now; but her smile was charming.

"You do not look like the little, wan boy I saw that morning in bed, so long ago. Do you remember?"

"I should say I did. I think I should have died that morning but for you. I have never forgotten it a moment since." The rising color in his cheeks took away the baldness of the speech.

She bowed with the most gracious smile, the color stealing up into her cheeks and making her look younger.

"I am not used to such compliments. Young men nowadays do not take the trouble to flatter old ladies."

Her face, though faded, still bore the unmistakable stamp of distinction. Calm, gray eyes and a strong mouth and chin recalled Norman's face. The daintiest of caps rested on her gray hair like a crown, and several little ringlets about her ears gave the charm of quaintness to the patrician face. Her voice was deep and musical. When she first spoke it was gracious rather than cordial; but after the inspective look she had given him it softened, and from this time Keith felt her warmth.

The easy, cordial, almost confidential manner in which she soon began to talk to him made Keith feel as if they had been friends always, and in a moment, in response to a question from her, he was giving quite frankly his impression of the big city: of its brilliance, its movement, its rush, that keyed up the nerves like the sweep of a swift torrent.

"It almost takes my breath away," he said. "I feel as if I were on the brink of a torrent and had an irresistible desire to jump into it and swim against it."

She looked at the young man in silence for a moment, enjoying his sparkling eyes, and then her face grew grave.

"Yes, it is interesting to get the impression made on a fresh young mind. But so many are dashed to pieces, it appears to me of late to be a maelstrom that engulfs everything in its resistless and terrible sweep. Fortune, health, peace, reputation, all are caught and swept away; but the worst is its heartlessness—and its emptiness."

She sighed so deeply that the young man wondered what sorrow could touch her, intrenched and enthroned in that beautiful mansion, surrounded by all that wealth and taste and affection could give. Years afterwards, that picture of the old-time gentlewoman in her luxurious home came back to him.

Just then a cheery voice was heard calling outside:

"Cousin?—cousin?—Matildy Carroll, where are you?"

It was the voice of an old lady, and yet it had something in it familiar to Keith.

Mrs. Wentworth rose, smiling.

"Here I am in the drawing-room," she said, raising her voice the least bit. "It is my cousin, a dear old friend and schoolmate," she explained to Keith. "Here I am. Come in here." She advanced to the door, stretching out her hand to some one who was coming down the stair.

"Oh, dear, this great, grand house will be the death of me yet!" exclaimed the other lady, as she slowly descended.

"Why, it is not any bigger than yours," protested Mrs. Wentworth.

"It's twice as large, and, besides, I was born in that and learned all its ups and downs and passages and corners when I was a child, just as I learned the alphabet. But this house! It is as full of devious ways and pitfalls as the way in 'Pilgrim's Progress,' and I would never learn it any more than I could the multiplication table. Why, that second-floor suite you have given me is just like six-times-nine. When you first put me in there I walked around to learn my way, and, on my word, I thought I should never get back to my own room. I thought I should have to sleep in a bath-tub. I escaped from the bath-room only to land in the linen-closet. That was rather interesting. Then when I had calculated all your sheets and pillow-cases, I got out of that to what I recognized as my own room. No! it was the broom-closet—eight-times-seven! That was the only familiar thing I saw. I could have hugged those brooms. But, my dear, I never saw so many brooms in my life! No wonder you have to have all those servants. I suppose some of them are to sweep the other servants up. But you really must shut off those apartments and just give me one little room to myself, or, now that I have escaped from the labyrinth, I shall put on my bonnet and go straight home."

All this was delivered from the bottom step with a most amusing gravity.

"Well, now that you have escaped, come in here," said Mrs. Wentworth, laughing. "I want a friend of mine to know you—a young man—"

"A gentleman!"

"Yes; a young gentleman from—"

"My dear!" exclaimed the other lady. "I am not fit to see a young gentleman—I haven't on my new cap. I really could not."

"Oh, yes, you can. Come in. I want you to know him, too. He is—m—m—m—"

This was too low for Keith to hear. The next second Mrs. Wentworth turned and reëntered the room, holding by the hand Keith's old lady of the train.

As she laid her eyes on Keith, she stopped with a little shriek, shut both eyes tight, and clutched Mrs. Wentworth's arm.

"My dear, it's my robber!"

"It's what?"

"My robber! He's the young man I told you of who was so suspiciously civil to me on the train. I can never look him in the face—never!" Saying which, she opened

170

her bright eyes and walked straight up to Keith, holding out her hand. "Confess that you are a robber and save me."

Keith laughed and took her hand.

"I know you took me for one." He turned to Mrs. Wentworth and described her making him count her bundles.

"You will admit that gentlemen were much rarer on that train than ruffians or those who looked like ruffians?" insisted the old lady, gayly. "I came through the car, and not one soul offered me a seat. You deserve all the abuse you got for being so hopelessly unfashionable as to offer any civility to a poor, lonely, ugly old woman."

"Abby, Mr. Keith does not yet know who you are. Mr. Keith, this is my cousin, Miss Brooke."

"Miss Abigail Brooke, spinster," dropping him a quaint little curtsy.

So this was little Lois's old aunt, Dr. Balsam's sweetheart —the girl who had made him a wanderer; and she was possibly the St. Abigail of whom Alice Yorke used to speak!

The old lady turned to Mrs. Wentworth.

"He is losing his manners; see how he is staring. What did I tell you? One week in New York is warranted to break any gentleman of good manners."

"Oh, not so bad as that," said Mrs. Wentworth. "Now you sit down there and get acquainted with each other."

So Keith sat down by Miss Brooke, and she was soon telling him of her niece, who, she said, was always talking of him and his father.

"Is she as pretty as she was as a child?" Keith asked.

"Yes—much too pretty; and she knows it, too," smiled the old lady. "I have to hold her in with a strong hand, I tell you. She has got her head full of boys already."

Other callers began to appear just then. It was Mrs. Wentworth's day, and to call on Mrs. Wentworth was in some sort the cachet of good society. Many, it was true, called there who were not in "society" at all,—serene and self-contained old residents, who held themselves above the

171

newly-rich who were beginning to crowd "the avenues" and force their way with a golden wedge,—and many who lived in splendid houses on the avenue had never been admitted within that dignified portal. They now began to drop in, elegantly dressed women and handsomely appointed girls. Mrs. Wentworth received them all with that graciousness that was her native manner. Miss Brooke, having secured her "new cap," was seated at her side, her faded face tinged with rising color, her keen eyes taking in the scene with quite as much avidity as Gordon's. Gordon had fallen back quite to the edge of the group that encircled the hostess, and was watching with eager eyes in the hope that, among the visitors who came in in little parties of twos and threes, he might find the face for which he had been looking. The name Wickersham presently fell on his ear.

"She is to marry Ferdy Wickersham," said a lady near him to another. They were looking at a handsome, statuesque girl, with a proud face, who had just entered the room with her mother, a tall lady in black with strong features and a refined voice, and who were making their way through the other guests toward the hostess. Mrs. Wentworth greeted them cordially, and signed to the elder lady to take a seat beside her.

"Oh, no ; she is flying for higher game than that." They both put up their lorgnons and gave her a swift glance.

"You mean— ?" She nodded over toward Mrs. Wentworth.

"Yes."

"Why, she would not allow him to. She has not a cent in the world. Her mother has spent every dollar her husband left her, trying to get her off."

"Yes ; but she has spent it to good purpose. They are old friends. Mrs. Wentworth does not care for money. She has all she needs. She has never forgotten that her grandfather was a general in the Revolution, and Mrs. Caldwell's grandfather was one also, I believe. She looks down on the upper end of Fifth Avenue—the Wickershams and such. Don't you know what Mrs. Wentworth's cousin said when she heard that the Wickershams had a coat-of-arms? She said, 'Her father must have made it.'"

Something about the placid voice and air of the lady, and the knowledge she displayed of the affairs of others, awoke old associations in Keith, and turning to take a good look at her, he recognized Mrs. Nailor, the inquiring lady with the feline manner and bell-like voice, who used to mouse around the verandah at Gates's during Alice Yorke's convalescence.

He went up to her and recalled himself. She apparently had some difficulty in remembering him, for at first she gave not the slightest evidence of recognition; but after the other lady had moved away she was more fortunate in placing him.

"You have known the Wentworths for some time?"

Keith did not know whether this was a statement or an inquiry. She had a way of giving a tone of interrogation to her statements. He explained that he and Norman Wentworth had been friends as boys.

"A dear fellow, Norman?" smiled Mrs. Nailor. "Quite one of our rising young men? He wanted, you know, to give up the most brilliant prospects to help his father, who had been failing for some time. Not failing financially?" she explained with the interrogation-point again. "Of course, I don't believe those rumors; I mean in health?"

Keith had so understood her.

"Yes, he has quite gone. Completely shattered?" She sighed deeply. "But Norman is said to be wonderfully clever, and has gone in with his father into the bank?" she pursued. "The girl over there is to marry him—if her mother can arrange it? That tall, stuck-up woman." She indicated Mrs. Caldwell, who was sitting near Mrs. Wentworth. "Do you think her handsome?"

Keith said he did. He thought she referred to the girl,

who looked wonderfully handsome in a tailor-made gown under a big white hat.

"Romance is almost dying out?" she sighed. "It is so beautiful to find it? Yes?"

Keith agreed with her about its charm, but hoped it was not dying out. He thought of one romance he knew.

"You used to be very romantic? Yes?"

Keith could not help blushing.

"Have you seen the Yorkes lately?" she continued. Keith had explained that he had just arrived. "You know Alice is a great belle? And so pretty, only she knows it too well; but what pretty girl does not? The town is divided now as to whether she is going to marry Ferdy Wickersham or Mr. Lancaster of Lancaster & Company. He is one of our leading men, considerably older than herself, but immensely wealthy and of a distinguished family. Ferdy Wickersham was really in love with"— she lowered her voice—"that girl over there by Mrs. Wentworth; but she preferred Norman Wentworth; at least, her mother did, so Ferdy has gone back to Alice? You say you have not been to see her? No? You are going, of course? Mrs. Yorke was so fond of you?"

"Which is she going to—I mean, which do people say she prefers?" inquired Keith, his voice, in spite of himself, betraying his interest.

"Oh, Ferdy, of course. He is one of the eligibles, so good-looking, and immensely rich, too. They say he is really a great financier. Has his father's turn? You know he came from a shop?"

Keith admitted his undeniable good looks and knew of his wealth; but he was so confounded by the information he had received that he was in quite a state of confusion.

Just then a young clergyman crossed the room toward them. He was a stout young man, with reddish hair and a reddish face. His plump cheeks, no less than his well-filled waistcoat, showed that the Rev. Mr. Rimmon was no anchoret.

"Ah, my dear Mrs. Nailor, so glad to see you! How well you look! I haven't seen you since that charming evening at Mrs. Creamer's."

"Do you call that charming? What did you think of the dinner?" asked Mrs. Nailor, dryly.

He laughed, and, with a glance around, lowered his voice.

"Well, the champagne was execrable after the first round. Didn't you notice that? You didn't notice it? Oh, you are too amiable to admit it. I am sure you noticed it, for no one in town has such champagne as you."

He licked his lips with reminiscent satisfaction.

"No, I assure you, I am not flattering you. One of my cloth! How dare you charge me with it!" he laughed. "I have said as much to Mrs. Yorke. You ask her if I haven't."

"How is your uncle's health?" inquired Mrs. Nailor.

The young man glanced at her, and the glance appeared to satisfy him.

"Robust isn't the word for it. He bids fair to rival the patriarchs in more than his piety."

Mrs. Nailor smiled. "You don't appear as happy as a dutiful nephew might."

"But he is so good—so pious. Why should I wish to withhold him from the joys for which he is so ripe?"

Mrs. Nailor laughed.

"You are a sinner," she declared.

"We are all miserable sinners," he replied. "Have you seen the Yorkes lately?"

"No; but I'll be bound you have."

"What do you think of the story about old Lancaster?"

"Oh, I think she'll marry him if mamma can arrange it."

"'Children, obey your parents,'" quoted Mr. Rimmon, with a little smirk as he sidled away.

"He is one of our rising young clergymen, nephew of the noted Dr. Little," explained Mrs. Nailor. "You know of him, of course? A good deal better man than his nephew." This under her breath. "He is his uncle's assistant and is waiting to step into his shoes. He wants to marry your friend, Alice Yorke. He is sure of his uncle's church if flattery can secure it."

Just then several ladies passed near them, and Mrs. Nailor, seeing an opportunity to impart further knowledge, with a slight nod moved off to scatter her information and inquiries, and Keith, having made his adieus to Mrs. Wentworth, withdrew. He was not in a happy frame of mind over what he had heard.

The next visit that Keith paid required more thought and preparation than that to the Wentworth house. He had thought of it, had dreamed of it, for years. He was seized with a sort of nervousness when he found himself actually on the avenue, in sight of the large brown-stone mansion which he knew must be the abode of Miss Alice Yorke.

He never forgot the least detail of his visit, from the shining brass rail of the outside steps and the pompous little hard-eyed servant in a striped waistcoat and brass buttons, who looked at him insolently as he went in, to the same servant as he bowed to him obsequiously as he came out. He never forgot Alice Yorke's first appearance in the radiance of girlhood, or Mrs. Yorke's affable imperviousness, that baffled him utterly.

The footman who opened the door to Keith looked at him with keenness, but ended in confusion of mind. He stood, at first, in the middle of the doorway and gave him a glance of swift inspection. But when Keith asked if the ladies were in he suddenly grew more respectful. The visitor was not up to the mark in appointment, but there was that in his air and tone which Bower recognized. He would see. Would he be good enough to walk in?

When he returned after a few minutes, indifference had given place to servility.

KEITH IN NEW YORK

Would Mr. Keats please be good enough to walk into the drawing-room? Thankee, sir. The ladies would be down in a few moments.

Keith did not know that this change in bearing was due to the pleasure expressed above-stairs by a certain young lady who had flatly refused to accept her mother's suggestion that they send word they were not at home.

Alice Yorke was not in a very contented frame of mind that day. For some time she had been trying to make up her mind on a subject of grave importance to her, and she had not found it easy to do. Many questions confronted her. Curiously, Keith himself had played a part in the matter. Strangely enough, she was thinking of him at the very time his card was brought up. Mrs. Yorke, who had not on her glasses, handed the card to Alice. She gave a little scream at the coincidence.

"Mr. Keith! How strange!"

"What is that?" asked her mother, quickly. Her ears had caught the name.

"Why, it is Mr. Keith. I was just—." She stopped, for Mrs. Yorke's face spoke disappointment.

"I do not think we can see him," she began.

"Why, of course, I must see him, mamma. I would not miss seeing him for anything in the world. Go down, Bower, and say I will be down directly." The servant disappeared.

"Now, Alice," protested her mother, who had already exhausted several arguments, such as the inconvenience of the hour, the impoliteness of keeping the visitor waiting, as she would have to do to dress, and several other such excuses as will occur to mammas who have plans of their own for their daughters and unexpectedly receive the card of a young man who, by a bare possibility, may in ten minutes upset the work of nearly two years—"Now, Alice, I think it very wrong in you to do anything to give that young man any idea that you are going to reopen that old affair."

Alice protested that she had no idea of doing anything like that. There was no "old affair." She did not wish to be rude when he had taken the trouble to call—that was all.

"Fudge!" exclaimed Mrs. Yorke. "Trouble to call! Of course, he will take the trouble to call. He would call a hundred times if he thought he could get—" she caught her daughter's eye and paused—"could get you. But you have no right to cause him unhappiness."

"Oh, I guess I couldn't cause him much unhappiness now. I fancy he is all over it now," said the girl, lightly. "They all get over it. It's a quick fever. It doesn't last, mamma. How many have there been?"

"You know better. Isn't he always sending you books and things? He is not like those others. What would Mr. Lancaster say?"

"Oh, Mr. Lancaster! He has no right to say anything," pouted the girl, her face clouding a little. "Mr. Lancaster will say anything I want him to say," she added as she caught sight of her mother's unhappy expression. "I wish you would not always be holding him up to me. I like him, and he is awfully good to me—much better than I deserve; but I get awfully tired of him sometimes: he is so serious. Sometimes I feel like breaking loose and just doing things. I do!" She tossed her head and stamped her foot with impatience like a spoiled child.

"Well, there is Ferdy?—" began her mother.

The girl turned on her.

"I thought we had an understanding on that subject, mamma. If you ever say anything more about my marrying Ferdy, I *will* do things! I vow I will!"

"Why, I thought you professed to like Ferdy, and he is certainly in love with you."

"He certainly is not. He is in love with Lou Caldwell as much as he could be in love with any one but himself; but if you knew him as well as I do you would know he is not in love with any one but Ferdy."

Mrs. Yorke knew when to yield, and how to do it. Her face grew melancholy and her voice pathetic as she protested that all she wished was her daughter's happiness.

"Then please don't mention that to me again," said the girl.

The next second her daughter was leaning over her, soothing her and assuring her of her devotion.

"I want to invite him to dinner, mamma."

Mrs. Yorke actually gasped.

"Nonsense! Why, he would be utterly out of place. This is not Ridgely. I do not suppose he ever had on a dress-coat in his life!" Which was true, though Keith would not have cared a button about it.

"Well, we can invite him to lunch," said Alice, with a sigh.

But Mrs. Yorke was obdurate. She could not undertake to invite an unknown young man to her table. Thus, the want of a dress-suit limited Mrs. Yorke's hospitality and served a secondary and more important purpose for her.

"I wish papa were here; he would agree with me," sighed the girl.

When the controversy was settled Miss Alice slipped off to gild the lily. The care she took in the selection of a toilet, and the tender pats and delicate touches she gave as she turned before her cheval-glass, might have belied her declaration to her mother, a little while before, that she was indifferent to Mr. Keith, and might even have given some comfort to the anxious young man in the drawing-room below, who, in default of books, was examining the pictures with such interest. He had never seen such a sumptuous house.

Meantime, Mrs. Yorke executed a manœuvre. As soon as Alice disappeared, she descended to the drawing-room. But she slipped on an extra diamond ring or two. Thus she had a full quarter of an hour's start of her daughter.

The greeting between her and the young man was more cordial than might have been expected. Mrs. Yorke was surprised to find how Keith had developed. He had broadened, and though his face was thin, it had undeniable distinction. His manner was so dignified that Mrs. Yorke was almost embarrassed.

"Why, how you have changed!" she exclaimed.

What she said to herself was: "What a bother for this boy to come here now, just when Alice is getting her mind settled! But I will get rid of him."

She began to question him as to his plans.

What Keith had said to himself when the step on the stair and the rustling gown introduced Mrs. Yorke's portly figure was: "Heavens! it's the old lady! I wonder what the old dragon will do, and whether I am not to see Her!" He observed her embarrassment as she entered the room, and took courage.

The next moment they were fencing across the room, and Keith was girding himself like another young St. George.

How was his school coming on? she asked.

He was not teaching any more. He had been to college, and had now taken up engineering. It offered such advantages.

She was so surprised. She would have thought teaching the very career for him. He seemed to have such a gift for it.

Keith was not sure that this was not a "touch." He quoted Dr. Johnson's definition that teaching was the universal refuge of educated indigents. "I do not mean to remain an indigent all my life," he added, feeling that this was a touch on his part.

Mrs. Yorke pondered a moment.

"But that was not his name. His name was Balsam. I know, because I had some trouble getting a bill out of him."

Keith changed his mind about the touch.

Just then there was another rustle on the stair and another step,—this time a lighter one,—and the next moment appeared what was to the young man a vision.

Keith's face, as he rose to greet her, showed what he

180

thought. For a moment, at least, the dragon had disappeared, and he stood in the presence only of Alice Yorke.

The girl was, indeed, as she paused for a moment just in the wide doorway under its silken hangings,—the minx! how was he to know that she knew how effective the position was?—a picture to fill a young man's eye and flood his face with light, and even to make an old man's eye grow young again. The time that had passed had added to the charm of both face and figure ; and, arrayed in her daintiest toilet of blue and white, Alice Yorke was radiant enough to have smitten a much harder heart than that which was at the moment thumping in Keith's breast and looking forth from his eager eyes. The pause in the doorway gave just time for the picture to be impressed forever in Keith's mind.

Her eyes were sparkling, and her lips parted with a smile of pleased surprise.

"How do you do?" She came forward with outstretched arm and a cordial greeting.

Mrs. Yorke could not repress a mother's pride at seeing the impression that her daughter's appearance had made. The expression on Keith's face, however, decided her that she would hazard no more such meetings.

The first words, of course, were of the surprise Alice felt at finding him there. "How did you remember us?"

"I was not likely to forget you," said Keith, frankly enough. "I am in New York on business, and I thought that before going home I would see my friends." This with some pride, as Mrs. Yorke was present.

"Where are you living?"

Keith explained that he was an engineer and lived in Gumbolt.

"Ah, I think that is a splendid profession," declared Miss Alice. "If I were a man I would be one. Think of building great bridges across mighty rivers, tunnelling great mountains!"

"Maybe even the sea itself," said Mr. Keith, who, so long

as Alice's eyes were lighting up at the thought of his profession, cared not what Mrs. Yorke thought.

"I doubt if engineers would find much to do in New York," put in Mrs. Yorke. "I think the West would be a good field—the far West," she explained.

"It was so good in you to look us up," Miss Alice said sturdily and, perhaps, a little defiantly, for she knew what her mother was thinking.

"If that is being good," said Keith, "my salvation is assured." He wanted to say, as he looked at her, "In all the multitude in New York there is but one person that I really came to see, and I am repaid," but he did not venture so far. In place of it he made a mental calculation of the chances of Mrs. Yorke leaving, if only for a moment. A glance at her, however, satisfied him that the chance of it was not worth considering, and gloom began to settle on him. If there is anything that turns a young man's heart to lead and encases it in ice, it is, when he has travelled leagues to see a girl, to have mamma plant herself in the room and mount guard. Keith knew now that Mrs. Yorke had mounted guard, and that no power but Providence would dislodge her. The thought of the cool woods of the Ridge came to him like a mirage, torturing him.

He turned to the girl boldly.

"Sha'n't you ever come South again?" he asked. "The humming-birds are waiting."

Alice smiled, and her blush made her charming.

Mrs. Yorke answered for her. She did not think the South agreed with Alice.

Alice protested that she loved it.

"How is my dear old Doctor? Do you know, he and I have carried on quite a correspondence this year?"

Keith did not know. For the first time in his life he envied the Doctor.

"He is your—one of your most devoted admirers. The last time I saw him he was talking of you."

"What did he say of me? Do tell me!" with exaggerated eagerness.

Keith smiled, wondering what she would think if she knew.

"Too many things for me to tell."

His gray eyes said the rest.

While they were talking a sound of wheels was heard outside, followed by a ring at the door. Keith sat facing the door, and could see the gentleman who entered the hall. He was tall and a little gray, with a pleasant, self-contained face. He turned toward the drawing-room, taking off his gloves as he walked.

"Her father. He is quite distinguished-looking," thought Keith. "I wonder if he will come in here? He looks younger than the dragon." He was in some trepidation at the idea of meeting Mr. Yorke.

When Keith looked at the ladies again some change had taken place in both of them. Their faces wore a different expression: Mrs. Yorke's was one of mingled disquietude and relief, and Miss Alice's an expression of discontent and confusion. Keith settled himself and waited to be presented.

The gentleman came in with a pleased air as his eye rested on the young lady.

"There is where she gets her high-bred looks—from her father," thought Keith, rising.

The next moment the gentleman was shaking hands warmly with Miss Alice and cordially with Mrs. Yorke. And then, after a pause,—a pause in which Miss Alice had looked at her mother,—the girl introduced "Mr. Lancaster." He turned and spoke to Keith pleasantly.

"Mr. Keith is—an acquaintance we made in the South when we were there winter before last," said Mrs. Yorke.

"A friend of ours," said the girl. She turned back to Keith.

"Tell me what Dr. Balsam said."

"Mr. Keith knows the Wentworths—I believe you know

the Wentworths very well?" Mrs. Yorke addressed Mr. Keith.

"Yes; I have known Norman since we were boys. I have met his mother, but I never met his father."

Mrs. Yorke was provoked at the stupidity of denying so advantageous an acquaintance. But Mr. Lancaster took more notice of Keith than he had done before. His dark eyes had a gleam of amusement in them as he turned and looked at the young man. Something in him recalled the past.

"From the South, you say?"

"Yes, sir." He named his State with pride.

"Did I catch your name correctly? Is it Keith?"

"Yes, sir."

"I used to know a gentleman of that name—General Keith."

"There were several of them," answered the young man, with pride. "My father was known as 'General Keith of Elphinstone.'"

"That was he. I captured him. He was desperately wounded, and I had the pleasure of having him attended to, and afterwards of getting him exchanged. How is he? Is he still living?"

"Yes, sir."

Mr. Lancaster turned to the ladies. "He was one of the bravest men I have known," he said. "I was once a recipient of his gracious hospitality. I went South to look into some matters there," he explained to the ladies.

The speech brought a gratified look into Keith's eyes.

Mrs. Yorke was divided between her feeling of relief that Mr. Lancaster should know of Keith's social standing and her fear that such praise might affect Alice. After a glance at the girl's face the latter predominated.

"Men have no sense at all," she said to herself. Had she known it, the speech made the girl feel more kindly toward her older admirer than she had ever done before.

Gordon's face was suffused with tenderness, as it always was at any mention of his father. He stepped forward.

"May I shake hands with you, sir?" He grasped the hand of the older man. "If I can ever be of any service to you—of the least service—I hope you will let my father's son repay a part of his debt. You could not do me a greater favor." As he stood straight and dignified, grasping the older man's hand, he looked more of a man than he had ever done. Mr. Lancaster was manifestly pleased.

"I will do so," he said, with a smile.

Mrs. Yorke was in a fidget. "This man will ruin every-thing," she said to herself.

Seeing that his chance of seeing Alice alone was gone, Keith rose and took leave with some stateliness. At the last moment Alice boldly asked him to take lunch with them next day.

"Thank you," said Keith, "I lunch in Sparta to-morrow. I am going South to-night." But his allusion was lost on the ladies.

When Keith came out, a handsome trap was standing at the door, with a fine pair of horses and a liveried groom.

And a little later, as Keith was walking up the avenue looking at the crowds that thronged it in all the bravery of fine apparel, he saw the same pair of high-steppers threading their way proudly among the other teams. He suddenly became aware that some one was bowing to him, and there was Alice Yorke sitting up beside Mr. Lancaster, bowing to him from under a big hat with great white plumes. For one moment he had a warm feeling about his heart, and then, as the turnout was swallowed up in the crowd, Keith felt a sudden sense of loneliness, and he positively hated Mrs. Yorke. A little later he passed Ferdy Wickersham, in a long coat and a high hat, walking up the avenue with the girl he had seen at Mrs. Went-worth's. He took off his hat as they passed, but appar-ently they did not see him. And once more that overwhelming loneliness swept over him.

He did not get over the feeling till he found himself in Dr. Templeton's study. He had promised provisionally to go back and take supper with the old clergyman, and had only not promised it absolutely because he had thought he might be invited to the Yorkes'. He was glad enough now to go, and as he received the old gentleman's cordial greeting, he felt his heart grow warm again. Here was Sparta, too. This, at least, was hospitality. He was introduced to two young clergymen, both earnest fellows who were working among the poor. One of them was a High-churchman and the other a Presbyterian, and once or twice they began to discuss warmly questions as to which they differed; but the old Rector appeared to know just how to manage them.

"Come, my boys; no division here," he said, with a smile, "Remember, one flag, one union, one Commander. Titus is still before the walls."

CHAPTER XIV

THE HOLD-UP

KEITH returned home that night. He now and then thought of Lancaster with a little misgiving. It was apparent that Mrs. Yorke was his friend; but, after all, Alice would never think of marrying a gray-haired man. She could not do it.

His father's pleasure when he told him of the stand he had taken with Mr. Wickersham reassured him.

"You did exactly right, sir; as a gentleman should have done," he said, as his face lighted up with pride and affection. "Go back and make your own way. Owe no man anything."

Gordon went back to his little office filled with a determination to succeed. He had now a double motive : he would win Alice Yorke, and he would show Mr. Wickersham who he was. A visit from Squire Rawson not long after he returned gave him new hope. The old man chuckled as he told him that he had had an indirect offer from Wickersham for his land, much larger than he had expected. It had only confirmed him in his determination to hold on.

"If it's worth that to him," he said, "it's worth that to me. We'll hold on awhile, and let him open a track for us. You look up the lines and keep your eye on 'em. Draw me some pictures of the lands. I reckon Phrony will have a pretty good patrimony before I'm through." He gave Keith a shrewd glance which, however, that young man did not see.

Not long afterwards Gordon received an invitation to Norman's wedding. He was to marry Miss Caldwell.

When Gordon read the account of the wedding, with the church "banked with flowers," and the bridal couple preceded by choristers, chanting, he was as interested as if it had been his brother's marriage. He tried to picture Alice Yorke in her bridesmaid's dress, "with the old lace draped over it and the rosebuds festooned about her."

He glanced around his little room with grim amusement as he thought of the difference it might make to him if he had what Mrs. Yorke had called "an establishment." He would yet be Keith of Elphinstone.

One fact related disturbed him. Ferdy Wickersham was one of the ushers, and it was stated that he and Miss Yorke made a handsome couple.

Norman had long ago forgotten Ferdy's unfriendly action at college, and wishing to bury all animosities and start his new life at peace with the whole world, he invited Ferdy to be one of his ushers, and Ferdy, for his own reasons, accepted. Ferdy Wickersham was now one of the most talked-of young men in New York. He had fulfilled the promise of his youth at least in one way, for he was one of the handsomest men in the State. Mrs. Wickersham, in whose heart defeat rankled, vowed that she would never bow so low as to be an usher at that wedding. But her son was of a deeper nature. He declared that he was "abundantly able to manage his own affairs."

At the wedding he was one of the gayest of the guests, and he and Miss Yorke were, as the newspapers stated, undoubtedly the handsomest couple of all the attendants. No one congratulated Mrs. Wentworth with more fervid words. To be sure, his eyes sought the bride's with a curious expression in them ; and when he spoke with her apart a little later, there was an air of cynicism about him that remained in her memory. The handsomest jewel she received outside of the Wentworth family was from him. Its centre was a heart set with diamonds.

For a time Louise Wentworth was in the seventh heaven of ecstasy over her good fortune. Her beautiful house, her carriages, her gowns, her husband, and all the equipage of her new station filled her heart. She almost immediately took a position that none other of the young brides had. She became the fashion. In Norman's devotion she might have quite forgotten Ferdy Wickersham, had Ferdy been willing that she should do so. But Ferdy had no idea of allowing himself to be forgotten. For a time he paid quite devoted attention to Alice Yorke; but Miss Alice looked on his attentions rather as a joke. She said to him :

"Now, Ferdy, I am perfectly willing to have you send me all the flowers in New York, and go with me to the theatre every other night, and offer me all the flattery you have left over from Louise; but I am not going to let it be thought that I am going to engage myself to you; for I am not, and you don't want me."

"I suppose you reserve that for my fortunate rival, Mr. Lancaster?" said the young man, insolently.

Alice's eyes flashed. "At least not for you."

So Ferdy gradually and insensibly drifted back to Mrs. Wentworth. For a little while he was almost tragic; then he settled down into a state of cold cynicism which was not without its effect. He never believed that she cared for Norman Wentworth as much as she cared for him. He believed that her mother had made the match, and deep in his heart he hated Norman with the hate of wounded pride. Moreover, as soon as Mrs. Wentworth was beyond him, he began to have a deeper feeling for her than he had ever admitted before. He set before himself very definitely just what he wanted to do, and he went to work about it with a patience worthy of a better aim. He flattered her in many ways which, experience had told him, were effective with the feminine heart.

Ferdy Wickersham estimated Mrs. Wentworth's vanity at its true value; but he underestimated her uprightness and her pride. She was vain enough to hazard wrecking her happiness; but her pride was as great as her vanity.

Thus, though Ferdy Wickersham flattered her vanity by his delicate attentions, his patient waiting, he found himself, after long service, in danger of being balked by her pride. His apparent faithfulness had enlisted her interest; but she held him at a distance with a resolution which he would not have given her credit for.

Most men, under such circumstances, would have retired and confessed defeat; but not so with Ferdy Wickersham. To admit defeat was gall and wormwood to him. His love for Louise had given place to a feeling almost akin to a desire for revenge. He would show her that he could conquer her pride. He would show the world that he could humble Norman Wentworth. His position appeared to him impregnable. At the head of a great business, the leader of the gayest set in the city, and the handsomest and coolest man in town—he was bound to win. So he bided his time, and went on paying Mrs. Wentworth little attentions that he felt must win her in the end. And soon he fancied that he began to see the results of his patience. Old Mr. Wentworth's health had failed rapidly, and Norman was so wholly engrossed in business, that he found himself unable to keep up with the social life of their set. If, however, Norman was too busy to attend all the entertainments, Ferdy was never too busy to be on hand, a fact many persons were beginning to note.

Squire Rawson's refusal of the offer for his lands began to cause Mr. Aaron Wickersham some uneasiness. He had never dreamed that the old countryman would be so intractable. He refused even to set a price on them. He "did not want to sell," he said.

Mr. Wickersham conferred with his son. "We have got to get control of those lands, Ferdy. We ought to have got them before we started the railway. If we wait till we get through, we shall have to pay double. The best thing is for you to go down there and get them. You know the chief owner and you know that young Keith. You ought to be able to work them. We shall have to employ Keith if necessary. Sometimes a very small lever will work a big one."

"Oh, I can work them easy enough," said the young man; "but I don't want to go down there just now—the weather's cold, and I have a lot of engagements and a matter on hand that requires my presence here now."

His father's brow clouded. Matters had not been going well of late. The Wentworths had been growing cooler both in business and in social life. In the former it had cost him a good deal of money to have the Wentworth interest against him; in the latter it had cost Mrs. Wickersham a good deal of heart-burning. And Aaron Wickersham attributed it to the fact, of which rumors had come to him, that Ferdy was paying young Mrs. Wentworth more attention than her husband and his family liked, and they took this form of resenting it.

"I do not know what business engagement you can have more important than a matter in which we have invested some millions which may be saved by prompt attention or lost. What engagements have you?"

"That is my affair," said Ferdy, coolly.

"Your affair! Isn't your affair my affair?" burst out his father.

"Not necessarily. There are several kinds of affairs. I should be sorry to think that all of my affairs you had an interest in."

He looked so insolent as he sat back with half-closed eyes and stroked his silken, black moustache that his father lost his temper.

"I know nothing about your affairs of one kind," he burst out angrily, "and I do not wish to know; but I want to tell you that I think you are making an ass of yourself to be hanging around that Wentworth woman, having every one talking about you and laughing at you."

191

The young man's dark face flushed angrily.

"What's that?" he said sharply.

"She is another man's wife. Why don't you let her alone?" pursued the father.

"For that very reason," said Ferdy, recovering his composure and his insolent air.

"—— it! Let the woman alone," said his father. "Your fooling around her has already cost us the backing of Wentworth & Son—and, incidentally, two or three hundred thousand."

The younger man looked at the other with a flash of rage. This quickly gave way to a colder gleam.

"Really, sir, I could not lower myself to measure a matter of sentiment by so vulgar a standard as your —— money."

His air was so intolerable that the father's patience quite gave way.

"Well, by ——! you'd better lower yourself, or you'll have to stoop lower than that. Creamer, Crustback & Company are out with us; the Wentworths have pulled out; so have Kestrel and others. Your deals and corners have cost me a fortune. I tell you that unless we pull through that deal down yonder, and unless we get that railroad to earning something, so as to get a basis for rebonding, you'll find yourself wishing you had my 'damned money.'"

"Oh, I guess we'll pull it through," said the young man. He rose coolly and walked out of the office.

The afternoon he spent with Mrs. Norman. He had to go South, he told her, to look after some large interests they had there. He made the prospects so dazzling that she laughingly suggested that he had better put a little of her money in there for her. She had quite a snug sum that the Wentworths had given her.

"Why do not you ask Norman to invest it?" he inquired, with a laugh.

"Oh, I don't know. He says bonds are the proper investment for women."

"He rather underestimates your sex, some of them," said Wickersham. And as he watched the color come in her cheeks, he added: "I tell you what I will do: I will put in fifty thousand for you on condition that you never mention it to a soul."

"I promise," she said half gratefully, and they shook hands on it.

That evening he informed his father that he would go South. "I'll get those lands easy enough," he said.

A few days later Ferdy Wickersham got off the train at Ridgely, now quite a flourishing little health-resort, and in danger of becoming a fashionable one, and that afternoon he drove over to Squire Rawson's.

A number of changes had taken place in the old white-pillared house since Ferdy had been an inmate. New furniture of black walnut supplanted, at least on the first floor, the old horsehair sofa and split-bottomed chairs and pine tables; a new plush sofa and a new piano glistened in the parlor; large mirrors with dazzling frames hung on the low walls, and a Brussels carpet as shiny as a bed of tulips, and as stiff as the stubble of a newly cut hay-field, was on the floor.

But great as were these changes, they were not as great as that which had taken place in the young person for whom they had been made.

When Ferdy Wickersham drove up to the door, there was a cry and a scurry within, as Phrony Tripper, after a glance out toward the gate, dashed up the stairs.

When Miss Euphronia Tripper, after a half-hour or more of careful and palpitating work before her mirror, descended the old straight stairway, she was a very different person from the round-faced, plump school-girl whom Ferdy, as a lad, had flirted with under the apple-trees three or four years before. She was quite as different as was the new piano with its deep tones from the rattling old instrument that jingled and clanged out of tune, or as the cool, self-contained, handsome young man in faultless attire was from the slim, uppish boy who used to strum on it. It was a very pretty and blushing young country maiden who now entered quite accidentally the parlor where sat Mr. Ferdy Wickersham in calm and indifferent discourse with her grandfather on the crops, on cattle, and on the effect of the new railroad on products and prices.

Several sessions at a boarding-school of some pretension, with ambition which had been awakened years before under the apple-trees, had given Miss Phrony the full number of accomplishments that are to be gained by such means. The years had also changed the round, school-girl plumpness into a slim yet strong figure ; and as she entered the parlor,—quite casually, be it repeated,—with a large basket of flowers held carelessly in one hand and a great hat shading her face, the blushes that sprang to her cheeks at the wholly unexpected discovery of a visitor quite astonished Wickersham.

"By Jove ! who would have believed it !" he said to himself.

Within two minutes after she had taken her seat on the sofa near Wickersham, that young envoy had conceived a plan which had vaguely suggested itself as a possibility during his journey South. Here was an ally to his hand ; he could not doubt it ; and if he failed to win he would deserve to lose.

The old squire had no sooner left the room than the visitor laid the first lines for his attack.

Why was she surprised to see him ? He had large interests in the mountains, and could she doubt that if he was within a thousand miles he would come by to see her ?

The mantling cheeks and dancing eyes showed that this took effect.

"Oh, you came down on business ? That was all ! I know," she said.

Wickersham looked her in the eyes.

Business was only a convenient excuse. Old Halbrook could have attended to the business ; but he preferred to come himself. Possibly she could guess the reason ? He looked handsome and sincere enough as he leant over and gazed in her face to have beguiled a wiser person than Phrony.

She, of course, had not the least idea.

Then he must tell her. To do this he found it necessary to sit on the sofa close to her. What he told her made her blush very rosy again, and stammer a little as she declared her disbelief in all he said, and was sure there were the prettiest girls in the world in New York, and that he had never thought of her a moment. And no, she would not listen to him—she did not believe a word he said ; and— yes, of course, she was glad to see any old friend ; and no, he should not go. He must stay with them. They ex- pected him to do so.

So Ferdy sent to Ridgely for his bags, and spent several days at Squire Rawson's, and put in the best work he was capable of during that time. He even had the satisfaction of seeing Phrony treat coldly and send away one or two country bumpkins who rode up in all the bravery of long broad-cloth coats and kid gloves.

But if at the end of this time the young man could con- gratulate himself on success in one quarter, he knew that he was balked in the other. Phrony Tripper was heels over head in love with him ; but her grandfather, though easy and pliable enough to all outward seeming, was in a land- deal as dull as a ditcher. Wickersham spread out before him maps and plats showing that he owned surveys which overlapped those under which the old man claimed.

"Don't you see my patents are older than yours ? "

"Looks so," said the old man, calmly. "But patents is somethin' like folks : they may be too old."

The young man tried another line.

The land was of no special value, he told him ; he only wanted to quiet their titles, etc. But the squire not only refused to sell an acre at the prices offered him, he would place no other price whatever on it.

In fact, he did not want to sell. He had bought the land

for mountain pasture, and he didn't know about these railroads and mines and such like. Phrony would have it after his death, and she could do what she wished with it after he was dead and gone.

"He is a fool!" thought Wickersham, and set Phrony to work on him; but the old fellow was obdurate. He kissed Phrony for her wheedling, but told her that women-folks didn't understand about business. So Wickersham had to leave without getting the lands.

The influx of strangers was so great now at Gumbolt that there was a stream of vehicles running between a point some miles beyond Eden, which the railroad had reached, and Gumbolt. Wagons, ambulances, and other vehicles of a nondescript character on good days crowded the road, filling the mountain pass with the cries and oaths of their drivers and the rumbling and rattling of their wheels, and filling Mr. Gilsey's soul with disgust. But the vehicle of honor was still "Gilsey's stage." It carried the mail and some of the express, had the best team in the mountains, and was known as the "reg'lar." On bad nights the road was a little less crowded. And it was a bad night that Ferdy Wickersham took for his journey to Gumbolt.

Keith had been elected marshal, but had appointed Dave Dennison his deputy, and on inclement nights Keith still occasionally relieved Tim Gilsey, for in such weather the old man was sometimes too stiff to climb up to his box.

"The way to know people," said the old driver to him, "is to travel on the road with 'em. There is many a man decent enough to pass for a church deacon; git him on the road, and you see he is a hog, and not of no improved breed at that. He wants to gobble everything": an observation that Keith had some opportunity to verify.

Terpsichore appeared suddenly to have a good deal of business over in Eden, and had been on the stage several times of late when Keith was driving it, and almost always took the box-seat. This had occurred often enough for some of his acquaintances in Gumbolt to rally him about it.

"You will have to look out for Mr. Bluffy again," they said. "He's run J. Quincy off the track, and he's still in the ring. He's layin' low; but that's the time to watch a mountain cat. He's on your track."

Mr. Plume, who was always very friendly with Keith, declared that it was not Bluffy, but Keith, who had run him off the track. "It's a case where virtue has had its reward," he said to Keith. "You have overthrown more than your enemy, Orlando. You have captured the prize we were all trying for. Take the goods the gods provide, and while you live, live. The epicurean is the only true philosopher. Come over and have a cocktail? No? Do you happen to have a dollar about your old clothes? I have not forgotten that I owe you a little account; but you are the only man of soul in this —— Gehenna except myself, and I'd rather owe you ten dollars than any other man living."

Keith's manner more than his words shut up most of his teasers. Nothing would shut up J. Quincy Plume.

Keith always treated Terpsichore with all the politeness he would have shown to any lady. He knew that she was now his friend, and he had conceived a sincere liking for her. She was shy and very quiet when a passenger on his stage, ready to do anything he asked, obedient to any suggestion he gave her.

It happened that, the night Wickersham chose for his trip to Gumbolt, Keith had relieved old Gilsey, and he found her at the Eden end of the route among his passengers. She had just arrived from Gumbolt by another vehicle and was now going straight back. As Keith came around, the young woman was evidently preparing to take the box-seat. He was conscious of a feeling of embarrassment, which was not diminished by the fact that Jake Dennison, his old pupil, was also going over. Jake as well as Dave was now living at Gumbolt. Jake was in all the

197

splendor of a black coat and a gilded watch-chain, for he
had been down to the Ridge to see Miss Euphronia Tripper.

It had been a misty day, and toward evening the
mist had changed into a drizzle.

Keith said to Terpsichore, with some annoyance :

"You had better go inside.   It's going to be a bad night."

A slight change came over her face, and she hesitated.
But when he insisted, she said quietly, "Very well."

As the passengers were about to take their seats in the
coach, a young man enveloped in a heavy ulster came
hurriedly out of the hotel, followed by a servant with
several bags in his hands, and pushed hastily into the
group, who were preparing to enter the coach in a
more leisurely fashion.   His hat partly concealed his
face, but something about him called up memories to
Keith that were not wholly pleasant.   When he reached
the coach door Jake Dennison and another man were just
on the point of helping in one of the women.   The young
man squeezed in between them.

"I beg your pardon," he said.

The two men stood aside at the polite tone, and the other
stepped into the stage and took the back seat, where he
proceeded to make himself comfortable in a corner.   This,
perhaps, might have passed but for the presence of the
women.   Woman at this mountain Eden was at a premium, as she was in the first.

Jake Dennison and his friend both asserted promptly
that there was no trouble about three of the ladies getting
back seats, and Jake, putting his head in at the door, said
briefly :

"Young man, there are several ladies out here.   You will
have to give up that seat."

As there was no response to this, he put his head in again.

"Didn't you hear?   I say there are some ladies out here.
You will have to take another seat."

To this the occupant of the stage replied that he had
paid for his seat ; but there were plenty of other seats that

they could have. This was repeated on the outside, and thereupon one of the women said she supposed they would have to take one of the other seats.

Women do not know the power of surrender. This surrender had no sooner been made than every man outside was her champion.

"You will ride on that back seat to Gumbolt to-night, or I'll ride in Jim Digger's hearse. I am layin' for him anyhow." The voice was Jake Dennison's.

"And I'll ride with him. Stand aside, Jake, and let me git in there. I'll yank him out," said his friend.

But Jake was not prepared to yield to any one the honor of "yanking." Jake had just been down to Squire Rawson's, and this young man was none other than Mr. Ferdy Wickersham. He had been there, too.

Jake had left with vengeance in his heart, and this was his opportunity. He was just entering the stage head foremost, when the occupant of the coveted seat decided that discretion was the better part of valor, and announced that he would give up the seat, thereby saving Keith the necessity of intervening, which he was about to do.

The ejected tenant was so disgruntled that he got out of the stage, and, without taking any further notice of the occupants, called up to know if there was a seat outside.

"Yes. Let me give you a hand," said Gordon, leaning down and helping him up. "How are you?"

Wickersham looked at him quickly as he reached the boot.

"Hello! You here?" The rest of his sentence was a malediction on the barbarians in the coach below and a general consignment of them all to a much warmer place than the boot of the Gumbolt stage.

"What are you doing here?" Wickersham asked.

"I am driving the stage."

"Regularly?" There was something in the tone and look that made Keith wish to say no, but he said doggedly:

"I have done it regularly, and was glad to get the opportunity."

He was conscious of a certain change in Wickersham's manner toward him.

As they drove along he asked Wickersham about Norman and his people, but the other answered rather curtly.

Norman had married.

"Yes." Keith had heard that. "He married Miss Caldwell, didn't he? She was a very pretty girl."

"What do you know about her?" Wickersham asked. His tone struck Keith.

"Oh, I met her once. I suppose they are very much in love with each other?"

Wickersham gave a short laugh. "In love with Norman! Women don't fall in love with a lump of ice."

"I do not think he is a lump of ice," said Keith, firmly.

Wickersham did not answer at first, then he said sharply:

"Well, she's worth a thousand of him. She married him for his money. Certainly not for his brains."

"Norman has brains—as much as any one I know," defended Keith.

"You think so!"

Keith remembered a certain five minutes out behind the stables at Elphinstone.

He wanted to ask Wickersham about another girl who was uppermost in his thoughts, but something restrained him. He could not bear to hear her name on his lips. By a curious coincidence, Wickersham suddenly said: "You used to teach at old Rawson's. Did you ever meet a girl named Yorke—Alice Yorke? She was down this way once."

Keith said that he had met "Miss Yorke." He had met her at Ridgely Springs and also in New York. He was glad that it was dark, and that Wickersham could not see his face. "A very pretty girl," he hazarded as a leader, now that the subject was broached.

"Yes, rather. Going abroad—title-hunting."

"I don't expect Miss Yorke cares about a title," said Keith, stiffly.

"Mamma does. Failing that, she wants old Lancaster and perquisites."

"Who does? Why, Mr. Lancaster is old enough to be her father!"

"Pile's old, too," said Wickersham, dryly.

"She doesn't care about that either," said Keith, shortly.

"Oh, doesn't she! You know her mother?"

"No; I don't believe she does. Whatever her mother is, she is a fine, high-minded girl."

Ferdy gave a laugh which might have meant anything. It made Keith hot all over. Keith, fearing to trust himself further, changed the subject and asked after the Rawsons, Wickersham having mentioned that he had been staying with them.

"Phrony is back at home, I believe? She has been off to school. I hear she is very much improved?"

"I don't know; I didn't notice her particularly," said Wickersham, indifferently.

"She is very pretty. Jake Dennison thinks so," laughed Keith.

"Jake Dennison? Who is he?"

"He's an old scholar of mine. He is inside now on the front seat; one of your friends."

"Oh, that's the fellow! I thought I had seen him before. Well, he had better try some other stock, I guess. He may find that cornered. She is not going to take a clod like that."

Wickersham went off into a train of reflection.

"I say, Keith," he began unexpectedly, "maybe, you can help me about a matter, and if so I will make it worth your while."

"About what matter?" asked Keith, wondering.

"Why, about that old dolt Rawson's land. You see, the governor has got himself rather concerned. When he got this property up here in the mountains and started to build the railroad, some of these people here got wind of it. That fool, Rhodes, talked about it too much, and they bought up the lands around the old man's property. They think the governor has got to buy 'em out. Old Rawson is the head of 'em. The governor sent Halbrook down to get it; but Halbrook is a fool, too. He let him know he wanted to buy him out, and, of course, he raised. You and he used to be very thick. He was talking of you the other night."

"He and I are great friends. I have a great regard for him, and a much higher opinion of his sense than you appear to have. He is a very shrewd man."

"Shrewd the deuce! He's an old blockhead. He has stumbled into the possession of some property which I am ready to pay him a fair price for. He took it for a cow-pasture. It isn't worth anything. It would only be a convenience to us to have it and prevent a row in the future, perhaps. That is the only reason I want it. Besides, his title to it ain't worth a ——, anyhow. We have patents that antedate his. You can tell him that the land is not worth anything. I will give you a good sum if you get him to name a price at, say, fifty per cent. on what he gave for it. I know what he gave for it. You can tell him it ain't worth anything to him and that his title is faulty."

"No, I could not," said Keith, shortly.

"Why not?"

"Because I think it is very valuable and his title perfect. And he knows it."

Wickersham glanced at him in the dusk.

"It isn't valuable at all," he said after a pause. "I will give you a good fee if you will get through a deal for it at any price we may agree on. Come!"

"No," said Keith; "not for all the money you own. My advice to you is to go to Squire Rawson and either offer to take him in with you to the value of his lands, or else make him a direct offer for what those lands are really worth. He knows as much about the value of those lands as you or Mr. Halbrook or any one else knows. Take my word for it."

"Rats!" ejaculated Wickersham, briefly. "I tell you what," he added presently: "if he don't sell us that land he'll never get a cent out of it. No one else will ever take it. We have him cornered. We've got the land above him, and the water, too, and, what is more, his title is not worth a damn ! "

"Well, that is his lookout. I expect you will find him able to take care of himself."

Wickersham gave a grunt, then he asked Keith suddenly :

"Do you know a man named Plume over there at Gumbolt ? "

"Yes," said Keith ; "he runs the paper there."

"Yes ; that's he. What sort of a man is he ? "

Keith gave a brief estimate of Mr. Plume : "You will see him and can judge for yourself."

"I always do," said Wickersham, briefly. "Know anybody can work him ? The governor and he fell out some time ago, but I want to get hold of him."

Keith thought he knew one who might influence Mr. Plume ; but he did not mention the name or sex.

"Who is that woman inside ? " demanded Wickersham. "I mean the young one, with the eyes."

"They call her Terpsichore. She keeps the dance-hall."

"Friend of yours ? "

"Yes." Keith spoke shortly.

The stage presently began to descend Hellstreak Hill, which Keith mentioned as the scene of the robbery which old Tim Gilsey had told him of. As it swung down the long descent, with the lights of the lamps flashing on the big tree-tops, and with the roar of the rushing water below them coming up as it boiled over the rocks, Wickersham conceived a higher opinion of Keith than he had had before, and he mentally resolved that the next time he came over that road he would make the trip in the daytime. They had just crossed the little creek which dashed over the rocks toward the river, and had begun to ascend another hill, when Wickersham, who had been talking about his drag, was pleased to have Keith offer him the reins. He took them with some pride, and Keith dived down into the boot. When he sat up again he had a pistol in his hand.

"It was just about here that that 'hold-up' occurred."

"Suppose they should try to hold you up now, what would you do?" asked Wickersham.

"Oh, I don't think there is any danger now," said Keith. "I have driven over here at all hours and in all weathers. We are getting too civilized for that now, and most of the express comes over in a special wagon. It's only the mail and small packages that come on this stage."

"But if they should?" demanded Wickersham.

"Well, I suppose I'd whip up my horses and cut for it," said Keith.

"I wouldn't," asserted Wickersham. "I'd like to see any man make me run when I have a gun in my pocket."

Suddenly, as if in answer to his boast, there was a flash in the road, and the report of a pistol under the very noses of the leaders, which made them swerve aside with a rattling of the swingle-bars, and twist the stage sharply over to the side of the road. At the same instant a dark figure was seen in the dim light which the lamp threw on the road, close beside one of the horses, and a voice was heard:

"I've got you now, —— you!"

It was all so sudden that Wickersham had not time to think. It seemed to him like a scene in a play rather than a reality. He instinctively shortened the reins and pulled up the frightened horses. Keith seized the reins with one hand and snatched at the whip with the other; but it was too late. Wickersham, hardly conscious of what he was doing, was clutching the reins with all his might, trying to control the leaders, whilst pandemonium broke out inside, cries from the women and oaths from the men.

There was another volley of oaths and another flash, and Wickersham felt a sharp little burn on the arm next Keith.

"Hold on!" he shouted. "For God's sake, don't shoot! Hold on! Stop the horses!"

204

Sprang over the edge of the road into the thick bushes below.

At the same moment Keith disappeared over the wheel. He had fallen or sprung from his seat.

"The —— coward!" thought Wickersham. "He is running."

The next second there was a report of a pistol close beside the stage, and the man in the road at the horses' heads fired again. Another report, and Keith dashed forward into the light of the lantern and charged straight at the robber, who fired once more, and then, when Keith was within ten feet of him, turned and sprang over the edge of the road into the thick bushes below. Keith sprang straight after him, and the two went crashing through the underbrush, down the steep side of the hill.

The inmates of the stage poured out into the road, all talking together, and Wickersham, with the aid of Jake Dennison, succeeded in quieting the horses. The noise of the flight and the pursuit had now grown more distant, but once more several shots were heard, deep down in the woods, and then even they ceased.

It had all happened so quickly that the passengers had seen nothing. They demanded of Wickersham how many robbers there were. They were divided in their opinion as to the probable outcome. The men declared that Keith had probably got the robber if he had not been killed himself at the last fire.

Terpsichore was in a passion of rage because the men had not jumped out instantly to Keith's rescue, and one of them had held her in the stage and prevented her from poking her head out to see the fight. In the light of the lantern Wickersham observed that she was handsome. He watched her with interest. There was something of the tiger in her lithe movement. She declared that she was going down into the woods herself to find Keith. She was sure he had been killed.

The men protested against this, and Jake Dennison and another man started to the rescue, whilst a grizzled, weather-beaten fellow caught and held her.

"Why, my darlint, I couldn't let you go down there. Why, you'd ruin your new bonnet," he said.

The young woman snatched the bonnet from her head and slung it in his face.

"You coward! Do you think I care for a bonnet when the best man in Gumbolt may be dying down in them woods?"

With a cuff on the ear as the man burst out laughing and put his hand on her to soothe her, she turned and darted over the bank into the woods. Fortunately for the rest of her apparel, which must have suffered as much as the dishevelled bonnet,—which the grizzled miner had picked up and now held in his hand as carefully as if it were one of the birds which ornamented it,—some one was heard climbing up through the bushes toward the road a little distance ahead.

The men stepped forward and waited, each one with his hand in the neighborhood of his belt, whilst the women instinctively fell to the rear. The next moment Keith appeared over the edge of the road. As he stepped into the light it was seen that his face was bleeding and that his left arm hung limp at his side.

The men called to Terpy to come back : that Keith was there. A moment later she emerged from the bushes and clambered up the bank.

"Did you get him?" was the first question she asked.

"No." Keith gave the girl a swift glance, and turning quietly, he asked one of the men to help him off with his coat. In the light of the lamp he had a curious expression on his white face.

"Terpy was that skeered about you, she swore she was goin' down there to help you," said the miner who still held the hat.

A box on the ear from the young woman stopped whatever further observation he was going to make.

"Shut up. Don't you see he's hurt?" She pushed away the man who was helping Keith off with his coat, and took his place.

THE HOLD-UP

No one who had seen her as she relieved Keith of the coat
and with dexterous fingers, which might have been a
trained nurse's, cut away the bloody shirt-sleeve, would
have dreamed that she was the virago who, a few moments
before, had been raging in the road, swearing like a trooper,
and cuffing men's ears.

When the sleeve was removed it was found that Keith's
arm was broken just above the elbow, and the blood was
pouring from two small wounds. Terpy levied imperiously
on the other passengers for handkerchiefs ; then, not waiting for their contributions, suddenly lifting her skirt,
whipped off a white petticoat, and tore it into strips. She
soon had the arm bound up, showing real skill in her
surgery. Once she whispered a word in his ear—a single
name. Keith remained silent, but she read his answer, and
went on with her work with a grim look on her face. Then
Keith mounted his box against the remonstrances of every
one, and the passengers having reëntered the stage, Wickersham drove on into Gumbolt. His manner was more
respectful to Keith than it had ever been before.

Within a half-hour after their arrival the sheriff and his
party, with Dave Dennison at the head of the posse, were
on their horses, headed for the scene of the "hold-up."
Dave could have had half of Gumbolt for posse had he desired it. They attempted to get some information from
Keith as to the appearance of the robber ; but Keith
failed to give any description by which one man might
have been distinguished from the rest of the male sex.

"Could they expect a man to take particular notice of
how another looked under such circumstances? He
looked like a pretty big man."

Wickersham was able to give a more explicit description.

The pursuers returned a little after sunrise next morning without having found the robber.

CHAPTER XV

MRS. YORKE MAKES A MATCH

THE next day Keith was able to sit up, though the Doctor refused to let him go out of the house. He was alone in his room when a messenger announced that a woman wished to see him. When the visitor came up it was Terpy. She was in a state of suppressed excitement. Her face was white, her eyes glittered. Her voice as she spoke was tremulous with emotion.

"They're on to him," she said in a husky voice. "That man that comed over on the stage with you give a description of him, this mornin', 't made 'em tumble to him after we had throwed 'em off the track. If I ever git a show at him! They knows 'twas Bill. That little devil Dennison is out ag'in."

"Oh, they won't catch him," said Keith; but as he spoke his face changed. "What if he should get drunk and come into town?" he asked himself.

"If they git him, they'll hang him," pursued the girl, without heeding him. "They're all up. You are so popular."

"Me?" exclaimed Keith, laughing.

"It's so," said the girl, gravely. "That Dave Dennison would kill anybody for you, and they're ag'in' Bill, all of 'em."

"Can't you get word to him?" began Keith, and paused. He looked at her keenly. "You must keep him out of the way."

208

"He's wounded. You got him in the shoulder. He's got to see a doctor. The ball's still in there."

"I knew it," said Keith, quietly.

The girl gazed at him a moment, and then looked away.

"That was the reason I have been a-pesterin' you, goin' back'ards and for'ards. I hope you will excuse me of it," she said irrelevantly.

Keith sat quite still for a moment, as it all came over him. It was, then, him that the man was after, not robbery, and this girl, unable to restrain her discarded suitor without pointing suspicion to him, had imperilled her life for Keith, when he was conceited enough to more than half accept the hints of strangers that she cared for him.

"We must get him away," he said, rising painfully. "Where is he?"

"He's hid in a house down the road. I have flung 'em off the track by abusin' of him. They know I am against him, and they think I am after you," she said, looking at him with frank eyes; "and I have been lettin' 'em think it," she added quietly.

Keith almost gasped. Truly this girl was past his comprehension.

"We must get him away," he said.

"How can we do it?" she asked. "They suspicion he's here, and the pickets are out. If he warn't hit in the shoulder so bad, he could fight his way out. He ain't afraid of none of 'em," she added, with a flash of the old pride. "I could go with him and help him; I have done it before; but I would have to break up here. He's got to see a doctor."

Keith sat in reflection for a moment.

"Tim Gilsey is going to drive the stage over to Eden to-night. Go down and see if the places are all taken."

"I have got a place on it," she said, "on the boot."

As Keith looked at her, she added in explanation :

"I take it regular, so as to have it when I want it."

Under Keith's glance she turned away her eyes.

"I am going to Eden to-night," said Keith.

She looked puzzled.

"If you could get old Tim to stop at that house for five minutes till I give Bluffy a letter to Dr. Balsam over at the Springs, I think we might arrange it. My clothes will fit him. You will have to see Uncle Tim."

Her countenance lit up.

"You mean you would stop there and let him take your place?"

"Yes."

The light of craft that must have been in Delilah's eyes when Samson lay at her feet was in her face. She sprang up.

"I will never forgit you, and Bill won't neither. He knows now what a hound he has been. When you let him off last night after he had slipped on the rock, he says that was enough for him. Before he will ever pull a pistol on you ag'in, he says he will blow his own brains out; and he will, or I will for him." She looked capable of it as she stood with glowing eyes and after a moment held out her hand. She appeared about to speak, but reflected and turned away.

When the girl left Keith's room a few moments later, she carried a large bundle under her arm, and that night the stage stopped in the darkness at a little shanty at the far end of the fast-growing street, and Keith descended painfully and went into the house. Whilst the stage waited, old Tim attempted to do something to the lamp on that side, and in turning it down he put it out. Just then Keith, with his arm in a sling and wrapped in a heavy coat, came out, and was helped by old Tim up to the seat beside him. The stage arrived somewhat ahead of time at the point which the railroad had now reached, and old Tim, without waiting for daylight, took the trouble to hire a buggy and send the wounded man on, declaring that it was important that he should get to a hospital as soon as possible.

Amusements were scarce in Gumbolt, and Ferdy Wicker-sham had been there only a day or two when, under Mr. Plume's guidance, he sought the entertainment of Terp-sichore's Hall. He had been greatly struck by Terpy that night on the road, when she had faced down the men and had afterwards bound up Keith's arm. He had heard from Plume rumors of her frequent trips over the road and jests of her fancy for Keith. He would test it. It would break the monotony and give zest to the pursuit to make an inroad on Keith's preserve. When he saw her on the little stage he was astonished at her dancing. Why, the girl was an artist! As good a figure, as active a tripper, as high a kicker, as dainty a pair of ankles as he had seen in a long time, not to mention a keen pair of eyes with the devil peep-ing from them. To his surprise, he found Terpy stony to his advances. Her eyes glittered with dislike for him.

He became one of the highest players that had ever en-tered the gilded apartment on Terpsichore's second floor; he ordered more champagne than any man in Gumbolt; but for all this he failed to ingratiate himself with its pre-siding genius. Terpsichore still looked at him with level eyes in which was a cold gleam, and when she showed her white teeth it was generally to emphasize some gibe at him. One evening, after a little passage at arms, Wicker-sham chucked her under the chin and called her "Dar-ling." Terpsichore wheeled on him.

"Keep your dirty hands to yourself," she said, with a flash in her eye, and gave him such a box on the ear as made his head ring. The men around broke into a guffaw.

Wickersham was more than angry; he was enraged. He had heard a score of men call her by endearing names. He had also seen some of them get the same return that he received; but none so vicious. He sprang to his feet, his face flushed. The next second his senses returned, and he saw that he must make the best of it.

"You vixen!" he said, with a laugh, and caught the girl by the wrist. "I will make you pay for that." As he tried to draw her to him, she whipped from her dress a small stiletto which she wore as an ornament, and drew it back.

"Let go, or I'll drive it into you," she said, with fire darting from her eyes; and Wickersham let go amid the laughter and jeers of those about them, who were egging the girl on and calling to her to "give it to him."

Wickersham after this tried to make his peace, but without avail. Though he did not know it, Terpsichore had in her heart a feeling of hate which was relentless. It was his description that had set the sheriff's posse on the track of her dissipated lover, and though she had "washed her hands of Bill Bluffy," as she said, she could not forgive the man who had injured him.

Then Wickersham, having committed one error, committed another. He tried to get revenge, and the man who sets out to get revenge on a woman starts on a sad journey. At least, it was so with Wickersham.

He attributed the snubbing he had received to the girl's liking for Keith, and he began to meditate how he should get even with them. The chance presented itself, as he thought, when one night he attended a ball at the Windsor. It was a gay occasion, for the Wickershams had opened their first mine, and Gumbolt's future was assured. The whole of Gumbolt was there—at least, all of those who did not side with Mr. Drummond, the Methodist preacher. Terpsichore was there, and Keith, who danced with her. She was the handsomest-dressed woman in the throng, and, to Wickersham's surprise, she was dressed with some taste, and her manners were quiet and subdued.

Toward morning the scene became hilarious, and a call was made for Terpsichore to give a Spanish dance. The girl held back, but her admirers were in no mood for refusal, and the call became insistent. Keith had gone to his room, but Wickersham was still there, and his champagne had flowed freely. At length the girl yielded, and, after a few words with the host of the Windsor, she stepped forward and began to dance.

She danced in such a way that the applause made the brass chandeliers ring. Even Wickersham, though he hated her, could not but admire her.

Keith, who had found it useless to try to sleep even in a remote corner of the hotel, returned just then, and whether it was that Terpsichore caught sight of him as she glanced his way, or that she caught sight of Wickersham's hostile face, she faltered and stopped suddenly.

Wickersham thought she had broken down, and, under the influence of the champagne, turned with a jeer to Plume.

"She can't dance, Plume," he called across to the editor, who was at some little distance in the crowd.

Those nearest to the dancer urged her to continue, but she had heard Wickersham's jeer, and she suddenly faced him and, pointing her long, bare arm toward him, said : "Put that man out, or I won't go on."

Wickersham gave a laugh. "Go on? You can't go on," he said, trying to steady himself on his feet. "You can't dance any more than a cow."

He had never heard before the hum of an angry crowd.

"Throw him out! Fling him out of the window!" were the words he caught.

In a second a score of men were about him, and more than a score were rushing in his direction with a sound that brought him quickly to his senses.

Fortunately two men with cool heads were near by. With a spring Keith and a short, stout young fellow with gray eyes were making their way to his side, dragging men back, throwing them aside, expostulating, ordering, and, before anything else had happened than the tearing of his coat half off of his back, Wickersham found himself with Keith and Dave Dennison standing in front of him, defendiı g him against the angry revellers.

The determined air of the two officers held the assailants

213

in check long enough for them to get their attention, and, after a moment, order was restored on condition that Wickersham should "apologize to the lady and leave town."

This Wickersham, well sobered by the handling he had received, was willing to do, and he was made to walk up and offer a humble apology to Terpsichore, who accepted it with but indifferent grace.

That winter the railroad reached Gumbolt, and Gumbolt, or New Leeds, as it was now called, sprang at once, so to speak, from a chrysalis to a full-fledged butterfly with wings unfolding in the sun of prosperity.

Lands that a year or two before might have been had for a song, and mineral rights that might have been had for less than a song, were now held at fabulous prices.

Keith was sitting at his table, one day, writing, when there was a heavy step outside, and Squire Rawson walked in on him.

When all matters of mutual interest had been talked over, the squire broached the real object of his visit; at least, he began to approach it. He took out his pipe and filled it.

"Well, it's come," he said.

"What has come?"

"The railroad. That young man Rhodes said 'twas comin', and so it's done. He was something of a prophet." The old fellow chuckled softly and lit his pipe. "That there friend of yours, Mr. Wickersham, is been down here ag'in. Kind o' hangs around. What's he up to?"

Keith laughed.

"Well, it's pretty hard to tell what Wickersham is up to,—at least, by what he says,—especially when you don't tell me what he is doing."

The old man looked pleased. Keith had let him believe that he did not know what he was talking of, and had expressed an opinion in which he agreed.

"That's what I think. Well, it's about my land up here."
Keith looked relieved.

"Has he made you another offer for it?"

"No; he ain't done that, and he won't do it. That's what I tells him. If he wants it, let him make me a good offer; but he won't do that. He kind o' circles around like a pigeon before he lights, and talks about what I paid for it, and a hundred per cent. advance, and all that. I give a sight for that land he don't know nothin' about—years of hard work on the mountain-side, sweatin' o' days, and layin' out in the cold at nights, lookin' up at the stars and wonderin' how I was to git along—studyin' of folks jest as I studied cattle. That's what I paid for that land. He wants me to set him a price, and I won't do that—he might give it." He looked shrewdly at Keith. "Ain't I right?"

"I think so."

"He wants me to let him have control of it; but I ain't a-goin' to do that neither."

"That's certainly right," said Keith, heartily.

"I tell him I'm a-goin' to hold to that for Phrony. Phrony says she wants me to sell it to him, too. But women-folks don't know about business."

Keith wondered what effect this piece of information had on Wickersham, and also what further design the old squire had in mind.

"I think it's about time to do something with that land. If all he says is true,—not about *my* land (he makes out as *my* land is situate too far away ever to be much account—fact is, he don't allow I've got any land; he says it's all his anyway), but about other lands—everybody else's land but mine,—it might be a good time to look around. I know as my land is the best land up here. I holds the key to the situation. That's what we used to call it durin' the war.

"Well, there ain't but three ways to git to them coal-lands back up yonder in the Gap: one's by way of heaven, and I 'lows there ain't many land-speculators goin' by that way; the other is through hell, a way they'll know more about hereafter; and the third's through my land."

Keith laughed and waited.

"He seems to be hangin' around Phrony pretty considerable?"

Keith caught the gleam in the old fellow's deep eye, and looked away.

"I can't make it out. Phrony she likes him."

Keith fastened his gaze on something out of the window.

"I don't know him," pursued the squire. "But I don't think—he'd suit Phrony. His ways ain't like ours, and—." He lapsed into reflection, and Keith, with his eyes still fastened on something outside the window, sighed to think of the old man's innocence. That he should imagine that Wickersham had any serious idea of marrying the granddaughter of a backwoods magistrate! The old squire broke the silence.

"You don't suppose he could be hankerin' after Phrony for her property, do you?"

"No, I do not," said Keith, positively, relieved that at last a question was put which he could answer directly.

"Because she ain't got any," asserted the squire. "She's got prospects; but I'm goin' to remove them. It don't do for a young woman to have too much prospects. I'm goin' to sell that land and git it down in cash, where I can do what I want with it. And I want you to take charge of it for me."

This, then, was the real object of his visit. He wanted Keith to take charge of his properties. It was a tempting offer to make Keith. The old man had been a shrewd negotiator.

There is no success so sweet as that which comes to a young man.

That night Keith spent out under the stars. Success had come. And its other name was Alice Yorke.

The way before Keith still stretched steep enough, but the light was on it, the sunshine caught peak after peak high up among the clouds themselves, and crowning the highest point, bathed in perpetual sunlight, was the image of Alice Yorke.

Alice Yorke had been abroad now for some time ; but he had followed her. Often when his work was done he had locked his door and shut himself in from the turmoil of the bustling, noisy throng outside to dream of her—to read and study that he might become worthy of her.

He had just seen by the papers that Alice Yorke had returned.

She had escaped the dangers of a foreign service ; but, by the account, she was the belle of the season at the watering-place which she was honoring with her presence. As he read the account, a little jealousy crept into the satisfaction which he had felt as he began. Mr. Lancaster was spoken of too pointedly ; and there was mention of too many yacht-parties and entertainments in which their names appeared together.

In fact, the forces exerted against Alice Yorke had begun to tell. Her mother, overawed by her husband's determination, had reluctantly abandoned her dreams of a foreign title with its attendant honors to herself, and, of late, had turned all her energies to furthering the suit of Mr. Lancaster. It would be a great establishment that he would give Alice, and no name in the country stood higher. He was the soul of honor, personal and commercial ; and in an age when many were endeavoring to amass great fortunes and make a dazzling display, he was content to live modestly, and was known for his broad-minded philanthropy. What did it matter that he was considerably older than Alice ? reflected Mrs. Yorke. Mrs. Creamer and half the mothers she knew would give their eyes to secure him for their daughters ; and certainly he had shown that he knew how to enter into Alice's feelings.

Even Mr. Yorke had begun to favor Mr. Lancaster after Mrs. Yorke had skilfully pointed out that Alice's next most attentive admirer was Ferdy Wickersham.

"Why, I thought he was still trying to get that Caldwell girl," said he.

"You know he cannot get her; she is married," replied Mrs. Yorke.

"I guess that would make precious little difference to that young man, if she would say the word. I wish he would keep away from here."

"Oh, Ferdy is no worse than some others; you were always unjust to him. Most young men sow their wild oats."

No man likes to be charged with injustice by his wife, and Mr. Yorke's tone showed that he was no exception to this rule.

"He is worse than most others *I* know, and the crop of oats he is sowing, if he does not look out, he will reap somewhere else besides in New York. Alice shall marry whom she pleases, provided it is not that young man; but she shall not marry him if she wants to."

"She does not want to marry him," said Mrs. Yorke; "if she had she could have done it long ago."

"Not while I lived," said Mr. Yorke, firmly. But from this time Mr. Yorke began to acquiesce in his wife's plans touching Mr. Lancaster.

Finally Alice herself began to yield. The influences were very strong, and were skilfully exerted. The only man who had ever made any lasting impression on her heart was, she felt, out of the question. The young school-teacher, with his pride and his scorn of modern ways, had influenced her life more than any one else she had ever known, and though under her mother's management the feeling had gradually subsided, and had been merged into what was merely a cherished recollection, Memory, stirred at times by some picture or story of heroism and devotion, reminded her that she too might, under other conditions, have had a real romance. Still, after two or three years, her life appeared to have been made for her by Fate, and she yielded, not recognizing that Fate was only a very ambitious and somewhat short-sighted mamma aided by the conditions of an artificial state of life known as fashionable society.

Keith wrote Alice Yorke a letter congratulating her upon her safe return; but a feeling, part shyness, part pride, seized him. He had received no acknowledgment of his last letter. Why should he write again? He mailed the letter in the waste-basket. Now, however, that success had come to him, he wrote her a brief note congratulating her upon her return, a stiff little plea for remembrance. He spoke of his good fortune: he was the agent for the most valuable lands in that region, and the future was beginning to look very bright. Business, he said, might take him North before long, and the humming-birds would show him the way to the fairest roses. The hope of seeing her shone in every line. It reached Alice Yorke in the midst of preparation for her marriage.

Alice Yorke sat for some time in meditation over this letter. It brought back vividly the time which she had never wholly forgotten. Often, in the midst of scenes so gay and rich as to amaze her, she had recalled the springtime in the budding woods, with an ardent boy beside her, worshipping her with adoring eyes. She had lived close to Nature then, and Content once or twice peeped forth at her from its covert with calm and gentle eyes. She had known pleasure since then, joy, delight, but never content. However, it was too late now. Mr. Lancaster and her mother had won the day; she had at last accepted him and an establishment. She had accepted her fate or had made it.

She showed the letter to her mother. Mrs. Yorke's face took on an inscrutable expression.

"You are not going to answer it, of course?" she said.

"Of course, I am; I am going to write him the nicest letter that I know how to write. He is one of the best friends I ever had."

"What will Mr. Lancaster say?"

"Mr. Lancaster quite understands. He is going to be reasonable; that is the condition."

This appeared to be satisfactory to Mrs. Yorke, or, at least, she said no more.

Alice's letter to Keith was friendly and even kind. She had never forgotten him, she said. Some day she hoped to meet him again. Keith read this with a pleasant light in his eyes. He turned the page, and his face suddenly whitened. She had a piece of news to tell him which might surprise him. She was engaged to be married to an old friend of her family's, Mr. Lancaster. He had met Mr. Lancaster, she remembered, and was sure he would like him, as Mr. Lancaster had liked him so much.

Keith sat long over this letter, his face hard set and very white. She was lost to him. He had not known till then how largely he had built his life upon the memory of Alice Yorke. Deep down under everything that he had striven for had lain the foundation of his hope to win her. It went down with a crash. He went to his room, and unlocking his desk, took from his drawer a small package of letters and other little mementos of the past that had been so sweet. These he put in the fire and, with a grim face, watched them blaze and burn to ashes. She was dead to him. He reserved nothing.

The newspapers described the Yorke-Lancaster wedding as one of the most brilliant affairs of the season. They dwelt particularly on the fortunes of both parties, the value of the presents, and the splendor of the dresses worn on the occasion. One journal mentioned that Mr. Lancaster was considerably older than the bride, and was regarded as one of the best, because one of the safest, matches to be found in society.

Keith recalled Mr. Lancaster: dignified, cultivated, and coldly gracious. Then he recalled his gray hair, and found some satisfaction in it. He recalled, too, Mrs. Yorke's friendliness for him. This, then, was what it meant. He wondered to himself how he could have been so blind to it.

When he came to think of it, Mr. Lancaster came nearer possessing what others strove for than any one else he knew.

Yet, Youth looks on Youth as peculiarly its own, and Keith found it hard to look on Alice Yorke's marriage as anything but a sale.

"They talk about the sin of selling negroes," he said; "that is as very a sale as ever took place at a slave-auction."

For a time he plunged into the gayest life that Gumbolt offered. He even began to visit Terpsichore. But this was not for long. Mr. Plume's congratulations were too distasteful to him for him to stomach them; and Terpy began to show her partiality too plainly for him to take advantage of it. Besides, after all, though Alice Yorke had failed him, it was treason to the ideal he had so long carried in his heart. This still remained to him.

He went back to his work, resolved to tear from his heart all memory of Alice Yorke. She was married and forever beyond his dreams. If he had worked before with enthusiasm, he now worked with fury. Mr. Lancaster, as wealthy as he was, as completely equipped with all that success could give, lacked one thing that Keith possessed : he lacked the promise of the Future. Keith would show these Yorkes who he was.

CHAPTER XVI

KEITH VISITS NEW YORK, AND MRS. LANCASTER SEES A GHOST

FOR the next year or two the tide set in very strong toward the mountains, and New Leeds advanced with giant strides. What had been a straggling village a year or two before was now a town, and was beginning to put on the airs of a city. Brick buildings quite as pretentious as the town were springing up where a year before there were unsightly frame boxes; the roads where hogs had wallowed in mire not wholly of their own kneading were becoming well-paved streets. Out on the heights, where had been a forest, were sprinkled sightly dwellings in pretty yards. The smoke of panting engines rose where but a few years back old Tim Gilsey drew rein over his steaming horses. Pretty girls and well-dressed women began to parade the sidewalks where formerly Terpsichore's skirts were the only feminine attire seen. And "Gordon Keith, civil and mining engineer," with his straight figure and tanned, manly face, was not ignored by them. But locked in his heart was the memory of the girl he had found in the Spring woods. She was forever beyond him; but he still clung to the picture he had enshrined there.

When he saw Dr. Balsam, no reference was made to the verification of the latter's prophecy; but the young man knew from the kind tone in the older man's voice that he had heard of it. Meantime Keith had not been idle. Surveys and plats had been made, and everything done to facilitate placing the Rawson properties on the market.

When old man Rawson came to New Lee
made Keith's little office his headquarters,
quaint philosophy Keith learned from him.

"I reckon it's about time to try our cattle
York market," he said at length to Keith. It
he never gave up. "You go up there and look around,
and if you have any trouble send for me."

So, taking his surveys and reports and a few letters of
introduction Keith went to New York.

Only one thought marred Keith's joy : the dearest aim he
had so long had in view had disappeared. The triumph of
standing before Alice Yorke and offering her the reward
of his endeavor was gone. All he could do was to show
her what she had lost. This he would do; he would win
life's highest honors. He grew grim with resolve.

Something of this triumphant feeling showed in his mien
and in his face as he plunged into the crowded life of the
city. From the time he passed into the throng that
streamed up the long platforms of the station and poured
into the wide ferry-boats, like grain pouring through a
mill, he felt the thrill of the life. This was what he had
striven for. He would take his place here and show what
was in him.

He had forgotten how gay the city life was. Every place
of public resort pleased him : theatres, hotels, beer-gardens ;
but best of all the streets. He took them all in with absolute freedom and delight.

Business was the watchword, the trade-mark. It buzzed
everywhere, from the Battery to the Park. It thronged
the streets, pulsating through the outlets and inlets at
ferries and railway-stations and crossings, and through the
great buildings that were already beginning to tower in
the business sections. It hummed in the chief centres.
And through it all and beyond it all shone opulence, opulence gilded and gleaming and dazzling in its glitter :
in the big hotels; in the rich shops; in the gaudy
theatres ; along the fine avenues : a display of wealth to

make the eyes ache; an exhibition of riches never seen before. It did Keith good at first just to stand in the streets and watch the pageant as it passed like a gilded panorama. Of the inner New York he did not yet know: the New York of luxurious homes; of culture and of art; of refinement and elegance. The New York that has grown up since, with its vast wealth, its brazen glitter, its tides that roll up riches as the sea rolls up the sand, was not yet. It was still in its infancy, a chrysalis as yet sleeping within its golden cocoon.

Keith had no idea there were so many handsome and stylish young women in the world as he now saw. He had forgotten how handsome the American girl is in her best appointment. They sailed down the avenue looking as fine as young fillies at a show, or streamed through the best shopping streets as though not only the shops, but the world belonged to them, and it were no longer the meek, but the proud, that inherit the earth.

If in the throngs on the streets there were often marked contrasts, Keith was too exhilarated to remark it—at least, at first. If women with worn faces and garments unduly thin in the frosty air, carrying large bundles in their pinched hands, hurried by as though hungry, not only for food, but for time in which to earn food; if sad-eyed men with hollow cheeks, sunken chests, and threadbare clothes shambled eagerly along, he failed to note them in his first keen enjoyment of the pageant. Old clothes meant nothing where he came from; they might be the badge of perilous enterprise and well-paid industry, and food and fire were at least common to all.

Keith, indeed, moved about almost in a trance, absorbing and enjoying the sights. It was Humanity in flood; Life at full tide.

Many a woman and not a few men turned to take a second look at the tanned, eager face and straight, supple figure, as, with smiling, yet keen, eyes, he stalked along with the free, swinging gait caught on the mountains, so different from the quick, short steps of the city man. Beggars, and some who from their look and apparel might not have been beggars, applied to him so often that he said to one of them, a fairly well-dressed man with a nose of a slightly red tinge:

"Well, I must have a very benevolent face or a very credulous one?"

"You have," said the man, with brazen frankness, pocketing the half-dollar given him on his tale of a picked pocket and a remittance that had gone wrong.

Keith laughed and passed on.

Meantime, Keith was making some discoveries. He did not at first call on Norman Wentworth. He had a feeling that it might appear as if he were using his friendship for a commercial purpose. He presented his business letters. His letters, however, failed to have the weight he had expected. The persons whom he had met down in New Leeds, during their brief visits there, were, somehow, very different when met in New York. Some whom he called on were civil enough to him; but as soon as he broached his business they froze up. The suggestion that he had coal-property to sell sent them down to zero. Their eyes would glint with a shrewd light and their faces harden into ice. One or two told him plainly that they had no money to embark in "wild-cat schemes."

Mr. Creamer of Creamer, Crustback & Company, Capitalists, a tall, broad-shouldered man, with a strongly cut nose and chin and keen, gray eyes, that, through long habitude, weighed chances with an infallible appraisement, to whom Keith had a letter from an acquaintance, one of those casual letters that mean anything or nothing, informed him frankly that he had "neither time nor inclination to discuss enterprises, ninety-nine out of every hundred of which were frauds, and the hundredth generally a failure."

"This is not a fraud," said Keith, hotly, rising. "I do not indorse frauds, sir." He began to draw on his gloves. "If I cannot satisfy any reasonable man of the fact I state, I am willing to fail. I ought to fail." With a bow, he turned to the door.

Something in Keith's assurance went further with the shrewd-eyed capitalist than his politeness had done. He shot a swift glance as he was retiring toward the door.

"Why didn't Wickersham make money down there?" he demanded, half in query, half in denial, gazing keenly over his gold-rimmed glasses. "He usually makes money, even if others lose it."

Mr. Creamer had his own reasons for not liking Wickersham.

Keith was standing at the door.

"For two or three reasons. One was that he underestimated the people who live down there, and thought he could force them into selling him their lands, and so lost the best properties there."

"The lands you have, I suppose?" said the banker, looking again at Keith quickly.

"Yes, the lands I have, though you don't believe it," said Keith, looking him calmly in the eyes.

The banker was gazing at the young man ironically; but, as he observed him, his credulity began to give way.

That stamp of truth which men recognize was written on him unmistakably. Mr. Creamer's mind worked quickly.

"By the way, you came from down there. Did you know a young man named Rhodes? He was an engineer. Went over the line."

Keith's eyes brightened. "He is one of my best friends. He is in Russia now."

Mr. Creamer nodded. "What do you think of him?"

"He is one of the best."

Mr. Creamer nodded. He did not think it necessary to tell Keith that Rhodes was paying his addresses to his daughter.

"You write to him," said Keith. "He will tell you just what I have. Tell him they are the Rawson lands."

Keith opened the door. "Good morning, sir."

"One moment!" Mr. Creamer leaned back in his chair. "Whom else do you know here?" he asked after a second.

Keith reflected a moment.

"I know Mr. Wentworth."

"Norman Wentworth?"

"Yes; I know him very well. He is an old friend of mine."

"Have you been to him?"

"No, sir."

"Why not?"

"Because my relations with him are entirely personal. We used to be warm friends, and I did not wish to use his friendship for me as a ground on which to approach him in a commercial enterprise."

Mr. Creamer's countenance expressed more incredulity than he intended to show.

"He might feel under obligations to do for me what he would not be inclined to do otherwise," Keith explained.

"Oh, I don't think you need have any apprehension on that score," Mr. Creamer said, with a glint of amusement in his eyes. "It is a matter of business, and I don't think you will find business men here overstepping the bounds of prudence from motives of sentiment."

"There is no man whom I would rather have go into it with me; but I shall not ask him to do it, for the reason I have given. Good morning."

The banker did not take his eyes from the door until the sound of Keith's steps had died away through his outer office. Then he reflected for a moment. Presently he touched a bell, and a clerk appeared in the door.

"Write a note to Mr. Norman Wentworth and ask him to drop in to see me—any time this afternoon."

"Yes, sir."

When Norman Wentworth called at Mr. Creamer's office he found the financier in a good humor. The market had gone well of late, and Mr. Creamer's moods were not altogether unlike the mercury. His greeting was more cordial than usual. After a brief discussion of recent events, he pushed a card across to his visitor and asked casually:

"What do you know about that man?"

"Gordon Keith!" exclaimed the younger man, in surprise. "Is he in New York, and I have not seen him! Why, I know all about him. He used to be an old friend of mine. We were boys together ever so long ago."

He went on to speak warmly of him.

"Well, that was long ago," said Mr. Creamer, doubtfully. "Many things have happened in that time. He has had time to change."

"He must have changed a good deal if he is not straight," declared Norman. "I wonder why he has not been to see me?"

"Well, I'll tell you what he said," began Mr. Creamer. He gave Keith's explanation.

"Did he say that? Then it's true. You ought to know his father. He is a regular old Don Quixote."

"The Don was not particularly practical. He would not have done much with coal and iron lands," observed the banker. "What do you know about this man's knowledge of such things?"

Norman admitted that on this point he had no information.

"He says he knows Wickersham—your friend," said Mr. Creamer, with a sly look at Norman.

"Yes, I expect he does—if any one knows him. He used to know him. What does he say of him?"

"Oh, I think he knows him. Well, I am much obliged to you for coming around," he said in a tone of dismissal. "You are coming to dine with us soon, I believe? The Lancasters are coming, too. And we expect Rhodes home. He's due next week."

"One member of your family will be glad to see him," said Norman, smiling. "The wedding is to take place in a few weeks, I believe?"

"I hear so," said the father. "Fine young man, Rhodes? Your cousin, isn't he? Been very successful?"

"Yes."

Once, as Keith passed along down Broadway, just where

some of the great shops were at that time, before the tide had rolled so far up-town, a handsome carriage and pair drew up in front of one of the big shops, and a lady stepped from it just behind him. She was a very pretty young woman, and richly dressed. A straight back and a well-set head, with a perfect toilet, gave her distinction even among the handsomely appointed women who thronged the street that sunny morning, and many a woman turned and looked at her with approval or envy.

The years, that had wrought Keith from a plain country lad into a man of affairs of such standing in New Leeds that a shrewd operator like Rawson had selected him for his representative, had also wrought a great change in Alice Lancaster. Alice had missed what she had once begun to expect, romance and all that it meant; but she had filled with dignity the place she had chosen. If Mr. Lancaster's absorption in serious concerns left her life more sombre than she had expected, at least she let no one know it. Association with a man like Mr. Lancaster had steadied and elevated her. His high-mindedness had lifted her above the level of her worldly mother and of many of those who constituted the set in which she lived.

He admired her immeasurably. He was constantly impressed by the difference between her and her shallow-minded and silly mother, or even between her and such a young woman as Mrs. Wentworth, who lived only for show and extravagance, and appeared in danger of ruining her husband and wrecking his happiness.

It was Mrs. Lancaster who descended from her carriage as Keith passed by. Just as she was about to enter the shop, a well-knit figure with square shoulders and springy step, swinging down the street, caught her eye. She glanced that way and gave an exclamation. The door was being held open for her by a blank-faced automaton in a many-buttoned uniform; so she passed in, but pausing just inside, she glanced back through the window. The next instant she left the shop and gazed down the street again. But

Keith had turned a corner, and so Alice Lancaster did not see him, though she stood on tiptoe to try and distinguish him again in the crowd.

"Well, I would have sworn that that was Gordon Keith," she said to herself, as she turned away, "if he had not been so broad-shouldered and good-looking." And wherever she moved the rest of the day her eyes wandered up and down the street.

Once, as she was thus engaged, Ferdy Wickersham came up. He was dressed in the tip of the fashion and looked very handsome.

"Who is the happy man?"

The question was so in keeping with her thought that she blushed unexpectedly.

"No one."

"Ah, not me, then? But I know it was some one. No woman looks so expectant and eager for 'no one.'"

"Do you think I am like you, perambulating streets trying to make conquests?" she said, with a smile.

"You do not have to try," he answered lazily. "You do it simply by being on the street. I am playing in great luck to-day."

"Have you seen Louise this morning?" she asked.

He looked her full in the face. "I see no one but you when you are around."

She laughed lightly.

"Ferdy, you will begin to believe that after a while, if you do not stop saying it so often."

"I shall never stop saying it, because it is true," he replied imperturbably, turning his dark eyes on her, the lids a little closed.

"You have got so in the habit of saying it that you repeat it like my parrot that I taught once, when I was younger and vainer, to say, 'Pretty Alice.' He says it all the time."

"Sensible bird," said Mr. Wickersham, calmly. "Come and drive me up to the Park and let's have a stroll. I know such a beautiful walk. There are so many people out to-day. I saw the lady of the 'cat-eyes and cat-claws' go by just now, seeking some one whom she can turn again and rend." It was the name she had given Mrs. Nailor.

"I do not care who is out. Are you going to the Wentworths' this evening?" she asked irrelevantly.

"No; I rarely go there. Will you mention that to Mrs. Nailor? She apparently has not that confidence in my word that I could have expected in one so truthful as herself."

Mrs. Lancaster laughed.

"Ferdy—" she began, and then paused irresolute. "However—"

"Well, what is it? Say it."

"You ought not to go there so often as you do."

"Why?" His eyes were full of insolence.

"Good-by. Drive home," she said to the coachman, in a tone intentionally loud enough for her friend to hear.

Ferdy Wickersham strolled on down the street, and a few minutes later was leaning in at the door of Mrs. Wentworth's carriage, talking very earnestly to the lady inside.

Mr. Wickersham's attentions to Louise Wentworth had begun to be the talk of the town. Young Mrs. Wentworth was not a person to allow herself to be shelved. She did not propose that the older lady who bore that name should be known by it. She declared she would play second fiddle to no one. But she discovered that the old lady who lived in the old mansion on Washington Square was "Mrs. Wentworth," and that Mrs. Wentworth occupied a position from which she was not to be moved. After a little she herself was known as "Mrs. Norman." It was the first time Mrs. Norman had ever had command of much money. Her mother had made a good appearance and dressed her daughter handsomely, but to carry out her plans she had had to stint and scrape to make both ends meet. Mrs. Caldwell told one of her friends that her rings knew the way to the pawnbroker's so well that if she threw them in the street they would roll into his shop.

This struggle Louise had witnessed with that easy indifference which was part her nature and part her youth. She had been brought up to believe she was a beauty, and she did believe it. Now that she had the chance, she determined to make the most of her triumph. She would show people that she knew how to spend money; embellishment was the aim of her life, and she did show them. Her toilets were the richest; her equipage was the handsomest and best appointed. Her entertainments soon were among the most splendid in the city.

Those who were accustomed to wealth and to parade wondered both at Mrs. Norman's tastes and at her gratification of them.

All the town applauded. They had had no idea that the Wentworths, as rich as they knew them to be, had so much money.

"She must have Aladdin's lamp," they said.

Only old Mrs. Wentworth looked grave and disapproving at the extravagance of her daughter-in-law. Still she never said a word of it, and when the grandson came she was too overjoyed to complain of anything.

It was only of late that people had begun to whisper of the frequency with which Ferdy Wickersham was seen with Mrs. Norman. Certain it was that he was with her a great deal.

That evening Alice Lancaster was dining with the Norman Wentworths. She was equally good friends with them and with their children, who on their part idolized her and considered her to be their especial property. Her appearance was always the signal for a romp. Whenever she went to the Wentworths' she always paid a visit to the nursery, from which she would return breathless and dishevelled, with an expression of mingled happiness and pain in her blue eyes. Louise Wentworth knew well why the longing look was there, and though usually cold and statuesque, she always softened to Alice Lancaster the more than she was wont to do.

"Alice pines for children," she said to Norman, who pinched her cheek and, like a man, told her she thought every one as romantic and as affectionate as herself. Had Mrs. Nailor heard this speech she would have blinked her innocent eyes and have purred with silent thoughts on the blindness of men.

This evening Mrs. Lancaster had come down from the nursery, where shouts of childish merriment had told of her romps with the ringletted young brigand who ruled there, and was sitting quite silent in the deep arm-chair in an attitude of profound reflection, her head thrown back, her white arms resting languidly on the arms of the chair, her face unusually thoughtful, her eyes on the gilded ceiling.

Mrs. Wentworth watched her for a moment silently, and then said :

"You must not let the boy tyrannize over you so."

Mrs. Lancaster's reply was complete :

"I love it; I just love it!"

Presently Mrs. Wentworth spoke again.

"What is the matter with you this evening? You seem quite distraite."

"I saw a ghost to-day." She spoke without moving.

Mrs. Wentworth's face took on more interest.

"What do you mean? Who was it?"

"I mean I saw a ghost; I might say two ghosts, for I saw in imagination also the ghost of myself as I was when a girl. I saw the man I was in love with when I was seventeen."

"I thought you were in love with Ferdy then?"

"No; never." She spoke with sudden emphasis.

"How interesting! And you congratulated yourself on your escape? We always do. I was violently in love with a little hotel clerk, with oily hair, a snub-nose, and a waxed black moustache, in the Adirondacks when I was that age."

Mrs. Lancaster made no reply to this, and her hostess looked at her keenly.

"Where was it? How long before—?" She started to ask, how long before she was married, but caught herself. "What did he look like? He must have been good-looking, or you would not be so pensive."

"He looked like—a man."

"How old was he—I mean, when he fell in love with you?" said Mrs. Wentworth, with a sort of gasp, as she recalled Mr. Lancaster's gray hair and elderly appearance.

"Rather young. He was only a few years older than I was; a young—what's his name?—Hercules, that brought me down a mountain in his arms the second time I ever saw him."

"Alice Lancaster!"

"I had broken my leg—almost. I had got a bad fall from a horse and could not walk, and he happened to come along."

"Of course. How romantic! Was he a doctor? Did you do it on purpose?"

Mrs. Lancaster smiled.

"No; a young schoolmaster up in the mountains. He was not handsome—not then. But he was fine-looking, eyes that looked straight at you and straight through you; the whitest teeth you ever saw; and shoulders! He could carry a sack of salt!" At the recollection a faint smile flickered about her lips.

"Why didn't you marry him?"

"He had not a cent in the world. He was a poor young school-teacher, but of a very distinguished family. However, mamma took fright, and whisked me away as if he had been a pestilence."

"Oh, naturally!"

"And he was too much in love with me. But for that I think I should not have given him up. I was dreadfully cut up for a little while. And he—" She did not finish the sentence.

On this Mrs. Wentworth made no observation, though the expression about her mouth changed.

"He made a reputation afterwards. I knew he would. He was bound to succeed. I believed in him even then. He had ideals. Why don't men have ideals now?"

"Some of them do," asserted Mrs. Wentworth.

"Yes; Norman has. I mean unmarried men. I heard he made a fortune, or was making one—or something."

"Oh!"

"He knew more than any one I ever saw—and made you want to know. All I ever read he set me to. And he is awfully good-looking. I had no idea he would be so good-looking. But I tell you this: no woman that ever saw him ever forgot him."

"Is he married?"

"I don't think so—no. If he had been I should have heard it. He really believed in me."

Mrs. Wentworth glanced at her with interest.

"Where is he staying?"

"I do not know. I saw him through a shop-window."

"What! Did you not speak to him?"

"I did not get a chance. When I came out of the shop he was gone."

"That was sad. It would have been quite romantic, would it not? But, perhaps, after all, he did not make his fortune?" Mrs. Wentworth looked complacent.

"He did if he set his mind to it," declared Mrs. Lancaster.

"How about Ferdy Wickersham?" The least little light of malevolence crept into Mrs. Wentworth's eyes.

Mrs. Lancaster gave a shrug of impatience, and pushed a photograph on a small table farther away, as if it incommoded her.

"Oh, Ferdy Wickersham! Ferdy Wickersham to that man is a heated room to the breath of hills and forests." She spoke with real warmth, and Mrs. Wentworth gazed at her curiously for a few seconds.

"Still, I rather fancy for a constancy you'd prefer the heated rooms to the coldness of the hills. Your gowns would not look so well in the forest."

It was a moment before Mrs. Lancaster's face relaxed.

"I suppose I should," she said slowly, with something very like a sigh. "He was the only man I ever knew who made me do what I did not want to do and made me wish to be something better than I was," she added absently.

Mrs. Wentworth glanced at her somewhat impatiently, but she went on :

"I was very romantic then ; and you should have heard him read the 'Idylls of the King.' He had the most beautiful voice. He made you live in Arthur's court, because he lived there himself."

Mrs. Wentworth burst into laughter, but it was not very merry.

"My dear Alice, you must have been romantic. How old were you, did you say ? "

"It was three years before I was married," said Mrs. Lancaster, firmly.

Her friend gazed at her with a puzzled expression on her face.

"Oh ! Now, my dear Alice, don't let's have any more of this sentimentalizing. I never indulge in it ; it always gives me a headache. One might think you were a school-girl."

At the word a wood in all the bravery of Spring sprang into Alice's mind. A young girl was seated on the mossy ground, and outstretched at her feet was a young man, fresh-faced and clear-eyed, quoting a poem of youth and of love.

"Heaven knows I wish I were," said Mrs. Lancaster, soberly. "I might then be something different from what I am ! "

"Oh, nonsense ! You do nothing of the kind. Here are you, a rich woman, young, handsome, with a great establishment ; perfectly free, with no one to interfere with you in any way. Now, I—"

"That's just it," broke in Mrs. Lancaster, bitterly. "Free ! Free from what my heart aches for. Free to dress in sables and diamonds and die of loneliness." She had sat up, and her eyes were glowing and her color flashing in her cheeks in her energy.

Mrs. Wentworth looked at her with a curious expression in her eyes.

"I want what you have, Louise Caldwell. In that big house with only ourselves and servants—sometimes I could wish I were dead. I envy every woman I see on the street with her children. Yes, I am free—too free! I married for respect, and I have it. But—I want devotion, sympathy. You have it. You have a husband who adores you, and children to fill your heart, cherish it." The light in her eyes was almost fierce as she leaned forward, her hands clasped so tightly that the knuckles showed white, and a strange look passed for a moment over Mrs. Wentworth's face.

"You are enough to give one the blue-devils!" she exclaimed, with impatience. "Let's have a liqueur." She touched a bell, but Mrs. Lancaster rose.

"No; I will go."

"Oh, yes; just a glass." A servant appeared like an automaton at the door.

"What will you have, Alice?" But Mrs. Lancaster was obdurate. She declined the invitation, and declared that she must go, as she was going to the opera; and the next moment the two ladies were taking leave of each other with gracious words and the formal manner that obtains in fashionable society, quite as if they had known each other just fifteen minutes.

Mrs. Lancaster drove home, leaning very far back in her brougham.

Mrs. Wentworth, too, appeared rather fatigued after her guest departed, and sat for fifteen minutes with the social column of a newspaper lying in her lap unscanned.

"I thought she and Ferdy liked each other," she said to herself; "but he must have told the truth. They cannot have cared for each other. I think she must have been in love with that man."

CHAPTER XVII

KEITH MEETS NORMAN

THE day after Keith's interview with Mr. Creamer he was walking up-town more slowly than was his wont; for gloom was beginning to take the place where disappointment had for some time been holding session. His experience that day had been more than usually disheartening. These people with all their shrewdness appeared to him to be in their way as contracted as his mountaineers. They lived to amass wealth, yet went like sheep in flocks, and were so blind that they could not recognize a great opportunity when it was presented. They were mere machines that ground through life as monotonously as the wheels in their factories, turning out riches, riches, riches.

This morning Keith had come across an article in a newspaper which, in a measure, explained his want of success. It was an article on New Leeds. It praised, in florid sentences, the place and the people, gave a reasonably true account of the rise of the town, set forth in a veiled way a highly colored prospectus of the Wickersham properties, and asserted explicitly that all the lands of value had been secured by this company, and that such as were now being offered outside were those which Wickersham had refused as valueless after a thorough and searching examination. The falsity of the statements made Keith boil with rage. Mr. J. Quincy Plume immediately flashed into his mind.

As he walked along, the newspaper clutched in his hand,

a man brushed against him. Keith's mind was far away on Quincy Plume and Ferdy Wickersham; but instinctively, as his shoulder touched the stranger's, he said:

"I beg your pardon."

At the words the other turned and glanced at him casually; then stopped, turned and caught up with him, so as to take a good look at his face. The next second a hand was on Keith's shoulder.

"Why, Gordon Keith!"

Keith glanced up in a maze at the vigorous-looking, well-dressed young man who was holding out his gloved hand to him, his blue eyes full of a very pleasant light. Keith's mind had been so far away that for a second it did not return. Then a light broke over his face. He seized the other's hand.

"Norman Wentworth!"

The greeting between the two was so cordial that men hurrying by turned to look back at the pleasant faces, and their own set countenances softened.

Norman demanded where Keith had just come from and how long he had been in town, piling his questions one on the other with eager cordiality.

Keith looked sheepish, and began to explain in a rather shambling fashion that he had been there some time and "intended to hunt him up, of course"; but he had "been so taken up with business," etc., etc.

"I heard you were here on business. That was the way I came to know you were in town," explained Norman, "and I have looked everywhere for you. I hope you have been successful?" He was smiling. But Keith was still sore from the treatment he had received in one or two offices that morning.

"I have not been successful," he said, "and I felt sure that I should be. I have discovered that people here are very much like people elsewhere; they are very like sheep."

"And very suspicious, timid sheep at that," said Norman.

"They have often gone for wool and got shorn. So every one has to be tested. An unknown man has a hard time here. I suppose they would not look into your plan?"

"They classed me with 'pedlers, book-agents, and beggars' —I saw the signs up ; looked as if they thought I was a thief. I am not used to being treated like a swindler."

"The same old Keith! You must remember how many swindlers they have to deal with, my boy. It is natural that they should require a guarantee—I mean an introduction of some kind. You remember what one of them said not long ago? 'A man spends one part of his life making a fortune and the rest of it trying to keep others from stealing it from him.' You ought to have come to me. You must come and dine with me this evening, and we will talk it over. Perhaps, I can help you. I want to show you my little home, and I have the finest boy in the world."

At the tone of cordial sincerity in his voice, Keith softened. He laid his hand on the back of Norman's and closed it tightly.

"I knew I could always count on you, and I meant, of course, to come and see you. The reason I have not come before I will explain to you sometime. I was feeling a little sore over a matter—sheer lies that some one has written." He shook the newspaper in his hand.

"Oh, don't mind that paper," said Norman. "The columns of that paper are for hire. They belong at present to an old acquaintance of ours. They do *me* the honor to pay their compliments to my affairs now and then."

Keith walked up the street with a warm feeling about his heart. That friendly face and kindly pressure of the hand had cheered him like sunshine in a wintry day, and transformed the cold, cheerless city into an abode of life and happiness. The crowds that thronged by him once more took on interest for him. The faces once more softened into human fellowship.

That evening, when Keith arrived at Norman Wentworth's, he found that what he had termed his "little house" was, in fact, a very ample and commodious mansion on one of the most fashionable avenues in the city.

Outside there was nothing to distinguish it particularly from the scores of other handsome houses that stretched for blocks up and down the street with ever-recurrent brown-stone monotony. They were as much alike as so many box-stalls in a stable.

"If I had to live in one of these," thought Keith, as he was making his way to keep his appointment, "I should have to begin and count my house from the corner. No wonder the people are all so much alike!"

Inside, however, the personal taste of the owner counted for much more, and when Keith was admitted by the vel-vety-stepped servant, he found himself in a scene of luxury for which nothing that Norman had said had prepared him.

A hall, rather contracted, but sumptuous in its furnish-ings, opened on a series of drawing-rooms absolutely splen-did with gilt and satin. One room, all gold and yellow, led into another all blue satin, and that into one where the light filtered through soft-tinted shades on tapestries and rugs of deep crimson.

Keith could not help thinking what a fortunate man Norman was, and the difference between his friend's situa-tion in this bower of roses, and his own in his square, bare little box on the windy mountain-side, insensibly flashed over him. This was "an establishment"! How unequally Fortune scattered her gifts! Just then, with a soft rustle of silk, the portières were parted, and Mrs. Wentworth appeared. She paused for a second just under the arch, and the young man wondered if she knew how effective she was. She was a vision of lace and loveliness. A figure straight and sinuous, above the middle height, which would have been quite perfect but for being slightly too full, and which struck one before one looked at the face; coloring that was rich to brilliance; abundant, beautiful hair with a glint of lustre on it; deep hazel eyes, the least bit too close together; and features that were good and only just missed being fine. Keith had remembered her as beautiful, but as Mrs. Wentworth stood beneath the azure portières, her long, bare arms outstretched, her lips parted in a half-smile of welcome, she was much more striking-looking than Keith's memory had recorded. As he gazed on her, the expression on his face testified his admiration.

She came forward with the same gratified smile on her face and greeted him with formal words of welcome as Norman's old friend. Her thought was, "What a strong-looking man he is! Like a picture I have seen somewhere. Why doesn't Ferdy like him?"

As she sank into a soft divan, and with a sudden twist her train fell about her feet, making an artistic drapery, Keith experienced a sense of delight. He did not dream that Mrs. Wentworth knew much better than he precisely the pose to show the curve of her white full throat and round arm. The demands of notorious beauty were already beginning to tell on her, and even while she spoke gracious words of her husband's friendship for him, she from time to time added a touch here and a soft caress there with her long white hands to make the arrangement the more complete. It was almost too perfect to be unconscious.

Suddenly Keith heard Norman's voice outside, apparently on the stair, calling cheerily "Good-by" to some one, and the next second he came hastily into the drawing-room. His hair was rumpled and his necktie a trifle awry. As he seized and wrung Keith's hand with unfeigned heartiness, Keith was suddenly conscious of a change in everything. This was warmth, sincerity, and the beautiful room suddenly became a home. Mrs. Wentworth appeared somewhat shocked at his appearance.

"Well, Norman, you are a sight! Just look at your necktie!"

"That ruffian!" he laughed, feeling at his throat and trying to adjust the crooked tie.

"What will Mr. Keith think?"

"Oh, pshaw! Keith thinks all right. Keith is one of the men I don't have to apologize to. But if I do"—he turned to Keith, smiling—"I'll show you the apology. Come along." He seized Keith by the hand and started toward the door.

"You are not going to take Mr. Keith up-stairs!" exclaimed his wife. "Remember, Mr. Keith may not share your enthusiasm."

"Wait until he sees the apology. Come along, Keith." He drew Keith toward the door.

"But, Norman, I don't think—" began Mrs. Wentworth.

What she did not think was lost to the two men; for Norman, not heeding her, had, with the eagerness of a boy, dragged his visitor out of the door and started up the stairs, telling him volubly of the treat that was in store for him in the perfections of a certain small young gentleman who had been responsible for his tardiness in appearing below.

When Norman threw back a silken portière up-stairs and flung open a door, the scene that greeted Keith was one that made him agree that Norman was fully justified. A yellow-haired boy was rolling on the floor, kicking up his little pink legs in all the abandon of his years, while a blue-eyed little girl was sitting in a nurse's lap, making strenuous efforts to join her brother on the floor.

At sight of his father, the boy, with a whoop, scrambled to his feet, and, with outstretched arms and open mouth, showing all his little white teeth, made a rush for him, while the young lady suddenly changed her efforts to descend, and began to jump up and down in a frantic ecstasy of delight.

Norman gathered the boy up, and as soon as he could disentwine his little arms from about his neck, turned him toward Keith. The child gave the stranger one of those calm, scrutinizing looks that children give, and then, his face suddenly breaking into a smile, with a rippling laugh of good-comradeship, he sprang into Keith's outstretched arms. That gentleman's necktie was in danger of undergoing the same damaging process that had incurred Mrs. Norman's criticism, when the youngster discovered that lady herself, standing at the door. Scrambling down from his perch on Keith's shoulder, the boy, with a shout, rushed toward his mother. Mrs. Wentworth, with a little shriek, stopped him and held him off from her; she could not permit him to disarrange her toilet; her coiffure had cost too much thought; but the pair were evidently on terms of good-fellowship, and the light in the mother's eyes even as she restrained the boy's attempt at caresses changed her, and gave Keith a new insight into her character.

Keith and the hostess returned to the drawing-room before Norman, and she was no longer the professional beauty, the cold woman of the world, the mere fashionable hostess. The doors were flung open more than once as Keith talked warmly of the boy, and within Keith got glimpses of what was hidden there, which made him rejoice again that his friend had such a treasure. These glimpses of unexpected softness drew him nearer to her than he had ever expected to be, and on his part he talked to her with a frankness and earnestness which sank deep into her mind and opened the way to a warmer friendship than she usually gave.

"Norman is right," she said to herself. "This is a man.'

At the thought a light flashed upon her. It suddenly came to her.

This is "the ghost"! Yet could it be possible? She solved the question quickly.

"Mr. Keith, did you ever know Alice Lancaster?"

"Alice Lancaster—?" For a bare second he looked puzzled. "Oh, Miss Alice Yorke? Yes, a long time ago. He was conscious that his expression had changed. So he added: "I used to know her very well."

"Decidedly, this is the ghost," reflected Mrs. Wentworth to herself, as she scanned anew Keith's strong features and sinewy frame. "Alice said if a woman had ever seen him she would not be likely to forget him, and I think she was right."

"Why do you ask me?" inquired Keith, who had now quite recovered from his little confusion. "Of course, you know her?"

"Yes, very well. We were at school together. She is my best friend, almost." She shut her mouth as firmly as though this were the last sentence she ever proposed to utter; but her eyes, as they rested on Keith's face, had the least twinkle in them. Keith did not know how much of their old affair had been told her, but she evidently knew something, and it was necessary to show her that he had recovered from it long ago and yet retained a friendly feeling for Mrs. Lancaster.

"She was an old sweetheart of mine long ago; that is, I used to think myself desperately in love with her a hundred years ago or so, before she was married—and I was, too," he added.

He gained not the least idea of the impression this made on Mrs. Wentworth.

"She was talking to me about you only the other day," she said casually.

Keith again made a feint to open her defence.

"I hope she said kind things about me? I deserve some kindness at her hands, for I have only pleasant memories of her."

"I wonder what he means by that?" questioned Mrs. Wentworth to herself, and then added:

"Oh, yes; she did. Indeed, she was almost enthusiastic about your—friendship." Her eyes scanned his face lightly.

"Has she fulfilled the promise of beauty that she gave as a school-girl? I used to think her one of the most beautiful creatures in the world; but I don't know that I was capable of judging at that time," he added, with a smile, "for I remember I was quite desperate about her for a little while." He tried to speak naturally.

Mrs. Wentworth's eyes rested on his face for a moment.

"Why, yes; many think her much handsomer than she ever was. She is one of the married beauties, you know." Her eyes just swept Keith's face.

"She was also one of the sweetest girls I ever knew," Keith said, moved for some reason to add this tribute.

"Well, I don't know that every one would call her that. Indeed, I am not quite sure that I should call her that myself always; but she can be sweet. My children adore her, and I think that is always a good sign."

"Undoubtedly. They judge correctly, because directly."

The picture of a young girl in a riding-habit kneeling in the dust with a chubby, little, ragged child in her arms flashed before Keith's mental vision. And he almost gave a gasp.

"Is she married happily?" he asked. "I hope she is happy."

"Oh, as happy as the day is long," declared Mrs. Wentworth, cheerfully. Deep down in her eyes was a wicked twinkle of malice. Her face wore a look of content. "He is not altogether indifferent yet," she said to herself. And when Keith said firmly that he was very glad to hear it, she did him the honor to disbelieve him.

"Of course, you know that Mr. Lancaster is a good deal older than Alice?"

Yes, Keith had heard so.

"But a charming man, and immensely rich."

"Yes." Keith began to look grim.

"Aren't you going to see her?" inquired Mrs. Wentworth, finding that Keith was not prepared to say any more on the subject.

Keith said he should like to do so very much. He hoped to see her before going away; but he could not tell.

"She is married now, and must be so taken up with her new duties that I fear she would hardly remember me," he added, with a laugh. "I don't think I ever made much impression on her."

"Alice Yorke is not one to forget her friends. Why, she spoke of you with real friendship," she said, smiling, thinking to herself, Alice likes him, and he is still in love with her. This begins to be interesting.

"A woman does not have to give up all her friends when she marries?" she added, with her eyes on Keith.

Keith smiled.

"Oh, no; only her lovers, unless they turn into friends."

"Of course, those," said Mrs. Wentworth, who, after a moment's reflection, added, "They don't always do that. Do you believe a woman ever forgets entirely a man she has really loved?"

"She does if she is happily married and if she is wise."

"But all women are not happily married."

"And, perhaps, all are not wise," said Keith.

Some association of ideas led him to say suddenly:

"Tell me something about Ferdy Wickersham. He was one of your ushers, wasn't he?" He was surprised to see Mrs. Wentworth's countenance change. Her eyelids closed suddenly as if a glare were turned unexpectedly on them, and she caught her breath.

"Yes—I have known him since we were children. Of course, you know he was desperately in love with Alice Lancaster?"

Keith said he had heard something of the kind.

"He still likes her."

"She is married," said Keith, decisively.

"Yes."

A moment later Mrs. Wentworth drew a long breath and moistened her lips.

"You knew him at the same time that you first knew Norman, did you not?" She was simply figuring for time.

"Yes, I met him first then," said Keith.

"Don't you think Ferdy has changed since he was a boy?" she demanded after a moment's reflection.

"How do you mean?" Keith was feeling very uncomfortable, and, to save himself an answer, plunged along:

"Of course he has changed." He did not say how, nor did he give Mrs. Wentworth time to explain herself. "I will tell you one thing, though," he said earnestly : "he never was worthy to loose the latchet of your husband's shoe."

Mrs. Wentworth's face changed again ; she glanced down for a second, and then said :

"You and Norman have a mutual admiration society."

"We have been friends a long time," said Keith, thoughtfully.

"But even that does not always count for so much. Friendships seem so easily broken these days."

"Because there are so few Norman Wentworths. That man is blessed who has such a friend," said the young man, earnestly.

Mrs. Wentworth looked at him with a curious light in her eyes, and as she gazed her face grew more thoughtful. Then, as Norman reappeared she changed the subject abruptly.

After dinner, while they were smoking, Norman made Keith tell him of his coal-lands and the business that had brought him to New York. To Keith's surprise, he seemed to know something of it already.

"You should have come to me at first," he said. "I might, at least, have been able to counteract somewhat the adverse influence that has been working against you." His brow clouded a little.

"Wickersham appears to be quite a personage here. I wonder he has not been found out," said Keith after a little reverie.

Norman shifted slightly in his chair. "Oh, he is not worth bothering about. Give me your lay-out now."

Keith put him in possession of the facts, and he became deeply interested. He had, indeed, a dual motive : one of friendship for Keith ; the other he as yet hardly confessed even to himself.

The next day Keith met Norman by appointment and

gave him his papers. And a day or two afterwards he met a number of his friends at lunch.

They were capitalists and, if General Keith's old dictum, that gentlemen never discussed money at table, was sound, they would scarcely have met his requirement; for the talk was almost entirely of money. When they rose from the table, Keith, as he afterwards told Norman, felt like a squeezed orange. The friendliest man to him was Mr. Yorke, whom Keith found to be a jovial, sensible little man with kindly blue eyes and a humorous mouth. His chief cross-examiner was a Mr. Kestrel, a narrow-faced, parch-ment-skinned man with a thin white moustache that looked as if it had led a starved existence on his bloodless lip.

"Those people down there are opposed to progress," he said, buttoning up his pockets in a way he had, as if he were afraid of having them picked. "I guess the Wicker-shams have found that out. I don't see any money in it."

"It is strange that Kestrel doesn't see money in this," said Mr. Yorke, with a twinkle in his eye; "for he usually sees money in everything. I guess there were other rea-sons than want of progress for the Wickershams not paying dividends."

A few days later Norman informed Keith that the money was nearly all subscribed; but Keith did not know until afterwards how warmly he had indorsed him.

"You said something about sheep the other day; well, a sheep is a solitary and unsocial animal to a city-man with money to invest. My grandfather's man used to tell me: 'Sheep is kind of gregarious, Mr. Norman. Coax the first one through and you can't keep the others out.' Even Kestrel is jumping to get in."

CHAPTER XVIII

MRS. LANCASTER

KEITH had not yet met Mrs. Lancaster. He meant to call on her before leaving town; for he would show her that he was successful, and also that he had recovered. Also he wanted to see her, and in his heart was a lurking hope that she might regret having lost him. A word that Mrs. Wentworth had let fall the first evening he dined there had kept him from calling before.

A few evenings later Keith was dining with the Norman Wentworths, and after dinner Norman said:

"By the way, we are going to a ball to-night. Won't you come along? It will really be worth seeing."

Keith, having no engagement, was about to accept, but he was aware that Mrs. Wentworth, at her husband's words, had turned and given him a quick look of scrutiny, that swept him from the top of his head to the toe of his boot.

He had had that swift glance of inspection sweep him up and down many times of late, in business offices. The look, however, appeared to satisfy his hostess; for after a bare pause she seconded her husband's invitation.

That pause had given Keith time to reflect, and he declined to go. But Norman, too, had seen the glance his wife had given, and he urged his acceptance so warmly and with such real sincerity that finally Keith yielded.

"This is not one of *the* balls," said Norman, laughingly. "It is only *a* ball, one of our subscription dances, so you need have no scruples about going along."

Keith looked a little mystified.

"Mrs. Creamer's balls are *the* balls, my dear fellow. There, in general, only the rich and the noble enter—rich in prospect and noble in title—"

"Norman, how can you talk so!" exclaimed Mrs. Wentworth, with some impatience. "You know better than that. Mrs. Creamer has always been particularly kind to us. Why, she asks me to receive with her every winter."

But Norman was in a bantering mood. "Am not I rich and you noble?" he laughed. "Do you suppose, my dear, that Mrs. Creamer would ask you to receive with her if we lived two or three squares off Fifth Avenue? It is as hard for a poor man to enter Mrs. Creamer's house as for a camel to pass through the needle's eye. Her motions are sidereal and her orbit is as regulated as that of a planet."

Mrs. Wentworth protested.

"Why, she has all sorts of people at her house—!"

"Except the unsuccessful. Even planets have a little eccentricity of orbit."

An hour or two later Keith found himself in such a scene of radiance as he had never witnessed before in all his life. Though, as Norman had said, it was not one of the great balls, to be present at it was in some sort a proof of one's social position and possibly of one's pecuniary condition.

Keith was conscious of that same feeling of novelty and exhilaration that had come over him when he first arrived in the city. It came upon him when he first stepped from the cool outer air into the warm atmosphere of the brilliantly lighted building and stood among the young men, all perfectly dressed and appointed, and almost as similar as the checks they were receiving from the busy servants in the cloak-room. The feeling grew stronger as he mounted the wide marble stairway to the broad landing, which was a bower of palms and flowers, with handsome women passing in and out like birds in gorgeous plumage, and gay voices sounding in his ears. It swept over him like a flood when he entered the spacious ball-room and gazed upon the dazzling scene before him.

"This is Aladdin's palace," he declared as he stood looking across the large ball-room. "The Arabian Nights have surely come again."

Mrs. Wentworth, immediately after presenting Keith to one or two ladies who were receiving, had been met and borne off by Ferdy Wickersham, and was in the throng at the far end of the great apartment, and some one had stopped Norman on the stairway. So Keith was left for a moment standing alone just inside the door. He had a sense of being charmed. Later, he tried to account for it. Was it the sight before him? Even such perfect harmony of color could hardly have done it. It must be the dazzling radiance of youth that almost made his eyes ache with its beauty. Perhaps, it was the strain of the band hidden in the gallery among those palms. The waltz music that floated down always set him swinging back in the land of memory. He stood for a moment quite entranced. Then he was suddenly conscious of being lonely. In all the throng before him he could not see one soul that he knew. His friends were far away.

Suddenly the wheezy strains of the fiddles and the blare of the horns in the big dining-room of the old Windsor back in the mountains sounded in his ears, and the motley but gay and joyous throng that tramped and capered and swung over the rough boards, setting the floor to swinging and the room to swaying, swam in a dim mist before his eyes. Girls in ribbons so gay that they almost made the eyes ache, faces flushed with the excitement and joy of the dance; smiling faces, snowy teeth, dishevelled hair, tarlatan dresses, green and pink and white; ringing laughter and whoops of real merriment—all passed before his senses.

As he stood looking on the scene of splendor, he felt lost, lonely, and for a moment homesick. Here all was formal, stiff, repressed; that gayety was real, that merriment was sincere. With all their crudeness, those people in that condition were all human, hearty, strong, real. He wondered if refinement and elegance meant necessarily a suppression of all these. There, men came not only to enjoy but to make others enjoy as well. No stranger could have stood a moment alone without some one stepping to his side and drawing him into a friendly talk. This mood soon changed.

Still, standing alone near the door waiting for Norman to appear, Keith found entertainment watching the groups, the splendidly dressed women, clustered here and there or moving about inspecting or speaking to each other. One figure at the far end of the room attracted his eye again and again. She was standing with her back partly toward him, but he knew that she was a pretty woman as well as a handsome one, though he saw her face only in profile, and she was too far off for him to see it very well. Her hair was arranged simply; her head was set beautifully on her shoulders. She was dressed in black, the bodice covered with spangles that with her slightest movement shimmered and reflected the light like a coat of flexible mail. A number of men were standing about her, and many women, as they passed, held out their hands to her in the way that ladies of fashion have. Keith saw Mrs. Wentworth approach her, and a very animated conversation appeared to take place between them, and the lady in black turned quickly and gazed about the room; then Mrs. Wentworth started to move away, but the other caught and held her, asking her something eagerly. Mrs. Wentworth must have refused to answer, for she followed her a few steps; but Mrs. Wentworth simply waved her hand to her and swept away with her escort, laughing back at her over her shoulder.

Keith made his way around the room toward Mrs. Wentworth. There was something about the young lady in black which reminded him of a girl he had once seen standing straight and defiant, yet very charming, in a woodland path under arching pine-boughs. Just then, however, a waltz struck up and Mrs. Wentworth began to dance, so Keith stood leaning against the wall. Presently a member of a group of young men near Keith said:

"The Lancaster looks well to-night."

"She does. The old man's at home, Ferdy's on deck."

"Ferdy be dashed! Besides, where is Mrs. Went—?"

"Don't lay any money on that."

"She's all right. Try to say anything to her and you'll find out."

The others laughed, and one of them asked:

"Been trying yourself, Stirling?"

"No. I know better, Minturn."

"Why doesn't she shake Ferdy then?" demanded the other. "He's always hanging around when he isn't around the other."

"Oh, they have been friends all their lives. She is not going to give up a friend, especially when others are getting down on him. Can't you allow anything to friendship?"

"Ferdy's friendship is pretty expensive," said his friend, sententiously.

Keith took a glance at the speakers to see if he could by following their gaze place Mrs. Lancaster. The one who defended the lady was a jolly-looking man with a merry eye and a humorous mouth. The other two were as much alike as their neckties, their collars, their shirt-fronts, their dress-suits, or their shoes, in which none but a tailor could have discovered the least point of difference. Their cheeks were smooth, their chins were round, their hair as perfectly parted and brushed as a barber's. Keith had an impression that he had seen them just before on the other side of the room, talking to the lady in black; but as he looked across, he saw the other young men still there, and there were yet others elsewhere. At the first glance they nearly all looked alike. Just then he became conscious that a couple had stopped close beside him. He glanced at them; the lady was the same to whom he had seen Mrs. Wentworth speaking at the other end of the room. Her face was turned away, and all he saw was an almost perfect figure with shoulders that looked dazzling in contrast with her shimmering black gown. A single red rose was stuck in her hair. He was waiting to get a look at her face, when she turned toward him.

"Why, Mr. Keith!" she exclaimed, her blue eyes open wide with surprise. She held out her hand. "I don't believe you know me?"

"Then you must shut your eyes," said Keith, smiling his pleasure.

"I don't believe I should have known you? Yes, I should; I should have known you anywhere."

"Perhaps, I have not changed so much," smiled Keith.

She gave him just the ghost of a glance out of her blue eyes.

"I don't know. Have you been carrying any sacks of salt lately?" She assumed a lighter air.

"No; but heavier burdens still."

"Are you married?"

Keith laughed.

"No; not so heavy as that—yet."

"So heavy as that *yet!* Oh, you are engaged?"

"No; not engaged either—except engaged in trying to make a lot of people who think they know everything understand that there are a few things that they don't know."

"That is a difficult task," she said, shaking her head, "if you try it in New York."

"'John P. Robinson, he
Says they don't know everything down in Judee,'"

put in the stout young man who had been standing by waiting to speak to her.

"But this isn't Judee yet," she laughed, "for I assure you we do know everything here, Mr. Keith." She held out her hand to the gentleman who had spoken, and after greeting him introduced him to Keith as "Mr. Stirling."

"You ought to like each other," she said cordially.

Keith professed his readiness to do so.

"I don't know about that," said Stirling, jovially. "You are too friendly to him."

"What are you doing? Where are you staying? How long are you going to be in town?" demanded Mrs. Lancaster, turning to Keith.

"Mining.—At the Brunswick.—Only a day or two," said Keith, laughing.

"Mining? Gold-mining?"

"No ; not yet."

"Where?"

"Down South at a place called New Leeds. It's near the place where I used to teach. It's a great city. Why, we think New York is jealous of us."

"Oh, I know about that. A friend of mine put a little money down there for me. You know him? Ferdy Wickersham?"

"Yes, I know him."

"Most of us know him," observed Mr. Stirling, turning his eyes on Keith.

"Of course, you must know him. Are you in with him? He tells me that they own pretty much everything that is good in that region. They are about to open a new mine that is to exceed anything ever known. Ferdy tells me I am good for I don't know how much. The stock is to be put on the exchange in a little while, and I got in on the ground-floor. That's what they call it—the lowest floor of all, you know?"

"Yes ; some people call it the ground-floor," said Keith, wishing to change the subject.

"You know there may be a cellar under a ground-floor," observed Mr. Stirling, demurely.

Keith looked at him, and their eyes met.

Fortunately, perhaps, for Keith, some one came up just then and claimed a dance with Mrs. Lancaster. She moved away, and then turned back.

"I shall see you again?"

"Yes. Why, I hope so—certainly."

She stopped and looked at him.

"When are you going away?"

"Why, I don't exactly know. Very soon. Perhaps, in a day or two."

"Well, won't you come to see us? Here, I will give you my address. Have you a card?" She took the pencil he offered her and wrote her number on it. "Come some afternoon—about six; Mr. Lancaster is always in then," she said sedately. "I am sure you will like each other."

Keith bowed.

She floated off smiling. What she had said to Mrs. Wentworth occurred to her.

"Yes; he looks like a man." She became conscious that her companion was asking a question.

"What is the matter with you?" he said. "I have asked you three times who that man was, and you have not said a word."

"Oh, I beg your pardon. Mr. Keith, an old friend of mine," she said, and changed the subject.

As to her old friend, he was watching her as she danced, winding in and out among the intervening couples. He wondered that he could ever have thought that a creature like that could care for him and share his hard life. He might as soon have expected a bird-of-paradise to live by choice in a coal-bunker.

He strolled about, looking at the handsome women, and presently found himself in the conservatory. Turning a clump of palms, he came on Mrs. Wentworth and Mr. Wickersham sitting together talking earnestly. Keith was about to go up and speak to Mrs. Wentworth, but her escort said something under his breath to her, and she looked away. So Keith passed on.

A little later, Keith went over to where Mrs. Lancaster stood. Several men were about her, and just after Keith joined her, another man walked up, if any movement so lazy and sauntering could be termed walking.

"I have been wondering why I did not see you," he drawled as he came up.

Keith recognized the voice of Ferdy Wickersham. He turned and faced him; but if Mr. Wickersham was aware of his presence, he gave no sign of it. His dark eyes were on Mrs. Lancaster. She turned to him.

"Perhaps, Ferdinand, it was because you did not use your eyes. That is not ordinarily a fault of yours."

"I never think of my eyes when yours are present," said he, lazily.

"Oh, don't you?" laughed Mrs. Lancaster. "What were you doing a little while ago in the conservatory—with—?"

"Nothing. I have not been in the conservatory this evening. You have paid some one else a compliment."

"Tell that to some one who does not use her eyes," said Mrs. Lancaster, mockingly.

"There are occasions when you must disbelieve the sight of your eyes." He was looking her steadily in the face, and Keith saw her expression change. She recovered herself.

"Last time I saw you, you vowed you had eyes for none but me, you may remember?" she said lightly.

"No. Did I? Life is too awfully short to remember. But it is true. It is the present in which I find my pleasure."

Up to this time neither Mrs. Lancaster nor Mr. Wickersham had taken any notice of Keith, who stood a little to one side, waiting, with his eyes resting on the other young man's face. Mrs. Lancaster now turned.

"Oh, Mr. Keith." She now turned back to Mr. Wickersham. "You know Mr. Keith?"

Keith was about to step forward to greet his old acquaintance; but Wickersham barely nodded.

"Ah, how do you do? Yes, I know Mr. Keith.—If I can take care of the present, I let the past and the future take care of themselves," he continued to Mrs. Lancaster. "Come and have a turn. That will make the present worth all of the past."

"Ferdy, you are discreet," said one of the other men, with a laugh.

"My dear fellow," said the young man, turning, "I assure you, you don't know half my virtues."

"What are your virtues, Ferdy?"

"One is not interfering with others." He turned back to Mrs. Lancaster. "Come, have a turn." He took one of his hands from his pocket and held it out.

"I am engaged," said Mrs. Lancaster.

"Oh, that makes no difference. You are always engaged; come," he said.

"I beg your pardon. It makes a difference in *this* case," said Keith, coming forward. "I believe this is my turn, Mrs. Lancaster?"

Wickersham's glance swept across, but did not rest on him, though it was enough for Keith to meet it for a second, and, without looking, the young man turned lazily away.

"Shall we find a seat?" Mrs. Lancaster asked as she took Keith's arm.

"Delighted, unless you prefer to dance."

"I did not know that dancing was one of your accomplishments," she said as they strolled along.

"Maybe, I have acquired several accomplishments that you do not know of. It has been a long time since you knew me," he answered lightly. As they turned, his eyes fell on Wickersham. He was standing where they had left him, his eyes fastened on them malevolently. As Keith looked he started and turned away. Mrs. Lancaster had also seen him.

"What is there between you and Ferdy?" she asked.

"Nothing."

"There must be. Did you ever have a row with him?"

"Yes; but that was long ago."

"I don't know. He has a good memory. He doesn't like you." She spoke reflectively.

"Doesn't he?" laughed Keith. "Well, I must try and sustain it as best I can."

"And you don't like him? Few men like him. I wonder why that is?"

"And many women?" questioned Keith, as for a moment he recalled Mrs. Wentworth's face when he spoke of him.

"Some women," she corrected, with a quick glance at him. She reflected, and then went on: "I think it is partly because he is so bold and partly that he never appears to know any one else. It is the most insidious flattery in the world. I like him because I have known him all my life. I know him perfectly."

"Yes?" Keith spoke politely.

She read his thought. "You wonder if I really know him? Yes, I do. But, somehow, I cling to those I knew in my girlhood. You don't believe that, but I do." She glanced at him and then looked away.

"Yes, I do believe it. Then let's be friends—old friends," said Keith. He held out his hand, and when she took it grasped hers firmly.

"Who is here with you to-night?" he asked.

"No one. Mr. Lancaster does not care for balls."

"Won't you give me the pleasure of seeing you home?"

She hesitated for a moment, and then said:

"I will drop you at your hotel. It is right on my way home."

Just then some one came up and joined the group.

"Ah, my dear Mrs. Lancaster! How well you are looking this evening!"

The full voice, no less than the words, sounded familiar to Keith, and turning, he recognized the young clergyman whom he had met at Mrs. Wentworth's when he passed through New York some years before. The years had plainly used Mr. Rimmon well. He was dressed in an evening suit with a clerical waistcoat which showed that his plump frame had taken on an extra layer, and a double chin was beginning to rest on his collar.

Mrs. Lancaster smiled as she returned his greeting.

"You are my stand-by, Mr. Rimmon. I always know that, no matter what others may say of me, I shall be sure of at least one compliment before the evening is over if you are present."

"That is because you always deserve it." He put his head on one side like an aldermanic robin. "Ah, if you knew how many compliments I do pay you which you never hear! My entire life is a compliment to you," declared Mr. Rimmon.

"Not your entire life, Mr. Rimmon. You are like some other men. You confound me with some one else; for I am sure I heard you saying the same thing five minutes ago to Louise Wentworth."

"Impossible. Then I must have confounded her with you," sighed Mr. Rimmon, with such a look at Mrs. Lancaster out of his languishing eyes that she gave him a laughing tap with her fan.

"Go and practise that on a débutante. I am an old married woman, remember."

"Ah, me!" sighed the gentleman. " 'Marriage and Death and Division make barren our lives.' "

"Where does that come from?" asked Mrs. Lancaster.

"Ah! from—ah—" began Mr. Rimmon, then catching Keith's eyes resting on him with an amused look in them, he turned red.

She addressed Keith. "Mr. Keith, you quoted that to me once; where does it come from? From the Bible?"

"No."

"I read it in the newspaper and was so struck by it that I remembered it," said Mr. Rimmon.

"I read it in 'Laus Veneris,'" said Keith, dryly, with his eyes on the other's face. It pleased him to see it redden.

Keith, as he passed through the rooms, caught sight of an old lady over in a corner. He could scarcely believe his senses; it was Miss Abigail. She was sitting back against the wall, watching the crowd with eyes as sharp as needles. Sometimes her thin lips twitched, and her bright eyes snapped with inward amusement. Keith made his way over to her. She was so much engaged that he stood beside her a moment without her seeing him. Then she turned and glanced at him.

" 'A chiel's amang ye takin' notes,' " he said, laughing and holding out his hand.

" 'An', faith! she'll prent 'em,' " she answered, with a nod. "How are you? I am glad to see you. I was just wishing I had somebody to enjoy this with me, but not a man. I ought to be gone; and so ought you, young man. I started, but I thought if I could get in a corner by myself where there were no men I might stay a little while and look at it; for I certainly never saw anything like this before, and I don't think I ever shall again. I certainly do not think you ought to see it."

Keith laughed, and she continued:

"I knew things had changed since I was a girl; but I didn't know it was as bad as this. Why, I don't think it ought to be allowed."

"What?" asked Keith.

"This." She waved her hand to include the dancing throng before them. "They tell me all those women dancing around there are married."

"I believe many of them are."

"Why don't those young women have partners?"

"Why, some of them do. I suppose the others are not attractive enough, or something."

"Especially *something*," said the old lady. "Where are their husbands?"

"Why, some of them are at home, and some are here."

"Where?" The old lady turned her eyes on a couple that sailed by her, the man talking very earnestly to his companion, who was listening breathlessly. "Is that her husband?"

"Well, no; that is not, I believe."

"No; I'll be bound it is not. You never saw a married man talking to his wife in public in that way—unless they were talking about the last month's bills. Why, it is perfectly brazen."

Keith laughed.

"Where is *her* husband?" she demanded, as Mrs. Wentworth floated by, a vision of brocaded satin and lace and white shoulders, supported by Ferdy Wickersham, who was talking earnestly and looking down into her eyes languishingly.

"Oh, her husband is here."

"Well, he had better take her home to her little children. If ever I saw a face that I distrusted it is that man's."

"Why, that is Ferdy Wickersham. He is one of the leaders of society. He is considered quite an Adonis," observed Keith.

"And I don't think Adonis was a very proper person for a young woman with children to be dancing with in attire in which only her husband should see her." She shut her lips grimly. "I know him," she added. "I know all about them for three generations. One of the misfortunes of age is that when a person gets as old as I am she knows so much evil about people. I knew that young man's grandfather when he was a worthy mechanic. His wife was an uppish hussy who thought herself better than her husband, and their daughter was a pretty girl with black eyes and rosy cheeks. They sent her off to school, and after the first year or two she never came back. She had got above them. Her father told me as much. The old man cried about it. He said his wife thought it was all right; that his girl had married a smart young fellow who was a clerk in a bank; but that if he had a hundred other children he'd never teach them any more than to read, write, and figure. And to think that her son should be the Adonis dancing with my cousin Everett Wentworth's daughter-in-law! Why, my Aunt Wentworth would rise from her grave if she knew it!"

"Well, times have changed," said Keith, laughing. "You see they are as good as anybody now."

"Not as good as anybody—you mean as rich as anybody."

"That amounts to about the same thing here, doesn't it?"

"I believe it does, here," said the old lady, with a sniff. "Well," she said after a pause, "I think I will go back and tell Matilda what I have seen. And if you are wise you will come with me, too. This is no place for plain, country-bred people like you and me."

Keith, laughing, said he had an engagement, but he would like to have the privilege of taking her home, and then he could return.

"With a married woman, I suppose? Yes, I will be bound it is," she added as Keith nodded. "You see the danger of evil association. I shall write to your father and tell him that the sooner he gets you out of New York the better it will be for your morals and your manners. For you are the only man, except Norman, who has been so provincial as to take notice of an unknown old woman."

So she went chatting merrily down the stairway to her carriage, making her observations on whatever she saw with the freshness of a girl.

"Do you think Norman is happy?" she suddenly asked Keith.

"Why—yes; don't you think so? He has everything on earth to make him happy," said Keith, with some surprise. But even at the moment it flitted across his mind that there was something which he had felt rather than observed in Mrs. Wentworth's attitude toward her husband.

"Except that he has married a fool," said the old lady, briefly. "Don't you marry a fool, you hear?"

"I believe she is devoted to Norman and to her children," Keith began, but Miss Abigail interrupted him.

"And why shouldn't she be? Isn't she his wife? She gives him, perhaps, what is left over after her devotion to herself, her house, her frocks, her jewels, and—Adonis."

"Oh, I don't believe she cares for him," declared Keith. "It is impossible."

"I don't believe she does either, but she cares for herself, and he flatters her. The idea of a Norman-Wentworth's wife being flattered by the attention of a tinker's grandson!"

When the ball broke up and Mrs. Lancaster's carriage was called, several men escorted her to it. Wickersham, who was trying to recover ground which something told him he had lost, followed her down the stairway with one or two other men, and after she had entered the carriage stood leaning in at the door while he made his adieus and peace at the same moment.

"You were not always so cruel to me," he said in a low tone.

Mrs. Lancaster laughed genuinely.

"I was never cruel to you, Ferdy; you mistake leniency for harshness."

"No one else would say that to me."

"So much the more pity. You would be a better man if you had the truth told you oftener."

"When did you become such an advocate of Truth? Is it this man?"

"What man?"

"Keith. If it is, I want to tell you that he is not what he pretends."

A change came over Mrs. Lancaster's face.

"He is a gentleman," she said coldly.

"Oh, is he? He was a stage-driver."

Mrs. Lancaster drew herself up.

"If he was—" she began. But she stopped suddenly, glanced beyond Wickersham, and moved over to the further side of the carriage.

Just then a hand was laid on Wickersham's arm, and a voice behind him said :

"I beg your pardon."

Wickersham knew the voice, and without looking around stood aside for the speaker to make his adieus. Keith stepped into the carriage and pulled to the door before the footman could close it.

At the sound the impatient horses started off, leaving

three men standing in the street looking very blank. Stirling was the first to speak ; he turned to the others in amazement.

"Who is Keith?" he demanded.

"Oh, a fellow from the South somewhere."

"Well, Keith knows his business!" said Mr. Stirling, with a nod of genuine admiration.

Wickersham uttered an imprecation and turned back into the house.

Next day Mr. Stirling caught Wickersham in a group of young men at the club, and told them the story.

"Look out for Keith," he said. "He gave me a lesson."

Wickersham growled an inaudible reply.

"Who was the lady? Wickersham tries to capture so many prizes, what you say gives us no light," said Mr. Minturn, one of the men.

"Oh, no. I'll only tell you it's not the one you think," said the jolly bachelor. "But I am going to take lessons of that man Keith. These countrymen surprise me sometimes."

"He was a d—d stage-driver," said Wickersham.

"Then you had better take lessons from him, Ferdy," said Stirling. "He drives well. He's a veteran."

When Keith reached his room he lit a cigar and flung himself into a chair. Somehow, the evening had not left a pleasant impression on his mind. Was this the Alice Yorke he had worshipped, revered? Was this the woman whom he had canonized throughout these years? Why was she carrying on an affair with Ferdy Wickersham? What did he mean by those last words at the carriage? She said she knew him. Then she must know what his reputation was. Now and then it came to Keith that it was nothing to him. Mrs. Lancaster was married, and her affairs could not concern him. But they did concern him. They had agreed to be old friends—old friends. He would be a true friend to her.

He rose and threw away his half-smoked cigar.

Keith called on Mrs. Lancaster just before he left for the South. Though he had no such motive when he put off his visit, he could not have done a wiser thing. It was a novel experience for her to invite a man to call on her and not have him jump at the proposal, appear promptly next day, frock-coat, kid gloves, smooth flattery, and all ; and when Keith had not appeared on the third day after the ball, it set her to thinking. She imagined at first that he must have been called out of town, but Mrs. Norman, whom she met, dispelled this idea. Keith had dined with them informally the evening before.

"He appeared to be in high spirits," added the lady. "His scheme has succeeded, and he is about to go South. Norman took it up and put it through for him."

"I know it," said Mrs. Lancaster, demurely.

Mrs. Wentworth's form stiffened slightly ; but her manner soon became gracious again. "Ferdy says there is nothing in it."

Could he be offended, or afraid—of himself? reflected Mrs. Lancaster. Mrs. Wentworth's next observation disposed of this theory also. "You ought to hear him talk of you. By the way, I have found out who that ghost was."

Mrs. Lancaster threw a mask over her face.

"He says you have more than fulfilled the promise of your girlhood : that you are the handsomest woman he has seen in New York, my dear," pursued the other, looking down at her own shapely figure. "Of course, I do not agree with him, quite," she laughed. "But, then, people will differ."

"Louise Wentworth, vanity is a deadly sin," said the other, smiling, "and we are told in the Commandments— I forget which one—to envy nothing of our neighbor's."

"He said he wanted to go to see you ; that you had kindly invited him, and he wished very much to meet Mr. Lancaster," said Mrs. Wentworth, blandly.

"Yes, I am sure they will like each other," said Mrs. Lancaster, with dignity. "Mamma also is very anxious to see him. She used to know him when—when he was a boy, and liked him very much, too, though she would not acknowledge it to me then." She laughed softly at some recollection.

"He spoke of your mother most pleasantly," declared Mrs. Wentworth, not without Mrs. Lancaster noticing that she was claiming to stand as Keith's friend.

"Well, I shall not be at home to-morrow," she began. "I have promised to go out to-morrow afternoon."

"Oh, sha'n't you? Why, what a pity! because he said he was going to pay his calls to-morrow, as he expected to leave to-morrow night. I think he would be very sorry not to see you."

"Oh, well, then, I will stay in. My other engagement is of no consequence."

Her friend looked benign.

Recollecting Mrs. Wentworth's expression, Mrs. Lancaster determined that she would not be at home the following afternoon. She would show Mrs. Wentworth that she could not gauge her so easily as she fancied. But at the last moment, after putting on her hat, she changed her mind. She remained in, and ended by inviting Keith to dinner that evening, an invitation which was so graciously seconded by Mr. Lancaster that Keith, finding that he could take a later train, accepted. Mrs. Yorke was at the dinner, too, and how gracious she was to Keith! She "could scarcely believe he was the same man she had known a few years before." She "had heard a great deal of him, and had come around to dinner on purpose to meet him." This was true.

"And you have done so well, too, I hear. Your friends are very pleased to know of your success," she said graciously.

Keith smilingly admitted that he had had, perhaps, better fortune than he deserved; but this Mrs. Yorke amiably would by no means allow.

"Mrs. Wentworth—not Louise—I mean the elder Mrs.

Wentworth—was speaking of you. You and Norman were great friends when you were boys, she tells me. They were great friends of ours, you know, long before we met you."

He wondered how much the Wentworths' indorsement counted for in securing Mrs. Yorke's invitation. For a good deal, he knew ; but as much credit as he gave it he was within the mark.

It was only her environment. She could no more escape from that than if she were in prison. She gauged every one by what others thought, and she possessed no other gauge. Yet there was a certain friendliness, too, in Mrs. Yorke. The good lady had softened with the years, and at heart she had always liked Keith.

Most of her conversation was of her friends and their position. Alice was thinking of going abroad soon to visit some friends on the other side, "of a very distinguished family," she told Keith.

When Keith left the Lancaster house that night Alice Lancaster knew that he had wholly recovered.

CHAPTER XIX

WICKERSHAM AND PHRONY

KEITH returned home and soon found himself a much bigger man in New Leeds than when he went away. The mine opened on the Rawson property began to give from the first large promises of success.

Keith picked up a newspaper one day a little later. It announced in large head-lines, as befitted the chronicling of such an event, the death of Mr. William Lancaster, capitalist. He had died suddenly in his office. His wife, it was stated, was in Europe and had been cabled the sad intelligence. There was a sketch of his life and also of that of his wife. Their marriage, it was recalled, had been one of the "romances" of the season a few years before. He had taken society by surprise by carrying off one of the belles of the season, the beautiful Miss Yorke. The rest of the notice was taken up in conjectures as to the amount of his property and the sums he would be likely to leave to the various charitable institutions of which he had always been a liberal patron.

Keith laid the paper down on his knee and went off in a revery. Mr. Lancaster was dead! Of all the men he had met in New York he had in some ways struck him the most. He had appeared to him the most perfect type of a gentleman; self-contained, and inclined to be cold, but a man of elegance as well as of brains. He felt that he ought to be sorry Mr. Lancaster was dead, and he tried to be sorry for his wife. He started to write her a letter of condolence, but stopped at the first line, and could get no further. Yet several times a day, for many days, she recurred to him, each time giving him a feeling of dissatisfaction, until at length he was able to banish her from his mind.

Prosperity is like the tide. It comes, each wave higher and higher, until it almost appears that it will never end, and then suddenly it seems to ebb a little, comes up again, recedes again, and, before one knows it, is passing away as surely as it came.

Just when Keith thought that his tide was in full flood, it began to ebb without any apparent cause, and before he was aware of it, the prosperity which for the last few years had been setting in so steadily in those mountain regions had passed away, and New Leeds and he were left stranded upon the rocks.

Rumor came down to New Leeds from the North. The Wickersham enterprises were said to be hard hit by some of the failures which had occurred.

A few weeks later Keith heard that Mr. Aaron Wickersham was dead. The clerks said that he had had a quarrel with his son the day after the panic and had fallen in an apoplectic fit soon afterwards. But then the old clerks had been discharged immediately after his death. Young Wickersham said he did not want any dead-wood in his offices. Also he did not want any dead property. Among his first steps was the sale of the old Keith plantation. Gordon, learning that it was for sale, got a friend to lend him the money and bought it in, though it would scarcely have been known for the same place. The mansion had been stripped of its old furniture and pictures soon after General Keith had left there, and the plantation had gone down.

Rumor also said that Wickersham's affairs were in a bad way. Certainly the new head of the house gave no sign of it. He opened a yet larger office and began operations on a more extensive scale. The *Clarion* said that his Southern

271

enterprises would be pushed actively, and that the stock of the Great Gun Mine would soon be on the New York Exchange.

Ferdy Wickersham suddenly returned to New Leeds, and New Leeds showed his presence. Machinery was shipped sufficient to run a dozen mines. He not only pushed the old mines, but opened a new one. It was on a slip of land that lay between the Rawson property and the stream that ran down from the mountain. Some could not understand why he should run the shaft there, unless it was that he was bent on cutting the Rawson property off from the stream. It was a perilous location for a shaft, and Matheson, the superintendent, had protested against it.

Matheson's objections proved to be well founded. The mine was opened so near the stream that water broke through into it, as Matheson had predicted, and though a strong wall was built, the water still got in, and it was difficult to keep it pumped out sufficiently to work. Some of the men struck. It was known that Wickersham had nearly come to a rupture with the hard-headed Scotchman over it; but Wickersham won. Still, the coal did not come. It was asserted that the shafts had failed to reach coal. Wickersham laughed and kept on—kept on till coal did come. It was heralded abroad. The *Clarion* devoted columns to the success of the "Great Gun Mine" and Wickersham.

Wickersham naturally showed his triumph. He celebrated it in a great banquet at the New Windsor, at which speeches were made which likened him to Napoleon and several other generals. Mr. Plume declared him "greater than Themistocles, for he could play the lute and make a small city a great one."

Wickersham himself made a speech, in which he professed his joy that he had silenced the tongue of slander and wrested from detraction a victory not for himself, but for New Leeds. His enemies and the enemies of New Leeds were, he declared, the same. They would soon see his enemies suing for aid. He was applauded to the echo. All this and much more was in the *Clarion* next day, with some very pointed satire about "rival mines."

Keith, meantime, was busy poring over plats and verifying lines.

The old squire came to town a morning or two later.

"I see Mr. Wickersham's struck coal at last," he said to Keith, after he had got his pipe lit. His face showed that he was brimming with information.

"Yes—*our* coal." Keith showed him the plats. "He is over our line—I do not know just where, but in here somewhere."

The old fellow put on his spectacles and looked long and carefully.

"He says he owns it all; that he'll have us suin' for pardon?"

"Suing for damages."

The old squire gave a chuckle of satisfaction. "He is in and about *there*." He pointed with a stout and horny finger.

"How did you know?"

"Well, you see, little Dave Dennison—you remember Dave? You taught him."

"Perfectly—I mean, I remember him perfectly. He is now in New York."

"Yes. Well, Dave he used to be sweet on Phrony, and he seems to be still sweet on her."

Mr. Keith nodded.

"Well, of course, Phrony she's lookin' higher than Dave —but you know how women air?"

"I don't know—I know they are strange creatures," said Keith, almost with a sigh, as his past with one woman came vividly before him.

"Well, they won't let a man go, noway, not entirely— unless he's in the way. So, though Phrony don't keer nothin' in the world about Dave, she sort o' kep' him on-an'-off-like till this here young Wickersham come down here. You know, I think she and him like each other?"

273

He's been to see her twicet and is always a-writin' to her?"
His voice had an inquiry in it; but Keith took no notice
of it, and the old man went on.

"Well, since then she's sort of cooled off to Dave—won't
have him around—and Dave's got sort of sour. Well, he
hates Wickersham, and he up and told her t'other night 't
Wickersham was the biggest rascal in New York; that he
had 'most broke his father and had put the stock of this
here new mine on the market, an' that he didn't have coal
enough in it to fill his hat; that he'd been down in it an'
that the coal all come out of our mine."

Keith's eyes glistened.

"Exactly."

"Well, with that she got so mad with Dave, she wouldn't
speak to him; and Dave left, swearin' he'd settle Wickersham and show him up, and he'll do it if he can."

"Where is he?" asked Keith, in some anxiety. "Tell
him not to do anything till I see him."

"No; I got hold of him and straightened him out. He
told me all about it. He was right much cut up. He jest
cried about Phrony."

Keith wrote a note to Wickersham. He referred to the
current rumors that the cutting had run over on their
side, suggesting, however, that it might have been by in-
advertence.

When this letter was received, Wickersham was in conference with his superintendent, Mr. Matheson. The interview had been somewhat stormy, for the superintendent had just made the very statement that Keith's note
contained. He was not in a placid frame of mind, for the
work was going badly; and Mr. Plume was seated in an
arm-chair listening to his report. He did not like Plume,
and had wished to speak privately to Wickersham; but
Wickersham had told him to go ahead, that Plume was a
friend of his, and as much interested in the success of the
work as Matheson was. Plume's satisfaction and noncha-
lant air vexed the Scotchman. Just then Keith's note came,

and Wickersham, after reading it, tossed it over first to Plume. Plume read it and handed it back without the least change of expression. Then Wickersham, after some reflection, tossed it to Matheson.

"That's right," he nodded, when he had read it. "We are already over the line so far that the men know it."

Wickersham's temper gave way.

"Well, I know it. Do you suppose I am so ignorant as not to know anything? But I am not fool enough to give it away. You need not go bleating around about it everywhere."

Plume's eye glistened with satisfaction.

The superintendent's brow, which had clouded, grew darker. He had already stood much from this young man. He had followed his orders in running the mine beyond the lines shown on the plats; but he had accepted Wickersham's statement that the lines were wrong, not the workings.

"I wush you to understand one thing, Mr. Wickersham," he said. " I came here to superintend your mines and to do my work like an honest man; but I don't propose to soil my hands with any dirrty dealings, or to engage in any violation of the law; for I am a law-abiding, God-fearing man, and before I'll do it I'll go."

"Then you can go," said Wickersham, angrily. "Go, and be d—d to you! I will show you that I know my own business."

"Then I will go. I do not think you do know it. If you did, you would not—"

"Never mind. I want no more advice from you," snarled Wickersham.

"I would like to have a letter saying that the work that has been done since you took charge has been under your express orders."

"I'll see you condemned first. I suppose it was by my orders that the cutting ran so near to the creek that that work had to be done to keep the mine from being flooded?"

"It was, by your *express* orders."

"I deny it. I suppose it was by my orders that the men were set on to strike?"

"You were told of the danger and the probable consequences of your insisting."

"Oh, you are always croaking—"

"And I will croak once more," said the discharged official. "You will never make that mine pay, for there is no coal there. It is all on the other side of the line."

"I won't! Well, I will show you. I, at least, stand a better chance to make it pay than I ever did before. I suppose you propose now to go over to Keith and tell him all you know about our work. I imagine he would like to know it—more than he knows already."

"I am not in the habit of telling the private affairs of my employers," said the man, coldly. "He does not need any information from me. He is not a fool. He knows it."

"Oh, he does, does he! Then you told him," asserted Wickersham, furiously.

This was more than the Scotchman could bear. He had already stood much, and his face might have warned Wickersham. Suddenly it flamed. He took one step forward, a long one, and rammed his clinched and hairy fist under the young man's nose.

"You lie! And, —— you! you know you lie. I'm a law-abiding, God-fearing man; but if you don't take that back, I will break every bone in your face. I've a mind to do it anyhow."

Wickersham rolled back out of his chair as if the knotted fist under his nose had driven him. His face was white as he staggered to his feet.

"I didn't mean—I don't say—. What do you mean anyhow?" he stammered.

"Take it back." The foreman advanced slowly.

"Yes—I didn't mean anything. What are you getting so mad about?"

The foreman cut him short with a fierce gesture. "Write me that paper I want, and pay me my money."

"Write what — ? "

"That the lower shaft and the last drift was cut by your order. Write it ! " He pointed to the paper on the desk.

Wickersham sat down and wrote a few lines. His hand trembled.

"Here it is," he said sullenly.

"Now pay me," said the glowering Scotchman.

The money was paid, and Matheson, without a word, turned and walked out.

"D—— him ! I wish the mine had fallen in on him," Wickersham growled.

"You are well quit of him," said Mr. Plume, consolingly.

"I'll get even with him yet."

"You have to answer your other friend," observed Mr. Plume.

"I'll answer him." He seized a sheet of paper and began to write, annotating it with observations far from complimentary to Keith and Matheson. He read the letter to Plume. It was a curt inquiry whether Mr. Keith meant to make the charge that he had crossed his line. If so, Wickersham & Company knew their remedy and would be glad to know at last the source whence these slanderous reports had come.

"That will settle him."

Mr. Plume nodded. "It ought to do it."

Keith's reply to this note was sent that night.

It stated simply that he did make the charge, and if Mr. Wickersham wished it, he was prepared to prove it.

Wickersham's face fell. "Matheson's been to him."

"Or some one else," said Mr. Plume. "That Bluffy hates you like poison. You've got to do something and do it quick."

Wickersham glanced up at Plume. He met his eye steadily. Wickersham's face showed the shadow of a frown ; then it passed, leaving his face set and a shade paler. He looked at Plume again and licked his lips. Plume's eye was still on him.

"What do you know?" he asked Plume.

"Only what others know. They all know it or will soon."

Wickersham's face settled more. He cursed in a low voice and then relapsed into reflection.

"Get up a strike," said Plume. "They are ripe for it. Close her down and blow her up."

Wickersham's countenance changed, and presently his brow cleared.

"It will serve them right. I'll let them know who owns these mines."

Next morning there was posted a notice of a cut of wages in the Wickersham mines. There was a buzz of excitement in New Leeds and anger among the mining population. At dinner-time there were meetings and much talking. That night again there were meetings and whiskey and more talking,—louder talking,—speeches and resolutions. Next morning a committee waited on Mr. Wickersham, who received the men politely but coldly. He "thought he knew how to manage his own business. They must be aware that he had spent large sums in developing property which had not yet begun to pay. When it began to pay he would be happy, etc. If they chose to strike, all right. He could get others in their places."

That night there were more meetings. Next day the men did not go to work. By evening many of them were drunk. There was talk of violence. Bill Bluffy, who was now a miner, was especially savage.

Keith was surprised, a few days later, as he was passing along the street, to meet Euphronia Tripper. He spoke to her cordially. She was dressed showily and was handsomer than when he saw her last. The color mounted her face as he stopped her, and he wondered that Wickersham had not thought her pretty. When she blushed she was almost a beauty. He asked about her people at home, inquiring in a breath when she came, where she was staying, how long she was going to remain, etc.

She answered the first questions glibly enough; but when he inquired as to the length of her visit and where she was staying, she appeared somewhat confused.

"I have cousins here, the Turleys."

"Oh! You are with Mr. Turley?" Keith felt relieved.

"Ur—no—I am not staying with them. I am with some other friends." Her color was coming and going.

"What is their name?"

"Their name? Oh—uh—I don't know their names."

"Don't know their names!"

"No. You see it's a sort of private boarding-house, and they took me in."

"Oh, I thought you said they were friends," said Keith.

"Why, yes, they are, but—I have forgotten their names. Don't you understand?"

Keith did not understand.

"I only came a few days ago, and I am going right away."

Keith passed on. Euphronia had clearly not changed her nature. Insensibly, Keith thought of Ferdy Wickersham. Old Rawson's conversation months before recurred to him. He knew that the girl was vain and light-headed. He also knew Wickersham.

He mentioned to Mr. Turley having seen the girl in town, and the old fellow went immediately and took her out of the little boarding-house where she had put up, and brought her to his home.

Keith was not long in doubt as to the connection between her presence and Wickersham's.

Several times he had occasion to call at Mr. Turley's. On each occasion he found Wickersham there, and it was very apparent that he was not an unwelcome visitor.

It was evident to Keith that Wickersham was trying to make an impression on the young girl.

That evening so long ago when he had come on her and

Wickersham in the old squire's orchard came back to him, and the stalwart old countryman, with his plain ways, his stout pride, his straight ideas, stood before him. He knew his pride in the girl; how close she was to his heart; and what a deadly blow it would be to him should anything befall her. He knew, moreover, how fiercely he would avenge any injury to her.

He determined to give Wickersham a hint of the danger he was running, if, as he believed, he was simply amusing himself with the girl. He and Wickersham still kept up relations ostensibly friendly. Wickersham had told him he was going back to New York on a certain day; but three days later, as Keith was returning late from his mines, he came on Wickersham and Phrony in a byway outside of the town. His arm was about her. They were so closely engaged that they did not notice him until he was on them. Phrony appeared much excited. "Well, I will not go otherwise," Keith heard her say. She turned hastily away as Keith came up, and her face was scarlet with confusion, and even Wickersham looked disconcerted.

That night Keith waited for Wickersham at the hotel till a late hour, and when at length Wickersham came in he met him.

"I thought you were going back to New York?" he said.

"I find it pleasanter here," said the young man, with a significant look at him.

"You appear to find it pleasant."

"I always make it pleasant for myself wherever I go, my boy. You are a Stoic; I prefer the Epicurean philosophy."

"Yes? And how about others?"

"Oh, I make it pleasant for them too. Didn't it look so to-day?" The glance he gave him authorized Keith to go on.

"Did it ever occur to you that you might make it too pleasant for them—for a time?"

"Ah! I have thought of that. But that's their lookout."

"Wickersham," said Keith, calmly, "that's a very young

girl and a very ignorant girl, and, so far as I know, a very innocent one."

"Doubtless you know!" said the other, insolently.

"Yes, I believe she is. Moreover, she comes of very good and respectable people. Her grandfather—"

"My dear boy, I don't care anything about the grandfather! It is only the granddaughter I am interesting myself in. She is the only pretty girl within a hundred miles of here, unless you except your old friend of the dance-hall, and I always interest myself in the prettiest woman about me."

"Do you intend to marry her?"

Wickersham laughed, heartily and spontaneously.

"Oh, come now, Keith. Are you going to marry the dance-hall keeper, simply because she has white teeth?"

Keith frowned a little.

"Never mind about me. Do you propose to marry her? She, at least, does not keep a dance-hall."

"No; I shall leave that for you." His face and tone were insolent, and Keith gripped his chair. He felt himself flush. Then his blood surged back; but he controlled himself and put by the insolence for the moment.

"Leave me out of the matter. Do you know what you are doing?" His voice was a little unsteady.

"I know at least what you are doing: interfering in my business. I know how to take care of myself, and I don't need your assistance."

"I was not thinking of you, but of her—"

"That's the difference between us. I was," said Ferdy, coolly. He rolled a cigarette.

"Well, you will have need to think of yourself if you wrong that girl," said Keith. "For I tell you now that if anything were to happen to her, your life would not be worth a button in these mountains."

"There are other places besides the mountains," observed Wickersham. But Keith noticed that he had paled a little and his voice had lost some of its assurance.

"I don't believe the world would be big enough to hide you. I know two men who would kill you on sight."

"Who is the other one?" asked Wickersham.

"I am not counting myself—yet," said Keith, quietly. "It would not be necessary. The old squire and Dave Dennison would take my life if I interfered with their rights."

"You are prudent," said Ferdy.

"I am forbearing," said Keith.

Wickersham's tone was as insolent as ever, but as he leaned over and reached for a match, Keith observed that his hand shook slightly. And the eyes that were levelled at Keith through the smoke of his cigarette were unsteady.

Next morning Ferdy Wickersham had a long interview with Plume, and that night Mr. Plume had a conference in his private office with a man—a secret conference, to judge from the care with which doors were locked, blinds pulled down, and voices kept lowered. He was a stout, youngish fellow, with a low forehead, lowering eyes, and a sodden face. He might once have been good-looking, but drink was written on Mr. William Bluffy now in ineffaceable characters. Plume alternately cajoled him and hectored him, trying to get his consent to some act which he was unwilling to perform.

"I don't see the slightest danger in it," insisted Plume, "and you did not use to be afraid. Your nerves must be getting loose."

The other man's eyes rested on him with something like contempt.

"My nerves 're all right. I ain't skeered ; but I don't want to mix up in your —— business. If a man wants trouble with me, he can get it and he knows how to do it. I don't like yer man Wickersham—not a little bit. But I don't want to do it that way. I'd like to meet him fair and full on the street and settle which was the best man."

Plume began again. "You can't do that way here now. That's broke up. But the way I tell you is the real way."

He pictured Wickersham's wealth, his hardness toward his employés, his being a Yankee, his boast that he would injure Keith and shut up his mine.

"What've you got against him?" demanded Mr. Bluffy. "I thought you and him was thick as thieves?"

"It's a public benefit I'm after," declared Plume, unblushingly. "I am for New Leeds first, last, and all the time."

"You must think you are New Leeds," observed Bluffy.

Plume laughed.

"I've got nothing against him particularly, though he's injured me deeply. Hasn't he thrown all the men out of work!" He pushed the bottle over toward the other, and he poured out another drink and tossed it off. "You needn't be so easy about him. He's been mean enough to you. Wasn't it him that gave the description of you that night when you stopped the stage?"

Bill Bluffy's face changed, and there was a flash in his eye. "Who says I done it?"

Plume laughed. "I don't say you did it. You needn't get mad with me. He says you did it. Keith said he didn't know what sort of man it was. Wickersham described you so that everybody knew you. I reckon if Keith had back-stood him you'd have had a harder time than you did."

The cloud had gathered deeper on Bluffy's brow. He took another drink.

"—— him! I'll blow up his —— mine and him, too!" he growled. "How did you say 'twas to be done?"

Plume glanced around at the closed windows and lowered his voice as he made certain explanations.

"I'll furnish the dynamite."

"All right. Give me the money."

But Plume demurred.

"Not till it's done. I haven't any doubt about your doing it," he explained quickly, seeing a black look in Bluffy's eyes. "But you know yourself you're liable to get full, and you mayn't do it as well as you otherwise would."

"Oh, if I say I'll do it, I'll do it."

"You needn't be afraid of not getting your money."

"I ain't afraid," said Bluffy, with an oath. "If I don't get it I'll get blood." His eyes as they rested on Plume had a sudden gleam in them.

When Wickersham and Plume met that night the latter gave an account of his negotiation. "It's all fixed," he said, "but it costs more than I expected—a lot more," he said slowly, gauging Wickersham's views by his face.

"How much more? I told you my limit."

"We had to do it," said Mr. Plume, without stating the price.

Wickersham swore.

"He won't do it till he gets the cash," pursued Plume. "But I'll be responsible for him," he added quickly, noting the change in Wickersham's expression.

Again Wickersham swore; and Plume changed the subject.

"How'd you come out?" he asked.

"When—what do you mean?"

Plume jerked his thumb over his shoulder. "With the lady?"

Wickersham sniffed. "All right." He drifted for a moment into reflection. "The little fool's got conscientious doubts," he said presently, with a half-smile. "Won't go unless—." His eyes rested on Plume's with a gauging expression in them.

"Well, why not? That's natural enough. She's been brought up right. They're proud as anybody. Her grandfather—"

"You're a fool!" said Wickersham, briefly.

"You can get some one to go through a ceremony for you that would satisfy her and wouldn't peach afterwards—"

"What a damned scoundrel you are, Plume!" said Mr. Wickersham, coldly.

Plume's expression was between a smile and a scowl, but the smile was less pleasant than the frown.

"Get her to go to New York— When you've got her there you've got her. She can't come back. Or I could perform it myself? I've been a preacher—am one now," said Plume, without noticing the interruption further than by a cold gleam in his eyes.

Wickersham laughed derisively.

"Oh, no, not that. I may be given to my own diversions somewhat recklessly, but I'm not so bad as to let you touch any one I—I take an interest in."

"As you like," said Plume, curtly. "I just thought it might be a convenience to you. I'd help you out. I don't see 't you need be so —— squeamish. What you're doing ain't so pure an' lofty 't you can set up for Marcus Aurelius and St. Anthony at once."

"At least, it's better than it would be if I let you take a hand in it," sneered Wickersham.

The following afternoon Wickersham left New Leeds somewhat ostentatiously. A few strikers standing sullenly about the station jeered as he passed in. But he took no notice of them. He passed on to his train.

A few nights later a tremendous explosion shook the town, rattling the windows, awakening people from their beds, and calling the timid and the curious into the streets.

It was known next morning that some one had blown up the Great Gun Mine, opened at such immense cost. The dam that kept out the water was blown up ; the machinery had been wrecked, and the mine was completely destroyed.

The *Clarion* denounced it as the deed of the strikers. The strikers held a meeting and denounced the charge as a foul slander ; but the *Clarion* continued to denounce them as *hostes humani generis*.

It was, however, rumored around that it was not the strikers at all. One rumor even declared that it was done by the connivance of the company. It was said that Bill Bluffy had boasted of it in his cups. But when Mr. Bluffy was asked about it he denied the story in toto. He wasn't such a —— fool as to do such a thing as that, he said. For the rest, he cursed Mr. Plume with bell, book, and candle.

A rumor came to Keith one morning a few days later that Phrony Tripper had disappeared.

She had left New Leeds more than a week before, as was supposed by her relatives, the Turleys, to pay a visit to friends in the adjoining State before returning home. To others she had said that she was going to the North for a visit, whilst yet others affirmed that she had given another destination. However this might be, she had left not long after Wickersham had taken his departure, and her leaving was soon coupled with his name. One man even declared that he had seen the two together in New York.

Another name was connected with the girl's disappearance, though in a different way. Terpsichore suggested that Mr. Plume had had something to do with it, and that he could give information on the subject if he would. Mr. Plume had been away from New Leeds for several days about the time of Phrony's departure.

"He did that Wickersham's dirty work for him ; that is, what he didn't do for himself," declared the young woman.

Plume's statement was that he had been off on private business and had met with an accident. The nature of this "accident" was evident in his appearance.

Keith was hardly surprised when, a day or two after the rumor of the girl's disappearance reached him, a heavy step thumping outside his office door announced the arrival of Squire Rawson. When the old man opened the door, Keith was shocked to see the change in him. He was haggard and worn, but there was that in his face which made Keith feel that whoever might be concerned in his granddaughter's disappearance had reason to beware of meeting him.

"You have heard the news?" he said, as he sank into the chair which Keith offered him.

Keith said that he had heard it, and regretted it more than he could express. He had only waited, hoping that it might prove untrue, to write to him.

"Yes, she has gone," added the old man, moodily. "She's gone off and married without sayin' a word to me or any-body. I didn't think she'd 'a' done it."

Keith gasped with astonishment. A load appeared to be lifted from him. After all, she was married. The next moment this hope was dashed by the squire.

"I always thought," said the old man, "that that young fellow was hankerin' around her a good deal. I never liked him, because I didn't trust him. And I wouldn't 'a' liked him anyway," he added frankly; "and I certainly don't like him now. But—." He drifted off into reflection for a moment and then came back again—"Wo-men-folks are curious creatures. Phrony's mother she appeared to like him, and I suppose we will have to make up with him. So I hev come up here to see if I can git his address."

Keith's heart sank within him. He knew Ferdy Wick-ersham too well not to know on what a broken reed the old man leaned.

"Some folks was a-hintin'," pursued the old fellow, speak-ing slowly, "as, maybe, that young man hadn't married her; but I knowed better then that, because, even if Phrony warn't a good girl,—which she is, though she ain't got much sense,—he knowed *me*. They ain't none of 'em ever inti-mated that to *me*," he added explanatorily.

Keith was glad that he had not intimated it. As he looked at the squire, he knew how dangerous it would be. His face was settled into a grimness which showed how perilous it would be for the man who had deceived Phrony, if, as Keith feared, his apprehensions were well founded.

But at that moment both Phrony and Wickersham were far beyond Squire Rawson's reach.

The evening after Phrony Tripper left New Leeds, a young woman somewhat closely veiled descended from the train in Jersey City. Here she was joined on the platform a moment later by a tall man who had boarded the train at Washington, and who, but for his spruced appearance,

287

might have been taken for Mr. J. Quincy Plume. The young woman having intrusted herself to his guidance, he conducted her across the ferry, and on the other side they were met by a gentleman, who wore the collar of his overcoat turned up. After a meeting more or less formal on one side and cordial on the other, the gentleman gave a brief direction to Mr. Plume, and, with the lady, entered a carriage which was waiting and drove off, Mr. Plume following a moment later in another vehicle.

"Know who that is?" asked one of the ferry officials of another. "That's F. C. Wickersham, who has made such a pile of money. They say he owns a whole State down South."

"Who is the lady?"

The other laughed. "Don't ask me; you can't keep up with him. They say they can't resist him."

An hour or two later, Mr. Plume, who had been waiting for some time in the café of a small hotel not very far up-town, was joined by Mr. Wickersham, whose countenance showed both irritation and disquietude. Plume, who had been consoling himself with the companionship of a decanter of rye whiskey, was in a more jovial mood, which further irritated the other.

"You say she has balked? Jove! She has got more in her than I thought!"

"She is a fool!" said Wickersham.

Plume shut one eye. "Don't know about that. Madame de Maintenon said : 'There is nothing so clever as a good woman.' Well, what are you going to do?"

"I don't know."

"Take a drink," said Mr. Plume, to whom this was a frequent solvent of a difficulty.

Wickersham followed his advice, but remained silent.

In fact, Mr. Wickersham, after having laid most careful plans and reached the point for which he had striven, found himself, at the very moment of victory, in danger of being defeated. He had induced Phrony Tripper to come to New York.   She was desperately in love with him, and would have gone to the ends of the earth for him.   But he had promised to marry her; it was to marry him that she had come.   As strong as was her passion for him, and as vain and foolish as she was, she had one principle which was stronger than any other feeling—a sense of modesty. This had been instilled in her from infancy.   Among her people a woman's honor was ranked higher than any other feminine virtue.   Her love for Wickersham but strengthened her resolution, for she believed that, unless he married her, his life would not be safe from her relatives. Now, after two hours, in which he had used every persuasion, Wickersham, to his unbounded astonishment, found himself facing defeat.   He had not given her credit for so much resolution.   Her answer to all his efforts to overcome her determination was that, unless he married her immediately, she would return home; she would not remain in the hotel a single night.   "I know they will take me back," she said, weeping.

This was the subject of his conversation, now, with his agent, and he was making up his mind what to do, aided by more or less frequent applications to the decanter which stood between them.

"What she says is true," declared Plume, his courage stimulated by his liberal potations.   "You won't be able to go back down there any more.   There are a half-dozen men I know, would consider it their duty to blow your brains out."

Wickersham filled his glass and tossed off a drink.   "I am not going down there any more, anyhow."

"I suppose not.   But I don't believe you would be safe even up here.   There is that devil, Dennison: he hates you worse than poison."

"Oh—up here—they aren't going to trouble me up here."

"I don't know—if he ever got a show at you—   Why don't you let me perform the ceremony?" he began persuasively. "She knows I've been a preacher. That will satisfy her scruples, and then, if you ever had to make it known—? But no one would know then."

Wickersham declined this with a show of virtue. He did not mention that he had suggested this to the girl but she had positively refused it. She would be married by a regular preacher or she would go home.

"There must be some one in this big town," suggested Plume, "who will do such a job privately and keep it quiet? Where is that preacher you were talking about once that took flyers with you on the quiet? You can seal his mouth. And if the worst comes to the worst, there is Montana; you can always get out of it in six weeks with an order of publication. *I* did it," said Mr. Plume, quietly, "and never had any trouble about it."

"You did! Well, that's one part of your rascality I didn't know about."

"I guess there are a good many of us have little bits of history that we don't talk about much," observed Mr. Plume, calmly. "I wouldn't have told you now, but I wanted to help you out of the fix that—"

"That you have helped me get into," said Wickersham, with a sneer.

"There is no trouble about it," Plume went on. "You don't want to marry anybody else—now, and meantime it will give you the chance you want of controlling old Rawson's interest down there. The old fellow can't live long, and Phrony is his only heir. You will have it all your own way. You can keep it quiet if you wish, and if you don't, you can acknowledge it and bounce your friend Keith. If I had your hand I bet I'd know how to play it."

"Well, by ——! I wish you had it," said Wickersham, angrily.

Wickersham had been thinking hard during Plume's statement of the case, and what with his argument and an occasional application to the decanter of whiskey, he was beginning to yield. Just then a sealed note was handed him by a waiter. He tore it open and read:

"I am going home; my heart is broken. Good-by.
"PHRONY."

With an oath under his breath, he wrote in pencil on a card: "Wait; I will be with you directly."

"Take that to the lady," he said. Scribbling a few lines more on another card, he gave Plume some hasty directions and left him.

When, five minutes afterwards, Mr. Plume finished the decanter, and left the hotel, his face had a crafty look on it. "This should be worth a good deal to you, J. Quincy," he said.

An hour later the Rev. Mr. Rimmon performed in his private office a little ceremony, at which, besides himself, were present only the bride and groom and a witness who had come to him a half-hour before with a scribbled line in pencil requesting his services. If Mr. Rimmon was startled when he first read the request, the surprise had passed away. The groom, it is true, was, when he appeared, decidedly under the influence of liquor, and his insistence that the ceremony was to be kept entirely secret had somewhat disturbed Mr. Rimmon for a moment. But he remembered Mr. Plume's assurance that the bride was a great heiress in the South, and knowing that Ferdy Wickersham was a man who rarely lost his head,—a circumstance which the latter testified by handing him a roll of greenbacks amounting to exactly one hundred dollars,—and the bride being very pretty and shy, and manifestly most eager to be married, he gave his word to keep the matter a secret until they should authorize him to divulge it.

When the ceremony was over, the bride requested Mr. Rimmon to give her her "marriage lines." This Mr. Rimmon promised to do; but as he would have to fill out the blanks, which would take a little time, the bride and groom, having signed the paper, took their departure without waiting for the certificate, leaving Mr. Plume to bring it.

A day or two later a steamship of one of the less popular companies sailing to a Continental port had among its passengers a gentleman and a lady who, having secured their accommodations at the last moment, did not appear on the passenger list.

It happened that they were unknown to any of the other passengers, and as they were very exclusive, they made no acquaintances during the voyage. If Mrs. Wagram, the name by which the lady was known on board, had one regret, it was that Mr. Plume had failed to send her her marriage certificate, as he had promised to do. Her husband, however, made so light of it that it reassured her, and she was too much taken up with her wedding-ring and new diamonds to think that anything else was necessary.

CHAPTER XX

MRS. LANCASTER'S WIDOWHOOD

THE first two years of her widowhood Alice Lancaster spent in retirement. Even the busy tongue of Mrs. Nailor could find little to criticise in the young widow. To be sure, that accomplished critic made the most of this little, and disseminated her opinion that Alice's grief for Mr. Lancaster could only be remorse for her indifference to him during his life. Every one knew, she said, how she had neglected him.

The idea that Alice Lancaster was troubled with regrets was not as unfounded as the rest of Mrs. Nailor's ill-natured charge. She was attached to her husband, and had always meant to be a good wife to him.

She was as good a wife as her mother and her friends would permit her to be. Gossip had not spared some of her best friends. Even as proud a woman as young Mrs. Wentworth had not escaped. But Gossip had never yet touched the name of Mrs. Lancaster, and Alice did not mean that it should. It was not unnatural that she should have accepted the liberty which her husband gave her and have gone out more and more, even though he could accompany her less and less.

No maelstrom is more unrelenting in its grasp than is that of Society. Only those who sink, or are cast aside by its seething waves, escape. And before she knew it, Alice Lancaster had found herself drawn into the whirlpool.

An attractive proposal had been made to her to go abroad and join some friends of hers for a London season a year or two before. Grinnell Rhodes had married Miss Creamer, who was fond of European society, and they had taken a house in London for the season, which promised to be very gay, and had suggested to Mrs. Lancaster to visit them. Mr. Lancaster had found himself unable to go. A good many matters of importance had been undertaken by him, and he must see them through, he said. Moreover, he had not been very well of late, and he had felt that he should be rather a drag amid the gayeties of the London season. Alice had offered to give up the trip, but he would not hear of it. She must go, he said, and he knew who would be the most charming woman in London. So, having extracted from him the promise that, when his business matters were all arranged, he would join her for a little run on the Continent, she had set off for Paris, where "awful beauty puts on all its arms," to make her preparations for the campaign.

Mr. Lancaster had not told her of an interview which her mother had had with him, in which she had pointed out that Alice's health was suffering from her want of gayety and amusement. He was not one to talk of himself.

Alice Lancaster was still in Paris when a cable message announced to her Mr. Lancaster's death. It was only after his death that she awoke to the unselfishness of his life and to the completeness of his devotion to her.

His will, after making provision for certain charities with which he had been associated in his lifetime, left all his great fortune to her; and there was, besides, a sealed letter left for her in which he poured out his heart to her. From it she learned that he had suffered greatly and had known that he was liable to die at any time. He, however, would not send for her to come home, for fear of spoiling her holiday.

"I will not say I have not been lonely," he wrote. "For God knows how lonely I have been since you left. The light went with you and will return only when you come home. Sometimes I have felt that I could not endure it

and must send for you or go to you ; but the first would
have been selfishness and the latter a breach of duty. The
times have been such that I have not felt it right to leave,
as so many interests have been intrusted to me. . . . It is
possible that I may never see your face again. I have
made a will which I hope will please you. It will, at least,
show you that I trust you entirely. I make no restrictions ;
for I wish you greater happiness than I fear I have been
able to bring you. . . . In business affairs I suggest that
you consult with Norman Wentworth, who is a man of high
integrity and of a conservative mind. Should you wish
advice as to good charities, I can think of no better adviser
than Dr. Templeton. He has long been my friend."

In the first excess of her grief and remorse, Alice Lancaster came home and threw herself heart and soul into
charitable work. As Mr. Lancaster had suggested, she
consulted Dr. Templeton, the old rector of a small and
unfashionable church on a side street. Under his guidance she found a world as new and as diverse from that
in which she had always lived as another planet would
have been.

She found in some places a life where vice was esteemed
more honorable than virtue, because it brought more bread.
She found things of which she had never dreamed : things
which appeared incredible after she had seen them.
These things she found within a half-hour's walk of her
sumptuous home ; within a few blocks of the avenue and
streets where Wealth and Plenty took their gay pleasure and where riches poured forth in a riot of splendid
extravagance.

She would have turned back, but for the old clergyman's
inspiring courage ; she would have poured out her wealth
indiscriminately, but for his wisdom—but for his wisdom
and Norman Wentworth's.

"No, my dear," said the old man ; "to give lavishly without discrimination is to put a premium on beggary and
to subject yourself to imposture."

This Norman indorsed, and under their direction she soon found ways to give of her great means toward charities which were far-reaching and enduring. She learned also what happiness comes from knowledge of others and knowledge of how to help them.

It was surprising to her friends what a change came over the young woman. Her point of view, her manner, her face, her voice changed. Her expression, which had once been so proud as to mar somewhat her beauty, softened; her manner increased in cordiality and kindness; her voice acquired a new and sincerer tone.

Even Mrs. Nailor observed that the enforced retirement appeared to have chastened the young widow, though she would not admit that it could be for anything than effect.

"Black always was the most bewilderingly becoming thing to her that I ever saw. Don't you remember those effects she used to produce with black and just a dash of red? Well, she wears black so deep you might think it was poor Mr. Lancaster's pall; but I have observed that whenever I have seen her there is always something red very close at hand. She either sits in a red chair, or there is a red shawl just at her back, or a great bunch of red roses at her elbow. I am glad that great window has been put up in old Dr. Templeton's church to William Lancaster's memory, or I am afraid it would have been but a small one."

Almost the first sign that the storm, which, as related, had struck New York would reach New Leeds was the shutting down of the Wickersham mines. The *Clarion* stated that the shutting down was temporary and declared that in a very short time, when the men were brought to reason, they would be opened again; also that the Great Gun Mine, which had been flooded, would again be opened.

The mines belonging to Keith's company did not appear for some time to be affected; but the breakers soon began to reach even the point on which Keith had stood so securely. The first "roller" that came to him was when orders arrived to cut down the force, and cut down also the wages of those who were retained. This was done. Letters, growing gradually more and more complaining, came from the general office in New York.

Fortunately for Keith, Norman ran down at this time and looked over the properties again for himself. He did not tell Keith what bitter things were being said and that his visit down there was that he might be able to base his defence of Keith on facts in his own knowledge.

"What has become of Mrs. Lancaster?" asked Keith, casually. "Is she still abroad?"

"No; she came home immediately on hearing the news. You never saw any one so changed. She has gone in for charity."

Keith looked a trifle grim.

"If you thought her pretty as a girl, you ought to see her as a widow. She is ravishing."

"You are enthusiastic. I see that Wickersham has returned?"

Norman's brow clouded.

"He'd better not come back here," said Keith.

It is a trite saying that misfortunes rarely come singly, and it would not be so trite if there were not truth in it. Misfortunes are sometimes like blackbirds : they come in flocks.

Keith was on his way from his office in the town to the mines one afternoon, when, turning the shoulder of the hill that shut the opening of the mine from view, he became aware that something unusual had occurred. A crowd was already assembled about the mouth of the mine, above the tipple, among them many women ; and people were hurrying up from all directions.

"What is it?" he demanded of the first person he came to.

"Water. They have struck a pocket or something, and the drift over toward the Wickersham line is filling up."

"Is everybody out?" Even as he inquired, Keith knew they were not.

"No, sir ; all drowned."

Keith knew this could not be true. He hurried forward and pushed his way into the throng that crowded about the entrance. A gasp of relief went up as he appeared.

"Ah ! Here's the boss." It was the expression of a vague hope that he might be able to do something. They gave way at his voice and stood back, many eyes turning on him in helpless appeal. Women, with blankets already in hand, were weeping aloud ; children hanging to their skirts were whimpering in vague recognition of disaster ; men were growling and swearing deeply.

"Give way. Stand back, every one." The calm voice and tone of command had their effect, and as a path was opened through the crowd, Keith recognized a number of the men who had been in and had just come out. They were all talking to groups about them. One of them gave him the first intelligent account of the trouble. They were working near the entrance when they heard the cries of men farther in, and the first thing they knew there was a rush of water which poured down on them, sweeping everything before it.

"It must have been a river," said one, in answer to a question from Keith. "It was rising a foot a minute. The lights were all put out, and we just managed to get out in time."

According to their estimates, there were about forty men and boys still in the mine, most of them in the gallery off from the main drift. Keith was running over in his mind the levels. His face was a study, and the crowd about him watched him closely, as if to catch any ray of hope that he might hold out. As he reflected, his face grew whiter. Down the slant from the mine came the roar of the water. It was a desperate chance.

Half turning, he glanced at the white, stricken faces about him.

"It is barely possible some of the men may still be alive There are two elevations. I am going down to see."

At the words, the sound through the crowd hushed suddenly.

"Na, th' ben't one alive," said an old miner, contentiously. The murmur began again.

"I am going down to see," said Keith. "If one or two men will come with me, it will increase the chances of getting to them. If not, I am going alone. But I don't want any one who has a family."

A dead silence fell, then three or four young fellows began to push their way through the crowd, amid expostulations of some of the women and the urging of others.

Some of the women seized them and held on to them.

"There are one or two places where men may have been able to keep their heads above water if it has not filled the drift, and that is what I am going to see," said Keith, preparing to descend.

"My brother's down there and I'll go," said a young light-haired fellow with a pale face. He belonged to the night shift.

"I ain't got any family," said a small, grizzled man. He had a thin black band on the sleeve of his rusty, brown coat.

Several others now came forward, amid mingled expostulations and encouragement; but Keith took the first two, and they prepared to enter. The younger man took off his silver watch, with directions to a friend to send it to his sister if he did not come back. The older man said a few words to a bystander. They were about a woman's grave on the hillside. Keith took off his watch and gave it to one of the men, with a few words scribbled on a leaf from a memorandum-book, and the next moment the three volunteers, amid a deathly silence, entered the mine.

Long before they reached the end of the ascent to the shaft they could hear the water gurgling and lapping against the sides as it whirled through the gallery below them. As they reached the water, Keith let himself down into it. The water took him to about his waist and was rising.

"It has not filled the drift yet," he said, and started ahead. He gave a halloo; but there was no sound in answer, only the reverberation of his voice. The other men called to him to wait and talk it over. The strangeness of the situation appalled them. It might well have awed a strong man; but Keith waded on. The older man plunged after him, the younger clinging to the cage for a second in a panic. The lights were out in a moment. Wading and plunging forward through the water, which rose in places to his neck, and feeling his way by the sides of the drift, Keith waded forward through the pitch-darkness. He stopped at times to halloo; but there was no reply, only the strange hollow sound of his own voice as it was thrown back on him, or died almost before leaving his throat. He had almost made up his mind that further attempt was useless and that he might as well turn back, when he thought he heard a faint sound ahead. With another shout he plunged forward again, and the next time he called he heard a cry of joy, and he pushed ahead again, shouting to them to come to him.

Keith found most of the men huddled together on the first level, in a state of panic. Some of them were whimpering and some were praying fervently, whilst a few were silent, in a sort of dazed bewilderment. All who were working in that part of the mine were there, they said, except three men, Bill Bluffy and a man named Hennson and his boy, who had been cut off in the far end of the gallery and who must have been drowned immediately, they told Keith.

"They may not be," said Keith. "There is one point as high as this. I shall go on and see."

The men endeavored to dissuade him. It was "a useless risk of life," they assured him; "the others must have been swept away immediately. The water had come so sudden. Besides, the water was rising, and it might even now be too late to get out." But Keith was firm, and ordering them back in charge of the two men who had come in with him, he pushed on alone. He knew that the water was still rising, though, he hoped, slowly. He had no voice to shout now, but he prayed with all his might, and that soothed and helped him. Presently the water was a little shallower. It did not come so high up on him. He knew from this that he must be reaching the upper level. Now and then he spoke Bluffy's and Hennson's names, lest in the darkness he should pass them.

Presently, as he stopped for a second to take breath, he thought he heard another sound besides the gurgling of the water as it swirled about the timbers. He listened intently.

It was the boy's voice. "Hold me tight, father. Don't leave me."

Then he heard another voice urging him to go. "You can't do any good staying; try it." But Hennson was refusing.

"Hold on. I won't leave you."

"Hennson! Bluffy!" shouted Keith, or tried to shout, for his voice went nowhere; but his heart was bounding now, and he plunged on. Presently he was near enough to catch their words. The father was praying, and the boy was following him.

"'Thy will be done on earth, as it is in heaven,'" Keith heard him say.

"Hennson!" he cried again.

From the darkness he heard a voice.

"Who is that? Is that any one?"

"It is I,—Mr. Keith,—Hennson. Come quick, all of you; you can get out. Cheer up."

A cry of joy went up.

"I can't leave my boy," called the man.

"Bring him on your back," said Keith. "Come on, Bluffy."

"I can't," said Bluffy. "I'm hurt. My leg is broke."

"God have mercy!" cried Keith, and waded on.

After a moment more he was up with the man, feeling for him in the darkness, and asking how he was hurt.

They told him that the rush of the water had thrown him against a timber and hurt his leg and side.

"Take the boy," said Bluffy, "and go on; leave me here."

The boy began to cry.

"No," said Keith; "I will take you, too: Hennson can take the boy. Can you walk at all?"

"I don't think so."

Keith made Hennson take the boy and hold on to him on one side, and slipping his arm around the injured man, he lifted him and they started back. He had put new courage into them, and the force of the current was in their favor. They passed the first high level, where he had found the others. When they reached a point where the water was too deep for the boy, Keith made the father take him on his shoulder, and they waded on through the blackness. The water was now almost up to his chin, and he grew so tired under his burden that he began to think they should never get out; but he fought against it and kept on, steadying himself against the timbers. He knew that if he went down it was the end. Many thoughts came to him of the past. He banished them and tried to speak words of encouragement, though he could scarcely hear himself.

"Shout," he said hoarsely; and the boy shouted, though it was somewhat feeble.

A moment later, he gave a shout of an entirely different kind.

"There is a light!" he cried.

The sound revived Keith's fainting energies, and he tried to muster his flagging strength. The boy shouted again, and in response there came back, strangely flattened, the shrill cry of a woman. Keith staggered forward with Bluffy, at times holding himself up by the side-timbers. He was conscious of a light and of voices, but was too exhausted to know more. If he could only keep the man and the boy above water until assistance came! He summoned his last atom of strength.

"Hold tight to the timbers, Hennson," he cried; "I am going."

The rest was a confused dream. He was conscious for a moment of the weight being lifted from him, and he was sinking into the water as if into a soft couch. He thought some one clutched him, but he knew nothing more.

Terpsichore was out on the street when the rumor of the accident reached her. Any accident always came home to her, and she was prompt to do what she could to help, in any case. But this was Mr. Keith's mine, and rumor had it that he was among the lost. Terpsichore was not attired for such an emergency; when she went on the streets, she still wore some of her old finery, though it was growing less and less of late. She always acted quickly. Calling to a barkeeper who had come to his front door on hearing the news, to bring her brandy immediately, she dashed into a dry-goods store near by and got an armful of blankets, and when the clerk, a stranger just engaged in the store, made some question about charging them to her, she tore off her jewelled watch and almost flung it at the man.

"Take that, idiot! Men are dying," she said. "I have not time to box your jaws." And snatching up the blankets, she ran out, stopped a passing buggy, and flinging them into it, sprang in herself. With a nod of thanks to the barkeeper, who had brought out several bottles of brandy, she snatched the reins from the half-dazed driver, and heading the horse up the street that led out toward the mine, she lashed him into a gallop. She arrived at the scene of the accident just before the first men rescued reappeared. She learned of Keith's effort to save them. She would have gone into the mine herself had she not been restrained. Just then the men came out.

The shouts and cries of joy that greeted so unexpected a deliverance drowned everything else for a few moments; but as man after man was met and received half dazed into the arms of his family and friends, the name of Keith began to be heard on all sides. One voice, however, was more imperative than the others; one figure pressed to the front—that of the gayly dressed woman who had just been comforting and encouraging the weeping women about the mine entrance.

"Where is Mr. Keith?" she demanded of man after man.

The men explained. "He went on to try and find three more men who are down there—Bluffy and Hennson and his boy."

"Who went with him?"

"No one. He went alone."

"And you men let him go?"

"We could not help it. He insisted. We tried to make him come with us."

"You cowards!" she cried, tearing off her wrap. "Of course, he insisted, for he is a *man*. Had one woman been down there, she would not have let him go alone." She sprang over the fencing rope as lightly as a deer, and started toward the entrance. A cry broke from the crowd.

"She's going! Stop her! She's crazy! Catch her!"

Several men sprang over the rope and started after her. Hearing them, Terpsichore turned. With out-stretched arms spread far apart and blazing eyes, she faced them.

"If any man tries to stop me, I will kill him on the spot, as God lives!" she cried, snatching up a piece of iron bar that lay near by. "I am going to find that man, dead or alive. If there is one of you man enough to come with me, come on. If not, I will go alone."

"I will go with you!" A tall, sallow-faced man who had just come up pushed through the throng and overtook her. "You stay here; I will go." It was Tib Drummond, the preacher. He was still panting. The girl hardly noticed him. She waved him aside and dashed on.

A dozen men offered to go if she would come back.

"No; I shall go with you," she said; and knowing that every moment was precious, and thinking that the only way to pacify her was to make the attempt, the men yielded, and a number of them entered the mine with her, the lank preacher among them.

They had just reached the bottom when the faint outline of something black was seen in the glimmer that their lights threw in the distance. Terpy, with a cry, dashed forward, and was just in time to catch Keith as he sank beneath the black water.

When the rescuing party with their burdens reached the surface once more, the scene was one to revive even a flagging heart; but Keith and Bluffy were both too far gone to know anything of it.

The crowd, which up to this time had been buzzing with the excitement of the reaction following the first rescue, suddenly hushed down to an awed silence as Keith and Bluffy were brought out and were laid limp and unconscious on a blanket, which Terpsichore had snatched from a man in the front of the others. Many women pressed forward to offer assistance, but the girl waved them back.

"A doctor!" she cried, and reaching for a brandy-bottle, she pressed it first to Keith's lips. Turning to Drummond, the preacher, who stood gaunt and dripping above her, she cried fiercely : " Pray, man ; if you ever prayed, pray now. Pray, and if you save 'em, I'll leave town. I swear before God I will. Tell Him so."

But the preacher needed no urging. Falling on his knees, he prayed as possibly he had never prayed before. In a few moments Keith began to come to. But Bluffy was still unconscious, and a half-hour later the Doctor pronounced him past hope.

It was some time before Keith was able to rise from his bed, and during this period a number of events had taken place affecting him, and, more or less, affecting New Leeds. Among these was the sale of Mr. Plume's paper to a new rival which had recently been started in the place, and the departure of Mr. Plume (to give his own account of the matter) "to take a responsible position upon a great metropolitan journal." He was not a man, he said, "to waste his divine talents in the attempt to carry on his shoulders the blasted fortunes of a 'bursted boom,' when the world was pining for the benefit of his ripe experience." Another account of the same matter was that rumor had begun to connect Mr. Plume's name with the destruction of the Wickersham mine and the consequent disaster in the Rawson mine. His paper, with brazen effrontery, had declared that the accident in the latter was due to the negligence of the management. This was too much for the people of New Leeds in their excited condition. Bluffy was dead ; but Hennson, the man whom Keith had rescued, had stated that they had cut through into a shaft when the water broke in on them, and an investigation having been begun, not only of this matter, but of the previous explosion in the Wickersham mine, Mr. Plume had sold out his paper hastily and shaken the dust of New Leeds from his feet.

Keith knew nothing of this until it was all over. He was very ill for a time, and but for the ministrations of Dr. Balsam, who came up from Ridgely to look after him, and the care of a devoted nurse in the person of Terpsichore, this history might have ended then. Terpsichore had, immediately after Keith's accident, closed her establishment and devoted herself to his care. There were many other offers of similar service, for New Leeds was now a considerable town, and Keith might have had a fair proportion of the gentler sex to minister to him; but Dr. Balsam, to whom Terpsichore had telegraphed immediately after Keith's rescue, had, after his first interview with her in the sick-room, decided in favor of the young woman.

"She has the true instinct," said the Doctor to himself. "She knows when to let well enough alone, and holds her tongue."

Thus, when Keith was able to take notice again, he found himself in good hands.

A few days after he was able to get up, Keith received a telegram summoning him to New York to meet the officers of the company. As weak as he was, he determined to go, and, against the protestations of doctor and nurse, he began to make his preparations.

Just before Keith left, a visitor was announced, or rather announced himself, for Squire Rawson followed hard upon his knock at the door. His heavy boots, he declared, "were enough to let anybody know he was around, and give 'em time to stop anything they was ashamed o' doin'."

The squire had come over, as he said, "to hear about things." It was the first time he had seen Keith since the accident, though, after he had heard of it, he had written and invited Keith to come "and rest up a bit at his house."

When the old man learned of the summons that had come to Keith, he relit his pipe and puffed a moment in silence.

"Reckon they'll want to know why they ain't been a realizin' of their dreams?" he said, with a twinkle in his half-shut eyes. "Ever notice, when a man is huntin', if he gits what he aims at, it's himself; but if he misses, it's the blamed old gun?"

Keith smiled. He had observed that phenomenon.

"Well, I suspicionate they'll be findin' fault with their gun. I have been a-watchin' o' the signs o' the times. If they do, don't you say nothin' to them about it; but I'm ready to take back my part of the property, and I've got a leetle money I might even increase my herd with."

The sum he mentioned made Keith open his eyes.

"When hard times comes," continued the old man, after enjoying Keith's surprise, "I had rather have my money in land than in one of these here banks. I has seen wild-cat money and Confederate money, and land 's land. I don't know that it is much of a compliment to say that I has more confidence in you than I has in these here men what has come down from nobody-knows-where to open a bank on nobody-knows-what."

Keith expressed his appreciation of the compliment, but thought that they must have something to bank on.

"Oh, they've got something," admitted the capitalist. "But you know what it is. They bank on brass and credulity. That's what I calls it."

The old man's face clouded. "I had been puttin' that by for Phrony," he said. "But she didn't want it. *My* money warn't good enough for her. Some day she'll know better."

Keith waited for his humor to pass.

"I won't ever do nothin' for her; but if ever you see her, I'd like you to help her out if she needs it," he said huskily.

Keith promised faithfully that he would.

That afternoon Terpy knocked at his door, and came in with that mingled shyness and boldness which was characteristic of her.

Keith offered her a chair and began to thank her for having saved his life.

"Well, I am always becoming indebted to you anew for saving my life—"

"I didn't come for that," declared the girl. "I didn't save your life. I just went down to do what I could to help you. You know how that mine got flooded?"

"I do," said Keith.

"They done it to do you," she said; "and they made Bill believe it was to hurt Wickersham. Bill's dead now, an' I don't want you to think he had anything against you." She began to cry.

All this was new to Keith, and he said so.

"Well, you won't say anything about what I said about Bill. J. Quincy made him think 'twas against Wickersham, and he was that drunk he didn't know what a fool they was makin' of him.—You are going away?" she said suddenly.

"Oh, only for a very little while—I am going off about a little business for a short time. I expect to be back very soon."

"Ah! I heard—I am glad to hear that you are coming back." She was manifestly embarrassed, and Keith was wondering more and more what she wanted of him. "I just wanted to say good-by. I am going away." She was fumbling at her wrap. "And to tell you I have changed my business. I'm not goin' to keep a dance-house any longer."

"I am glad of that," said Keith, and then stuck fast again.

"I don't think a girl ought to keep a dance-house or a bank?"

"No; I agree with you. What are you going to do?"

"I don't know; I thought of trying a milliner. I know right smart about hats; but I'd wear all the pretty ones and give all the ugly ones away," she said, with a poor little smile. "And it might interfere with Mrs. Gaskins, and she is a widder. So I thought I'd go away. I thought of being a nurse—I know a little about that. I used to be about the hospital at my old home, and I've had some little experience since." She was evidently seeking his advice.

"You saved my life," said Keith. "Dr. Balsam says you are a born nurse."

She put this by without comment, and Keith went on.

"Where was your home?"

"Grofton."

"Grofton? You mean in England? In the West Country?"

She nodded. "Yes. I was the girl the little lady gave the doll to. You were there. Don't you remember? I ran away with it. I have it now—a part of it. They broke it up; but I saved the body."

Keith's eyes opened wide.

"That Lois Huntington gave it to?"

"Yes. I heard you were going to be married?" she said suddenly.

"I! Married! No! No such good luck for me." His laugh had an unexpected tone of bitterness in it. She gave him a searching glance in the dusk, and presently began again haltingly.

"I want you to know I am never going back to that any more."

"I am glad to hear it."

"You were the first to set me to thinkin' about it."

"I!"

"Yes; I want to live straight, and I'm goin' to."

"I am sure you are, and I cannot tell you how glad I am," he said cordially.

"Yes, thankee." She was looking down, picking shyly at the fringe on her wrap. "And I want you to know 'twas you done it. I have had a hard life—you don't know how hard—ever since I was a little bit of a gal—till I run away from home. And then 'twas harder. And they all treated me 's if I was just a—a dog, and the worst kind of a dog. So I lived like a dog. I learned how to bite, and then they treated me some better, because they found I would bite if they fooled with me. And then I learned what fools and cowards men were, and I used 'em. I used to love to play 'em, and I done it. I used to amuse 'em for money and hold 'em off. But I knew sometime I'd die like a dog as I lived like one—and then you came—." She paused and looked away out of the window, and after a gulp went on again: "They preached at me for dancin'. But I don't think there's any harm dancin'. And I love it better'n anything else in the worl'."

"I do not, either," said Keith.

"You was the only one as treated me as if I was—some'n' I warn't. I fought against you and tried to drive you out, but you stuck, and I knew then I was beat. I didn't know 'twas you when I—made such a fool of myself that time—."

Keith laughed.

"Well, I certainly did not know it was you."

"No—I wanted you to know that," she went on gravely, "because—because, if I had, I wouldn' 'a' done it—for old times' sake." She felt for her handkerchief, and not finding it readily, suddenly caught up the bottom of her skirt and wiped her eyes with it as she might have done when a little girl.

Keith tried to comfort her with words of assurance, the tone of which was at least consoling.

"I always was a fool about crying—an' I was thinkin' about Bill," she said brokenly. "Good-by." She wrung his hand, turned, and walked rapidly out of the room, leaving Keith with a warm feeling about his heart.

CHAPTER XXI

THE DIRECTORS' MEETING

KEITH found, on his arrival in New York to meet his directors, that a great change had taken place in business circles since his visit there when he was getting up his company.

Even Norman, at whose office Keith called immediately on his arrival, appeared more depressed than Keith had ever imagined he could be. He looked actually care-worn.

As they started off to attend the meeting, Norman warned Keith that the meeting might be unpleasant for him, but urged him to keep cool, and not mind too much what might be said to him.

"I told you once, you remember, that men are very unreasonable when they are losing." He smiled gloomily.

Keith told him of old Rawson's offer.

"You may need it," said Norman.

When Keith and Norman arrived at the office of the company, they found the inner office closed. Norman, being a director, entered at once, and finally the door opened and "Mr. Keith" was invited in. As he entered, a director was showing two men out of the room by a side door, and Keith had a glimpse of the back of one of them. The tall, thin figure suggested to him Mr. J. Quincy Plume ; but he was too well dressed to be Mr. Plume, and Keith put the matter from his mind as merely an odd resemblance. The other person he did not see.

Keith's greeting was returned, as it struck him, some

what coldly by most of them. Only two of the directors shook hands with him.

It was a meeting which Keith never forgot. He soon found that he had need of all of his self-control. He was cross-examined by Mr. Kestrel. It was evident that it was believed that he had wasted their money, if he had not done worse. The director sat with a newspaper in his lap, to which, from time to time, he appeared to refer. From the line of the questioning, Keith soon recognized the source of his information.

"You have been misled," Keith said coldly, in reply to a question. "I desire to know the authority for your statement."

"I must decline," was the reply. "I think I may say that it is an authority which is unimpeachable. You observe that it is one who knows what he is speaking of?" He gave a half-glance about him at his colleagues.

"A spy?" demanded Keith, coldly, his eye fixed on the other.

"No, sir. A man of position, a man whose sources of knowledge even you would not question. Why, this has been charged in the public prints without denial!" he added triumphantly.

"It has been charged in one paper," said Keith, "a paper which every one knows is for sale and has been bought—by your rival."

"It is based not only on the statement of the person to whom I have alluded, but is corroborated by others."

"By what others?" inquired Keith.

"By another," corrected Mr. Kestrel.

"That only proves that there are two men who are liars," said Keith, slowly. "I know but two men who I believe would have been guilty of such barefaced and brazen falsehoods. Shall I name them?"

"If you choose."

"They are F. C. Wickersham and a hireling of his, Mr. . Quincy Plume."

There was a stir among the directors. Keith had named both men. It was a fortunate shot.

"By Jove! Brought down a bird with each barrel," said Mr. Yorke, who was one of the directors, to another in an undertone.

Keith proceeded to give the history of the mine and of its rival mine, the Wickersham property.

During the cross-examination Norman sat a silent witness. Beyond a look of satisfaction when Keith made his points clearly or countered on his antagonist with some unanswerable fact, he had taken no part in the colloquy. Up to this time Keith had not referred to him or even looked at him, but he glanced at him now, and the expression on his face decided Keith.

"Mr. Wentworth, there, knows the facts. He knows F. C. Wickersham as well as I do, and he has been on the ground."

There was a look of surprise on the face of nearly every one present. How could he dare to say it!

"Oh, I guess we all know him," said one, to relieve the tension.

Norman bowed his assent.

Mr. Kestrel shifted his position.

"Never mind Mr. Wentworth; it's *your* part in the transaction that we are after," he said insolently.

The blood rushed to Keith's face; but a barely perceptible glance from Norman helped him to hold himself in check. The director glanced down at the newspaper.

"How about that accident in our mine? Some of us have thought that it was carelessness on the part of the local management. It has been charged that proper inspection would have indicated that the flooding of an adjacent mine should have given warning; in fact, had given warning." He half glanced around at his associates, and then fastened his eyes on Keith.

Keith's eyes met his unflinchingly and held them. He drew in his breath with a sudden sound, as a man might who has received a slap full in the face. Beyond this, there was no sound. Keith sat for a moment in silence. The blow had dazed him. In the tumult of his thought, as it returned, it seemed as if the noise of the stricken crowd was once more about him, weeping women and moaning men; and he was descending into the blackness of death. Once more the roar of that rushing water was in his ears; he was once more plunging through the darkness; once more he was being borne down into its depths; again he was struggling, gasping, floundering toward the light; once more he returned to consciousness, to find himself surrounded by eyes full of sympathy—of devotion. The eyes changed suddenly. The present came back to him. Hostile eyes were about him.

Keith rose from his chair slowly, and slowly turned from his questioner toward the others.

"Gentlemen, I have nothing further to say to you. I have the honor to resign my position under you."

"Resign!" exclaimed the director who had been badgering him. "Resign your position!" He leaned back in his chair and laughed.

Keith turned on him so quickly that he pushed his chair back as if he were afraid he might spring across the table on him.

"Yes. Resign!" Keith was leaning forward across the table now, resting his weight on one hand. "Anything to terminate our association. I am no longer in your employ, Mr. Kestrel." His eyes had suddenly blazed, and held Mr. Kestrel's eyes unflinchingly. His voice was calm, but had the coldness of a steel blade.

There was a movement among the directors. They shifted uneasily in their chairs, and several of them pushed them back. They did not know what might happen. Keith was the incarnation of controlled passion. Mr. Kestrel seemed to shrink up within himself. Norman broke the silence.

"I do not wonder that Mr. Keith should feel aggrieved,"

he said, with feeling. "I have held off from taking part in this interview up to the present, because I promised to do so, and because I felt that Mr. Keith was abundantly able to take care of himself; but I think that he has been unjustly dealt with and has been roughly handled."

Keith's only answer was a slow wave of the arm in protest toward Norman to keep clear of the contest and leave it to him. He was standing quite straight now, his eyes still resting upon Mr. Kestrel's face, with a certain watchfulness in them, as if he were expecting him to stir again, and were ready to spring on him should he do so.

Unheeding him, Norman went on.

"I know that much that he says is true." Keith looked at him quickly, his form stiffening. "And I believe that *all* that he says is true," continued Norman; "and I am unwilling to stand by longer and see this method of procedure carried on."

Keith bowed. There flashed across his mind the picture of a boy rushing up the hill to his rescue as he stood by a rock-pile on a hillside defending himself against overwhelming assailants, and his face softened.

"Well, I don't propose to be dictated to as to how I shall conduct my own business," put in Mr. Kestrel, in a sneering voice. When the spell of Keith's gaze was lifted from him he had recovered.

If Keith heard him now, he gave no sign of it, nor was it needed, for Norman turned upon him.

"I think you will do whatever this board directs," he said, with almost as much contempt as Keith had shown.

He took up the defence of the management to such good purpose that a number of the other directors went over to his side.

They were willing to acquit Mr. Keith of blame, they said, and to show their confidence in him. They thought it would be necessary to have some one to look after the property and prevent further loss until better times should come, and they thought it would be best to get Mr. Keith to remain in charge for the present.

During this time Keith had remained motionless and silent, except to bow his acknowledgments to Norman. He received their new expression of confidence in silence, until the discussion had ceased and the majority were on his side. Then he faced Mr. Yorke.

"Gentlemen," he said, "I am obliged to you for your expression; but it comes too late. Nothing on earth could induce me ever again to assume a position in which I could be subjected to what I have gone through this morning. I will never again have any business association with—" he turned and looked at Mr. Kestrel—"Mr. Kestrel, or those who have sustained him."

Mr. Kestrel shrugged his shoulders.

"Oh, as to that," he laughed, "you need have no trouble. I shall get out as soon as I can. I have no more desire to associate with you than you have with me. All I want to do is to save what you mis—"

Keith's eyes turned on him quietly.

"—what I was misled into putting into your sink-hole down there. You may remember that you told me, when I went in, that you would guarantee me all I put in." His voice rose into a sneer.

"Oh, no. None of that, none of that!" interrupted Norman, quickly. "You may remember, Mr. Kestrel,—?"

But Keith interrupted him with a wave of his hand.

"I do remember. I have a good memory, Mr. Kestrel."

"That was all done away with," insisted Norman, his arm outstretched toward Mr. Kestrel. "You remember that an offer was made you of your input and interest, and you declined?"

"I am speaking to *him*," said Mr. Kestrel, not turning his eyes from Keith.

"I renew that offer now," said Keith, coldly.

"Then that's all right." Mr. Kestrel sat back in his chair. "I accept your proposal, principal and interest."

Protests and murmurs went around the board, but Mr. Kestrel did not heed them. Leaning forward, he seized a pen, and drawing a sheet of paper to him, began to scribble a memorandum of the terms, which, when finished, he pushed across the table to Keith.

Keith took it against Norman's protest, and when he had read it, picked up a pen and signed his name firmly.

"Here, witness it," said Mr. Kestrel to his next neighbor. "If any of the rest of you want to save your bones, you had better come in."

Several of the directors agreed with him.

Though Norman protested, Keith accepted their proposals, and a paper was drawn up which most of those present signed. It provided that a certain time should be given Keith in which to raise money to make good his offer, and arrangements were made provisionally to wind up the present company, and to sell out and transfer its rights to a new organization. Some of the directors prudently insisted on reserving the right to withdraw their proposals should they change their minds. It may be stated, however, that they had no temptation to do so. Times rapidly grew worse instead of better.

But Keith had occasion to know how sound was Squire Rawson's judgment when, a little later, another of the recurrent waves of depression swept over the country, and several banks in New Leeds went down, among them the bank in which old Rawson had had his money. The old man came up to town to remind Keith of his wisdom.

"Well, what do you think of brass and credulity now?" he demanded.

"Let me know when you begin to prophesy against me," said Keith, laughing.

"'Tain't no prophecy. It's jest plain sense. Some folks has it and some hasn't. When sense tells you a thing, hold on to it.

"Well, you jest go ahead and git things in shape, and don't bother about me. No use bein' in a hurry, neither. I have observed that when times gits bad, they generally gits worse. It's sorter like a fever; you've got to wait for the crisis and jest kind o' nurse 'em along. But I don't

318

reckon that coal is goin' to run away. It has been there some time, accordin' to what that young man used to say, and if it was worth what they gin for it a few years ago, it's goin' to be worth more a few years hence. When a wheel keeps turnin', the bottom's got to come up sometime, and if we can stick we'll be there. I think you and I make a pretty good team. You let me furnish the ideas and you do the work, and we'll come out ahead o' some o' these Yankees yet. Jest hold your horses; keep things in good shape, and be ready to start when the horn blows. It's goin' to blow sometime."

The clouds that had begun to rest in Norman Wentworth's eyes and the lines that had written themselves in his face were not those of business alone. Fate had brought him care of a deeper and sadder kind. Though Keith did not know it till later, the little rift within the lute, that he had felt, but had not understood, that first evening when he dined at Norman's house, had widened, and Norman's life was beginning to be overcast with the saddest of all clouds. Miss Abigail's keen intuition had discovered the flaw. Mrs. Wentworth had fallen a victim to her folly. Love of pleasure, love of admiration, love of display, had become a part of Mrs. Wentworth's life, and she was beginning to reap the fruits of her ambition.

For a time it was mighty amusing to her. To shop all morning, make the costliest purchases; to drive on the avenue or in the Park of an afternoon with the latest and most stylish turnout, in the handsomest toilet; to give the finest dinners; to spend the evening in the most expensive box; to cause men to open their eyes with admiration, and to make women grave with envy : all this gave her delight for a time—so much delight that she could not forego it even for her husband. Norman was so occupied of late that he could not go about with her as much as he had done. His father's health had failed, and then he had died, throwing all the business on Norman.

Ferdy Wickersham had returned home from abroad not long before—alone. Rumor had connected his name while abroad with some woman—an unknown and very pretty woman had "travelled with him." Ferdy, being rallied by his friends about it, shook his head. "Must have been some one else." Grinnell Rhodes, who had met him, said she declared herself his wife. Ferdy's denial was most conclusive —he simply laughed.

To Mrs. Wentworth he had told a convincing tale. It was a slander. Norman was against him, he knew, but she, at least, would believe he had been maligned.

Wickersham had waited for such a time in the affairs of Mrs. Wentworth. He had watched for it; striven to bring it about in many almost imperceptible ways; had tendered her sympathy; had been ready with help as she needed it; till he began to believe that he was making some impression. It was, of all the games he played, the dearest just now to his heart. It had a double zest. It had appeared to the world that Norman Wentworth had defeated him. He had always defeated him—first as a boy, then at college, and later when he had borne off the prize for which Ferdy had really striven. Ferdy would now show who was the real victor. If Louise Caldwell had passed him by for Norman Wentworth, he would prove that he still possessed her heart.

It was not long, therefore, before society found a delightful topic of conversation,—that silken-clad portion of society which usually deals with such topics,—the increasing intimacy between Ferdy Wickersham and Mrs. Wentworth.

Tales were told of late visits; of strolls in the dusk of evenings on unfrequented streets; of little suppers after the opera; of all the small things that deviltry can suggest and malignity distort. Wickersham cared little for having his name associated with that of any one, and he was certainly not going to be more careful for another's name than for his own. He had grown more reckless since his return, but it had not injured him with his set. It flattered his pride to be credited with the conquest of so cold and unapproachable a Diana as Louise Wentworth.

"What was more natural?" said Mrs. Nailor. After all, Ferdy Wickersham was her real romance, and she was his, notwithstanding all the attentions he had paid Alice Yorke. "Besides," said the amiable lady, "though Norman Wentworth undoubtedly lavishes large sums on his wife, and gives her the means to gratify her extravagant tastes, I have observed that he is seen quite as much with Mrs. Lancaster as with her, and any woman of spirit will resent this. You need not tell me that he would be so complacent over all that driving and strolling and box-giving that Ferdy does for her if he did not find his divertisement elsewhere."

Mrs. Nailor even went to the extent of rallying Ferdy on the subject.

"You are a naughty boy. You have no right to go around here making women fall in love with you as you do," she said, with that pretended reproof which is a real encouragement.

"One might suppose I was like David, who slew his tens of thousands," answered Ferdy. "Which of my victims are you attempting to rescue?"

"You know?"

As Ferdy shook his head, she explained further.

"I don't say that it isn't natural she should find you more—more—sympathetic than a man who is engrossed in business when he is not engrossed in dangling about a pair of blue eyes; but you ought not to do it. Think of her."

"I thought you objected to my thinking of her?" said Mr. Wickersham, lightly.

Mrs. Nailor tapped him with her fan to show her displeasure.

"You are so provoking. Why won't you be serious?"

"Serious? I never was more serious in my life. Suppose I tell you I think of her all the time?" He looked at her keenly, then broke into a laugh as he read her delight in the speech. "Don't you think I am competent to attend to my own affairs, even if Louise Caldwell is the soft and unsophisticated creature you would make her? I am glad you did not feel it necessary to caution me about her husband?" His eyes gave a flash.

Mrs. Nailor hastened to put herself right—that is, on the side of the one present, for with her the absent was always in the wrong.

Wickersham improved his opportunities with the ability of a veteran. Little by little he excited Mrs. Wentworth's jealousy. Norman, he said, necessarily saw a great deal of Alice Lancaster, for he was her business agent. It was, perhaps, not necessary for him to see her every day, but it was natural that he should. The arrow stuck and rankled. And later, at an entertainment, when she saw Norman laughing and enjoying himself in a group of old friends, among whom was Alice Lancaster, Mrs. Norman was on fire with suspicion, and her attitude toward Alice Lancaster changed.

So, before Norman was aware of it, he found life completely changed for him. As a boatman on a strange shore in the night-time drifts without knowing of it, he, in the absorption of his business, drifted away from his old relation without marking the process. His wife had her life and friends, and he had his. He made at times an effort to recover the old relation, but she was too firmly held in the grip of the life she had chosen for him to get her back.

His wife complained that he was out of sympathy with her, and he could not deny it. She resented this, and charged him with neglecting her. No man will stand such a charge, and Norman defended himself hotly.

"I do not think it lies in your mouth to make such a charge," he said, with a flash in his eye. "I am nearly always at home when I am not necessarily absent. You can hardly say as much. I do not think my worst enemy would charge me with that. Even Ferdy Wickersham would not say that."

She fired at the name.

"You are always attacking my friends," she declared. "I think they are quite as good as yours."

Norman turned away. He looked gloomily out of the window for a moment, and then faced his wife again.

"Louise," he said gravely, "if I have been hard and unsympathetic, I have not meant to be. Why can't we start all over again? You are more than all the rest of the world to me. I will give up whatever you object to, and you give up what I object to. That is a good way to begin." His eyes had a look of longing in them, but Mrs. Wentworth did not respond.

"You will insist on my giving up my friends," she said.

"Your friends? I do not insist on your giving up any friend on earth. Mrs. Nailor and her like are not your friends. They spend their time tearing to pieces the characters of others when you are present, and your character when you are absent. Wickersham is incapable of being a friend."

"You are always so unjust to him," said Mrs. Wentworth, warmly.

"I am not unjust to him. I have known him all my life, and I tell you he would sacrifice any one and every one to his pleasure."

Mrs. Wentworth began to defend him warmly, and so the quarrel ended worse than it had begun.

CHAPTER XXII

MRS. CREAMER'S BALL

THE next few years passed as the experience of old Rawson had led him to predict. Fortunes went down; but Fortune's wheel is always turning, and, as the old countryman said, "those that could stick would come up on top again."

Keith, however, had prospered. He had got the Rawson mine to running again, and even in the hardest times had been able to make it pay expenses. Other properties had failed and sold out, and had been bought in by Keith's supporters, when Wickersham once more appeared in New Leeds affairs. It was rumored that Wickersham was going to start again. Old Adam Rawson's face grew dark at the rumor. He said to Keith:

"If that young man comes down here, it's him or me. I'm an old man, and I ain't got long to live; but I want to live to meet him once. If he's got any friends, they'd better tell him not to come." He sat glowering and puffing his pipe morosely.

Keith tried to soothe him; but the old fellow had received a wound that knew no healing.

"I know all you say, and I'm much obliged to you; but I can't accept it. It's an eye for an eye and a tooth for a tooth with me. He has entered my home and struck me in the dark. Do you think I done all I have done jest for the money I was makin'! No; I wanted revenge. I have set on my porch of a night and seen her wanderin' about in them fureign cities, all alone, trampin' the streets—trampin', trampin', trampin'; tired, and, maybe, sick and hungry, not able to ask them outlandish folks for even a piece of bread—her that used to set on my knee and hug me with her little arms and call me grand-dad, and claim all the little calves for hers—jest the little ones; and that I've ridden many a mile over the mountains for, thinkin' how she was goin' to run out to meet me when I got home. And now even my old dog's dead—died after she went away.

"No!" he broke out fiercely. "If he comes back here, it's him or me! By the Lord! if he comes back here, I'll pay him the debt I owe him. If she's his wife, I'll make her a widow, and if she ain't, I'll revenge her."

He mopped the beads of sweat that had broken out on his brow, and without a word stalked out of the door.

But Ferdy Wickersham had no idea of returning to New Leeds. He found New York quite interesting enough for him about this time.

The breach between Norman and his wife had grown of late.

Gossip divided the honors between them, and some said it was on Ferdy Wickersham's account; others declared that it was Mrs. Lancaster who had come between them. Yet others said it was a matter of money—that Norman had become tired of his wife's extravagance and had re-fused to stand it any longer.

Keith knew vaguely of the trouble between Norman and his wife; but he did not know the extent of it, and he studiously kept up his friendly relations with her as well as with Norman. His business took him to New York from time to time, and he was sensible that the life there was growing more and more attractive for him. He was fitting into it too, and enjoying it more and more. He was like a strong swimmer who, used to battling in heavy waves, grows stronger with the struggle, and finds ever new enjoyment and courage in his endeavor. He felt that he was now quite a man of the world. He was aware that his point of view had changed and (a little) that he had changed. As flattering as was his growth in New Leeds, he had a much more infallible evidence of his success in the favor with which he was being received in New York.

The favor that Mrs. Lancaster had shown Keith, and, much more, old Mrs. Wentworth's friendship, had a marked effect throughout their whole circle of acquaintance. That a man had been invited to these houses meant that he must be something. There were women who owned large houses, wore priceless jewels, cruised in their own yachts, had their own villas on ground as valuable as that which fronted the Roman Forum in old days, who would almost have licked the marble steps of those mansions to be admitted to sit at their dinner-tables and have their names appear in the Sunday issues of the newly established society journals among the blessed few. So, as soon as it appeared that Gordon was not only an acquaintance, but a friend of these critical leaders, women who had looked over his head as they drove up the avenue, and had just tucked their chins and lowered their eyelids when he had been presented, began to give him invitations. Among these was Mrs. Nailor. Truly, the world appeared warmer and kinder than Keith had thought.

To be sure, it was at Mrs. Lancaster's that Mrs. Nailor met him, and Keith was manifestly on very friendly terms with the pretty widow. Even Mrs. Yorke, who was present on the occasion with her "heart," was impressively cordial to him. Mrs. Nailor had no idea of being left out. She almost gushed with affection, as she made a place beside her on a divan.

"You do not come to see all your friends," she said, with her winningest smile and her most bird-like voice. "You appear to forget that you have other old friends in New York besides Mrs. Lancaster and Mrs. Yorke. Alice dear, you must not be selfish and engross all his time. You must let him come and see me, at least, sometimes. Yes?" This with a peculiarly innocent smile and tone.

Keith declared that he was in New York very rarely, and Mrs. Lancaster, with a slightly heightened color, repudiated the idea that she had anything to do with his movements.

"Oh, I hear of you here very often," declared Mrs. Nailor, roguishly. "I have a little bird that brings me all the news about my friends."

"A little bird, indeed!" said Alice to herself, and to Keith later. "I'll be bound she has not. If she had a bird, the old cat would have eaten it."

"You are going to the Creamers' ball, of course?" pursued Mrs. Nailor.

No, Keith said : he was not going ; he had been in New York only two days, and, somehow, his advent had been overlooked. He was always finding himself disappointed by discovering that New York was still a larger place than New Leeds.

"Oh, but you must go ! We must get you an invitation, mustn't we, Alice?" Mrs. Nailor was always ready to promise anything, provided she could make her engagement in partnership and then slip out and leave the performance to her friend.

"Why, yes ; there is not the least trouble about getting an invitation. Mrs. Nailor can get you one easily."

Keith looked acquiescent.

"No, my dear ; you write the note. You know Mrs. Creamer every bit as well as I," protested Mrs. Nailor, "and I have already asked for at least a dozen. There are Mrs. Wyndham and Lady Stobbs, who were here last winter ; and that charming Lord Huckster, who was at Newport last summer ; and I don't know how many more —so you will have to get the invitation for Mr. Keith."

Keith, with some amusement, declared that he did not wish any trouble taken ; he had only said he would go because Mrs. Nailor had appeared to desire it so much.

Next morning an invitation reached Keith,—he thought he knew through whose intervention,—and he accepted it.

That evening, as Keith, about dusk, was going up the avenue on his way home, a young girl passed him, walking very briskly. She paused for a moment just ahead of him to give some money to a poor woman who, doubled up on the pavement in a black shawl, was grinding out from a wheezy little organ a thin, dirge-like strain.

"Good evening. I hope you feel better to-day," Keith heard her say in a kind tone, though he lost all of the other's reply except the "God bless you."

She was simply dressed in a plain, dark walking-suit, and something about her quick, elastic step and slim, trim figure as she sailed along, looking neither to the right nor to the left, attracted his attention. Her head was set on her shoulders in a way that gave her quite an air, and as she passed under a lamp the light showed the flash of a fine profile and an unusual face. She carried a parcel in her hand that might have been a roll of music, and from the lateness of the hour Keith fancied her a shop-girl on her way home, or possibly a music-teacher.

Stirred by the glimpse of the refined face, and even more by the carriage of the little head under the dainty hat, Keith quickened his pace to obtain another glance at her. He had almost overtaken her when she stopped in front of a well-lighted window of a music-store. The light that fell on her face revealed to him a face of unusual beauty. Something about her graceful pose as, with her dark brows slightly knitted, she bent forward and scanned intently the pieces of music within, awakened old associations in Keith's mind, and sent him back to his boyhood at Elphinstone. And under an impulse, which he could better justify to himself than to her, he did a very audacious and improper thing. Taking off his hat, he spoke to her. She had been so absorbed that for a moment she did not comprehend that it was she he was addressing. Then

328

as it came to her that it was she to whom this stranger was speaking, she drew herself up and gave him a look of such withering scorn that Keith felt himself shrink. Next second, with her head high in the air, she had turned without a word and sped up the street, leaving Keith feeling very cheap and subdued.

But that glance from dark eyes flashing with indignation had filled Keith with a sensation to which he had long been a stranger. Something about the simple dress, the high-bred face with its fine scorn; something about the patrician air of mingled horror and contempt, had suddenly cleaved through the worldly crust that had been encasing him for some time, and reaching his better self, awakened an emotion that he had thought gone forever. It was like a lightning-flash in the darkness. He knew that she had entered his life. His resolution was taken on the instant. He would meet her, and if she were what she looked to be—again Elphinstone and his youth swept into his mind. He already was conscious of a sense of protection; he felt curiously that he had the right to protect her. If he had addressed her, might not others do so? The thought made his blood boil. He almost wished that some one would attempt it, that he might assert his right to show her what he was, and thus retrieve himself in her eyes. Besides, he must know where she lived. So he followed her at a respectful distance till she ran up the steps of one of the better class of houses and disappeared within. He was too far off to be able to tell which house it was that she entered, but it was in the same block with Norman Wentworth's house.

Keith walked the avenue that night for a long time, pondering how he should find and explain his conduct to the young music-teacher, for a music-teacher he had decided she must be. The next evening, too, he strolled for an hour on the avenue, scanning from a distance every fair passer-by, but he saw nothing of her.

Mrs. Creamer's balls were, as Norman had once said, *the* balls of the season. "Only the rich and the noble were expected."

Mrs. Creamer's house was one of the great, new, brownstone mansions which had been built within the past ten years upon "the avenue." It had cost a fortune. Within, it was so sumptuous that a special work has been "gotten up," printed, and published by subscription, of its "art treasures," furniture, and upholstery.

Into this palatial residence—for flattery could not have called it a home—Keith was admitted, along with some hundreds of other guests.

To-night it was filled with, not flowers exactly, but with floral decorations; for the roses and orchids were lost in the designs—garlands, circles, and banks formed of an infinite number of flowers.

Mrs. Creamer, a large, handsome woman with good shoulders, stood just inside the great drawing-room. She was gorgeously attired and shone with diamonds until the eyes ached with her splendor. Behind her stood Mr. Creamer, looking generally mightily bored. Now and then he smiled and shook hands with the guests, at times drawing a friend out of the line back into the rear for a chat, then relapsing again into indifference or gloom.

Keith was presented to Mrs. Creamer. She only nodded to him. Keith moved on. He soon discovered that a cordial greeting to a strange guest was no part of the convention in that society. One or two acquaintances spoke to him, but he was introduced to no one; so he sauntered about and entertained himself observing the people. The women were in their best, and it was good.

Keith was passing from one room to another when he became aware that a man, who was standing quite still in the doorway, was, like himself, watching the crowd. His face was turned away; but something about the compact figure and firm chin was familiar to him. Keith moved to take a look at his face. It was Dave Dennison.

He had a twinkle in his eye as he said : "Didn't expect to see me here?"

"Didn't expect to see myself here," said Keith.

"I'm one of the swells now"; and Dave glanced down at his expensive shirt-front and his evening suit with complacency. "Wouldn't Jake give a lot to have such a bosom as that? I think I look just as well as some of 'em?" he queried, with a glance about him.

Keith thought so too. "You are dressed for the part," he said. Keith's look of interest inspired him to go on.

"You see, 'tain't like 'tis down with us, where you know everybody, and everything about him, to the number of drinks he can carry."

"Well, what do you do here?" asked Keith, who was trying to follow Mr. Dennison's calm eye as, from time to time, it swept the rooms, resting here and there on a face or following a hand. He was evidently not merely a guest.

"Detective."

"A detective!" exclaimed Keith.

Dave nodded. "Yes; watchin' the guests, to see they don't carry off each other. It is the new ones that puzzle us for a while," he added. "Now, there is a lady acting very mysteriously over there." His eye swept over the room and then visited, in that casual way it had, some one in the corner across the room. "I don't just seem to make her out. She looks all right—but—?"

Keith followed the glance, and the blood rushed to his face and then surged back again to his heart, for there, standing against the wall, was the young girl whom he had spoken to on the street a few evenings before, who had given him so merited a rebuff. She was a patrician-looking creature and was standing quite alone, observing the scene with keen interest. Her girlish figure was slim; her eyes, under straight dark brows, were beautiful; and her mouth was almost perfect. Her fresh face expressed unfeigned interest, and though generally grave as she glanced about her, she smiled at times, evidently at her own thoughts.

"I don't just make her out," repeated Mr. Dennison, softly. "I never saw her before, as I remember, and yet— ?" He looked at her again.

"Why, I do not see that she is acting at all mysteriously," said Keith. "I think she is a music-teacher. She is about the prettiest girl in the room. She may be a stranger, like myself, as no one is talking to her."

"Don't no stranger git in here," said Mr. Dennison, decisively. "You see how different she is from the others. Most of them don't think about anything but themselves. She ain't thinkin' about herself at all; she is watchin' others. She may be a reporter—she appears mighty interested in clothes."

"A reporter!"

The surprise in Keith's tone amused his old pupil. "Yes, a sassiety reporter. They have curious ways here. Why, they pay money to git themselves in the paper."

Just then so black a look came into his face for a second that Keith turned and followed his glance. It rested on Ferdy Wickersham, who was passing at a little distance, with Mrs. Wentworth on his arm.

"There's one I am watchin' on my own account," said the detective. "I'm comin' up with him, and some day I'm goin' to light on him." His eye gave a flash and then became as calm and cold as usual. Presently he spoke again :

"I don't forgit nothin'—'pears like I can't do it." His voice had a new subtone in it, which somehow sent Keith's memory back to the past. "I don't forgit a kindness, anyway," he said, laying his hand for a second on Keith's arm. "Well, see you later, sir." He moved slowly on. Keith was glad that patient enemy was not following him.

Keith's inspection of the young girl had inflamed his interest. It was an unusual face— high-bred and fine. Humor lurked about the corners of her mouth ; but resolution also might be read there. And Keith knew how those big, dark eyes could flash. And she was manifestly having a good time all to herself. She was dressed much more simply than any other woman he saw, in a plain muslin dress; but she made a charming picture as she stood against the wall, her dark eyes alight with interest. Her brown hair was drawn back from a brow of snowy whiteness, and her little head was set on her shoulders in a way that recalled to Keith an old picture. She would have had an air of distinction in any company. Here she shone like a jewel.

Keith's heart went out to her. At sight of her his youth appeared to flood over him again. Keith fancied that she looked weary, for every now and then she lifted her head and glanced about the rooms as though looking for some one. A sense of protection swept over him. He must meet her. But how? She did not appear to know any one. Finally he determined on a bold expedient. If he succeeded it would give him a chance to recover himself as nothing else could; if he failed he could but fail. So he made his way over to her. But it was with a beating heart.

"You look tired. Won't you let me get you a chair?" His voice sounded strange even to himself.

"No, thank you; I am not tired." She thanked him civilly enough, but scarcely looked at him. "But I should like a glass of water."

"It is the only liquid I believe I cannot get you," said Keith. "There are three places where water is scarce: the desert, a ball-room, and the other place where Dives was."

She drew herself up a little.

"But I will try," he added, and went off. On his return with a glass of water, she took it.

As she handed the glass back to him, she glanced at him, and he caught her eye. Her head went up, and she flushed to the roots of her brown hair.

"Oh!—I beg your pardon! I—I—really—I don't—

Thank you very much. I am very sorry." She turned away stiffly.

"Why?" said Keith, flushing in spite of himself. "You have done me a favor in enabling me to wait on you. May I introduce myself? And then I will get some one to do it in person—Mrs. Lancaster or Mrs. Wentworth. They will vouch for me."

The girl looked up at him, at first with a hostile expression on her face, which changed suddenly to one of wonder.

"Isn't this Gordon Keith?"

Gordon's eyes opened wide. How could she know him? "Yes."

"You don't know me?" Her eyes were dancing now, and two dimples were flitting about her mouth. Keith's memory began to stir. She put her head on one side.

"'Lois, if you'll kiss me I'll let you ride my horse,'" she said cajolingly.

"Lois Huntington! It can't be!" exclaimed Keith, delighted. "You are just so high." Keith measured a height just above his left watch-pocket. "And you have long hair down your back."

With a little twist she turned her head and showed him a head of beautiful brown hair done up in a Grecian knot just above the nape of a shapely little neck.

"—And you have the brightest—"

She dropped her eyes before his, which were looking right into them—though not until she had given a little flash from them, perhaps to establish their identity.

"—And you used to say I was your sw—"

"Did I?" (this was very demurely said). "How old was I then?"

"How old are you now?"

"Eighteen," with a slight straightening of the slim figure.

"Impossible!" exclaimed Keith, enjoying keenly the picture she made.

"All of it," with a flash of the eyes.

"For me you are just all of seven years old."

"Do you know who I thought you were?" Her face dimpled.

"Yes; a waiter!"

She nodded brightly.

"It was my good manners. The waiters have struck me much this evening," said Keith.

She smiled, and the dimples appeared again.

"That is their business. They are paid for it."

"Oh, I see. Is that the reason others are—what they are? Well, I am more than paid. My recompense is—you."

She looked pleased. "You are the first person I have met!—Did you have any idea who I was the other evening?" she asked suddenly.

Keith would have given five years of his life to be able to answer yes. But he said no. "I only knew you were some one who needed protection," he said, trying to make the best of a bad situation. You are too young to be on the street so late."

"So it appeared. I had been out for a walk to see old Dr. Templeton and to get a piece of music, and it was later than I thought."

"Whom are you here with?" inquired Keith, to get off of delicate ground. "Where are you staying?"

"With my cousin, Mrs. Norman Wentworth. It is my first introduction into New York life."

Just then there was a movement toward the supper-room.

Keith suggested that they should go and find Mrs. Norman. Miss Huntington said, however, she thought she had better remain where she was, as Mrs. Norman had promised to come back.

"I hope she will invite you to join our party," she said naïvely.

"If she does not, I will invite you both to join mine,"

declared Keith. "I have no idea of letting you escape for another dozen years."

Just then, however, Mrs. Norman appeared. She was with Ferdy Wickersham, who, on seeing Keith, looked away coldly. She smiled, greatly surprised to find Keith there. "Why, where did you two know each other?"

They explained.

"I saw you were pleasantly engaged, so I did not think it necessary to hasten back," she said to Lois.

Ferdy Wickersham said something to her in an undertone, and she held out her hand to the girl.

"Come, we are to join a party in the supper-room. We shall see you after supper, Mr. Keith?"

Keith said he hoped so. He was conscious of a sudden wave of disappointment sweeping over him as the three left him. The young girl gave him a bright smile.

Later, as he passed by, he saw only Ferdy Wickersham with Mrs. Norman. Lois Huntington was at another table, so Keith joined her.

After the supper there was to be a novel kind of entertainment: a sort of vaudeville show in which were to figure a palmist, a gentleman set down in the programme with its gilt printing as the "Celebrated Professor Cheireman"; several singers; a couple of acrobatic performers; and a danseuse: "Mlle. Terpsichore."

The name struck Keith with something of sadness. It recalled old associations, some of them pleasant, some of them sad. And as he stood near Lois Huntington, on the edge of the throng that filled the large apartment where the stage had been constructed, during the first three or four numbers he was rather more in Gumbolt than in that gay company in that brilliant room.

"Professor Cheireman" had shown the wonders of the trained hand and the untrained mind in a series of tricks that would certainly be wonderful did not so many men perform them.

Mlle. de Voix performed hardly less wonders with her

336

voice, running up and down the scale like a squirrel in a cage, introducing trills into songs where there were none, and making the simplest melodies appear as intricate as pieces of opera. The Burlystone Brothers jumped over and skipped under each other in a marvellous and "absolutely unrivalled manner." And presently the danseuse appeared.

Keith was standing against the wall thinking of Terpy and the old hall with its paper hangings in Gumbolt, and its benches full of eager, jovial spectators, when suddenly there was a roll of applause, and he found himself in Gumbolt. From the side on which he stood walked out his old friend, Terpy herself. He had not been able to see her until she was well out on the stage and was making her bow. The next second she began to dance.

After the first greeting given her, a silence fell on the room, the best tribute they could pay to her art, her grace, her abandon. Nothing so audacious had ever been seen by certainly half the assemblage. Casting aside the old tricks of the danseuse, the tipping and pirouetting and grimacing for applause, the dancer seemed oblivious of her audience and as though she were trying to excel herself. She swayed and swung and swept from side to side as though on wings.

Round after round of applause swept over the room. Men were talking in undertones to each other; women buzzed behind their fans.

She stopped, panting and flushed with pride, and with a certain scorn in her face and mien glanced over the audience. Just as she was poising herself for another effort, her eye reached the side of the room where Keith stood just beside Miss Huntington. A change passed over her face. She nodded, hesitated for a second, and then began again. She failed to catch the time of the music and danced out of time. A titter came from the rear of the room. She looked in that direction, and Keith did the same. Ferdy Wickersham, with a malevolent gleam in his eye, was laughing. The dancer flushed deeply, frowned, lost her self-possession, and stopped. A laugh of derision sounded at the rear.

"For shame! It is shameful!" said Lois Huntington in a low voice to Keith.

"It is. The cowardly scoundrel!" He turned and scowled at Ferdy.

At the sound, Terpy took a step toward the front, and bending forward, swept the audience with her flashing eyes.

"Put that man out."

A buzz of astonishment and laughter greeted her outbreak.

"Cackle, you fools!"

She turned to the musicians.

"Play that again and play it right, or I'll wring your necks!"

She began to dance again, and soon danced as she had done at first.

Applause was beginning again; but at the sound she stopped, looked over the audience disdainfully, and turning, walked coolly from the stage.

"Who is she?" "Well, did you ever see anything like that!" "Well, I never did!" "The insolent creature!" "By Jove! she can dance if she chooses!" buzzed over the room.

"Good for her," said Keith, his face full of admiration.

"Did you know her?" asked Miss Huntington.

"Well."

The girl said nothing, but she stiffened and changed color slightly.

"You know her, too," said Keith.

"I! I do not."

"Do you remember once, when you were a tot over in England, giving your doll to a little dancing-girl?—When your governess was in such a temper?"

Lois nodded.

"That is she. She used to live in New Leeds. She was almost the only woman in Gumbolt when I went there. Had a man laughed at her there then, he would never have left the room alive. Mr. Wickersham tried it once, and came near getting his neck broken for it. He is getting even with her now."

As the girl glanced up at him, his face was full of suppressed feeling. A pang shot through her.

Just then the entertainment broke up and the guests began to leave. Mrs. Wentworth beckoned to Lois. Wickersham was still with her.

"I will not trust myself to go within speaking distance of him now," said Keith; "so I will say good-by, here." He made his adieus somewhat hurriedly, and moved off as Mrs. Wentworth approached.

Wickersham, who, so long as Keith remained with Miss Huntington, had kept aloof, and was about to say good night to Mrs. Wentworth, had, on seeing Keith turn away, followed Mrs. Wentworth.

Every one was still chatting of the episode of the young virago.

"Well, what did you think of your friend's friend?" asked Wickersham of Lois.

"Of whom?"

"Of your friend Mr. Keith's young lady. She is an old flame of his," he said, turning to Mrs. Wentworth and speaking in an undertone, just loud enough for Lois to hear. "They have run her out of New Leeds, and I think he is trying to force her on the people here. He has cheek enough to do anything; but I think to-night will about settle him."

"I do not know very much about such things; but I think she dances very well," said Lois, with heightened color, moved to defend the girl under an instinct of opposition to Wickersham.

"So your friend thinks, or thought some time ago," said Wickersham. "My dear girl, she can't dance at all. She

339

is simply a disreputable young woman, who has been run out of her own town, as she ought to be run out of this, as an impostor, if nothing else." He turned to Mrs. Wentworth : "A man who brought such a woman to a place like this ought to be kicked out of town."

"If you are speaking of Mr. Keith, I don't believe that of him," said Lois, coldly.

Wickersham looked at her for a moment. A curious light was in his eyes as he said :

"I am not referring to any one. I am simply generalizing." He shrugged his shoulders and turned away.

As Mrs. Wentworth and Lois entered their carriage, a gentleman was helping some one into a hack just behind Mrs. Wentworth's carriage. The light fell on them at the moment that Lois stepped forward, and she recognized Mr. Keith and the dancer, Mlle. Terpsichore. He was handing her in with all the deference that he would have shown the highest lady in the land.

Lois Huntington drove home in a maze. Life appeared to have changed twice for her in a single evening. Out of that crowd of strangers had come one who seemed to be a part of her old life. They had taken each other up just where they had parted. The long breach in their lives had been bridged. He had seemed the old friend and champion of her childhood, who, since her aunt had revived her recollection of him, had been a sort of romantic hero in her dreams. Their meeting had been such as she had sometimes pictured to herself it would be. She believed him finer, higher, than others. Then, suddenly, she had found that the vision was but an idol of clay. All that her aunt had said of him had been dashed to pieces in a trice. He was not worthy of her notice. He was not a gentleman. He was what Mr. Wickersham had called him. He had boasted to her of his intimacy with a common dancing-girl. He had left her to fly to her and escort her home.

As Keith had left the house, Terpsichore had come out of the side entrance, and they had met. Keith was just wondering how he could find her, and he considered the meeting a fortunate one. She was in a state of extreme agitation. It was the first time that she had undertaken to dance at such an entertainment. She had refused, but had been over-persuaded, and she declared it was all a plot between Wickersham and her manager to ruin her. She would be even with them both, if she had to take a pistol to right her wrongs.

Keith had little idea that the chief motive of her acceptance had been the hope that she might find him among the company. He did what he could to soothe her, and having made a promise to call upon her, he bade her good-by, happily ignorant of the interpretation which she who had suddenly sprung uppermost in his thoughts had, upon Wickersham's instigation, put upon his action.

Keith walked home with a feeling to which he had been long a stranger. He was somehow happier than he had been in years. A young girl had changed the whole entertainment for him—the whole city—almost his whole outlook on life. He had not felt this way for years—not since Alice Yorke had darkened life for him. Could love be for him again?

The dial appeared to have turned back for him. He felt younger, fresher, more hopeful. He walked out into the street and tried to look up at the stars. The houses obscured them; they were hardly visible. The city streets were no place for stars and sentiment. He would go through the park and see them. So he strolled along and turned into a park. The gas-lamps shed a yellow glow on the trees, making circles of feeble light on the walks, and the shadows lay deep on the ground. Most of the benches were vacant; but here and there a waif or a belated home-goer sat in drowsy isolation. The stars were too dim even from this vantage-ground to afford Keith much satisfaction. His thoughts flew back to the mountains and the great blue canopy overhead, spangled with stars, and a blue-eyed girl amid pillows whom he used to worship. An arid waste of years cut them off from the present, and his thoughts came back to a sweet-faced girl with dark eyes, claiming him as her old friend. She appeared to be the old ideal rather than the former.

All next day Keith thought of Lois Huntington. He wanted to go and see her; but he waited until the day after. He would not appear too eager.

He called at Norman's office for the pleasure of talking of her; but Norman was still absent. The following afternoon he called at Norman's house. The servant said Mrs. Norman was out.

"Miss Huntington?"

"She left this morning."

Keith walked up the street feeling rather blank. That night he started for the South. But Lois Huntington was much in his thoughts. He wondered if life would open for him again. When a man wonders about this, life has already opened.

By the time he reached New Leeds, he had already made up his mind to write and ask Miss Abby for an invitation to Brookford, and he wrote his father a full account of the girl he had known as a child, over which the old General beamed.

He forgave people toward whom he had hard feelings. The world was better than he had been accounting it. He even considered more leniently than he had done Mrs. Wentworth's allowing Ferdy Wickersham to hang around her. It suddenly flashed on him that, perhaps, Ferdy was in love with Lois Huntington. Crash! went his kind feelings, his kind thoughts. The idea of Ferdy making love to that pure, sweet, innocent creature! It was horrible! Her innocence, her charming friendliness, her sweetness, all swept over him, and he thrilled with a sense of protection.

Could he have known what Wickersham had done to poison her against him, he would have been yet more enraged. As it was, Lois was at that time back at her old home; but with how different feelings from those which she had had but a few days before! Sometimes she hated Keith, or, at least, declared to herself that she hated him; and at others she defended him against her own charge. And more and more she truly hated Wickersham.

"So you met Mr. Keith?" said her aunt, abruptly, a day or two after her return. "How did you like him?"

"I did not like him," said Lois, briefly, closing her lips with a snap, as if to keep the blood out of her cheeks.

"What! you did not like him? Girls are strange creatures nowadays. In my time, a girl—a girl like you—would have thought him the very pink of a man. I suppose you liked that young Wickersham better?" she added grimly.

"No, I did not like him either. But I think Mr. Keith is perfectly horrid."

"Horrid!" The old lady's black eyes snapped. "Oh, he didn't ask you to dance! Well, I think, considering he knew you when you were a child, and knew you were my niece, he might—"

"Oh, yes, I danced with him; but he is not very nice. He—ah— Something I saw prejudiced me."

Miss Abby was so insistent that she should tell her what had happened that she yielded.

"Well, I saw him on the street helping a woman into a carriage."

"A woman? And why shouldn't he help her in? He probably was the only man you saw that would do it, if you saw the men I met."

"A dis—reputable woman," said Lois, slowly.

"And, pray, what do you know of disreputable women? Not that there are not enough of them to be seen!"

"Some one told me—and she looked it," said Lois, blushing. The old lady unexpectedly whipped around and took her part so warmly that Lois suddenly found herself defending Gordon. She could not bear that others should attack him, though she took frequent occasion to tell herself that she hated him. In fact, she hated him so that she wanted to see him to show him how severe she would be.

The occasion might have come sooner than she expected ; but alas ! Fate was unkind.

Keith was not conscious until he found that Lois Huntington had left town how much he had thought of her. Her absence appeared suddenly to have emptied the city. By the time he had reached his room he had determined to follow her home. That rift of sunshine which had entered his life should not be shut out again. He sat down and wrote to her : a friendly letter, expressing warmly his pleasure at having met her, picturing jocularly his disappointment at having failed to find her. He made a single allusion to the Terpsichore episode. He had done what he could, he said, to soothe his friend's ruffled feelings ; but, though he thought he had some influence with her, he could not boast of having had much success in this.

In the light in which Lois read this letter, the allusion to the dancing-girl outweighed all the rest, and though her heart had given a leap when she first saw that she had a letter from Keith, when she laid it down her feeling had changed. She would show him that she was not a mere country chit to be treated as he had treated her. His "friend" indeed !

When Keith, to his surprise, received no reply to his letter, he wrote again more briefly, asking if his former letter had been received ; but this shared the fate of the first.

Meantime Lois had gone off to visit a friend. Her mind was not quite as easy as it should have been. She felt that if she had it to go over, she would do just the same thing ; but she began to fancy excuses for Keith. She even hunted up the letters he had written her as a boy.

It is probable that Lois's failure to write did more to raise her in Keith's estimation and fix her image in his mind than anything else she could have done. Keith knew that something untoward had taken place, but what it was

344

he could not conceive. At least, however, it proved to him that Lois Huntington was different from some of the young women he had met of late. So he sat down and wrote to Miss Brooke, saying that he was going abroad on a matter of importance, and asking leave to run down and spend Sunday with them before he left. Miss Brooke's reply nearly took his breath away. She not only refused his request, but intimated that there was a good reason why his former letters had not been acknowledged and why he would not be received by her.

It was rather incoherent, but it had something to do with "inexplicable conduct." On this Keith wrote Miss Brooke, requesting a more explicit charge and demanding an opportunity to defend himself. Still he received no reply ; and, angry that he had written, he took no further steps about it.

By the time Lois reached home she had determined to answer his letter. She would write him a severe reply.

Miss Abby, however, announced to Lois, the day of her return, that Mr. Keith had written asking her permission to come down and see them. The blood sprang into Lois's face, and if Miss Abby had had on her spectacles at that moment, she must have read the tale it told.

"Oh, he did ! And what — ?" She gave a swallow to restrain her impatience. "What did you say to him, Aunt Abby ? Have you answered the letter ?" This was very demurely said.

"Yes. Of course, I wrote him not to come. I preferred that he should not come."

Could she have but seen Lois's face !

"Oh, you did ! "

"Yes. I want no hypocrites around me." Her head was up and her cap was bristling. "I came very near telling him so, too. I told him that I had it from good authority that he had not behaved in altogether the most gentlemanly way—consorting openly with a hussy on the street ! I think he knows whom I referred to."

"But, Aunt Abby, I do not know that she was. I only heard she was," defended Lois.

"Who told you?"

"Mr. Wickersham."

"Well, *he* knows," said Miss Abigail, with decision. "Though I think he had very little to do to discuss such matters with you."

"But, Aunt Abby, I think you had better have let him come. We could have shown him our disapproval in our manner. And possibly he might have some explanation?"

"I guess he won't make any mistake about that. The hypocrite! To sit up and talk to me as if he were a bishop! I have no doubt he would have explanation enough. They always do."

CHAPTER XXIII

GENERAL KEITH VISITS STRANGE LANDS

JUST then the wheel turned. Interest was awaking in England in American enterprises, and, fortunately for Keith, he had friends on that side.

Grinnell Rhodes now lived in England, dancing attendance on his wife, the daughter of Mr. Creamer of Creamer, Crustback & Company, who was aspiring to be in the fashionable set there.

Matheson, the former agent of the Wickershams, with whom Ferdy had quarrelled, had gone back to England, and had acquired a reputation as an expert.

By one of the fortuitous happenings so hard to account for, about this time Keith wrote to Rhodes, and Rhodes consulted Matheson, who knew the properties. Ferdy had incurred the Scotchman's implacable hate, and the latter was urged on now by a double motive. To Rhodes, who was bored to death with the life he was leading, the story told by the Wickershams' old superintendent was like a trumpet to a war-horse.

Out of the correspondence with Rhodes grew a suggestion to Keith to come over and try to place the Rawson properties with an English syndicate. Keith had, moreover, a further reason for going. He had not recovered from the blow of Miss Brooke's refusal to let him visit Lois. He knew that in some way it was connected with his attention to Terpsichore ; he knew that there was a misunderstanding, and felt that Wickersham was somehow connected with it. But he was too proud to make any further attempt to explain it.

Accordingly, armed with the necessary papers and powers, he arranged to go to England. He had control of and options on lands which were estimated to be worth several millions of dollars at any fair valuation.

Keith had long been trying to persuade his father to accompany him to New York on some of his visits; but the old gentleman had never been able to make up his mind to do so.

"I have grown too old to travel in strange lands," he said. "I tried to get there once, but they stopped me just in sight of a stone fence on the farther slope beyond Gettysburg." A faint flash glittered in his quiet eyes. "I think I had better restrain my ambition now to migrations from the blue bed to the brown, and confine my travels to 'the realms of gold'!"

Now, after much urging, as Gordon was about to go abroad to try and place the Rawson properties there, the General consented to go to New York and see him off. It happened that Gordon was called to New York on business a day or two before his father was ready to go. So he exacted a promise that he would follow him, and went on ahead. Though General Keith would have liked to back out at the last moment, as he had given his word, he kept it. He wrote his son that he must not undertake to meet him, as he could not tell by what train he should arrive.

"I shall travel slowly," he said, "for I wish to call by and see one or two old friends on my way, whom I have not seen for years."

The fact was that he wished to see the child of his friend, General Huntington, and determined to avail himself of this opportunity to call by and visit her. Gordon's letter about her had opened a new vista in life.

The General found Brookford a pleasant village, lying on the eastern slope of the Piedmont, and having written to ask permission to call and pay his respects, he was graciously received by Miss Abby, and more than graciously received by her niece. Miss Lois would probably have met any visitor at the train; but she might not have had so palpitating a heart and so rich a color in meeting many a young man.

Few things captivate a person more than to be received with real cordiality by a friend immediately on alighting at a strange station from a train full of strangers. But when the traveller is an old and somewhat unsophisticated man, and when the friend is a young and very pretty girl, and when, after a single look, she throws her arms around his neck and kisses him, the capture is likely to be as complete as any that could take place in life. When Lois Huntington, after asking about his baggage, and exclaiming because he had sent his trunk on to New York and had brought only a valise, as if he were only stopping off between trains, finally settled herself down beside the General and took the reins of the little vehicle that she had come in, there was, perhaps, not a more pleased old gentleman in the world than the one who sat beside her.

"How you have grown!" he said, gazing at her with admiration. "Somehow, I always thought of you as a little girl—a very pretty little girl."

She thought of what his son had said at their meeting at the ball.

"But you know one must grow some, and it has been eleven years since then. Think how long that has been!"

"Eleven years! Does that appear so long to you?" said the old man, smiling. "So it is in our youth. Gordon wrote me of his meeting you and of how you had changed."

I wonder what he meant by that, said Lois to herself, the color mounting to her cheek. "He thought I had changed, did he?" she asked tentatively, after a moment, a trace of grimness stealing into her face, where it lay like a little cloud in May.

"Yes; he hardly knew you. You see, he did not have the greeting that I got."

"I should think not!" exclaimed Lois. "If he had, I don't know what he might have thought!" She grew as grave as she could.

"He said you were the sweetest and prettiest girl there, and that all the beauty of New York was there, even the beautiful Mrs.—what is her name? She was Miss Yorke."

Lois's face relaxed suddenly with an effect of sunshine breaking through a cloud.

"Did he say that?" she exclaimed.

"He did, and more. He is a young man of some discernment," observed the old fellow, with a chuckle of gratification.

"Oh, but he was only blinding you. He is in love with Mrs. Lancaster."

"Not he."

But Lois protested guilefully that he was.

A little later she asked the General:

"Did you ever hear of any one in New Leeds who was named Terpsichore?"

"Terpsichore?" Of course. Every one knows her there. I never saw her until she became a nurse, when she was nursing my son. She saved his life, you know?"

"Saved his life!" Her face had grown almost grim. "No, I never heard of it. Tell me about it."

"Saved his life twice, indeed," said the old General. "She has had a sad past, but she is a noble woman." And unheeding Lois's little sniff, he told the whole story of Terpsichore, and the brave part she had played. Spurred on by his feeling, he told it well, no less than did he the part that Keith had played. When he was through, there had been tears in Lois's eyes, and her bosom was still heaving.

"Thank you," she said simply, and the rest of the drive was in silence.

When General Keith left Brookford he was almost as much in love with his young hostess as his son could have been, and all the rest of his journey he was dreaming of what life might become if Gordon and she would but take a fancy to each other, and once more return to the old place. It would be like turning back the years and reversing the consequences of the war.

The General, on his arrival in New York, was full of his visit to Brookford and of Lois. "There is a girl after my own heart," he declared to Gordon, with enthusiasm. "Why don't you go down there and get that girl?"

Gordon put the question aside with a somewhat grim look. He was very busy, he said. His plans were just ripening, and he had no time to think about marrying. Besides, "a green country girl" was not the most promising wife. There were many other women who, etc., etc.

"Many other women!" exclaimed the General. "There may be; but I have not seen them lately. As to 'a green country girl'—why, they make the best wives in the world if you get the right kind. What do you want? One of these sophisticated, fashionable, strong-minded women— a woman's-rights woman? Heaven forbid! When a gentleman marries, he wants a lady and he wants a wife, a woman to love him; a lady to preside over his home, not over a woman's meeting."

Gordon quite agreed with him as to the principle; but he did not know about the instance cited.

"Why, I thought you had more discernment," said the old gentleman. "She is the sweetest creature I have seen in a long time. She has both sense and sensibility. If I were forty years younger, I should not be suggesting her to you, sir. I should be on my knees to her for myself." And the old fellow buttoned his coat, straightened his figure, and looked quite spirited and young.

At the club, where Gordon introduced him, his father soon became quite a toast. Half the habitués of the "big room" came to know him, and he was nearly always surrounded by a group listening to his quaint observations of life, his stories of old times, his anecdotes, his quotations from Plutarch or from "Dr. Johnson, sir."

An evening or two after his appearance at the club, Norman Wentworth came in, and when the first greetings were over, General Keith inquired warmly after his wife.

"Pray present my compliments to her. I have never had the honor of meeting her, sir, but I have heard of her charms from my son, and I promise myself the pleasure of calling upon her as soon as I have called on your mother, which I am looking forward to doing this evening."

Norman's countenance changed a little at the unexpected words, for half a dozen men were around. When, however, he spoke it was in a very natural voice.

"Yes, my mother is expecting you," he said quietly. Mrs. Wentworth also would, he said, be very glad to see him. Her day was Thursday, but if General Keith thought of calling at any other time, and would be good enough to let him know, he thought he could guarantee her being at home. He strolled away.

"By Jove! he did it well," said one of the General's other acquaintances when Norman was out of ear-shot.

"You know, he and his wife have quarrelled," explained Stirling to the astonished General.

"Great Heavens!" The old gentleman looked inexpressibly shocked.

"Yes—Wickersham."

"That scoundrel!"

"Yes; he is the devil with the women."

Next evening, as the General sat with Stirling among a group, sipping his toddy, some one approached behind him.

Stirling, who had become a great friend of the General's, greeted the newcomer.

"Hello, Ferdy! Come around; let me introduce you to General Keith, Gordon Keith's father."

The General, with a pleasant smile on his face, rose from his chair and turned to greet the newcomer. As he did so he faced Ferdy Wickersham, who bowed coldly. The old gentleman stiffened, put his hand behind his back, and with uplifted head looked him full in the eyes for a second, and then turned his back on him.

"I beg your pardon, Mr. Stirling, for declining to recognize any one whom you are good enough to wish to introduce to me, but that man I must decline to recognize. He is not a gentleman."

"I doubt if you know one," said Ferdy, with a shrug, as he strolled away with affected indifference. But a dozen men had seen the cut.

"I guess you are right enough about that, General," said one of them.

When the General reflected on what he had done, he was overwhelmed with remorse. He apologized profusely to Stirling for having committed such a solecism.

"I am nothing but an irascible old idiot, sir, and I hope you will excuse my constitutional weakness, but I really could not recognize that man."

Stirling's inveterate amiability soon set him at ease again.

"It is well for Wickersham to hear the truth now and then," he said. "I guess he hears it rarely enough. Most people feed him on lies."

Some others appeared to take the same view of the matter, for the General was more popular than ever.

Gordon found a new zest in showing his father about the city. Everything astonished him. He saw the world with the eyes of a child. The streets, the crowds, the shop-windows, the shimmering stream of carriages that rolled up and down the avenue, the elevated railways which had just been constructed, all were a marvel to him.

"Where do these people get their wealth?" he asked.

"Some of them get it from rural gentlemen who visit the town," said Gordon, laughing.

The old fellow smiled. "I suspect a good many of them get it from us countrymen. In fact, at the last we furnish it all. It all comes out of the ground."

"It is a pity that we did not hold on to some of it," said Gordon.

The old gentleman glanced at him. "I do not want any of it. My son, Agar's standard was the best: 'neither poverty nor riches.' Riches cannot make a gentleman."

Keith laughed and called him old-fashioned, but he knew in his heart that he was right.

The beggars who accosted him on the street never turned away empty-handed. He had it not in his heart to refuse the outstretched hand of want.

"Why, that man who pretended that he had a large family and was out of work is a fraud," said Gordon. "I'll bet that he has no family and never works."

"Well, I didn't give him much," said the old man. "But remember what Lamb said: 'Shut not thy purse-strings always against painted distress. It is good to believe him. Give, and under the personate father of a family think, if thou pleasest, that thou hast relieved an indigent bachelor.'"

A week later Gordon was on his way to England and the General had returned home.

It was just after this that the final breach took place between Norman Wentworth and his wife. It was decided that for their children's sake there should be no open separation; at least, for the present. Norman had business which would take him away for a good part of the time, and the final separation could be left to the future. Meanwhile, to save appearances somewhat, it was arranged that Mrs. Wentworth should ask Lois Huntington to come up and spend the winter in New York, partly as her companion and partly as governess for the children. This might stop the mouths of some persons.

When the proposal first reached Miss Abigail, she rejected it without hesitation; she would not hear of it. Curiously enough, Lois suddenly appeared violently anxious to go. But following the suggestion came an invitation from Norman's mother asking Miss Abigail to pay her a long visit. She needed her, she said, and she asked as a favor that she would let Lois accept her daughter-in-law's invitation. So Miss Abby consented. "The Lawns" was shut up for the winter, and the two ladies went up to New York.

As Norman left for the West the very day that Lois was installed, she had no knowledge of the condition of affairs in that unhappy household, except what Gossip whispered about her. This would have been more than enough, but for the fact that the girl stiffened as soon as any one approached the subject, and froze even such veterans as Mrs. Nailor.

Mrs. Wentworth was far too proud to refer to it. All Lois knew, therefore, was that there was trouble and she was there to help tide it over, and she meant, if she could, to make it up. Meanwhile, Mrs. Wentworth was very kind, if formal, to her, and the children, delighted to get rid of the former governess, whom they insisted in describing as an "old cat," were her devoted slaves.

Yet Lois was not as contented as she had fondly expected to be.

She learned soon after her arrival that one object of her visit to New York would be futile. She would not see Mr. Keith. He had gone abroad.—"In pursuit of Mrs. Lancaster," said Mrs. Nailor; for Lois was willing enough to hear all that lady had to say on this subject, and it was a good deal. "You know, I believe she is going to marry him. She will unless she can get a title."

"I do not believe a title would make any difference to her," said Lois, rather sharply, glad to have any sound reason for attacking Mrs. Nailor.

"Oh, don't you believe it! She'd snap one up quick enough if she had the chance."

"She has had a plenty of chances," asserted Lois.

"Well, it may serve Mr. Keith a good turn. He looked very low down for a while last Spring—just after that big Creamer ball. But he had quite perked up this Fall, and, next thing I heard, he had gone over to England after

Alice Lancaster, who is spending the winter there. It was time she went, too, for people were beginning to talk a good deal of the way she ran after Norman Wentworth."

"I must go," said Lois, suddenly rising; "I have to take the children out."

"Poor dears!" sighed Mrs. Nailor. "I am glad they have some one to look after them." Lois's sudden change prevented any further condolence. Fortunately, Mrs. Nailor was too much delighted with the opportunity to pour her information into quite fresh ears to observe Lois's expression.

The story of the trouble between Mr. and Mrs. Wentworth was soon public property. Wickersham's plans appeared to him to be working out satisfactorily. Louise Wentworth must, he felt, care for him to sacrifice so much for him. In this assumption he let down the barriers of prudence which he had hitherto kept up, and, one evening when the opportunity offered, he openly declared himself. To his chagrin and amazement, she appeared to be shocked and even to resent it.

Yes, she liked him—liked him better than almost any one, she admitted; but she did not, she could not, love him. She was married.

Wickersham ridiculed the idea.

Married! Well, what difference did that make? Did not many married women love other men than their husbands? Had not her husband gone after another?

Her eyes closed suddenly; then her eyelids fluttered.

"Yes; but I am not like that. I have children." She spoke slowly.

"Nonsense," cried Wickersham. "Of course, we love each other and belong to each other. Send the children to your husband."

Mrs. Wentworth recoiled in horror. There was that in his manner and look which astounded her. "Abandon her children?" How could she? Her whole manner changed. "You have misunderstood me."

"Sit down. I want to talk to you."

Wickersham grew angry.

"Don't be a fool, Louise. You have broken with your husband. Now, don't go and throw away happiness for a priest's figment. Get a divorce and marry me, if you want to; but at least accept my love."

But he had overshot the mark. He had opened her eyes. Was this the man she had taken as her closest friend! —for whom she had quarrelled with her husband and defied the world!

Wickersham watched her as her doubt worked its way in her mind. He could see the process in her face. He suddenly seized her and drew her to him.

"Here, stop this! Your husband has abandoned you and gone after another woman."

She gave a gasp, but made no answer.

She pushed him away from her slowly, and after a moment rose and walked from the room as though dazed.

It was so unexpected that Wickersham made no attempt to stop her.

A moment later Lois entered the room. She walked straight up to him. Wickersham tried to greet her lightly, but she remained grave.

"Mr. Wickersham, I do not think you—ought to come here—as often as you do."

"And, pray, why not?" he demanded.

Her brown eyes looked straight into his and held them steadily.

"Because people talk about it."

"I cannot help people talking. You know what they are," said Wickersham, amused.

"You can prevent giving them occasion to talk. You are too good a friend of Cousin Louise to cause her unhappiness." The honesty of her words was undoubted. It spoke in every tone of her voice and glance of her eyes. "She is most unhappy."

Wickersham conceived a new idea. How lovely she was in her soft blue dress!

"Very well; I will do what you say. There are few things I would not do for you." He stepped closer to her and gazed in her eyes. "Sit down. I want to talk to you."

"Thank you ; I must go now."

Wickersham tried to detain her, but she backed away, her hands down and held a little back.

"Good-by."

"Miss Huntington—Lois—" he said ; "one moment."

But she opened the door and passed out.

Wickersham walked down the street in a sort of maze.

CHAPTER XXIV

KEITH TRIES HIS FORTUNES IN
ANOTHER LAND

IN fact, as usual, Mrs. Nailor's statement to Lois had some foundation, though very little. Mrs. Lancaster had gone abroad, and Keith had followed her.

Keith, on his arrival in England, found Rhodes somewhat changed, at least in person. Years of high living and ease had rounded him, and he had lost something of his old spirit. At times an expression of weariness or discontent came into his eyes.

He was as cordial as ever to Keith, and when Keith unfolded his plans he entered into them with earnestness.

"You have come at a good time," he said. "They are beginning to think that America is all a bonanza."

After talking over the matter, Rhodes invited Keith down to the country.

"We have taken an old place in Warwickshire for the hunting. An old friend of yours is down there for a few days,"—his eyes twinkled,—"and we have some good fellows there. Think you will like them—some of them," he added.

"Who is my friend?" asked Keith.

"Her name was Alice Yorke," he replied, with his eyes on Keith's face.

At the name another face sprang to Keith's mind. The eyes were brown, not blue, and the face was the fresh face of a young girl. Yet Keith accepted.

Rhodes did not tell him that Mrs. Lancaster had not accepted their invitation until after she had heard that he was to be invited. Nor did he tell him that she had authorized him to subscribe largely to the stock of the new syndicate.

On reaching the station they were met by a rich equipage with two liveried servants, and, after a short drive through beautiful country, they turned into a fine park, and presently drove up before an imposing old country house; for "The Keep" was one of the finest mansions in all that region. It was also one of the most expensive. It had broken its owners to run it. But this was nothing to Creamer of Creamer, Crustback & Company; at least, it was nothing to Mrs. Creamer, or to Mrs. Rhodes, who was her daughter. She had plans, and money was nothing to her. Rhodes was manifestly pleased at Keith's exclamations of appreciation as they drove through the park with its magnificent trees, its coppices and coverts, its stretches of emerald sward and roll of gracious hills, and drew up at the portal of the mansion. Yet he was inclined to be a little apologetic about it, too.

"This is rather too rich for me," he said, between a smile and a sigh. "Somehow, I began too late."

It was a noble old hall into which he ushered Keith, the wainscoting dark with age, and hung with trophies of many a chase and forgotten field. A number of modern easy-chairs and great rich rugs gave it an air of comfort, even if they were not altogether harmonious.

Keith did not see Mrs. Rhodes till the company were all assembled in the drawing-room for dinner. She was a rather pretty woman, distinctly American in face and voice, but in speech more English than any one Keith had seen since landing. Her hair and speech were arranged in the extreme London fashion. She was "awfully keen on" everything she fancied, and found most things English "ripping." She greeted Keith with somewhat more formality than he had expected from Grinnell Rhodes's wife, and introduced him to Colonel Campbell, a handsome, broad-shouldered man, as "an American," which Keith thought rather unnecessary, since no one could have been in doubt about it.

Keith found, on his arrival in the drawing-room, that the house was full of company, a sort of house-party assembled for the hunting.

Suddenly there was a stir, followed by a hush in the conversation, and monocles and lorgnons went up.

"Here she comes," said a man near Keith.

"Who is she?" asked a thin woman with ugly hands, dropping her monocle with the air of a man.

"La belle Américaine," replied the man beside her, "a friend of the host."

"Oh! Not of the hostess?"

"Oh, I don't know. I met her last night—"

"Steepleton is ahead—wins in a walk."

"Oh, she's rich? The castle needs a new roof? Will it be in time for next season?"

The gentleman said he knew nothing about it.

Keith turned and faced Alice Lancaster.

She was dressed in a black gown that fitted perfectly her straight, supple figure, the soft folds clinging close enough to show the gracious curves, and falling away behind her in a train that, as she stood with her head uplifted, gave her an appearance almost of majesty. Her round arms and perfect shoulders were of dazzling whiteness; her abundant brown hair was coiled low on her snowy neck, showing the beauty of her head; and her single ornament was one rich red rose fastened in her bodice with a small diamond clasp. It was the little pin that Keith had found in the Ridgely woods and returned to her so long ago; though Keith did not recognize it. It was the only jewel about her, and was worn simply to hold the rose, as though that were the thing she valued. Keith's thoughts sprang to the first time he ever saw her with a red rose near her heart —the rose he had given her, which the humming-bird had sought as its chalice.

The other ladies were all gowned in satin and velvet of

rich colors, and were flaming in jewels, and as Mrs. Lancaster stood among them and they fell back a little on either side to look at her, they appeared, as it were, a setting for her.

After the others were presented, Keith stepped forward to greet her, and her face lit up with a light that made it suddenly young.

"I am so glad to see you." She clasped his hand warmly. "It is so good to see an old friend from our ain countree."

"I do not need to say I am glad to see you," said Keith, looking her in the eyes. "You are my ain countree here."

At that moment the rose fell at her feet. It had slipped somehow from the clasp that held it. A half-dozen men sprang forward to pick it up, but Keith was ahead of them. He took it up, and, with his eyes looking straight into hers, handed it to her.

"It is your emblem; it is what I always think of you as being." The tone was too low for any one else to hear; but her mounting color and the light in her eyes told that she caught it.

Still looking straight into his eyes without a word, she stuck the rose in her bodice just over her heart.

Several women turned their gaze on Keith and scanned him with sudden interest, and one of them, addressing her companion, a broad-shouldered man with a pleasant, florid face, said in an undertone:

"That is the man you have to look out for, Steepleton."

"A good-looking fellow. Who is he?"

"Somebody, I fancy, or our hostess wouldn't have him here."

The dinner that evening was a function. Mrs. Rhodes would rather have suffered a serious misfortune than fail in any of the social refinements of her adopted land. Rhodes had suggested that Keith be placed next to Mrs. Lancaster, but Mrs. Rhodes had another plan in mind. She liked Alice Lancaster, and she was trying to do by her as she would have been done by. She wanted her to make a brilliant match. Lord Steepleton appeared designed by Providence for this especial purpose : the representative of an old and distinguished house, owner of a famous—indeed, of an historic—estate, unhappily encumbered, but not too heavily to be relieved by a providential fortune. Hunting was his most serious occupation. At present he was engaged in the most serious hunt of his career : he was hunting an heiress.

Mrs. Rhodes was his friend, and as his friend she had put him next to Mrs. Lancaster.

Ordinarily, Mrs. Lancaster would have been extremely pleased to be placed next the lion of the occasion. But this evening she would have liked to be near another guest. He was on the other side of the board, and appeared to be, in the main, enjoying himself, though now and then his eyes strayed across in her direction, and presently, as he caught her glance, he lifted his glass and smiled. Her neighbor observed the act, and putting up his monocle, looked across the table ; then glanced at Mrs. Lancaster, and then looked again at Keith more carefully.

"Who is your friend ? " he asked.

Mrs. Lancaster smiled, with a pleasant light in her eyes.

"An old friend of mine, Mr. Keith."

"Ah ! Fortunate man. Scotchman ? "

"No ; an American."

"Oh !— You have known him a long time ? "

"Since I was a little girl."

"Oh !— What is he ? "

"A gentleman."

"Yes." The Englishman took the trouble again to put up his monocle and take a fleeting glance across the table. "He looks it," he said. "I mean, what does he do ? Is he a capitalist like—like our host ? Or is he just getting to be a capitalist ? "

"I hope he is," replied Mrs. Lancaster, with a twinkle in

her eyes that showed she enjoyed the Englishman's mystification. "He is engaged in mining."

She gave a rosy picture of the wealth in the region from
which Keith came.

"All your men do something, I believe?" said the gentleman.

"All who are worth anything," assented Mrs. Lancaster.

"No wonder you are a rich people."

Something about his use of the adjective touched her.

"Our people have a sense of duty, too, and as much courage as any others, only they do not make any to-do about
it. I have a friend—a *gentleman*—who drove a stage-coach
through the mountains for a while rather than do nothing,
and who was held up one night and jumped from the stage
on the robber, and chased him down the mountains and
disarmed him."

"Good!" exclaimed the gentleman. "Nervy thing!"

"Rather," said Mrs. Lancaster, with mantling cheeks,
stirred by what she considered a reflection on her people.
And that was not all he did. "He had charge of a mine,
and one day the mine was flooded while the men were at
work, and he went in in the darkness and brought the men
out safe."

"Good!" said the gentleman. "But he had others with
him? He did not go alone?"

"He started alone, and two men volunteered to go with
him. But he sent them back with the first group they
found, and then, as there were others, he waded on by himself to where the others were, and brought them out, bringing on his shoulder the man who had attempted his life."

"Fine!" exclaimed the gentleman. "I've been in some
tight places myself; but I don't know about that. What
was his name?"

"Keith."

"Oh!"

Her eyes barely glanced his way; but the Earl of Steepleton saw in them what he had never been able to bring there.

The Englishman put up his monocle and this time gazed long at Gordon.

"Nervy chap!" he said quietly. "Won't you present me after dinner?"

In his slow mind was dawning an idea that, perhaps, after all, this quiet American who had driven his way forward had found a baiting-place which he, with all his titles and long pedigrees, could not enter. His honest, outspoken admiration had, however, done more to make him a place in that guarded fortress than all Mrs. Rhodes's praises had effected.

A little later the guests had all departed or scattered. Those who remained were playing cards and appeared settled for a good while.

"Keith, we are out of it. Let's have a game of billiards," said the host, who had given his seat to a guest who had just come in after saying good night on the stair to one of the ladies.

Keith followed him to the billiard-room, a big apartment finished in oak, with several large tables in it, and he and Rhodes began to play. The game, however, soon languished, for the two men had much to talk about.

"Houghton, you may go," said Rhodes to the servant who attended to the table. "I will ring for you when I want you to shut up."

"Thank you, sir"; and he was gone.

"Now tell me all about everything," said Rhodes. "I want to hear everything that has happened since I came away—came into exile. I know about the property and the town that has grown up just as I knew it would. Tell me about the people—old Squire Rawson and Phrony, and Wickersham, and Norman and his wife."

Keith told him about them. "Rhodes," he said, as he ended, "you started it and you ought to have stayed with it. Old Rawson says you foretold it all."

Suddenly Rhodes flung his cue down on the table and straightened up. "Keith, this is killing me. Sometimes

I think I can't stand it another day. I've a mind to chuck up the whole business and cut for it."

Keith gazed at him in amazement. The clouded brow, the burning eyes, the drawn mouth, all told how real that explosion was and from what depths it came. Keith was quite startled.

"It all seems to me so empty, so unreal, so puerile. I am bored to death with it. Do you think this is real?" He waved his arms impatiently about him. "It is all a sham and a fraud. I am nothing—nobody. I am a puppet on a hired stage, playing to amuse—not myself!—the Lord knows I am bored enough by it!—but a lot of people who don't care any more about me than I do about them. I can't stand this. D—n it! I don't want to make love to any other man's wife any more than I will have any of them making love to my wife. I think they are beginning to understand that. I showed a little puppy the front door not long ago—an earl, too, or next thing to it, an earl's eldest son—for doing what he would no more have dared to do in an Englishman's house than he would have tried to burn it. After that, I think, they began to see I might be something. Keith, do you remember what old Rawson said to us once about marrying?"

Keith had been thinking of it all the evening.

"Keith, I was not born for this; I was born to *do* something. But for giving up I might have been like Stevenson or Eads or your man Maury, whom they are all belittling because he did it all himself instead of getting others to do it. By George! I hope to live till I build one more big bridge or run one more long tunnel. Jove! to stand once more up on the big girders, so high that the trees look small below you, and see the bridge growing under your eyes where the old croakers had said nothing would stand!"

Keith's eyes sparkled, and he reached out his hand; and the other grasped it.

When Keith returned home, he was already in sight of victory.

The money had all been subscribed. His own interest in the venture was enough to make him rich, and he was to be general superintendent of the new company, with Matheson as his manager of the mines. All that was needed now was to complete the details of the transfer of the properties, perfect his organization, and set to work. This for a time required his presence more or less continuously in New York, and he opened an office in one of the office buildings down in the city, and took an apartment in a pleasant up-town hotel.

When Keith returned to New York that Autumn, it was no longer as a young man with eyes aflame with hope and expectation and face alight with enthusiasm. The eager recruit had changed to the veteran. He had had experience of a world where men lived and died for the most sordid of all rewards—money, mere money.

The fight had left its mark upon him. The mouth had lost something of the smile that once lurked about its corners, but had gained in strength. The eyes, always direct and steady, had more depth. The shoulders had a squarer set, as though they had been braced against adversity. Experience of life had sobered him.

Sometimes it had come to him that he might be caught by the current and might drift into the same spirit, but self-examination up to this time had reassured him. He knew that he had other motives : the trust reposed in him by his friends, the responsibility laid upon him, the resolve to justify that confidence, were still there, beside his eager desire for success.

He called immediately to see Norman. He was surprised to find how much he had aged in this short time. His hair was sprinkled with gray. He had lost all his lightness. He was distrait and almost morose.

"You men here work too hard," asserted Keith. "You ought to have run over to England with me. You'd have learned that men can work and live too. I spent some of the most profitable time I was over there in a deer forest, which may have been Burnam-wood, as all the trees had disappeared—gone somewhere, if not to Dunsinane."

Norman half smiled, but he answered wearily :

"I wish I had been anywhere else than where I was."

He turned away while he was speaking and fumbled among the papers on his desk. Keith rose, and Norman rose also.

"I will send you cards to the clubs. I shall not be in town to-night, but to-morrow night, or the evening after, suppose you dine with me at the University. I'll have two or three fellows to meet you—or, perhaps, we'll dine alone. What do you say? We can talk more freely."

Keith said that this was just what he should prefer, and Norman gave him a warm handshake and, suddenly seating himself at his desk, dived quickly into his papers.

Keith came out mystified. There was something he could not understand. He wondered if the trouble of which he had heard had grown.

Next morning, looking over the financial page of a paper, Keith came on a paragraph in which Norman's name appeared. He was mentioned as one of the directors of a company which the paper declared was among those that had disappointed the expectations of investors. There was nothing very tangible about the article ; but the general tone was critical, and to Keith's eye unfriendly.

When, the next afternoon, Keith rang the door-bell at Norman's house, and asked if Mrs. Wentworth was at home, the servant who opened the door informed him that no one of that name lived there. They used to live there, but had moved. Mrs. Wentworth lived somewhere on Fifth Avenue near the Park. It was a large new house near such a street, right-hand side, second house from the corner.

Keith had a feeling of disappointment. Somehow, he had hoped to hear something of Lois Huntington.

Keith, having resolved to devote the afternoon to the call on his friend's wife, and partly in the hope of learning where Lois was, kept on, and presently found himself in front of a new double house, one of the largest on the block. Keith felt reassured.

"Well, this does not look as if Wentworth were altogether broke," he thought.

A strange servant opened the door. Mrs. Wentworth was not at home. The other lady was in—would the gentleman come in? There was the flutter of a dress at the top of the stair.

Keith said no. He would call again. The servant looked puzzled, for the lady at the top of the stair had seen Mr. Keith cross the street and had just given orders that he should be admitted, as she would see him. Now, as Keith walked away, Miss Lois Huntington descended the stair.

"Why didn't you let him in, Hucless?" she demanded.

"I told him you were in, Miss; but he said he would not come in."

Miss Huntington turned and walked slowly back up to her room. Her face was very grave; she was pondering deeply.

A little later Lois Huntington put on her hat and went out.

Lois had not found her position at Mrs. Wentworth's the most agreeable in the world. Mrs. Wentworth was moody and capricious, and at times exacting.

She had little idea how often that quiet girl who took her complaints so calmly was tempted to break her vow of silence, answer her upbraidings, and return home. But her old friends were dropping away from her. And it was on this account and for Norman's sake that Lois put up with her capriciousness. She had promised Norman to stay with her, and she would do it.

Mrs. Norman's quarrel with Alice Lancaster was a sore trial to Lois. Many of her friends treated Lois as if she were a sort of upper servant, with a mingled condescension and hauteur. Lois was rather amused at it, except when it became too apparent, and then she would show her little claws, which were sharp enough. But Mrs. Lancaster had always been sweet to her, and Lois had missed her sadly. She no longer came to Mrs. Wentworth's. Lois, however, was always urged to come and see her, and an intimacy had sprung up between the two. Lois, with her freshness, was like a breath of Spring to the society woman, who was a little jaded with her experience ; and the elder lady, on her part, treated the young girl with a warmth that was half maternal, half the cordiality of an elder sister. What part Gordon Keith played in this friendship must be left to surmise.

It was to Mrs. Lancaster's that Lois now took her way. Her greeting was a cordial one, and Lois was soon confiding to her her trouble ; how she had met an old friend after many years, and then how a contretemps had occurred. She told of his writing her, and of her failure to answer his letters, and how her aunt had refused to allow him to come to Brookford to see them.

Mrs. Lancaster listened with interest.

"My dear, there was nothing in that. Yes, that was just one of Ferdy's little lies," she said, in a sort of reverie.

"But it was so wicked in him to tell such falsehoods about a man," exclaimed Lois, her color coming and going, her eyes flashing.

Mrs. Lancaster shrugged her shoulders.

"Ferdy does not like Mr. Keith, and he does like you, and he probably thought to prevent your liking him."

"I detest him."

The telltale color rushed up into her cheeks as Mrs. Lancaster's eyes rested on her, and as it mounted, those blue eyes grew a little more searching.

"I can scarcely bear to see him when he comes there," said Lois.

"Has he begun to go there again?" Mrs. Lancaster inquired, in some surprise.

"Yes ; and he pretends that he is coming to see me !" said

the girl, with a flash in her eyes. "You know that is not true?"

"Don't you believe him," said the other, gravely. Her eyes, as they rested on the girl's face, had a very soft light in them.

"Well, we must make it up," she said presently. "You are going to Mrs. Wickersham's?" she asked suddenly.

"Yes; Cousin Louise is going and says I must go. Mr. Wickersham will not be there, you know."

"Yes." She drifted off into a reverie.

CHAPTER XXV

THE DINNER AT MRS. WICKERSHAM'S

KEITH quickly discovered that Rumor was busy with Ferdy Wickersham's name in other places than gilded drawing-rooms. He had been dropped from the board of more than one big corporation in which he had once had a potent influence. Knowing men, like Stirling and his club friends, began to say that they did not see how he had kept up. But up-town he still held on—held on with a steady eye and stony face that showed a nerve worthy of a better man. His smile became more constant,—to be sure, it was belied by his eyes: that cold gleam was not mirth,—but his voice was as insolent as ever.

Several other rumors soon began to float about. One was that he and Mrs. Wentworth had fallen out. As to the cause of this the town was divided. One story was that the pretty governess at Mrs. Wentworth's was in some way concerned with it.

However this was, the Wickersham house was mortgaged, and Rumor began to say even up-town that the Wickersham fortune had melted away.

The news of Keith's success in England had reached home as soon as he had. His friends congratulated him, and his acquaintances greeted him with a warmth that, a few years before, would have cheered his heart and have made him their friend for life. Mrs. Nailor, when she met him, almost fell on his neck. She actually called him her "dear boy."

"Oh, I have been hearing about you!" she said archly.

"You must come and dine with us at once and tell us all about it."

"About what?" inquired Keith.

"About your great successes on the other side. You see, your friends keep up with you!"

"They do, indeed, and sometimes get ahead of me," said Keith.

"How would to-morrow suit you? No, not to-morrow— Saturday? No; we are going out Saturday. Let me see— we are so crowded with engagements I shall have to go home and look at my book. But you must come very soon. You have heard the news, of course? Isn't it dreadful?"

"What news?" He knew perfectly what she meant.

"About the Norman-Wentworths getting a divorce? Dreadful, isn't it? Perfectly dreadful! But, of course, it was to be expected. Any one could see that all along?"

"I could not," said Keith, dryly; "but I do not claim to be any one."

"Which side are you on? Norman's, I suppose?"

"Neither," said Keith.

"You know, Ferdy always was in love with her?" This with a glance to obtain Keith's views.

"No; I know nothing about it."

"Yes; always," she nodded oracularly. "Of course, he is making love to Alice Lancaster, too, and to the new governess at the Wentworths'."

"Who is that?" asked Keith, moved by some sudden instinct to inquire.

"That pretty country cousin of Norman's, whom they brought there to save appearances when Norman first left. Huntington is her name."

Keith suddenly grew hot.

"Yes, Ferdy is making love to her, too. Why, they say that is what they have quarrelled about. Louise is insanely jealous, and she is very pretty. Yes—you know, Ferdy is like some other men? Just gregarious? Yes? But

Louise Wentworth was always his *grande passion*. He is just amusing himself with the governess, and she, poor little fool, supposes she has made a conquest. You know how it is?"

"I really know nothing about it," declared Keith, in a flame.

"Yes; and he was always her *grande passion*? Don't you think so?"

"No, I do not," said Keith, firmly. "I know nothing about it; but I believe she and Norman were devoted,—as devoted a couple as I ever saw,—and I do not see why people cannot let them alone. I think none too well of Ferdy Wickersham, but I don't believe a word against her. She may be silly; but she is a hundred times better than some who calumniate her."

"Oh, you dear boy! You were always so amiable. It's a pity the world is not like you; but it is not."

"It is a pity people do not let others alone and attend to their own affairs," remarked Keith, grimly. "I believe more than half the trouble is made by the meddlers who go around gossiping."

"Don't they! Why, every one is talking about it. I have not been in a drawing-room where it is not being discussed."

"I suppose not," said Mr. Keith.

"And, you know, they say Norman Wentworth has lost a lot of money, too. But, then, he has a large account to fall back on. Alice Lancaster has a plenty."

"What's that?" Keith's voice had an unpleasant sharpness in it.

"Oh, you know, he is her trustee, and they are great friends. Good-by. You must come and dine with us sometime—sometime soon, too."

And Mrs. Nailor floated away, and in the first drawing-room she visited told of Keith's return and of his taking the story of Louise Wentworth and Ferdy Wickersham very seriously; adding, "And you know, I think he is a great

374

admirer of Louise himself—a very great admirer. Of course, he would like to marry Alice Lancaster, just as Ferdy would. They all want to marry her; but Louise Wentworth is the one that has their hearts. She knows how to capture them. You keep your eyes open. You ought to have seen the way he looked when I mentioned Ferdy Wickersham and her. My dear, a man doesn't look that way unless he feels something here." She tapped solemnly the spot where she imagined her heart to be, that dry and desiccated organ that had long ceased to know any real warmth.

A little time afterwards, Keith, to his great surprise, received an invitation to dine at Mrs. Wickersham's. He had never before received an invitation to her house, and when he had met her, she had always been stiff and repellent toward him. This he had regarded as perfectly natural; for he and Ferdy had never been friendly, and of late had not even kept up appearances.

He wondered why he should be invited now. Could it be true, as Stirling had said, laughing, that now he had the key and would find all doors open to him?

Keith had not yet written his reply when he called that evening at Mrs. Lancaster's. She asked him if he had received such an invitation. Keith said yes, but he did not intend to go. He almost thought it must have been sent by mistake.

"Oh, no; now come. Ferdy won't be there, and Mrs. Wickersham wants to be friendly with you. You and Ferdy don't get along; but neither do she and Ferdy. You know they have fallen out? Poor old thing! She was talking about it the other day, and she burst out crying. She said he had been her idol."

"What is the matter?"

"Oh, Ferdy's selfishness."

"He is a brute! Think of a man quarrelling with his mother! Why — !" He went into a reverie in which his face grew very soft, while Mrs. Lancaster watched him silently. Presently he started. "I have nothing against her except a sort of general animosity from boyhood, which I am sorry to have."

"Oh, well, then, come. As people grow older they outgrow their animosities and wish to make friends."

"You being so old as to have experienced it?" said Keith.

"I am nearly thirty years old," she said. "Isn't it dreadful?"

"Aurora is much older than that," said Keith.

"Ah, Sir Flatterer, I have a mirror." But her eyes filled with a pleasant light as Keith said:

"Then it will corroborate what needs no proof."

She knew it was flattery, but she enjoyed it and dimpled.

"Now, you will come? I want you to come." She looked at him with a soft glow in her face.

"Yes. On your invitation."

"Alice Lancaster, place one good deed to thy account: 'Blessed are the peacemakers,'" said Mrs. Lancaster.

When Keith arrived at Mrs. Wickersham's he found the company assembled in her great drawing-room—the usual sort to be found in great drawing-rooms of large new chateau-like mansions in a great and commercial city.

"Mr. Keats!" called out the prim servant. They always took this poetical view of his name.

Mrs. Wickersham greeted him civilly and solemnly. She had aged much since Keith saw her last, and had also grown quite deaf. Her face showed traces of the desperate struggle she was making to keep up appearances. It was apparent that she had not the least idea who he was; but she shook hands with him much as she might have done at a funeral had he called to pay his respects. Among the late arrivals was Mrs. Wentworth. She was the richest-dressed woman in the room, and her jewels were the finest, but she had an expression on her face, as she entered, which Keith had never seen there. Her head was high, and there was an air of defiance about her which challenged the eye at once.

"I don't think I shall speak to her," said a voice near Keith.

"Well, I have known her all my life, and until it becomes a public scandal I don't feel authorized to cut her—"

The speaker was Mrs. Nailor, who was in her most charitable mood.

"Oh, of course, I shall speak to her here, but I mean—I certainly shall not visit her."

"You know she has quarrelled with her friend, Mrs. Lancaster? About her husband." This was behind her fan.

"Oh, yes. She is to be here to-night. Quite brazen, isn't it? We shall see how they meet. I met a remarkably pretty girl down in the dressing-room," she continued; "one of the guests. She has such pretty manners, too. Really, I thought, from her politeness to me in arranging my dress, she must be one of the maids until Mrs. Wentworth spoke to her. Young girls nowadays are so rude! They take up the mirror the whole time, and never think of letting you see yourself. I wonder who she can be?"

"Possibly Mrs. Wentworth's companion. I think she is here. She has to have some one to do the proprieties, you know?" said Mrs. Nailor.

"I should think it might be as well," assented the other, with a sniff. "But she would hardly be here!"

"She is really her governess, a very ill-bred and rude young person," said Mrs. Nailor.

The other sighed.

"Society is getting so democratic now, one might say, so mixed, that there is no telling whom one may meet nowadays."

"No, indeed," pursued Mrs. Nailor. "I do not at all approve of governesses and such persons being invited out. I think the English way much the better. There the governess never dreams of coming to the table except to luncheon, and her friends are the housekeeper and the butler."

Keith, wearied of the banalities at his ear, crossed over

to where Mrs. Wentworth stood a little apart from the other ladies. One or two men were talking to her. She was evidently pleased to see him. She talked volubly, and with just that pitch in her voice that betrays a subcurrent of excitement.

From time to time she glanced about her, appearing to Keith to search the faces of the other women. Keith wondered if it were a fancy of his that they were holding a little aloof from her. Presently Mrs. Nailor came up and spoke to her.

Keith backed away a little, and found himself mixed up with the train of a lady behind him, a dainty thing of white muslin.

He apologized in some confusion, and turning, found himself looking into Lois Huntington's eyes. For a bare moment he was in a sort of maze. Then the expression in her face dispelled it. She held out her hand, and he clasped it; and before he had withdrawn his eyes from hers, he knew that his peace was made, and Mrs. Wickersham's drawing-room had become another place. This, then, was what Alice Lancaster meant when she spoke of the peace-makers.

"It does not in the least matter about the dress, I assure you," she said in reply to his apology. "My dressmaker, Lois Huntington, can repair it so that you will not know it has been torn. It was only a ruse of mine to attract your attention." She was trying to speak lightly. "I thought you were not going to speak to me at all. It seems to be a way you have of treating your old friends —your oldest friends," she laughed.

"Oh, the insolence of youth!" said Keith, wishing to keep away from a serious subject. "Let us settle this question of age here and now. I say you are seven years old."

"You are a Bourbon," she said; "you neither forget nor learn. Look at me. How old do I look?"

"Seven—"

"No. Look."

378

"I am looking—would I were Argus! You look like—perpetual Youth."

And she did. She was dressed in pure white. Her dark eyes were soft and gentle, yet with mischief lurking in them, and her straight brows, almost black, added to their lustre. Her dark hair was brushed back from her white forehead, and as she turned, Keith noted again, as he had done the first time he met her, the fine profile and the beautiful lines of her round throat, with the curves below it, as white as snow. "Perpetual Youth," he murmured.

"And do you know what you are?" she challenged him.

"Yes; Age."

"No. Flattery. But I am proof. I have learned that men are deceivers ever. You positively refused to see me when I had left word with the servant that I would see you if you called." She gave him a swift little glance to see how he took her charge.

"I did nothing of the kind. I will admit that I should know where you are by instinct, as Sir John knew the Prince; but I did not expect you to insist on my doing so. How was I to know you were in the city?"

"The servant told you."

"The servant told me?"

As Keith's brow puckered in the effort to unravel the mystery, she nodded.

"Um-hum—I heard him. I was at the head of the stair."

Keith tapped his head.

"It's old age—sheer senility."

"'No; I don't want to see the other lady,'" she said, mimicking him so exactly that he opened his eyes wide.

"I am staying at Mrs. Wentworth's—Cousin Norman's," she continued, with a little change of expression and the least little lift of her head.

Keith's expression, perhaps, changed slightly, too, for she added quietly: "Cousin Louise had to have some one with her, and I am teaching the children. I am the governess."

"I have always said that children nowadays have all the

best things," said Keith, desirous to get off delicate ground.
"You know, some one has said he never ate a ripe peach
in his life : when he was a boy the grown-ups had them,
and since he grew up the children have them all."

She laughed.

"I am very severe, I assure you."

"You look it. I should think you might be Herod
himself."

She smiled, and then the smile died out, and she glanced
around her.

"I owe you an apology," she said in a lowered voice.

"For what?"

"For—mis—for not answering your letters. But I mis—
I don't know how to say what I wish. Won't you accept
it without an explanation?" She held out her hand and
gave him the least little flitting glance of appeal.

"I will," said Keith. "With all my heart."

"Thank you. I have been very unhappy about it."
She breathed a little sigh of relief, which Keith caught.

Mrs. Lancaster did not arrive until all the other guests
had been there a little while. But when she entered she
had never looked handsomer. As soon as she had greeted
her hostess, her eyes swept around the room, and in their
circuit rested for a moment on Keith, who was talking to
Lois. She gave them a charming smile. The next moment, however, her eyes stole that way again, and this time
they bore a graver expression. The admiration that filled
the younger girl's eyes was unbounded and unfeigned.

"Don't you think she is the handsomest woman in the
room?" she asked, with a nod toward Mrs. Lancaster.

Keith was suddenly conscious that he did not wish to
commit himself to such praise. She was certainly very
handsome, he admitted, but there were others who would
pass muster, too, in a beauty show.

"Oh, but I know you must think so; every one says you
do," Lois urged, with a swift glance up at him, which,
somehow, Keith would have liked to avoid.

"Then, I suppose it must be so; for every one knows my innermost thoughts. But I think she was more beautiful when she was younger. I do not know what it is; but there is something in Society that, after a few years, takes away the bloom of ingenuousness and puts in its place just the least little shade of unreality."

"I know what you mean; but she is so beautiful that one would never notice it. What a power such beauty is! I should be afraid of it." Lois was speaking almost to herself, and Keith, as she was deeply absorbed in observing Mrs. Lancaster, gazed at her with renewed interest.

"I'd so much rather be loved for myself," the girl went on earnestly. "I think it is one of the compensations that those who want such beauty have—"

"Well, it is one of the things which you must always hold merely as a conjecture, for you can never know by experience."

She glanced up at him with a smile, half pleased, half reproving.

"Do you think I am the sort that likes flattery? I believe you think we are all silly. I thought you were too good a friend of mine to attempt that line with me."

Keith declared that all women loved flattery, but protested, of course, that he was not flattering her.

"Why should I?" he laughed.

"Oh, just because you think it will please me, and because it is so easy. It is so much less trouble. It takes less intellect, and you don't think I am worth spending intellect on."

This Keith stoutly denied.

She gave him a fleeting glance out of her brown eyes. "She, however, is as good as she is handsome," she said, returning to Mrs. Lancaster.

"Yes; she is one of those who 'do good by stealth, and blush to find it fame.'"

"There are not a great many like that around here," Lois smiled. "Here comes one now?" she added, as Mrs. Nailor moved up to them. She was "so glad" to see Miss Hunt-ington out. "You must like your Winter in New York?" she said, smiling softly. "You have such opportunities for seeing interesting people—like Mr. Keith, here?" She turned her eyes on Keith.

"Oh, yes. I do. I see so many entertaining people," said Lois, innocently.

"They are very kind to you?" purred the elder lady.

"Most condescending." Lois turned her eyes toward Keith with a little sparkle in them; but as she read his appreciation a smile stole into them.

Dinner was solemnly announced, and the couples swept out in that stately manner appropriate to solemn occasions, such as marriages, funerals, and fashionable dinners.

"Do you know your place?" asked Keith of Lois, to whom he had been assigned.

"Don't I? A governess and not know her place! You must help me through."

"Through what?"

"The dinner. You do not understand what a tremendous responsibility you have. This is my first dinner."

"I always said dinners were a part of the curse," said Keith, lightly, smiling down at her fresh face with sheer content. "I shall confine myself hereafter to breakfast and lunch—except when I receive invitations to Mrs. Wicker-sham's," he added.

Mrs. Lancaster was on the other side of Keith; so he found the dinner much pleasanter than he had expected. She soon fell to talking of Lois, a subject which Keith found very agreeable.

"You know, she is staying with Louise Wentworth? Louise had to have some one to stay with her, so she got her to come and teach the children this Winter. Louise says she is trying to make something of her."

"From my slight observation, it seems to me as if the Creator has been rather successful in that direction already. How does she propose to help Him out?"

Mrs. Lancaster bent forward and took a good look at the girl, who at the moment was carrying on an animated conversation with Stirling. Her color was coming and going, her eyes were sparkling, and her cheek was dimpling with fun.

"She looks as if she came out of a country garden, doesn't she?" she said.

"Yes, because she has, and has not yet been wired to a stick."

Mrs. Lancaster's eyes grew graver at Keith's speech.

Just then the conversation became more general.

Some one told a story of a man travelling with his wife and meeting a former wife, and forgetting which one he then had.

"Oh, that reminds me of a story I heard the other day. It was awfully good—but just a little wicked," exclaimed Mrs. Nailor.

Keith's smile died out, and there was something very like a cloud lowering on his brow. Several others appeared surprised, and Mr. Nailor, a small bald-headed man, said across the table : "Hally, don't you tell that story."

But Mrs. Nailor was not to be controlled.

"Oh, I must tell it! It is not going to hurt any of you. Let me see if there is any one here very young and innocent?" She glanced about the table. "Oh, yes; there is little Miss Huntington. Miss Huntington, you can stop your ears while I tell it."

"Thank you," said Lois, placidly. She leaned a little forward and put her fingers in her ears.

A sort of gasp went around the table, and then a shout of laughter, led by Stirling. Mrs. Nailor joined in it, but her face was red and her eyes were angry. Mrs. Wentworth looked annoyed.

"Good," said Mrs. Lancaster, in an undertone.

"Divine," said Keith, his eyes snapping with satisfaction.

"It was not so bad as that," said Mrs. Nailor, her face

very red. "Miss Huntington, you can take your hands down now ; I sha'n't tell it."

"Thank you," said Lois, and sat quietly back in her chair, with her face as placid as a child's.

Mrs. Nailor suddenly changed the conversation to Art. She was looking at a painting on the wall behind Keith, and after inspecting it a moment through her lorgnon, turned toward the head of the table.

"Where did you get that picture, Mrs. Wickersham? Have I ever seen it before?"

The hostess's gaze followed hers.

"That? Oh, we have had it ever so long. It is a portrait of an ancestor of mine. It belonged to a relative, a distant relative—another branch, you know, in whose family it came down, though we had even more right to it, as we were an older branch," she said, gaining courage as she went on.

Mrs. Lancaster turned and inspected the picture.

"I, too, almost seem to have seen it before," she said presently, in a reflective way.

"My dear, you have not seen it before," declared the hostess, positively. "Although we have had it for a good while, it was at our place in the country. Brush, the picture-dealer, says it is one of the finest 'old masters' in New York, quite in the best style of Sir Peter— What's his name?"

"Then I have seen some one so like it—? Who can it be?" said Mrs. Lancaster, her mind still working along the lines of reminiscence.

Nearly every one was looking now.

"Why, I know who it is!" said Lois Huntington, who had turned to look at it, to Mrs. Lancaster. "It is Mr. Keith." Her clear voice was heard distinctly.

"Of course, it is," said Mrs. Lancaster. Others agreed with her.

Keith, too, had turned and looked over his shoulder at the picture behind him, and for a moment he seemed in a dream. His father was gazing down at him out of the frame. The next moment he came to himself. It was the man-in-armor that used to hang in the library at Elphinstone. As he turned back, he glanced at Mrs. Lancaster, and her eyes gazed into his. The next moment he addressed Mrs. Wickersham and started a new subject of conversation.

"That is it," said Mrs. Lancaster to herself. Then turning to her hostess, she said : "No, I never saw it before ; I was mistaken."

But Lois knew that she herself had seen it before, and remembered where it was.

Mrs. Wickersham looked extremely uncomfortable, but Keith's calm courtesy set her at ease again.

When the gentlemen, after their cigars, followed the ladies into the drawing-room, Keith found Mrs. Lancaster and Lois sitting together, a little apart from the others, talking earnestly. He walked over and joined them.

They had been talking of the incident of the picture, but stopped as he came up.

"Now, Lois," said Mrs. Lancaster, gayly, "I have known Mr. Keith a long time, and I give you one standing piece of advice. Don't believe one word that he tells you ; for he is the most insidious flatterer that lives."

"On the contrary," said Keith, bowing and speaking gravely to the younger girl, "I assure you that you may believe implicitly every word that I tell you. I promise you in the beginning that I shall never tell you anything but the truth as long as I live. It shall be my claim upon your friendship."

"Thank you," said Lois, lifting her eyes to his face. Her color had deepened a little at his earnest manner. "I love a palpable truth."

"You do not get it often in Society," said Mrs. Lancaster.

"I promise you that you shall always have it from me," said Keith.

"Thank you," she said again, quite earnestly, looking him calmly in the eyes. "Then we shall always be friends."

"Always."

Just then Stirling came up and with a very flattering speech asked Miss Huntington to sing.

"I hear you sing like a seraph," he declared.

"I thought they always cried," she said, smiling; then, with a half-frightened look across toward her cousin, she sobered and declared that she could not.

"I have been meaning to have her take lessons," said Mrs. Wentworth, condescendingly, from her seat near by; "but I have not had time to attend to it. She will sing very well when she takes lessons." She resumed her conversation. Stirling was still pressing Miss Huntington, and she was still excusing herself, declaring that she had no one to play her accompaniments.

"Please help me," she said in an undertone to Keith. "I used to play them myself, but Cousin Louise said I must not do that; that I must always stand up to sing."

"Nonsense," said Keith. "You sha'n't sing if you do not wish to do so; but let me tell you: there is a deed of record in my State conveying a tract of land to a girl from an old gentleman on the expressed consideration that she had sung 'Annie Laurie' for him when he asked her to do it, without being begged."

She looked at him as if she had not heard, and then glanced at her cousin.

"Either sing or don't sing, my dear," said Mrs. Wentworth, with a slight frown. "You are keeping every one waiting."

Keith glanced over at her, and was about to say to Lois, "Don't sing"; but he was too late. Folding her hands before her, and without moving from where she stood near the wall, she began to sing "Annie Laurie." She had a lovely voice, and she sang as simply and unaffectedly as if she had been singing in her own room for her own pleasure.

When she got through, there was a round of applause throughout the company. Even Mrs. Wentworth joined in it ; but she came over and said :

"That was well done ; but next time, my dear, let some one play your accompaniment."

"Next time, don't you do any such thing," said Keith, stoutly. "You can never sing it so well again if you do. Please accept this from a man who would rather have heard you sing that song that way than have heard Albani sing in 'Lohengrin.'" He took the rosebud out of his buttonhole and gave it to her, looking her straight in the eyes.

"Is this the truth?" she asked, with her gaze quite steady on his face.

"The palpable truth," he said.

CHAPTER XXVI

A MISUNDERSTANDING

MISS LOIS HUNTINGTON, as she sank back in the corner of her cousin's carriage, on their way home, was far away from the rattling New York street. Mrs. Wentworth's occasional recurrence to the unfortunate incidents of stopping her ears and of singing the song without an accompaniment did not ruffle her. She knew she had pleased one man—the one she at that moment would rather have pleased than all the rest of New York. Her heart was eased of a load that had made it heavy for many a day. They were once more friends. Mrs. Wentworth's chiding sounded as if it were far away on some alien shore, while Lois floated serenely on a tide that appeared to begin away back in her childhood, and was bearing her gently, still gently, she knew not whither. If she tried to look forward she was lost in a mist that hung like a soft haze over the horizon. Might there be a haven yonder in that rosy distance? Or were those still the billows of the wide and trackless sea? She did not know or care. She would drift and meantime think of him, the old friend who had turned the evening for her into a real delight. Was he in love with Mrs. Lancaster? she wondered. Every one said he was, and it would not be unnatural if he were. It was on her account he had gone to Mrs. Wickersham's. She undoubtedly liked him. Many men were after her. If Mr. Keith was trying to marry her, as every one said, he must be in love with her. He would never marry

388

any one whom he did not love. If he were in love with Mrs. Lancaster, would she marry him? Her belief was that she would.

At the thought she for one moment had a pang of envy. Her reverie was broken in on by Mrs. Wentworth.

"Why are you so pensive? You have not said a word since we started."

"Why, I do not know. I was just thinking. You know, such a dinner is quite an episode with me."

"Did you have a pleasant time? Was Mr. Keith agreeable? I was glad to see you had him; for he is a very agreeable man when he chooses, but quite moody, and you never know what he is going to say."

"I think that is one of his—of his charms—that you don't know what he is going to say. I get so tired of talking to people who say just what you know they are going to say—just what some one else has just said and what some one else will say to-morrow. It is like reading an advertisement."

"Lois, you must not be so unconventional," said Mrs. Wentworth. "I must beg you not to repeat such a thing as your performance this evening. I don't like it."

"Very well, Cousin Louise, I will not," said the girl, a little stiffly. "I shall recognize your wishes; but I must tell you that I do not agree with you. I hate conventionality. We all get machine-made. I see not the least objection to what I did, except your wishes, of course, and neither did Mr. Keith."

"Well, while you are with me, you must conform to my wishes. Mr. Keith is not responsible for you. Mr. Keith is like other men—ready to flatter a young and unsophisticated girl."

"No; Mr. Keith is not like other men. He does not have to wait and see what others think and say before he forms an opinion. I am so tired of hearing people say what they think others think. Even Mr. Rimmon, at church, says what he thinks his congregation likes—just as when he meets them he flatters them and tells them what dear ladies they are, and how well they look, and how good their wine is. Why can't people think for themselves?"

"Well, on my word, Lois, you appear to be thinking for yourself! And you also appear to think very highly of Mr. Keith," said Mrs. Wentworth.

"I do. I have known Mr. Keith all my life," said the girl, gravely. "He is associated in my mind with all that I loved."

"There, I did not mean to call up sorrowful thoughts," said Mrs. Wentworth. "I wanted you to have a good time."

Next day Mr. Keith gave himself the pleasure of calling promptly at Mrs. Norman's. He remembered the time when he had waited a day or two before calling on Miss Huntington and had found her gone, with its train of misunderstandings. So he had no intention of repeating the error. In Love as in War, Success attends Celerity.

Miss Huntington was not at home, the servant said in answer to Keith's inquiries for the ladies; she had taken the children out to see Madam Wentworth. But Mrs. Wentworth would see Mr. Keith.

Mrs. Wentworth was more than usually cordial. She was undoubtedly more nervous than she used to be. She soon spoke of Norman, and for a moment grew quite excited.

"I know what people say about me," she exclaimed. "I know they say I ought to have borne everything and have gone on smiling and pretending I was happy even when I had the proof that he was—was—that he no longer cared for me, or for my—my happiness. But I could not— I was not constituted so. And if I have refused to submit to it I had good reason."

"Mrs. Wentworth," said Keith, "will you please tell me what you are talking about?"

"You will hear about it soon enough," she said, with a

390

bitter laugh. "All you have to do is to call on Mrs. Nailor or Mrs. Any-one-else for five minutes."

"If I hear what I understand you to believe, that Norman cares for some one else, I shall not believe it."

She laughed bitterly.

"Oh, you and Norman always swore by each other. I guess that you are no better than other men."

"We are, at least, better than some other men," said Keith, "and Norman is better than most other men."

She simply shrugged her shoulders and drifted into a reverie. It was evidently not a pleasant one.

Keith rose to go. And a half-hour later he quite casually called at old Mrs. Wentworth's, where he found the children having a romp. Miss Huntington looked as sweet as a rose, and Keith thought, or at least hoped, she was pleased to see him.

Keith promptly availed himself of Mrs. Wentworth's permission, and was soon calling every day or two at her house, and even on those days when he did not call he found himself sauntering up the avenue or in the Park, watching for the slim, straight, trim little figure he now knew so well. He was not in love with Lois. He said this to himself quite positively. He only admired her, and had a feeling of protection and warm friendship for a young and fatherless girl who had once had every promise of a life of ease and joy, and was by the hap of ill fortune thrown out on the cold world and into a relation of dependence. He had about given up any idea of falling in love. Love, such as he had once known it, was not for him. Love for love's sake—love that created a new world and peopled it with one woman—was over for him. At least, so he said.

And when he had reasoned thus, he would find himself hurrying along the avenue or in the Park, straining his eyes to see if he could distinguish her among the crowd of walkers and loungers that thronged the sidewalk or the foot-path a quarter of a mile away. And if he could not, he was conscious of disappointment; and if he did distinguish her, his heart would give a bound, and he would go racing along till he was at her side.

Oftenest, though, he visited her at Mrs. Wentworth's, where he could talk to her without the continual interruption of the children's busy tongues, and could get her to sing those old-fashioned songs that, somehow, sounded to him sweeter than all the music in the world.

In fact, he went there so often to visit her that he began to neglect his other friends. Even Norman he did not see as much of as formerly.

Once, when he was praising her voice to Mrs. Wentworth, she said to him: "Yes, I think she would do well in concert. I am urging her to prepare herself for that; not at present, of course, for I need her just now with the children; but in a year or two the boys will go to school and the two girls will require a good French governess, or I may take them to France. Then I shall advise her to try concert. Of course, Miss Brooke cannot take care of her always. Besides, she is too independent to allow her to do it."

Keith was angry in a moment. He had never liked Mrs. Wentworth so little. "I shall advise her to do nothing of the kind," he said firmly. "Miss Huntington is a lady, and to have her patronized and treated as an inferior by a lot of *nouveaux riches* is more than I could stand."

"I see no chance of her marrying," said Mrs. Wentworth. "She has not a cent, and you know men don't marry penniless girls these days."

"Oh, they do if they fall in love. There are a great many men in the world and even in New York, besides the small tuft-hunting, money-loving parasites that one meets at the so-called swell houses. If those you and I know were all, New York would be a very insignificant place. The brains and the character and the heart; the makers and leaders, are not found at the dinners and balls we are honored with invitations to by Mrs. Nailor and her like. Alice Lancaster was saying the other day—"

Mrs. Wentworth froze up.

"Alice Lancaster!" Her eyes flashed. "Do not quote her to me!" Her lips choked with the words.

"She is a friend of yours, and a good friend of yours," declared Keith, boldly.

"I do not want such friends as that," she said, flaming suddenly. "Who do you suppose has come between my husband and me?"

"Not Mrs. Lancaster."

"Yes."

"No," said Keith, firmly; "you wrong them both. You have been misled."

She rose and walked up and down the room in an excitement like that of an angry lioness.

"You are the only friend that would say that to me."

"Then I am a better friend than others." He went on to defend Mrs. Lancaster warmly.

When Keith left he wondered if that outburst meant that she still loved Norman.

It is not to be supposed that Mr. Keith's visits to the house of Mrs. Wentworth had gone unobserved or unchronicled. That portion of the set that knew Mrs. Wentworth best, which is most given to the discussion of such important questions as who visits whom too often, and who has stopped visiting whom altogether, with the reasons therefor, was soon busy over Keith's visits.

They were referred to in the society column of a certain journal recently started, known by some as "The Scandalmonger's Own," and some kind friend was considerate enough to send Norman Wentworth a marked copy.

Some suggested timidly that they had heard that Mr. Keith's visits were due to his opinion of the governess; but they were immediately suppressed.

Mrs. Nailor expressed the more general opinion when she declared that even a débutante would know that men like Ferdy Wickersham and Mr. Keith did not fall in love with unknown governesses. That sort of thing would do to put in books; but it did not happen in real life. They might visit them, but — ! After which she proceeded to say as many ill-natured things about Miss Lois as she could think of; for the story of Lois's stopping her ears had also gotten abroad.

Meantime, Keith pursued his way, happily ignorant of the motives attributed to him by some of those who smiled on him and invited him to their teas. A half-hour with Lois Huntington was reward enough to him for much waiting. To see her eyes brighten and to hear her voice grow softer and more musical as she spoke his name; to feel that she was in sympathy with him, that she understood him without explanation, that she was interested in his work : these were the rewards which lit up life for him and sent him to his rooms cheered and refreshed. He knew that she had no idea of taking him otherwise than as a friend. She looked on him almost as a contemporary of her father. But life was growing very sweet for him again.

It was not long before the truth was presented to him.

One of his club friends rallied him on his frequent visits in a certain quarter and the conquest which they portended. Keith flushed warmly. He had that moment been thinking of Lois Huntington. He had just been to see her, and her voice was still in his ears; so, though he thought it unusual in Tom Trimmer to refer to the matter, it was not unnatural. He attempted to turn the subject lightly by pretending to misunderstand him.

"I mean, I hear you have cut Wickersham out. Ferdy thought he had a little corner there."

Again Keith reddened. He, too, had sometimes thought that Ferdy was beginning to be attentive to Lois Huntington. Others manifestly thought so too.

"I don't know that I understand you," he said.

"Don't you?" laughed the other. "Haven't you seen the papers lately?"

Keith chilled instantly.

"Norman Wentworth is my friend," he said quietly.

"So they say is Mrs. Norm—" began Mr. Trimmer, with a laugh.

Before he had quite pronounced the name, Keith leaned forward, his eyes levelled right into the other's.

"Don't say that, Trimmer. I want to be friends with you," he said earnestly. "Don't you ever couple my name with that lady's. Her husband is my friend, and any man that says I am paying her any attention other than such as her husband would have me pay her says what is false."

"I know nothing about that," said Tom, half surlily. "I am only giving what others say."

"Well, don't you even do that." He rose to his feet, and stood very straight. "Do me the favor to say to any one you may hear intimate such a lie that I will hold any man responsible who says it."

"Jove!" said Mr. Trimmer, afterwards, to his friend Minturn, "must be some fire there. He was as hot as pepper in a minute. Wanted to fight any one who mentioned the matter. He'll have his hands full if he fights all who are talking about him and Ferdy's old flame. I heard half a roomful buzzing about it at Mrs. Nailor's. But it was none of my affair. If he wants to fight about another man's wife, let him. It's not the best way to stop the scandal."

"You know, I think Ferdy is a little relieved to get out of that," added Mr. Minturn. "Ferdy wants money, and big money. He can't expect to get money there. They say the chief cause of the trouble was Wentworth would not put up money enough for her. He has got his eye on the Lancaster-Yorke combine, and he is all devotion to the widow now."

"She won't look at him. She has too much sense. Besides, she likes Keith," said Stirling.

As Mr. Trimmer and his friend said, if Keith expected to silence all the tongues that were clacking with his name and affairs, he was likely to be disappointed. There are some people to whose minds the distribution of scandal is as great a delight as the sweetest morsel is to the tongue. Besides, there was one person who had a reason for spreading the report. Ferdy Wickersham had returned and was doing his best to give it circulation.

Norman Wentworth received in his mail, one morning, a thin letter over which a frown clouded his brow. The address was in a backhand. He had received a letter in the same handwriting not long previously—an anonymous letter. It related to his wife and to one whom he had held in high esteem. He had torn it up furiously in little bits, and had dashed them into the waste-basket as he had dashed the matter from his mind. He was near tearing this letter up without reading it; but after a moment he opened the envelope. A society notice in a paper the day before had contained the name of his wife and that of Mr. Gordon Keith, and this was not the only time he had seen the two names together. As his eye glanced over the single page of disguised writing, a deeper frown grew on his brow. It was only a few lines; but it contained a barbed arrow that struck and rankled:

> " When the cat's away
> The mice will play.
> If you have cut your wisdom-teeth,
> You'll know your mouse. His name is ——"

It was signed, "*A True Friend.*"

Norman crushed the paper in his hand, in a rage for having read it. But it was too late. He could not banish it from his mind: so many things tallied with it. He had heard that Keith was there a great deal. Why had he ceased speaking of it of late?

When Keith next met Norman there was a change in the latter. He was cold and almost morose; answered Keith absently, and after a little while rose and left him rather curtly.

When this had occurred once or twice Keith determined to see Norman and have a full explanation. Accordingly,

one day he went to his office. Mr. Wentworth was out, but
Keith said he would wait for him in his private office.

On the table lay a newspaper. Keith picked it up to
glance over it. His eye fell on a marked passage. It was a
notice of a dinner to which he had been a few evenings
before. Mrs. Wentworth's name was marked with a blue
pencil, and a line or two below it was his own name simi-
larly marked.

Keith felt the hot blood surge into his face, then a grip
came about his throat. Could this be the cause? Could
this be the reason for Norman's curtness? Could Norman
have this opinion of him? After all these years!

He rose and walked from the office and out into the
street. It was a blow such as he had not had in years.
The friendship of a lifetime seemed to have toppled down
in a moment.

Keith walked home in deep reflection. That Norman
could treat him so was impossible except on one theory :
that he believed the story which concerned him and Mrs.
Wentworth. That he could believe such a story seemed
absolutely impossible. He passed through every phase of
regret, wounded pride, and anger. Then it came to him
clearly enough that if Norman were laboring under any
such hallucination it was his duty to dispel it. He should
go to him and clear his mind. The next morning he went
again to Norman's office. To his sorrow, he learned that he
had left town the evening before for the West to see about
some business matters. He would be gone some days.
Keith determined to see him as soon as he returned.

Keith had little difficulty in assigning the scandalous
story to its true source, though he did Ferdy Wickersham
an injustice in laying the whole blame on him.

Meantime, Keith determined that he would not go to
Mrs. Wentworth's again until after he had seen Norman,
even though it deprived him of the chance of seeing Lois.
It was easier to him, as he was very busy now pushing
through the final steps of his deal with the English syndi-

cate. This he was the more zealous in as his last visit South
had shown him that old Mr. Rawson was beginning to
fail.

"I am just livin' now to hear about Phrony," said the
old man, "—and to settle with that man," he added, his
deep eyes burning under his shaggy brows.

Keith had little idea that the old man would ever live
to hear of her again, and he had told him so as gently as
he could.

"Then I shall kill him," said the old man, quietly.

Keith was in his office one morning when his attention
was arrested by a heavy step outside his door. It had
something familiar in it. Then he heard his name spoken
in a loud voice. Some one was asking for him, and the next
moment the door opened and Squire Rawson stood on the
threshold. He looked worn ; but his face was serene. Keith's
intuition told him why he had come ; and the old man did
not leave it in any doubt. His greeting was brief.

He had gotten to New York only that morning, and had
already been to Wickersham's office ; but the office was shut.

"I have come to find her," he said, "and I'll find her, or
I'll drag him through this town by his neck." He took
out a pistol and laid it by him on the table.

Keith was aghast. He knew the old man's resolution.
His face showed that he was not to be moved from it.
Keith began to argue with him. They did not do things
that way in New York, he said. The police would arrest
him. Or if he should shoot a man he would be tried, and
it would go hard with him. He had better give up his
pistol. "Let me keep it for you," he urged.

The old man took up the pistol and felt for his pocket.

"I'll find her or I'll kill him," he said stolidly. "I have
come to do one or the other. "If I do that, I don't much
keer what they do with me. But I reckon some of 'em
would take the side of a woman what's been treated so.
Well, I'll go on an' wait for him. How do you find this
here place?" He took out a piece of paper and, carefully

adjusting his spectacles, read a number. It was the number of Wickersham's office.

Keith began to argue again; but the other's face was set like a rock. He simply put up his pistol carefully. "I'll kill him if I don't find her. Well, I reckon somebody will show me the way. Good day." He went out.

The moment his footsteps had died away, Keith seized his hat and dashed out.

The bulky figure was going slowly down the street, and Keith saw him stop a man and show him his bit of paper. Keith crossed the street and hurried on ahead of him. Wickersham's office was only a few blocks away, and a minute later Keith rushed into the front office. The clerks looked up in surprise at his haste. Keith demanded of one of them if Mr. Wickersham was in. The clerk addressed turned and looked at another man nearer the door of the private office, who shook his head warningly. No, Mr. Wickersham was not in.

Keith, however, had seen the signal, and he walked boldly up to the door of the private office.

"Mr. Wickersham is in, but he is engaged," said the man, rising hastily.

"I must see him immediately," said Keith, and opening the door, walked straight in.

Wickersham was sitting at his desk poring over a ledger, and at the sudden entrance he looked up, startled. When he saw who it was he sprang to his feet, his face changing slightly. Just then one of the clerks followed Keith.

As Keith, however, spoke quietly, Wickersham's expression changed, and the next second he had recovered his composure and with it his insolence.

"To what do I owe the honor of this unexpected visit?" he demanded, with a curl of his lip.

Keith gave a little wave of his arm, as if he would sweep away his insolence.

"I have come to warn you that old Adam Rawson is in town hunting you."

Wickersham's self-contained face paled suddenly, and he stepped a little back. Then his eye fell on the clerk, who stood just inside the door. "What do you want?" he demanded angrily. "—— you! can't you keep out when a gentleman wants to see me on private business?"

The clerk hastily withdrew.

"What does he want?" he asked of Keith, with a dry voice.

"He is hunting for you. He wants to find his granddaughter, and he is coming after you."

"What the —— do I know about his granddaughter!" cried Wickersham.

"That is for you to say. He swears that he will kill you unless you produce her. He is on his way here now, and I have hurried ahead to warn you."

Wickersham's face, already pale, grew as white as death, for he read conviction in Keith's tone. With an oath he turned to a bell and rang it.

"Ring for a cab for me at once," he said to the clerk who appeared. "Have it at my side entrance."

As Keith passed out he heard him say to the clerk:

"Tell any one who calls I have left town. I won't see a soul."

A little later an old man entered Wickersham & Company's office and demanded to see F. C. Wickersham.

There was a flurry among the men there, for they all knew that something unusual had occurred; and there was that about the massive, grim old man, with his fierce eyes, that demanded attention.

On learning that Wickersham was not in, he said he would wait for him and started to take a seat.

There was a whispered colloquy between two clerks, and then one of them told him that Mr. Wickersham was not in the city. He had been called away from town the day before, and would be gone for a month or two. Would the visitor leave his name?

"Tell him Adam Rawson has been to see him, and that

he will come again." He paused a moment, then said slowly: "Tell him I'm huntin' for him and I'm goin' to stay here till I find him."

He walked slowly out, followed by the eyes of every man in the office.

The squire spent his time between watching for Wickersham and hunting for his granddaughter. He would roam about the streets and inquire for her of policemen and strangers, quite as if New York were a small village like Ridgely instead of a great hive in which hundreds of thousands were swarming, their identity hardly known to any but themselves. Most of those to whom he applied treated him as a harmless old lunatic. But he was not always so fortunate. One night, when he was tired out with tramping the streets, he wandered into one of the parks and sat down on a bench, where he finally fell asleep. He was awakened by some one feeling in his pocket. He had just been dreaming that Phrony had found him and had sat down beside him and was fondling him, and when he first came back to consciousness her name was on his lips. He still thought it was she who sat beside him, and he called her by name, "Phrony." The girl, a poor, painted, bedizened creature, was quick enough to answer to the name.

"I am Phrony; go to sleep again."

The joy of getting back his lost one aroused the old man, and he sat up with an exclamation of delight. The next second, at sight of the strange, painted face, he recoiled.

"You Phrony?"

"Yes. Don't you know me?" She snuggled closer beside him, and worked quietly at his big watch, which somehow had caught in his tight vest pocket.

"No, you ain't! Who are you, girl? What are you doin'?"

The young woman put her arms around his neck, and began to talk cajolingly. He was "such a dear old fellow," etc., etc. But the old man's wit had now returned to him. His disappointment had angered him.

401

"Get away from me, woman. What are you doin' to me?" he demanded roughly.

She still clung to him, using her poor blandishments. But the squire was angry. He pushed her off. "Go away from me, I say. What do you want? You ought to be ashamed of yourself. You don't know who I am. I am a deacon in the church, a trustee of Ridge College, and I have a granddaughter who is older than you. If you don't go away, I will tap you with my stick."

The girl, having secured his watch, with something between a curse and a laugh, went off, calling him "an old drunk fool."

Next moment the squire put his hand in his pocket to take out his watch, but it was gone. He felt in his other pockets, but they were empty, too. The young woman had clung to him long enough to rob him of everything. The squire rose and hurried down the walk, calling lustily after her; but it was an officer who answered the call. When the squire told his story he simply laughed and told him he was drunk, and threatened, if he made any disturbance, to "run him in."

The old countryman flamed out.

"Run who in?" he demanded. "Do you know who I am, young man?"

"No, I don't, and I don't keer a ——."

"Well, I'm Squire Rawson of Ridgely, and I know more law than a hundred consarned blue-bellied thief-hiders like you. Whoever says I am drunk is a liar. But if I was drunk is that any reason for you to let a thief rob me? What is your name? I've a mind to arrest you and run you in myself. I've run many a better man in."

It happened that the officer's record was not quite clear enough to allow him to take the chance of a contest with so bold an antagonist as the squire of Ridgely. He did not know just who he was, or what he might be able to do. So he was willing to "break even," and he walked off threatening, but leaving the squire master of the field.

A MISUNDERSTANDING

The next day the old man applied to Keith, who placed the matter in Dave Dennison's hands and persuaded the squire to return home.

Keith was very unhappy over the misunderstanding between Norman and himself. He wrote Norman a letter asking an interview as soon as he returned. But he received no reply. Then, having heard of his return, he went to his office one day to see him.

Yes, Mr. Wentworth was in. Some one was with him, but would Mr. Keith walk in? said the clerk, who knew of the friendship between the two. But Keith sent in his name.

The clerk came out with a surprised look on his face. Mr. Wentworth was "engaged."

Keith went home and wrote a letter, but his letter was returned unopened, and on it was the indorsement, "Mr. Norman Wentworth declines to hold any communication with Mr. Gordon Keith."

After this, Keith, growing angry, swore that he would take no further steps.

CHAPTER XXVII

PHRONY TRIPPER AND THE REV. MR. RIMMON

AS Keith stepped from his office one afternoon, he thought he heard his name called—called somewhat timidly. When, however, he turned and glanced around among the hurrying throng that filled the street, he saw no one whom he knew. Men and women were bustling along with that ceaseless haste that always struck him in New York—haste to go, haste to return, haste to hasten: the trade-mark of New York life: the hope of outstripping in the race.

A moment later he was conscious of a woman's step close behind him. He turned as the woman came up beside him, and faced—Phrony Tripper. She was so worn and bedraggled and aged that for a moment he did not recognize her. Then, as she spoke, he knew her.

"Why, Phrony!" He held out his hand. She seized it almost hungrily.

"Oh, Mr. Keith! Is it really you? I hardly dared hope it was. I have not seen any one I knew for so long —so long!" Her face worked, and she began to whimper; but Keith soothed her.

He drew her away from the crowded thoroughfare into a side street.

"You knew—?" she said, and gazed at him with a silent appeal.

"Yes, I knew. He deceived you and deluded you into running away with him."

"I thought he loved me, and he did when he married me. I am sure he did. But when he met that lady—"

"When he did what?" asked Keith, who could scarcely believe his own ears. "Did he marry you? Ferdy Wickersham? Who married you? When? Where was it? Who was present?"

"Yes; I would not come until he promised—"

"Yes, I knew he would promise. But did he marry you afterwards? Who was present? Have you any witnesses?"

"Yes. Oh, yes. I was married here in New York— one night—about ten o'clock—the night we got here. Mr. Plume was our only witness. Mr. Plume had a paper the preacher gave him; but he lost it."

"He did! Who married you? Where was it?"

"His name was Rimm—Rimm-something—I cannot remember much; my memory is all gone. He was a young man. He married us in his room. Mr. Plume got him for me. He offered to marry us himself—said he was a preacher; but I wouldn't have him, and said I would go home or kill myself if they didn't have a preacher. Then Mr. Plume went and came back, and we all got in a carriage and drove a little way, and got out and went into a house, and after some talk we were married. I don't know the street. But I would know him if I saw him. He was a young, fat man, that smiled and stood on his toes." The picture brought up to Keith the fat and unctuous Rimmon.

"Well, then you went abroad, and your husband left you over there?"

"Yes; I was in heaven for—for a little while, and then he left me—for another woman. I am sure he cared for me, and he did not mean to treat me so; but she was rich and so beautiful, and—what was I?" She gave an expressive gesture of self-abnegation.

"Poor fool!" said Keith to himself. "Poor girl!" he said aloud.

"I have written; but, maybe, he never got my letter. He would not have let me suffer so."

Keith's mouth shut closer.

She went on to tell of Wickersham's leaving her; of her hopes that after her child was born he would come back to her. But the child was born and died. Then of her despair; of how she had spent everything, and sold everything she had to come home.

"I think if I could see him and tell him what I have been through, maybe he would—be different. I know he cared for me for a while.—But I can't find him," she went on hopelessly. "I don't want to go to him where there are others to see me, for I'm not fit to see even if they'd let me in—which they wouldn't." (She glanced down at her worn and shabby frock.) "I have watched for him 'most all day, but I haven't seen him, and the police ordered me away."

"I will find him for you," said Keith, grimly.

"Oh, no! You mustn't—you mustn't say anything to him. It would make him—it wouldn't do any good, and he'd never forgive me." She coughed deeply.

"Phrony, you must go home," said Keith.

For a second a spasm shot over her face; then a ray of light seemed to flit across it, and then it died out.

She shook her head.

"No, I'll never go back there," she said.

"Oh, yes, you will—you must. I will take you back. The mountain air will restore you, and—" She was shaking her head, but the look in her eyes showed that she was thinking of something far off.

"No—no!"

"I will take you," repeated Keith. "Your grandfather will be—he will be all right. He has just been here hunting for you."

The expression on her face was so singular that Keith put his hand on her arm. To his horror, she burst into a laugh. It was so unreal that men passing glanced at her quickly, and, as they passed on, turned and looked back again.

"Well, good-by; I must find my husband," she said, holding out her hand nervously and speaking in a hurried manner. "He's got the baby with him. Tell 'em at home I'm right well, and the baby is exactly like grandmother, but prettier, of course." She laughed again as she turned away and started off hastily.

Keith caught up with her.

"But, Phrony—" But she hurried on, shaking her head, and talking to herself about finding her baby and about its beauty. Keith kept up with her, put his hand in his pocket, and taking out several bills, handed them to her.

"Here, you must take this, and tell me where you are staying."

She took the money mechanically.

"Where am I? Oh!—where am I staying? Sixteen Himmelstrasse, third floor—yes, that's it. No :—18 Rue Petits Champs, troisième étage. Oh, no :—241 Hill Street. I'll show you the baby. I must get it now." And she sped away, coughing.

Keith, having watched her till she disappeared, walked on in deep reflection, hardly knowing what course to take. Presently his brow cleared. He turned and went rapidly back to the great office building where Wickersham had his offices on the first floor. He asked for Mr. Wickersham. A clerk came forward. Mr. Wickersham was not in town. No, he did not know when he would be back.

After a few more questions as to the possible time of his return, Keith left his card.

That evening Keith went to the address that Phrony had given him. It was a small lodging-house of, perhaps, the tenth rate. The dowdy woman in charge remembered a young woman such as he described. She was ill and rather crazy and had left several weeks before. She had no idea where she had gone. She did not know her name.

Sometimes she called herself "Miss Tripper," sometimes "Mrs. Wickersham."

Keith took a cab and drove to the detective agency where Dave Dennison had his office. Keith told him why he had come, and Dave listened with tightened lips and eyes in which the flame burned deeper and deeper.

"I'll find her," he said.

Having set Dennison to work, Keith next directed his steps toward the commodious house to which the Rev. William H. Rimmon had succeeded, along with the fashionable church and the fashionable congregation which his uncle had left.

He was almost sure, from the name she had mentioned, that Mr. Rimmon had performed the ceremony. Rimmon had from time to time connected his name with matrimonial affairs which reflected little credit on him.

From the time Mr. Rimmon had found his flattery and patience rewarded, the pulpit from which Dr. Little had for years delivered a well-weighed, if a somewhat dry, spiritual pabulum had changed.

Mr. Rimmon knew his congregation too well to tax their patience with any such doctrinal sermons as his uncle had been given to. He treated his people instead to pleasant little discourses which were as much like Epictetus and Seneca as St. John or St. Paul.

Fifteen minutes was his limit,—eighteen at the outside,— weighed out like a ration. Doubtless, Mr. Rimmon had his own idea of doing good. His assistants worked hard in back streets and trod the dusty byways, succoring the small fry, while he stepped on velvet carpets and cast his net for the larger fish.

Was not Dives as well worth saving as Lazarus—and better worth it for Rimmon's purposes! And surely he was a more agreeable dinner-companion. Besides, nothing was really proved against Dives; and the crumbs from his table fed many a Lazarus.

But there were times when the Rev. William H. Rimmon

had a vision of other things : when the Rev. Mr. Rimmon,
with his plump cheeks and plump stomach, with his em-
broidered stoles and fine surplices, his rich cassocks and
hand-worked slippers, had a vision of another life. He remembered the brief period when, thrown with a number
of earnest young men who had consecrated their lives to
the work of their Divine Master, he had had aspirations for
something essentially different from the life he now led.
Sometimes, as he would meet some hard-working, threadbare brother toiling among the poor, who yet, for all his
toil and narrowness of means, had in his face that light
that comes only from feasting on the living bread, he envied
him for a moment, and would gladly have exchanged for
a brief time the "good things" that he had fallen heir to
for that look of peace. These moments, however, were
rare, and were generally those that followed some evening
of even greater conviviality than usual, or some report
that the stocks he had gotten Ferdy Wickersham to buy for
him had unexpectedly gone down, so that he must make up
his margins. When the margins had been made up and
the stocks had reacted, Mr. Rimmon was sufficiently well
satisfied with his own lot.

And of late Mr. Rimmon had determined to settle down.
There were those who said that Mr. Rimmon's voice took
on a peculiarly unctuous tone when a certain young widow,
as noted for her wealth as for her good looks and good
nature entered the portals of his church.

Keith now having rung the bell at Mr. Rimmon's
pleasant rectory and asked if he was at home, the servant
said he would see. It is astonishing how little servants in
the city know of the movements of their employers. How
much better they must know their characters !

A moment later the servant returned.

"Yes, Mr. Rimmon is in. He will be down directly ;
will the gentleman wait ?"

Keith took his seat and inspected the books on the table
—a number of magazines, a large work on Exegesis, several

volumes of poetry, the Social Register, and a society journal that contained the gossip and scandal of the town.

Presently Mr. Rimmon was heard descending the stair.
He had a light footfall, extraordinarily light in one so stout ;
for he had grown rounder with the years.

"Ah, Mr. Keith. I believe we have met before. What
can I do for you?" He held Keith's card in his hand, and
was not only civil, but almost cordial. But he did not ask
Keith to sit down.

Keith said he had come to him hoping to obtain a little
information which he was seeking for a friend. He was
almost certain that Mr. Rimmon could give it to him.

"Oh, yes. Well? I shall be very glad, I am sure, if I can
be of service to you. It is a part of our profession, you
know. What is it?"

"Why," said Keith, "it is in regard to a marriage ceremony—a marriage that took place in this city three or
four years ago, about the middle of November three years
ago. I think you possibly performed the ceremony."

"Yes, yes. What are the names of the contracting parties? You see, I solemnize a good many marriage cere-
monies. For some reason, a good many persons come to
me. My church is rather—popular, you see. I hate to
have 'fashionable' applied to holy things. I cannot tell
without their names."

"Why, of course," said Keith, struck by the sudden
assumption of a business manner. "The parties were
Ferdinand C. Wickersham and a young girl, named Euphronia Tripper."

Keith was not consciously watching Mr. Rimmon, but
the change in him was so remarkable that it astonished
him. His round jaw actually dropped for a second. Keith
knew instantly that he was the man. His inquiry had
struck home. The next moment, however, Mr. Rimmon
had recovered himself. A single glance shot out of his
eyes, so keen and suspicious that Keith was startled. Then
his eyes half closed again, veiling their flash of hostility.

"'F. C. Wickershaw and Euphronia Trimmer?'" he repeated half aloud, shaking his head. "No, I don't remember any such names. No, I never united in the bonds of matrimony any persons of those names. I am quite positive." He spoke decisively.

"No, not Wicker*shaw*—F. C. Wicker*sham* and Euphronia Tripper. Ferdy Wickersham—you know him. And the girl was named Tripper; she might have called herself 'Phrony' Tripper."

"My dear sir, I cannot undertake to remember the names of all the persons whom I happen to come in contact with in the performance of my sacred functions," began Mr. Rimmon. His voice had changed, and a certain querulousness had crept into it.

"No, I know that," said Keith, calmly; "but you must at least remember whether within four years you performed a marriage ceremony for a man whom you know as well as you know Ferdy Wickersham—?"

"Ferdy Wickersham! Why don't you go and ask him?" demanded the other, suddenly. "You appear to know him quite as well as I, and certainly Mr. Wickersham knows quite as well as I whether or not he is married. I know nothing of your reasons for persisting in this investigation. It is quite irregular, I assure you. I don't know that ever in the course of my life I knew quite such a case. A clergyman performs many functions simply as a ministerial official. I should think that the most natural way of procedure would be to ask Mr. Wickersham."

"Certainly it might be. But whatever my reason may be, I have come to ask you. As a matter of fact, Mr. Wickersham took this young girl away from her home. I taught her when she was a school-girl. Her grandfather, who brought her up, is a friend of mine. I wish to clear her good name. I have reason to think that she was legally married here in New York, and that you performed the ceremony, and I came to ask you whether you did so or not. It is a simple question. You can at least say whether you

411

did so or did not. I assumed that as a minister you would be glad to help clear a young woman's good name."

"And I have already answered you," said Mr. Rimmon, who, while Keith was speaking, had been forming his reply.

Keith flushed.

"Why, you have not answered me at all. If you have, you can certainly have no objection to doing me the favor of repeating it. Will you do me the favor to repeat it? Did you or did you not marry Ferdy Wickersham to a young girl about three years ago?"

"My dear sir, I have told you that I do not recognize your right to interrogate me in this manner. I know nothing about your authority to pursue this investigation, and I refuse to continue this conversation any longer."

"Then you refuse to give me any information whatever?" Keith was now very angry, and, as usual, very quiet, with a certain line about his mouth, and his eyes very keen.

"I do most emphatically refuse to give you any information whatever. I decline, indeed, to hold any further communication with you," (Keith was yet quieter,) "and I may add that I consider your entrance here an intrusion and your manner little short of an impertinence." He rose on his toes and fell on his heels, with the motion which Keith had remarked the first time he met him.

Keith fastened his eye on him.

"You do?" he said. "You think all that? You consider even my entrance to ask you, a minister of the Gospel, a question that any good man would have been glad to answer, 'an intrusion'? Now I am going; but before I go I wish to tell you one or two things. I have heard reports about you, but I did not believe them. I have known men of your cloth, the holiest men on earth, saints of God, who devoted their lives to doing good. I was brought up to believe that a clergyman must be a good man. I could not credit the stories I have heard coupled with your name. I now believe them true, or, at least, possible."

Mr. Rimmon's face was purple with rage. He stepped forward with uplifted hand.

"How dare you, sir!" he began.

"I dare much more," said Keith, quietly.

"You take advantage of my cloth— !"

"Oh, no; I do not. I have one more thing to say to you before I go. I wish to tell you that one of the shrewdest detectives in New York is at work on this case. I advise you to be careful, for when you fall you will fall far. Good day."

He left Mr. Rimmon shaken and white. His indefinite threats had struck him more deeply than any direct charge could have done. For Mr. Rimmon knew of acts of which Keith could not have dreamed.

When he rose he went to his sideboard, and, taking out a bottle, poured out a stiff drink and tossed it off. "I feel badly," he said to himself: "I have allowed that—that fellow to excite me, and Dr. Splint said I must not get excited. I did pretty well, though; I gave him not the least information, and yet I did not tell a falsehood, an actual falsehood."

With the composure that the stimulant brought, a thought occurred to him. He sat down and wrote a note to Wickersham, and, marking it, "Private," sent it by a messenger.

The note read:

"DEAR FERDY: I must see you without an hour's delay on a matter of the greatest possible importance. Tripper-business. Your friend K. has started investigation; claims to have inside facts. I shall wait at my house for reply. If impossible for you to come immediately, I will run down to your office.

"Yours,   RIMMON."

When Mr. Wickersham received this note, he was in his office. He frowned as he glanced at the handwriting. He said to himself:

"He wants more money, I suppose. He is always after money, curse him. He must deal in some other office as well as in this." He started to toss the note aside, but on second thought he tore it open. For a moment he looked puzzled, then a blank expression passed over his face.

He turned to the messenger-boy, who was waiting and chewing gum with the stolidity of an automaton.

"Did they tell you to wait for an answer?"

"Sure!"

He leant over and scribbled a line and sealed it. "Take that back."

"Yes, sir." The automaton departed, glancing from side to side and chewing diligently.

The note read: "Will meet you at club at five."

As the messenger passed up the street, a smallish man who had come down-town on the same car with him, and had been reading a newspaper on the street for some little time, crossed over and accosted him.

"Can you take a note for me?"

"Where to?"

"Up-town. Where are you going?"

The boy showed his note.

"Um—hum! Well, my note will be right on your way." He scribbled a line. It read: "Can't be back till eight. Look out for Shepherd. Pay boy 25 if delivered before four."

"You drop this at that number before four o'clock and you'll get a quarter."

Then he passed on.

That afternoon Keith walked up toward the Park. All day he had been trying to find Phrony, and laying plans for her relief when she should be found. The avenue was thronged with gay equipages and richly dressed women, yet among all his friends in New York there was but one woman to whom he could apply in such a case—Alice Lancaster. Old Mrs. Wentworth would have been another, but he could not go to her now, since his breach with Nor-

man. He knew that there were hundreds of good, kind
women; they were all about him, but he did not know
them. He had chosen his friends in another set. The fact
that he knew no others to whom he could apply struck a
sort of chill to his heart. He felt lonely and depressed.
He determined to go to Dr. Templeton. There, at least,
he was sure of sympathy.

He turned to go back down-town, and at a little distance
caught sight of Lois Huntington. Suddenly a light appeared to break in on his gloom. Here was a woman to
whom he could confide his trouble with the certainty of
sympathy. As they walked along he told her of Phrony;
of her elopement; of her being deserted; and of his chance
meeting with her and her disappearance again. He did
not mention Wickersham, for he felt that until he had the
proof of his marriage he had no right to do so.

"Why, I remember that old man, Mr. Rawson," said
Lois. "It was where my father stayed for a while?" Her
voice was full of tenderness.

"Yes. It is his granddaughter."

"I remember her kindness to me. We must find her.
I will help you." Her face was sweet with tender sympathy, her eyes luminous with firm resolve.

Keith gazed at her with a warm feeling surging about
his heart. Suddenly the color deepened in her cheeks;
her expression changed; a sudden flame seemed to dart
into her eyes.

"I wish I knew that man!"

"What would you do?" demanded Keith, smiling at her
fierceness.

"I'd make him suffer all his life." She looked the incarnation of vengeance.

"Such a man would be hard to make suffer," hazarded
Keith.

"Not if I could find him."

Keith soon left her to carry out his determination, and
Lois went to see Mrs. Lancaster, and told her the story she

had heard. It found sympathetic ears, and the next day
Lois and Mrs. Lancaster were hard at work quietly trying
to find the unfortunate woman. They went to Dr. Templeton; but, unfortunately, the old man was ill in bed.

The next afternoon, Keith caught sight of Lois walking
up the street with some one; and when he got nearer her
it was Wickersham. They were so absorbed that Keith
passed without either of them seeing him. He walked
on with more than wonder in his heart. The meeting,
however, had been wholly accidental on Lois's part.

Wickersham of late had frequently fallen in with Lois
when she was out walking. And this afternoon he had
hardly joined her when she began to speak of the subject
that had been uppermost in her mind all day. She did
not mention any names, but told the story just as she had
heard it.

Fortunately for Wickersham, she was so much engrossed
in her recital that she did not observe her companion's
face until he had recovered himself. He had fallen a little
behind her and did not interrupt her until he had quite
mastered himself. Then he asked quietly:

"Where did you get that story?"

"Mr. Keith told me."

"And he said the man who did that was a 'gentleman'?"

"No, he did not say that; he did not give me the least
idea who it was. Do you know who it was?"

The question was so unexpected that Wickersham for a
moment was confounded. Then he saw that she was quite
innocent. He almost gasped.

"I? How could I? I have heard that story—that is,
something of it. It is not as Mr. Keith related it. He
has some of the facts wrong. I will tell you the true story
if you will promise not to say anything about it."

Lois promised.

"Well, the truth is that the poor creature was crazy;
she took it into her head that she was married to some

one, and ran away from home to try and find him. At one time she said it was a Mr. Wagram ; then it was a man named Plume, a drunken sot; then I think she for a time fancied it was Mr. Keith himself; and "—he glanced at her quickly—"I am not sure she did not claim me once. I knew her slightly. Poor thing ! she was quite insane."

"Poor thing !" sighed Lois, softly. She felt more kindly toward Wickersham than she had ever done before.

"I shall do what I can to help you find her," he added.

"Thank you. I hope you may be successful."

"I hope so," said Wickersham, sincerely.

That evening Wickersham called on Mr. Rimmon, and the two were together for some time. The meeting was not wholly an amicable one. Wickersham demanded something that Mr. Rimmon was unwilling to comply with, though the former made him an offer at which his eyes glistened. He had offered to carry his stock for him as long as he wanted it carried. Mr. Rimmon showed him his register to satisfy him that no entry had been made there of the ceremony he had performed that night a few years before ; but he was unwilling to write him a certificate that he had not performed such a ceremony. He was not willing to write a falsehood.

Wickersham grew angry.

"Now look here, Rimmon," he said, "you know perfectly well that I never meant to marry that—to marry any one. You know that I was drunk that night, and did not know what I was doing, and that what I did was out of kindness of heart to quiet the poor little fool."

"But you married her in the presence of a witness," said Mr. Rimmon, slowly. "And I gave him her certificate."

"You must have been mistaken. I have the affidavit of the man that he signed nothing of the kind. I give you my word of honor as to that. Write me the letter I want." He pushed the decanter on the table nearer to Rimmon, who poured out a drink and took it slowly. It appeared to give him courage, for after a moment he shook his head.

"I cannot."

Wickersham looked at him with level eyes.

"You will do it, or I will sell you out," he said coldly.

"You cannot. You promised to carry that stock for me till I could pay up the margins."

"Write me that letter, or I will turn you out of your pulpit. You know what will happen if I tell what I know of you."

The other man's face turned white.

"You would not be so base."

Wickersham rose and buttoned up his coat.

"It will be in the papers day after to-morrow."

"Wait," gasped Rimmon. "I will see what I can say." He poured a drink out of the decanter, and gulped it down. Then he seized a pen and a sheet of paper and began to write. He wrote with care.

"Will this do?" he asked tremulously.

"Yes."

"You promise not to use it unless you have to?"

"Yes."

"And to carry the stock for me till it reacts and lets me out?"

"I will make no more promises."

"But you did promise—," began Mr. Rimmon.

Wickersham put the letter in his pocket, and taking up his hat, walked out without a word. But his eyes glinted with a curious light.

CHAPTER XXVIII

ALICE LANCASTER FINDS PHRONY

MR. RIMMON was calling at Mrs. Lancaster's a few days after his interview with Keith and the day following the interview with Wickersham. Mr. Rimmon called at Mrs. Lancaster's quite frequently of late. They had known each other a long time, almost ever since Mr. Rimmon had been an acolyte at his uncle Dr. Little's church, when the stout young man had first discovered the slim, straight figure and pretty face, with its blue eyes and rosy mouth, in one of the best pews, with a richly dressed lady beside her. He had soon learned that this was Miss Alice Yorke, the only daughter of one of the wealthiest men in town. Miss Alice was then very devout : just at the age and stage when she bent particularly low on all the occasions when such bowing is held seemly. And the mind of the young man was not unnaturally affected by her devoutness.

Since then Mr. Rimmon had never quite banished her from his mind, except, of course, during the brief interval when she had been a wife. When she became a widow she resumed her place with renewed power. And of late Mr. Rimmon had begun to have hope.

Now Mr. Rimmon was far from easy in his mind. He knew something of Keith's attention to Mrs. Lancaster ; but it had never occurred to him until lately that he might be successful. Wickersham he had feared at times ; but Wickersham's habits had reassured him. Mrs. Lancaster would hardly marry him. Now, however, he had an uneasy feeling that Keith might injure him, and he called partly to ascertain how the ground lay, and partly to forestall any possible injury Keith might do. To his relief, he found Mrs. Lancaster more cordial than usual. The line of conversation he adopted was quite spiritual, and he felt elevated by it. Mrs. Lancaster also was visibly impressed. Presently she said: "Mr. Rimmon, I want you to do me a favor."

"Even to the half of my kingdom," said Mr. Rimmon, bowing with his plump hand on his plump bosom.

"It is not so much as that; it is only a little of your time and, maybe, a little of your company. I have just heard of a poor young woman here who seems to be in quite a desperate way. She has been abandoned by her husband, and is now quite ill. The person who told me, one of those good women who are always seeking out such cases, tells me that she has rarely seen a more pitiable case. The poor thing is absolutely destitute. Mrs. King tells me she has seen better days."

For some reason, perhaps, that the circumstances called up not wholly pleasant associations, Mr. Rimmon's face fell a little at the picture drawn. He did not respond with the alacrity Mrs. Lancaster had expected.

"Of course, I will do it, if you wish it—or I could have some of our workers look up the case, and, if the facts warrant it, could apply some of our alms to its relief. I should think, however, the woman is rather a fit subject for a hospital. Why hasn't she been sent to a hospital, I wonder?"

"I don't know. No, that is not exactly what I meant," declared Mrs. Lancaster. "I thought I would go myself, and that, as Dr. Templeton is ill, perhaps you would go with me. She seems to be in great distress of mind, and possibly you might be able to comfort her. I have never forgotten what an unspeakable comfort your uncle was when we were in trouble years ago."

"Oh, of course, I will go with you," said the divine.

"There is no place, dear lady, where I would not go in such company," he added, his head as much on one side as his stout neck would allow, and his eyes as languishing as he dared make them.

Mrs. Lancaster, however, did not appear to notice this. Her face did not change.

"Very well, then : we will go to-morrow. I will come around and pick you up. I will get the address."

So the following morning Mrs. Lancaster's carriage stopped in front of the comfortable house which adjoined Mr. Rimmon's church, and after a little while that gentleman came down the steps. He was not in a happy frame of mind, for stocks had fallen heavily the day before, and he had just received a note from Ferdy Wickersham. However, as he settled his plump person beside the lady, the Rev. William H. Rimmon was as well-satisfied-looking as any man on earth could be. Who can blame him if he thought how sweet it would be if he could drive thus always !

The carriage presently stopped at the entrance of a narrow street that ran down toward the river. The coachman appeared unwilling to drive down so wretched an alley, and waited for further instructions. After a few words the clergyman and Mrs. Lancaster got out.

"You wait here, James ; we will walk." They made their way down the street, through a multitude of curious children with one common attribute, dirt, examining the numbers on either side, and commiserating the poor creatures who had to live in such squalor.

Presently Mrs. Lancaster stopped.

"This is the number."

It was an old house between two other old houses.

Mrs. Lancaster made some inquiries of a slatternly woman who sat sewing just inside the doorway, and the latter said there was such a person as she asked for in a room on the fourth floor. She knew nothing about her except that she was very sick and mostly out of her head.

The health-doctor had been to see her, and talked about sending her to a hospital.

The three made their way up the narrow stairs and through the dark passages, so dark that matches had to be lighted to show them the way. Several times Mr. Rimmon protested against Mrs. Lancaster going farther. Such holes were abominable; some one ought to be prosecuted for it. Finally the woman stopped at a door.

"She's in here." She pushed the door open without knocking, and walked in, followed by Mrs. Lancaster and Mr. Rimmon. It was a cupboard hardly more than ten feet square, with a little window that looked out on a dead-wall not more than an arm's-length away.

A bed, a table made of an old box, and another box which served as a stool, constituted most of the furniture, and in the bed, under a ragged coverlid, lay the form of the sick woman.

"There's a lady and a priest come to see you," said the guide, not unkindly. She turned to Mrs. Lancaster. "I don't know as you can make much of her. Sometimes she's right flighty."

The sick woman turned her head a little and looked at them out of her sunken eyes.

"Thank you. Won't you be seated?" she said, with a politeness and a softness of tone that sounded almost uncanny coming from such a source.

"We heard that you were sick, and have come to see if we could not help you," said Mrs. Lancaster, in a tone of sympathy, leaning over the bed.

"Yes," said Mr. Rimmon, in his full, rich voice, which made the little room resound; "it is our high province to minister to the sick, and through the kindness of this dear lady we may be able to remove you to more commodious quarters—to some one of the charitable institutions which noble people like our friend here have endowed for such persons as yourself."

Something about the full-toned voice with its rising in-

"It is he! 'Tis he!" she cried.

flection caught the invalid's attention, and she turned her eyes on him with a quick glance, and, half raising her head, scanned his face closely.

"Mr. Rimmon, here, may be able to help you in other ways too," Mrs. Lancaster again began ; but she got no further. The name appeared to electrify the woman.

With a shriek she sat up in bed.

"It is he ! 'Tis he !" she cried. "You are the very one. You will help me, won't you? You will find him and bring him back to me?" She reached out her thin arms to him in an agony of supplication.

"I will help you,—I shall be glad to do so,—but whom am I to bring back? How can I help you?"

"My husband—Ferdy—Mr. Wickersham. I am the girl you married that night to Ferdy Wickersham. Don't you remember? You will bring him back to me? I know he would come if he knew."

The effect that her words, and even more her earnestness, produced was remarkable. Mrs. Lancaster stood in speechless astonishment.

Mr. Rimmon for a moment turned ashy pale. Then he recovered himself.

"She is quite mad," he said in a low tone to Mrs. Lancaster. "I think we had better go. She should be removed to an asylum."

But Mrs. Lancaster could not go. Just then the woman stretched out her arms to her.

"You will help me? You are a lady. I loved him so. I gave up all for him. He married me. Didn't you marry us, sir? Say you did. Mr. Plume lost the paper, but you will give me another, won't you?"

The commiseration in Mr. Rimmon's pale face grew deeper and deeper. He rolled his eyes and shook his head sadly.

"Quite mad—quite mad," he said in an undertone. And, indeed, the next moment it appeared but too true, for with a laugh the poor creature began a babble of her child and its beauty. "Just like its father. Dark eyes and brown hair. Won't he be glad to see it when he comes? Have you children?" she suddenly asked Mrs. Lancaster.

"No." She shook her head.

Then a strange thing happened.

"I am so sorry for you," the poor woman said. And the next second she added: "I want to show mine to Alice Yorke. She is the only lady I know in New York. I used to know her when I was a young girl, and I used to be jealous of her, because I thought Ferdy was in love with her. But he was not, never a bit."

"Come away," said Mr. Rimmon to Mrs. Lancaster. "She is crazy and may become violent."

But he was too late; the whole truth was dawning on Mrs. Lancaster. A faint likeness had come to her, a memory of a far-back time. She ignored him, and stepped closer to the bed.

"What is your name?" she asked in a kind voice, bending toward the woman and taking her hand.

"Euphronia Tripper; but I am now Mrs. Wickersham. He married us." She turned her deep eyes on Mr. Rimmon. At sight of him a change came over her face.

"Where is my husband?" she demanded. "I wrote to you to bring him. Won't you bring him?"

"Quite mad—quite mad!" repeated Mr. Rimmon, shaking his head solemnly, and turning his gaze on Mrs. Lancaster. But he saw his peril. Mrs. Lancaster took no notice of him. She began to talk to the woman at the door, and gave her a few directions, together with some money. Then she advanced once more to the bed.

"I want to make you comfortable. I will send some one to take care of you." She shook hands with her softly, pulled down her veil, and then, half turning to Mr. Rimmon, said quietly, "I am ready."

As they stepped into the street, Mr. Rimmon observed at a little distance a man who had something familiar about him, but the next second he passed out of sight.

Mrs. Lancaster walked silently down the dirty street

without turning her head or speaking to the preacher, who stepped along a little behind her, his mind full of misgiving.

Mr. Rimmon, perhaps, did as hard thinking in those few minutes as he had ever done during the whole course of his life. It was a serious and delicate position. His reputation, his position, perhaps even his profession, depended on the result. He must sound his companion and placate her at any cost.

"That is one of the saddest spectacles I ever saw," he began.

To this Mrs. Lancaster vouchsafed no reply.

"She is quite mad."

"No wonder!"

"Ah, yes. What do you think of her?"

"That she is Ferdy Wickersham's wife—or ought to be."

"Ah, yes." Here was a gleam of light. "But she is so insane that very little reliance should be placed on anything that she says. In such instances, you know, women make the most preposterous statements and believe them. In her condition, she might just as well have claimed me for her husband."

Mrs. Lancaster recognized this, and looked just a little relieved. She turned as if about to speak, but shut her lips tightly and walked on to the waiting carriage. And during the rest of the return home she scarcely uttered a word.

An hour later Ferdy Wickersham was seated in his private office, when Mr. Rimmon walked in.

Wickersham greeted him with more courtesy than he usually showed him.

"Well," he said, "what is it?"

"Well, it's come."

Wickersham laughed unmirthfully. "What? You have been found out? Which commandment have you been caught violating?"

"No; it's you," said Mr. Rimmon, his eyes on Wickersham, with a gleam of retaliation in them. "Your wife has turned up." He was gratified to see Wickersham's cold face turn white. It was a sweet revenge.

"My wife! I have no wife." Wickersham looked him steadily in the eyes.

"You had one, and she is in town."

"I have no wife," repeated Wickersham, firmly, not taking his eyes from the clergyman's face. What he saw there did not satisfy him. "I have your statement."

The other hesitated and reflected.

"I wish you would give me that back. I was in great distress of mind when I gave you that."

"You did not give it," said Wickersham. "You sold it." His lip curled.

"I was—what you said you were when it occurred," said Mr. Rimmon. "I was not altogether responsible."

"You were sober enough to make me carry a thousand shares of weak stock for you till yesterday, when it fell twenty points," said Wickersham. "Oh, I guess you were sober enough."

"She is in town," said Rimmon, in a dull voice.

"Who says so?"

"I have seen her."

"Where is she?"—indifferently.

"She is ill. She is mad."

Wickersham's face settled a little. His eyes blinked as if a blow had been aimed at him nearly. Then he recovered his poise.

"How mad?"

"As mad as a March hare."

"You can attend to it," he said, looking the clergyman full in the face. "I don't want her to suffer. There will be some expense. Can you get her into a comfortable place for—for a thousand dollars?"

"I will try. The poor creature would be better off," said the other, persuading himself. "She cannot last long. She is a very ill woman."

Wickersham either did not hear or pretended not to hear.

"You go ahead and do it. I will send you the money the day after it is done," he said. "Money is very tight to-day, almost a panic at the board."

"That stock? You will not trouble me about it?"

Wickersham growled something about being very busy, and rose and bowed the visitor out. The two men shook hands formally at the door of the inner office; but it was a malevolent look that Wickersham shot at the other's stout back as he walked out.

As Mr. Rimmon came out of the office he caught sight of the short, stout man he had seen in the street to which he had gone with Mrs. Lancaster. Suddenly the association of ideas brought to him Keith's threat. He was shadowed. A perspiration broke out over him.

Wickersham went back to his private office, and began once more on his books. What he saw there was what he began to see on all sides: ruin. He sat back in his chair and reflected. His face, which had begun to grow thinner of late, as well as harder, settled more and more until it looked like gray stone. Presently he rose, and locking his desk carefully, left his office.

As he reached the street, a man, who had evidently been waiting for him, walked up and spoke to him. He was a tall, thin, shabby man, with a face and figure on which drink was written ineffaceably. Wickersham, without looking at him, made an angry gesture and hastened his step. The other, however, did the same, and at his shoulder began to whine.

"Mr. Wickersham, just a word."

"Get out," said Wickersham, still walking on. "I told you never to speak to me again."

"I have a paper that you'd give a million dollars to get hold of."

Wickersham's countenance showed not the least change.

"If you don't keep away from here, I'll hand you over to the police."

"If you'll just give me a dollar I'll swear never to trouble

427

you again. I have not had a mouthful to eat to-day. You won't let me starve?"

"Yes, I will. Starve and be —— to you!" He suddenly stopped and faced the other. "Plume, I wouldn't give you a cent if you were actually starving. Do you see that policeman? If you don't leave me this minute, I'll hand you over to him. And if you ever speak to me again or write to me again, or if I find you on the street about here, I'll arrest you and send you down for blackmail and stealing. Now do you understand?"

The man turned and silently shuffled away, his face working and a glint in his bleared eye.

An evening or two later Dave Dennison reported to Keith that he had found Phrony. Dave's face was black with hate, and his voice was tense with suppressed feeling.

"How did you find her?" inquired Keith.

"Shadowed the preacher. Knew he and that man had been confabbin'. She's clean gone," he added. "They've destroyed her. She didn't know me." His face worked, and an ominous fire burned in his eyes.

"We must get her home."

"She can't go. You'd never know her. We'll have to put her in an asylum."

Something in his voice made Keith look at him. He met his gaze.

"They're getting ready to do it—that man and the preacher. But I don't mean 'em to have anything more to do with her. They've done their worst. Now let 'em keep away from her."

Keith nodded his acquiescence.

That evening Keith went to see a doctor he knew, and next day, through his intervention, Phrony was removed to the private ward of an asylum, where she was made as comfortable as possible.

It was evident that she had not much longer to stay. But God had been merciful to her. She babbled of her baby and her happiness at seeing it soon. And a small, strongly built man with grave eyes sat by her in the ambulance, and told her stories of it with a fertility of invention that amazed the doctor who had her in charge.

When Mr. Rimmon's agents called next day to make the preliminary arrangements for carrying out his agreement with Wickersham, they found the room empty. The woman who had charge of the house had been duly "fixed" by Dave, and she told a story sufficiently plausible to pass muster. The sick woman had disappeared at night and had gone she did not know where. She was afraid she might have made away with herself, as she was out of her head. This was verified, and this was the story that went back to Mr. Rimmon and finally to Ferdy Wickersham. A little later the body of a woman was found in the river, and though there was nothing to identify her, it was stated in one of the papers that there was good ground for believing that she was the demented woman whose disappearance had been reported the week before.

CHAPTER XXIX

THE MARRIAGE CERTIFICATE

ONE day after Phrony was removed, Keith was sitting in the office he had taken in New York, working on the final papers which were to be exchanged when his deal should be completed, when there was a tap at the door. A knock at the door is almost as individual as a voice. There was something about this knock that awakened associations in Keith's mind. It was not a woman's tap, yet Terpy and Phrony Tripper both sprang into Keith's mind.

Almost at the same moment the door opened slowly, and pausing on the threshold stood J. Quincy Plume. But how changed from the Mr. Plume of yore, the jovial and jocund manager of the Gumbolt *Whistle*, or the florid and flowery editor of the New Leeds *Clarion!*

The apparition in the door was a shabby representation of what J. Quincy Plume had been in his palmy days. He bore the last marks of extreme dissipation; his eyes were dull, his face bloated, and his hair thin and long. His clothes looked as if they had served him by night as well as by day for a long time. His shoes were broken, and his hat, once the emblem of his station and high spirits, was battered and rusty.

"How are you, Mr. Keith?" he began boldly enough. But his assumption of something of his old air of bravado died out under Keith's icy and steady gaze, and he stepped only inside of the room, and, taking off his hat, waited uneasily.

"What do you want of me?" demanded Keith, leaning back in his chair and looking at him coldly.

"Well, I thought I would like to have a little talk with you about a matter—"

Keith, without taking his eyes from his face, shook his head slowly.

"About a friend of yours," continued Plume.

Again Keith shook his head very slowly.

"I have a little information that might be of use to you —that you'd like to have."

"I don't want it."

"You would if you knew what it was."

"No."

"Yes, you would. It's about Squire Rawson's grand-daughter—about her marriage to that man Wickersham."

"How much do you want for it?" demanded Keith.

Plume advanced slowly into the room and looked at a chair.

"Don't sit down. How much do you want for it?" repeated Keith.

"Well, you are a rich man now, and—"

"I thought so." Keith rose. "However rich I am, I will not pay you a cent." He motioned Plume to the door.

"Oh, well, if that's the way you take it!" Plume drew himself up and stalked to the door. Keith reseated himself and again took up his pen.

At the door Plume turned and saw that Keith had put him out of his mind and was at work again.

"Yes, Keith, if you knew what information I have—"

Keith sat up suddenly.

"Go out of here!"

"If you'd only listen—"

Keith stood up, with a sudden flame in his eyes.

"Go on, I say. If you do not, I will put you out. It is as much as I can do to keep my hands off you. You could not say a word that I would believe on any subject."

"I will swear to this."

"Your oath would add nothing to it."

Plume waited, and after a moment's reflection began in a different key.

"Mr. Keith, I did not come here to sell you anything—"

"Yes, you did."

"No, I did not. I did not come—only for that. If I could have sold it, I don't say I wouldn't, for I need money —the Lord knows how much I need it! I have not a cent in the world to buy me a mouthful to eat—or drink. I came to tell you something that only *I* know—"

"I have told you that I would not believe you on oath," began Keith, impatiently.

"But you will, for it is true; and I tell it not out of love for you (though I never disliked—I always liked you— would have liked you if you'd have let me), but out of hate for that—. That man has treated me shamefully—worse than a yellow dog! I've done for that man what I wouldn't have done for my brother. You know what I've done for him, Mr. Keith, and now when he's got no further use for me, he kicks me out into the street and threatens to give me to the police if I come to him again."

Keith's expression changed. There was no doubt now that for once Quincy Plume was sincere. The hate in his bleared eyes and bloated face was unfeigned.

"Give me to the police! I'll give him to the police!" he broke out in a sudden flame at Keith's glance of inspection. "He thinks he has been very smart in taking from me all the papers. He thinks no one will believe me on my mere word, but I've got a paper he don't know of." His hand went to the breast of his threadbare coat with an angry clutch. "I've got the marriage lines of his wife."

One word caught Keith, and his interest awoke.

"What wife?" he asked as indifferently as he could.

"His wife,—his lawful wife,—Squire Rawson's grand-daughter, Phrony Tripper. I was at the weddin'—I was a witness. He thought he could get out of it, and he was half drunk; but he married her."

"Where? When? You were present?"

"Yes. They were married by a preacher named Rimmon, and he gave me her certificate, and I swore to her I had lost it : *he* got me to do it—the scoundrel! He wanted me to give it to him ; but I swore to him I had lost it, too. I thought it would be of use some of these days." A gleam of the old craftiness shone in his eyes.

Keith gazed at the man in amazement. His unblushing effrontery staggered him.

"Would you mind letting me see that certificate?"

Plume hesitated and licked his lips like a dog held back from a bone. Keith noted it.

"I do not want you to think that I will give you any money for it, for I will not," he added quietly, his gray eyes on him.

For a moment Plume was so taken aback that his face became a blank. Then, whether it was that the very frankness of the speech struck home to him or that he wished to secure a fragment of esteem from Keith, he recovered himself.

"I don't expect any money for it, Mr. Keith. I don't want any money for it. I will not only show you this paper, I will give it to you."

"It is not yours to give," said Keith. "It belongs to Mrs. Wickersham. I will see that she gets it if you deliver it to me."

"That's so," ejaculated Plume, as if the thought had never occurred to him before. "I want her to have it, but you'd better keep it for her. That man will get it away from her. You don't know him as I do. You don't know what he'd do on a pinch. I tell you he is a gambler for life. I have seen him sit at the board and stake sums that would have made me rich for life. Besides," he added, as if he needed some other reason for giving it up, "I am afraid if he knew I had it he'd get it from me in some way."

He walked forward and handed the paper to Keith, who

saw at a glance that it was what Plume had declared it to be : a marriage certificate, dirty and worn, but still with signatures that appeared to be genuine. Keith's eyes flashed with satisfaction as he read the name of the Rev· William H. Rimmon and Plume's name, evidently written with the same ink at the same time.

"Now," said Keith, looking up from the paper, "I will see that Mrs. Wickersham's family is put in possession of this paper."

"Couldn't you lend me a small sum, Mr. Keith," asked Plume, wheedlingly, "just for old times' sake? I know I have done you wrong and given you good cause to hate me, but it wasn't my fault, an' I've done you a favor to-day, anyhow."

Keith looked at him for a second, and put his hand in his pocket.

"I'll pay you back, as sure as I live—" began Plume, cajolingly.

"No, you will not," said Keith, sharply. "You could not if you would, and would not if you could, and I would not lend you a cent or have a business transaction with you for all the money in New York. I will give you this—for the person you have most injured in life. Now, don't thank me for it, but go."

Plume took, with glistening eyes and profuse thanks, the bills that were handed out to him, and shambled out of the room.

That night Keith, having shown the signatures to a good expert, who pronounced them genuine, telegraphed Dr. Balsam to notify Squire Rawson that he had the proof of Phrony's marriage. The Doctor went over to see the old squire. He mentioned the matter casually, for he knew his man. But as well as he knew him, he found himself mistaken in him.

"I know that," he said quietly, "but what I want is to find Phrony." His deep eyes glowed for a while and suddenly flamed. "I'm a rich man," he broke out, "but I'd give every dollar I ever owned to get her back, and to get my hand once on that man."

The deep fire glowed for a while and then grew dull again, and the old man sank back into his former grim silence.

The Doctor looked at him commiseratingly. Keith had written him fully of Phrony and her condition, and he had decided to say nothing to the old grandfather.

CHAPTER XXX

"SNUGGLERS' ROOST"

WICKERSHAM began to renew his visits to Mrs. Wentworth, which he had discontinued for a time when he had found himself repulsed. The repulse had stimulated his desire to win her; but he had a further motive. Among other things, she might ask for an accounting of the money he had had of her, and he wanted more money. He must keep up appearances, or others might pounce upon him.

When he began again, it was on a new line. He appealed to her sympathy. If he had forgotten himself so far as to ask for more than friendship, she would, he hoped, forgive him. She could not find a truer friend. He would never offend her so again; but he must have her friendship, or he might do something desperate.

Fortunately for him, Wickersham had a good advocate at court. Mrs. Wentworth was very lonely and unhappy just then, and the plea prevailed. She forgave him, and Wickersham again began to be a visitor at the house.

But deeper than these lay another motive. While following Mrs. Wentworth he had been thrown with Lois Huntington. Her freshness, her beauty, the charm of her girlish figure, the unaffected gayety of her spirits, attracted him, and he had paused in his other pursuit to captivate her, as he might have stepped aside to pluck a flower beside the way. To his astonishment, she declined the honor;

more, she laughed at him. It teased him to find himself
balked by a mere country girl, and from this moment he
looked on her with new eyes. The unexpected revelation
of a deeper nature than most he had known astonished him.

Since their interview on the street Lois received him with
more friendliness than she had hitherto shown him. In
fact, the house was a sad one these days, and any diversion
was welcome. The discontinuance of Keith's visits had
been so sudden that Lois had felt it all the more. She
had no idea of the reason, and set it down to the score of
his rumored success with Mrs. Lancaster. She, too, could
play the game of pique, and she did it well. She accordingly showed Wickersham more favor than she had ever
shown him before. While, therefore, he kept up his visits
to Mrs. Norman, he was playing all the time his other
game with her cousin, knowing the world well enough to
be sure that it would not believe his attentions to the latter
had any serious object. In this he was not mistaken.
The buzz that coupled his name with Mrs. Wentworth's
was soon as loud as ever.

Finally Lois decided to take matters in her own hands.
She would appeal to Mr. Wickersham himself. He had
talked to her of late in a manner quite different from the
sneering cynicism which he aired when she first met him.
In fact, no one could hold higher sentiments than he had
expressed about women or about life. Mr. Keith himself
had never held loftier ideals than Mr. Wickersham had
declared to her. She began to think that the tittle-tattle
that she got bits of whenever she saw Mrs. Nailor or some
others was, perhaps, after all, slander, and that Mr. Wickersham was not aware of the injury he was doing Mrs. Wentworth. She would appeal to his better nature. She lay in
wait several times without being able to meet him in a
way that would not attract attention. At length she wrote
him a note, asking him to meet her on the street, as she
wished to speak to him privately.

When Wickersham met her that afternoon at the point

GORDON KEITH

she had designated, not far from the Park, he had a curious expression on his cold face.

She was dressed in a perfectly simple, dark street-costume
which fitted without a wrinkle her willowy figure, and a
big black hat with a single large feather shaded her face
and lent a shadow to her eyes which gave them an added
witchery. Wickersham thought he had never known her
so pretty or so chic. He had not seen as handsome a figure
that day, and he had sat at the club window and scanned
the avenue with an eye for fine figures.

She held out her hand in the friendliest way, and looking into his eyes quite frankly, said, with the most natural
of voices:

"Well, I know you think I have gone crazy, and are
consumed with curiosity to know what I wanted with you?"

"I don't know about the curiosity," he said, smiling at
her. "Suppose we call it interest. You don't have to be
told now that I shall be only too delighted if I am fortunate enough to be of any service to you." He bent down
and looked so deep into her eyes that she drew a little back.

"The fact is, I am plotting a little treason," she said, with
a blush, slightly embarrassed.

"By Jove! she is a real beauty," thought Wickersham,
noting, with the eye of a connoisseur, the white, round
throat, the dainty curves of the slim figure, and the purity
of the oval face, in which the delicate color came and went
under his gaze.

"Well, if this be treason, I'll make the most of it," he said,
with his most fascinating smile. "Treasons, stratagems,
and spoils are my game."

"But this may be treason partly against yourself?" She
gave a half-glance up at him to see how he took this.

"I am quite used to this, too, my dear girl, I assure you,"
he said, wondering more and more. She drew back a little
at the familiarity.

"Come and let us stroll in the Park," he suggested, and
though she demurred a little, he pressed her, saying it was

quieter there, and she would have a better opportunity of showing him how he could help her.

They walked along talking, he dealing in light badinage of a flattering kind, which both amused and disturbed her a little, and presently he turned into a somewhat secluded alley, where he found a bench sheltered and shadowed by the overhanging boughs of a tree.

"Well, here is a good place for confidences." He took her hand and, seating himself, drew her down beside him. "I will pretend that you are a charming dryad, and I— what shall I be?"

"My friend," she said calmly, and drew her hand away from him.

"*Votre ami?* *Avec tout mon cœur.* I will be your best friend." He held out his hand.

"Then you will do what I ask? You are also a good friend of Mrs. Wentworth?"

A little cloud flitted over his face; but she did not see it.

"We do not speak of the absent when the present holds all we care for," he said lightly.

She took no notice of this, but went on: "I do not think you would wittingly injure any one."

He laughed softly. "Injure any one? Why, of course I would not—I could not. My life is spent in making people have a pleasant time—though some are wicked enough to malign me."

"Well," she said slowly, "I do not think you ought to come to Cousin Louise's so often. You ought not to pay Cousin Louise as much attention as you do."

"What!" He threw back his head and laughed.

"You do not know what an injury you are doing her," she continued gravely. "You cannot know how people are talking about it?"

"Oh, don't I?" he laughed. Then, as out of the tail of his eye he saw her troubled face, he stopped and made his face grave. "And you think I am injuring her!" She did notice the covert cynicism.

"I am sure you are—unwittingly. You do not know how unhappy she is."

An expression very like content stole into his dark eyes. Lois continued:

"She has not been wise. She has been foolish and un-yielding and—oh, I hate to say anything against her, for she has been very kind to me!—She has allowed others to make trouble between her and her husband; but she loves him dearly for all that—and—"

"Oh, she does! You think so!" said Wickersham, with an ugly little gleam under his half-closed lids and a shrewd glance at Lois.

"Yes. Oh, yes, I am sure of it. I know it. She adores him."

"She does, eh?"

"Yes. She would give the world to undo what she has done and win him back."

"She would, eh?" Again that gleam in Wickersham's dark eyes as they slanted a glance at the girl's earnest face.

"I think she had no idea till—till lately how people talked about her, and it was a great shock to her. She is a very proud woman, you know?"

"Yes," he assented, "quite proud."

"She esteems you—your friendship—and likes you ever so much, and all that." She was speaking rapidly now, her sober eyes on Wickersham's face with an appealing look in them. "And she doesn't want to do anything to—to wound you; but I think you ought not to come so often or see her in a way to make people talk—and I thought I'd say so to you." A smile that was a plea for sympathy flickered in her eyes.

Wickersham's mind had been busy. This explained the change in Louise Wentworth's manner of late—ever since he had made the bold declaration of his intention to conquer her. Another idea suggested itself. Could the girl be jealous of his attentions to Mrs. Wentworth? He had had women play such a part; but none was like this girl. If it was a game it was a deep one. He took his line, and when she ended composed his voice to a low tone as he leant toward her.

"My dear girl, I have listened to every word you said. I am shocked to hear what you tell me. Of course I know people have talked about me,—curse them! they always will talk,—but I had no idea it had gone so far. As you know, I have always taken Mrs. Wentworth's side in the unhappy differences between her and her husband. This has been no secret. I cannot help taking the side of the woman in any controversy. I have tried to stand her friend, notwithstanding what people said. Sometimes I have been able to help her. But—" He paused and took a long breath, his eyes on the ground. Then, leaning forward, he gazed into her face.

"What would you say if I should tell you that my frequent visits to Mrs. Wentworth's house were not to see her —entirely?" He felt his way slowly, watching the effect on her. It had no effect. She did not understand him.

"What do you mean?"

He leant over, and taking hold of her wrist with one hand, he put his other arm around her. "Lois, can you doubt what I mean?" He threw an unexpected passion into his eyes and into his voice,—he had done it often with success,—and drew her suddenly to him.

Taken by surprise, she, with a little exclamation, tried to draw away from him, but he held her firmly.

"Do you think I went there to see her? Do you give me no credit for having eyes—for knowing the prettiest, sweetest, dearest little girl in New York? I must have concealed my secret better than I thought. Why, Lois, it is you I have been after." His eyes were close to hers and looked deep into them.

She gave an exclamation of dismay and tried to rise. "Oh, Mr. Wickersham, please let me go!" But he held her fast.

"Why, of course, it is yourself."

"Let me go—please let me go, Mr. Wickersham," she exclaimed as she struggled.

"Oh, now don't get so excited," he said, drawing her all the closer to him, and holding her all the tighter. "It is not becoming to your beautiful eyes. Listen to me, my darling. I am not going to hurt you. I love you too much, little girl, and I want your love. Sit down. Listen to me." He tried to kiss her, but his lips just touched her face.

"No ; I will not listen." She struggled to her feet, flushed and panting, but Wickersham rose too.

"I will kiss you, you little fool." He caught her, and clasping her with both arms, kissed her twice violently ; then, as she gave a little scream, released her. "There !" he said. As he did so she straightened herself and gave him a ringing box on his ear.

"There !" She faced him with blazing eyes.

Angry, and with his cheek stinging, Wickersham seized her again.

"You little devil !" he growled, and kissed her on her cheek again and again.

As he let her go, she faced him. She was now perfectly calm.

"You are not a gentleman," she said in a low, level tone, tears of shame standing in her eyes.

For answer he caught her again.

Then the unexpected happened. At that moment Keith turned a clump of shrubbery a few paces off, that shut out the alley from the bench which Wickersham had selected. For a second he paused, amazed. Then, as he took in the situation, a black look came into his face.

The next second he had sprung to where Wickersham stood, and seizing him by the collar, jerked him around and slapped him full in the face.

"You hound !" He caught him again, the light of fury in his eyes, the primal love of fight that has burned there when men have fought for a woman since the days of Adam, and with a fierce oath hurled him spinning back across the walk, where he measured his length on the ground.

Then Keith turned to the girl:

"Come; I will see you home."

The noise had attracted the attention of others besides Gordon Keith. Just at this juncture a stout policeman turned the curve at a double-quick.

As he did so, Wickersham rose and slipped away.

"What th' devil 'rre ye doin'?" the officer demanded in a rich brogue before he came to a halt. "I'll stop this racket. I'll run ye ivery wan in. I've got ye now, me foine leddy; I've been waitin' for ye for some time." He seized Lois by the arm roughly.

"Let her go. Take your hand off that lady, sir. Don't you dare to touch her." Keith stepped up to him with his eyes flashing and hand raised.

"And you too. I'll tache you to turn this park into—"

"Take your hand off her, or I'll make you sorry for it."

"Oh, you will!" But at the tone of authority he released Lois.

"What is your name? Give me your number. I'll have you discharged for insulting a lady," said Keith.

"Oh, me name's aall right. Me name's Mike Doherty—Sergeant Doherty. I guess ye'll find it on the rolls right enough. And as for insultin' a leddy, that's what I'm goin' to charrge against ye—that and—"

"Why, Mike Doherty!" exclaimed Keith. "I am Mr. Keith—Gordon Keith."

"Mr. Keith! Gordon Keith!" The big officer leant over and looked at Keith in the gathering dusk. "Be jabbers, and so it is! Who's your leddy friend?" he asked in a low voice. "Be George, she's a daisy!"

Keith stiffened. The blood rushed to his face, and he started to speak sharply. He, however, turned to Lois.

"Miss Huntington, this is an old friend of mine. This is Mike Doherty, who used to be the best man on the ship when I ran the blockade as a boy."

443

"The verry same," said Mike.

"He used to teach me boxing," continued Keith.

"I taaught him the left upper-cut," nodded the sergeant.

Keith went on and told the story of his coming on a man who was annoying Miss Huntington, but he did not give his name.

"Did ye give him the left upper-cut?" demanded Sergeant Doherty.

"I am not sure that I did not," laughed Keith. "I know he went down over there where you saw him lying—and I have ended one or two misunderstandings with it very satisfactorily."

"Ah, well, then, I'm glad I taaught ye. I'm glad ye've got such a good defender, ma'am. Ye'll pardon what I said when I first coomed up. But I was a little over-het. Ye see, this place is kind o' noted for—for— This place is called 'Snugglers' Roost.' Nobody comes here this time 'thout they'rre a little aff, and we has arders to look out for 'em."

"I am glad I had two such defenders," said Lois, innocently.

"I'm always glad to meet Mr. Keith's friends—and his inimies too," said the sergeant, taking off his helmet and bowing. "If I can sarve ye any time, sind worrd to Precin't XX, and I'll be proud to do it."

As Keith and Lois walked slowly homeward, Lois gave him an account of her interview with Wickersham. Only she did not tell him of his kissing her the first time. She tried to minimize the insult now, for she did not know what Keith might do. He had suddenly grown so quiet.

What she said to Keith, however, was enough to make him very grave. And when he left her at Mrs. Wentworth's house the gravity on his face deepened to grimness. That Wickersham should have dared to insult this young girl as he had done stirred Keith's deepest anger. What Keith did was, perhaps, a very foolish thing. He tried to find him, but failing in this, he wrote him a note in which he

444

told him what he thought of him, and added that if he felt aggrieved he would be glad to send a friend to him and arrange to give him any satisfaction which he might desire.

Wickersham, however, had left town. He had gone West on business, and would not return for some weeks, the report from his office stated.

On reaching home, Lois went straight to her room and thought over the whole matter. It certainly appeared grave enough to her. She determined that she would never meet Wickersham again, and, further, that she would not remain in the house if she had to do so. Her cheeks burned with shame as she thought of him, and then her heart sank at the thought that Keith might at that moment be seeking him.

Having reached her decision, she sought Mrs. Wentworth.

As soon as she entered the room, Mrs. Wentworth saw that something serious had occurred, and in reply to her question Lois sat down and quietly told the story of having met Mr. Wickersham and of his attempting to kiss her, though she did not repeat what Wickersham had said to her. To her surprise, Mrs. Wentworth burst out laughing.

"On my word, you were so tragic when you came in that I feared something terrible had occurred. Why, you silly creature, do you suppose that Ferdy meant anything by what he did?"

"He meant to insult me—and you," said Lois, with a lift of her head and a flash in her eye.

"Nonsense! He has probably kissed a hundred girls, and will kiss a hundred more if they give him the chance to do so."

"I gave him no chance," said Lois, sitting very straight and stiff, and with a proud dignity which the other might well have heeded.

"Now, don't be silly," said Mrs. Wentworth, with a little hauteur. "Why did you walk in a secluded part of the Park with him?"

445

"I thought I could help a friend of mine," said Lois.

"Mr. Keith, I suppose!"

"No; *not* Mr. Keith."

"A woman, perhaps?"

"Yes; a woman." She spoke with a hauteur which Mrs. Wentworth had never seen in her.

"Cousin Louise," she said suddenly, after a moment's reflection, "I think I ought to say to you that I will never speak to Mr. Wickersham again."

The color rushed to Mrs. Wentworth's face, and her eyes gave a flash. "You will never do what?" she demanded coldly, looking at her with lifted head.

"I will never meet Mr. Wickersham again."

"You appear to have met him once too often already. I think you do not know what you are saying or whom you are speaking to."

"I do perfectly," said Lois, looking her full in the eyes.

"I think you had better go to your room," said Mrs. Wentworth, angrily.

The color rose to Lois's face, and her eyes were sparkling. Then the color ebbed back again as she restrained herself.

"You mean you wish me to go?" Her voice was calm.

"I do. You have evidently forgotten your place."

"I will go home," she said. She walked slowly to the door. As she reached it she turned and faced Mrs. Wentworth. "I wish to thank you for all your kindness to me; for you have been very kind to me at times, and I wish—" Her voice broke a little, but she recovered herself, and walking back to Mrs. Wentworth, held out her hand. "Good-by."

Mrs. Wentworth, without rising, shook hands with her coldly. "Good-by."

Lois turned and walked slowly from the room.

As soon as she had closed the door she rushed up-stairs, and, locking herself in, threw herself on the bed and burst out crying. The strain had been too great, and the bent bow at last snapped.

An hour or two later there was a knock on her door. Lois opened it, and Mrs. Wentworth entered. She appeared rather surprised to find Lois packing her trunk.

"Are you really going away?" she asked.

"Yes, Cousin Louise."

"I think I spoke hastily to you. I said one or two things that I regret. I had no right to speak to you as I did," said Mrs. Wentworth.

"No, I do not think you had," said Lois, gravely; "but I will try and never think of it again, but only of your kindness to me."

Suddenly, to her astonishment, Mrs. Wentworth burst out weeping. "You are all against me," she exclaimed— "all! You are all so hard on me!"

Lois sprang toward her, her face full of sudden pity. "Why, Cousin Louise!"

"You are all deserting me. What shall I do! I am so wretched! I am so lonely—so lonely! Oh, I wish I were dead!" sobbed the unhappy woman. "Then, maybe, some one might be sorry for me even if they did not love me."

Lois slipped her arm around her and drew her to her, as if their ages had been reversed. "Don't cry, Cousin Louise. Calm yourself."

Lois drew her down to a sofa, and kneeling beside her, tried to comfort her with tender words and assurances of her affection. "There, Cousin Louise, I do love you—we all love you. Cousin Norman loves you."

Mrs. Wentworth only sobbed her dissent.

"I will stay. I will not go," said Lois. "If you want me."

The unhappy woman caught her in her arms and thanked her with a humility which was new to the girl. And out of the reconciliation came a view of her which Lois had never seen, and which hardly any one had seen often.

447

CHAPTER XXXI

TERPY'S LAST DANCE AND WICKER-SHAM'S FINAL THROW

CURIOUSLY enough, the interview between Mrs. Lancaster and Lois brought them closer together than before. The older woman seemed to find a new pleasure in the young girl's society, and as often as she could she had the girl at her house. Sometimes, too, Keith was of the party. He held himself in leash, and hardly dared face the fact that he had once more entered on the lane which, beginning among flowers, had proved so thorny in the end. Yet more and more he let himself drift into that sweet atmosphere whose light was the presence of Lois Huntington.

One evening they all went together to see a vaudeville performance that was being much talked about.

Keith had secured a box next the stage. The theatre was crowded. Wickersham sat in another box with several women, and Keith was aware that he was covertly watching his party. He had never appeared gayer or been handsomer.

The last number but one was a dance by a new danseuse, who, it was stated in the playbills, had just come over from Russia. According to the reports, the Russian court was wild about her, and she had left Europe at the personal request of the Czar. However this might be, it appeared that she could dance. The theatre was packed nightly, and she was the drawing-card.

As the curtain rose, the danseuse made her way to the centre of the stage. She had raven-black hair and brows; but even as she stood, there was something in the pose that

448

seemed familiar to Keith, and as she stepped forward and bowed with a little jerk of her head, and then, with a nod to the orchestra, began to dance, Keith recognized Terpy. That abandon was her own.

As she swept the boxes with her eyes, they fell on Keith, and she started, hesitated, then went on. Next moment she glanced at the box again, and as her eye caught Keith's she gave him a glance of recognition. She was not to be disconcerted now, however. She had never danced so well. And she was greeted with raptures of applause. The crowd was wild with delight.

At that moment, from one of the wings, a thin curl of smoke rose and floated up alongside a painted tamarind-tree. It might at first have been only the smoke of a cigar. Next moment, however, a flick of flame stole out and moved up the tree, and a draught of air blew the smoke across the stage. There were a few excited whispers, a rush in the wings; some one in the gallery shouted "Fire!" and just then a shower of sparks from the flaming scenery fell on the stage.

In a second the whole audience was on its feet. In a second more there would have been a panic which must have cost many lives. Keith saw the danger. "Stay in this box," he said. "The best way out is over the stage. I will come for you if necessary." He sprang on the stage, and, with a wave of his arm to the audience, shouted: "Down in your seats! It is all right."

Those nearest the stage, seeing a man stand between them and the fire, had paused, and the hubbub for a moment had ceased. Keith took advantage of it.

"This theatre can be emptied in three minutes if you take your time," he cried; "but the fire is under control."

Terpy had seized the burning piece of scenery and torn it down, and was tearing off the flaming edges with her naked hands. He sprang to Terpy's side. Her filmy dress caught fire, but Keith jerked off his coat and smothered the flame. Just then the water came, and the fire was subdued.

"Strike up that music again," Keith said to the musicians. Then to Terpy he said : "Begin dancing. Dance for your life !" The girl obeyed, and, all blackened as she was, began to dance again. She danced as she had never danced before, and as she danced the people at the rear filed out, while most of those in the body of the house stood and watched her. As the last spark of flame was extinguished the girl stopped, breathless. Thunders of applause broke out, but ceased as Terpy suddenly sank to the floor, clutching with her blackened hands at her throat. Keith caught her, and lowering her gently, straightened her dress. The next moment a woman sprang out of her box and knelt beside him ; a woman's arm slipped under the dancer's head, and Lois Huntington, on her knees, was loosening Terpy's bodice as if she had been a sister.

A doctor came up out of the audience and bent over her, and the curtain rang down.

That night Keith and Lois and Mrs. Lancaster all spent in the waiting-room of the Emergency Hospital. They knew that Terpy's life was ebbing fast. She had swallowed the flame, the doctor said. During the night a nurse came and called for Keith. The dying woman wanted to see him. When Keith reached her bedside, the doctor, in reply to a look of inquiry from him, said : "You can say anything to her ; it will not hurt her." He turned away, and Keith seated himself beside her. Her face and hands were swathed in bandages.

"I want to say good-by," she said feebly. "You don't mind now what I said to you that time?" Keith, for answer, stroked the coverlid beside her. "I want to go back home—to Gumbolt.—Tell the boys good-by for me."

Keith said he would—as well as he could, for he had little voice left.

"I want to see *her*," she said presently.

"Whom?" asked Keith.

"The younger one. The one you looked at all the time. I want to thank her for the doll. I ran away."

Lois was sent for, but when she reached the bedside Terpy was too far gone to speak so that she could be understood. But she was conscious enough to know that Lois was at her side and that it was her voice that repeated the Lord's Prayer.

The newspapers the next day rang with her praises, and that night Keith went South with her body to lay it on the hillside among her friends, and all of old Gumbolt was there to meet her.

Wickersham, on finding his attempt at explanation to Mrs. Wentworth received with coldness, turned his attentions in another direction. It was necessary. His affairs had all gone wrong of late. He had seen his great fortune disappear under his hands. Men who had not half his ability were succeeding where he had failed. Men who once followed him now held aloof, and refused to be drawn into his most tempting schemes. His enemies were working against him. He would overthrow them yet. Norman Wentworth and Gordon Keith especially he hated.

He began to try his fortune with Mrs. Lancaster again. Now, if ever, appeared a good time. She was indifferent to every man—unless she cared for Keith. He had sometimes thought she might; but he did not believe it. Keith, of course, would like to marry her; but Wickersham did not believe Keith stood any chance. Though she had refused Wickersham, she had never shown any one else any special favor. He would try new tactics and bear her off before she knew it. He began with a dash. He was quite a different man from what he had been. He even was seen in church, turning on Rimmon a sphinx-like face that a little disconcerted that eloquent person.

Mrs. Lancaster received him with the serene and unruffled indifference with which she received all her admirers, and there were many. She treated him, however, with the easy indulgence with which old friends are likely to be treated for old times' sake; and Wickersham was deceived. Fortune appeared suddenly to smile on him again. Hope sprang up once more.

Mrs. Nailor one day met Lois, and informed her that Mr. Wickersham was now a rival of Mr. Keith's with Mrs. Lancaster, and, what was more, that Norman Wentworth had learned that it was not Wickersham at all, but Mr. Keith who had really caused the trouble between Norman and his wife.

Lois was aghast. She denied vehemently that it was true; but Mrs. Nailor received her denial with amused indulgence.

"Oh, every one knows it," she said. "Mr. Keith long ago cut Fredy out; and Norman knows it."

Lois went home in a maze. This, then, explained why Mr. Keith had suddenly stopped coming to the house. When he had met her he had appeared as glad as ever to see her, but he had also appeared constrained. He had begun to talk of going away. He was almost the only man in New York that she could call her friend. To think of New York without him made her lonely. He was in love with Mrs. Lancaster, she knew—of that she was sure, notwithstanding Mrs. Nailor's statement. Could Mrs. Lancaster have treated him badly? She had not even cared for her husband, so people said; would she be cruel to Keith?

The more she pondered over it the more unhappy Lois became. Finally it appeared to her that her duty was plain. If Mrs. Lancaster had rejected Keith for Wickersham, she might set her right. She could, at least, set her right as to the story about him and Mrs. Wentworth.

That afternoon she called on Mrs. Lancaster. It was in the Spring, and she put on a dainty gown she had just made.

She was received with the sincere cordiality that Alice Lancaster always showed her. She was taken up to her boudoir, a nest of blue satin and sunshine. And there, of all occupations in the world, Mrs. Lancaster, clad in a soft lavender tea-gown, was engaged in mending old clothes. "For my orphans," she said, with a laugh and a blush that made her look charming.

A photograph of Keith stood on the table in a silver frame. When, however, Lois would have brought up the subject of Mr. Keith, his name stuck in her throat.

"I have what the children call 'a swap' for you," said the girl, smiling.

Mrs. Lancaster smiled acquiescingly as she bit off a thread.

"I heard some one say the other day that you were one of those who 'do good by stealth, and blush to find it fame.'"

"Oh, how nice! I am not, at all, you know. Still, it is pleasant to deceive people that way. Who said it?"

"Mr. Keith." Lois could not help blushing a little; but she had broken the ice.

"And I have one to return to you. I heard some one say that you had 'the rare gift of an absolutely direct mind.' That you were like George Washington: you couldn't tell a lie—that truth had its home in your eyes." Her eyes were twinkling.

"My! Who said that?" asked the girl.

"Mr. Keith."

Lois turned quickly under pretence of picking up something, but she was not quick enough to hide her face from her friend. The red that burned in her cheeks flamed down and made her throat rosy.

Mrs. Lancaster looked at the young girl. She made a pretty picture as she sat leaning forward, the curves of her slim, light-gowned figure showing against the background of blue. Her face was pensive, and she was evidently thinking deeply.

"What are you puzzling over so?"

At the question the color mounted into her cheeks, and the next second a smile lit up her face as she turned her eyes frankly on Mrs. Lancaster.

"You would be amused to know. I was wondering how long you had known Mr. Keith, and what he was like when he was young."

"When he was young! Do you call him old now? Why, he is only a little over thirty."

"Is that all! He always seems much older to me, I do not know why. But he has seen so much—done so much. Why, he appears to have had so many experiences! I feel as if no matter what might happen, he would know just what to do. For instance, that story that Cousin Norman told me once of his going down into the flooded mine, and that night at the theatre, when there was the fire—why, he just took charge. I felt as if he would take charge no matter what might happen."

Mrs. Lancaster at first had smiled at the girl's enthusiasm, but before Lois had finished, she had drifted away.

"He would—he would," she repeated, pensively.

"Then that poor girl—what he did for her. I just"—Lois paused, seeking for a word—"trust him!"

Mrs. Lancaster smiled.

"You may," she said. "That is exactly the word."

"Tell me, what was he like when—you first knew him?"

"I don't know—why, he was—he was just what he is now—you could have trusted him—"

"Why didn't you marry him?" asked Lois, her eyes on the other's face.

Mrs. Lancaster looked at her with almost a gasp.

"Why, Lois! What are you talking about? Who says—?"

"He says so. He said he was desperately in love with you."

"Why, Lois—!" began Mrs. Lancaster, with the color mounting to her cheeks. "Well, he has gotten bravely over it," she laughed.

"He has not. He is in love with you now," the young girl said calmly.

Mrs. Lancaster turned and faced her with her mouth open to speak, and read the girl's sincerity in her face. "With me!" She clasped her hands with a pretty gesture over her bosom. A warm feeling suddenly surged to her heart.

The younger woman nodded.

454

"Yes—and, oh, Mrs. Lancaster, don't treat him badly!" She laid both hands on her arm and looked at her earnestly. "He has loved you always," she continued.

"Loved me! Lois, you are dreaming." But as she said it, Alice's heart was beating.

"Yes, he was talking to me one evening, and he began to tell me of his love for a girl,—a young girl,—and what a part it had played in his life—"

"But I was married," put in Mrs. Lancaster, seeking for further proof rather than renouncing this.

"Yes, he said she did not care for him ; but he had always striven to keep her image in his heart—her image as she was when he knew her and as he imagined her."

Mrs. Lancaster's face for a moment was a study.

"Do you know whom he is in love with now?" she said presently.

"Yes ; with you."

"No—not with me ; with you." She put her hand on Lois's cheek caressingly, and gazed into her eyes.

The girl's eyes sank into her lap. Her face, which had been growing white and pink by turns, suddenly flamed.

"Mrs. Lancaster, I believe I—" she began in low tones. She raised her eyes, and they met for a moment Mrs. Lancaster's. Something in their depths, some look of sympathy, of almost maternal kindness, struck her, passed through to her long-stilled heart. With a little cry she threw herself into the other's arms and buried her burning face in her lap.

The expression on the face of the young widow changed. She glanced down for a moment at the little head in her lap, then bending down, she buried her face in the brown tresses, and drew her form close to her heart.

In a moment the young girl was pouring out her soul to her as if she had been her daughter.

The expression in Alice Lancaster's eyes was softer than it had been for a long time, for it was the light of self-sacrifice that shone in them.

"You have your happiness in your hands," she said tenderly.

Lois looked up with dissent in her eyes.

Mrs. Lancaster shook her head.

"No. He will never be in love with me again."

The girl gave a quick intaking of her breath, her hand clutching at her throat.

"Oh, Mrs. Lancaster!" She was thinking aloud rather than speaking. "I thought that you cared for him."

Alice Lancaster shook her head. She tried to meet frankly the other's eyes, but as they gazed deep into hers with an inquiry not to be put aside, hers failed and fell.

"No," she said, but it was with a gasp.

Lois's eyes opened wide, and her face changed.

"Oh!" she murmured, as the sense of what she had done swept over her. She rose to her feet and, bending down, kissed Mrs. Lancaster tenderly. One might have thought she was the elder of the two.

Lois returned home in deep thought. She had surprised Mrs. Lancaster's secret, and the end was plain. She allowed herself no delusions. The dream that for a moment had shed its radiance on her was broken. Keith was in love with Mrs. Lancaster, and Alice loved him. She prayed that they might be happy—especially Keith. She was angry with herself that she had allowed herself to become so interested in him. She would forget him. This was easier said than done. But she could at least avoid seeing him. And having made her decision, she held to it firmly. She avoided him in every way possible.

The strain, however, had been too much for Lois, and her strength began to go. The doctor advised Mrs. Wentworth to send her home. "She is breaking down, and you will have her ill on your hands," he said. Lois, too, was pining to get away. She felt that she could not stand the city another week. And so, one day, she disappeared from town.

When Wickersham met Mrs. Lancaster after her talk with Lois, he was conscious of the change in her. The old easy, indulgent attitude was gone; and in her eye, instead of the lazy, half-amused smile, was something very like scorn. Something had happened, he knew.

His thoughts flew to Keith, Norman, Rimmon, also to several ladies of his acquaintance. What had they told her? Could it be the fact that he had lost nearly everything —that he had spent Mrs. Wentworth's money? That he had written anonymous letters? Whatever it was, he would brave it out. He had been in some hard places lately, and had won out by his nerve. He assumed an injured and a virtuous air, and no man could do it better.

"What has happened? You are so strange to me. Has some one been prejudicing you against me? Some one has slandered me," he said, with an air of virtue.

"No. No one." Mrs. Lancaster turned her rings with a little embarrassment. She was trying to muster the courage to speak plainly to him. He gave it to her.

"Oh, yes; some one has. I think I have a right to demand who it is. Is it that man Keith?"

"No." She glanced at him with a swift flash in her eye. "Mr. Keith has not mentioned your name to me since I came home."

Her tone fired him with jealousy.

"Well, who was it, then? He is not above it. He hates me enough to say anything. He has never got over our buying his old place, and has never lost an opportunity to malign me since."

She looked him in the face, for the first time, quite steadily.

"Let me tell you, Mr. Keith has never said a word against you to me—and that is much more than I can say for you; so you need not be maligning him now."

A faint flush stole into Wickersham's face.

"You appear to be championing his cause very warmly."

"Because he is a friend of mine and an honorable gentleman."

457

He gave a hard, bitter laugh.

"Women are innocent!"

"It is more than men are," she said, fired, as women always are, by a fleer at the sex.

"Who has been slandering me?" he demanded, angered suddenly by her retort. "I have stood in a relation to you which gives me a right to demand the name."

"What relation to me?—Where is your wife?"

His face whitened, and he drew in his breath as if struck a blow,—a long breath,—but in a second he had recovered himself, and he burst into a laugh.

"So you have heard that old story—and believe it?" he said, with his eyes looking straight into hers. As she made no answer, he went on. "Now, as you have heard it, I will explain the whole thing to you. I have always wanted to do it; but—but—I hardly knew whether it were better to do it or leave it alone. I thought if you had heard it you would mention it to me—"

"I have done so now," she said coldly.

"I thought our relation—or, as you object to that word, our friendship—entitled me to that much from you."

"I never heard it till—till just now," she defended, rather shaken by his tone and air of candor.

"When?"

"Oh—very recently."

"Won't you tell me who told you?"

"No—o. Go on."

"Well, that woman—that poor girl—her name was—her name is—Phrony Tripper—or Trimmer. I think that was her name—she called herself Euphronia Tripper." He was trying with puckered brow to recall exactly. "I suppose that is the woman you are referring to?" he said suddenly.

"It is. You have not had more than one, have you?"

He laughed, pleased to give the subject a lighter tone.

"Well, this poor creature I used to know in the South when I was a boy—when I first went down there, you know?

She was the daughter of an old farmer at whose house we stayed. I used to talk to her. You know how a boy talks to a pretty girl whom he is thrown with in a lonesome old country place, far from any amusement." Her eyes showed that she knew, and he was satisfied and proceeded.

"But heavens! the idea of being in love with her! Why, she was the daughter of a farmer. Well, then I fell in with her afterwards—once or twice, to be accurate—when I went down there on business, and she was a pretty, vain country girl—"

"I used to know her," assented Mrs. Lancaster.

"You did!" His face fell.

"Yes; when I went there to a little Winter resort for my throat—when I was seventeen. She used to go to the school taught by Mr. Keith."

"She did? Oh, then you know her name? It was Tripper, wasn't it?"

She nodded.

"I thought it was. Well, she was quite pretty, you remember; and, as I say, I fell in with her again, and having been old friends—" He shifted in his seat a little as if embarrassed—"Why—oh, you know how it is. I began to talk nonsense to her to pass away the time,—told her she was pretty and all that,—and made her a few presents—and—" He paused and took a long breath. "I thought she was very queer. The first thing I knew, I found she was—out of her mind. Well, I stopped and soon came away, and, to my horror, she took it into her head that she was my wife. She followed me here. I had to go abroad, and I heard no more of her until, not long ago, I heard she had gone completely crazy and was hunting me up as her husband. You know how such poor creatures are?" He paused, well satisfied with his recital, for first surprise and then a certain sympathy took the place of incredulity in Mrs. Lancaster's face.

"She is absolutely mad, poor thing, I understand," he sighed, with unmistakable sympathy in his voice.

"Yes," Mrs. Lancaster assented, her thoughts drifting away.

He watched her keenly, and next moment began again.

"I heard she had got hold of Mr. Rimmon's name and declares that he married us."

Mrs. Lancaster returned to the present, and he went on :

"I don't know how she got hold of it. I suppose his being the fashionable preacher, or his name being in the papers frequently, suggested the idea. But if you have any doubt on the subject, ask him."

Mrs. Lancaster looked assent.

"Here— Having heard the story, and thinking it might be as well to stop it at once, I wrote to Mr. Rimmon to give me a statement to set the matter at rest, and I have it in my pocket." He took from his pocket-book a letter and spread it before Mrs. Lancaster. It read :

"DEAR MR. WICKERSHAM : I am sorry you are being annoyed. I cannot imagine that you should need any such statement as you request. The records of marriages are kept in the proper office here. Any one who will take the trouble to inspect those records will see that I have never made any such report. This should be more than sufficient.

"I feel sure this will answer your purpose.

"Yours sincerely,

"W. H. RIMMON."

"I think that settles the matter," said Wickersham, with his eyes on her face.

"It would seem so," said Mrs. Lancaster, gravely.

As she spoke slowly, Wickersham put in one more nail.

"Of course, you know there must be a witness to a marriage," he said. "If there be such a witness, let K—let those who are engaged in defaming me produce him."

"No, no," said Mrs. Lancaster, quickly. "Mr. Rimmon's statement—I think I owe you an apology for what I said. Of course, it appeared incredible ; but something occurred—

I can't tell you—I don't want to tell you what—that shocked me very much, and I suppose I judged too hastily and harshly. You must forget what I said, and forgive me for my injustice."

"Certainly I will," he said earnestly.

The revulsion in her belief inclined her to be kinder toward him than she had been in a long time.

The change in her manner toward him made Wicker-sham's heart begin to beat. He leant over and took her hand.

"Won't you give me more than justice, Alice?" he began. "If you knew how long I have waited—how I have hoped even against hope—how I have always loved you—" She was so taken aback by his declaration that, for a moment she did not find words to reply, and he swept on : "—you would not be so cold—so cruel to me. I have always thought you the most beautiful—the most charming woman in New York."

She shook her head. "No, you have not."

"I have ; I swear I have ! Even when I have hung around—around other women, I have done so because I saw you were taken up with—some one else. I thought I might find some one else to supplant you, but never for one moment have I failed to acknowledge your superiority—"

"Oh, no ; you have not. How can you dare to tell me that?" she smiled, recovering her self-possession.

"I have, Alice, ever since you were a girl—even when you were—were—when you were beyond me—I loved you more than ever—I—" Her face changed, and she recoiled from him.

"Don't," she said.

"I will." He seized her hand and held it tightly. "I loved you even then better than I ever loved in my life—better than your—than any one else did." Her face whitened.

"Stop !" she cried. "Not another word. I will not listen. Release my hand." She pulled it from him forcibly, and, as he began again, she, with a gesture, stopped him.

"No—no—no! It is impossible. I will not listen."

His face changed as he looked into her face. She rose from her seat and turned away from him, taking two or three steps up and down, trying to regain control of herself.

He waited and watched her, an angry light coming into his eyes. He misread her feelings. He had made love to married women before and had not been repulsed.

She turned to him now, and with level eyes looked into his.

"You never loved me in your life. I have had men in love with me, and know when they are; but you are not one of them."

"I was—I am—" he began, stepping closer to her; but she stopped him.

"Not for a minute," she went on, without heeding him. "And you had no right to say that to me."

"What?" he demanded.

"What you said. My husband loved me with all the strength of a noble, high-minded man, and notwithstanding the difference in our ages, treated me as his equal; and I loved him—yes, loved him devotedly," she said, as she saw a spark come into his eyes.

"You love some one else now," he said coolly.

It might have been anger that brought the rush of color to her face. She turned and looked him full in the face.

"If I do, it is not you."

The arrow went home. His eyes snapped with anger.

"You took such lofty ground just now that I should hardly have supposed the attentions of Mr. Wentworth meant anything so serious. I thought that was mere friendship."

This time there was no doubt that the color meant anger.

"What do you mean?" she demanded, looking him once more full in the eyes.

"I refer to what the world says, especially as he himself is such a model of all the Christian virtues."

"What the world says? What do you mean?" she persisted, never taking her eyes from his face.

He simply shrugged his shoulders.

"So I assume Mr. Keith is the fortunate suitor for the remnant of your affections : Keith the immaculate—Keith the pure and pious gentleman who trades on his affections. I wish you good luck."

At his insolence Mrs. Lancaster's patience suddenly snapped.

"Go," she said, pointing to the door. "Go."

When Wickersham walked out into the street, his face was white and drawn, and a strange light was in his eyes. He had played one of his last cards, and had played it like a fool. Luck had gone against him, and he had lost his head. His heart—that heart that had never known remorse and rarely dismay—began to sink. Luck had been going against him now for a long time, so long that it had swept away his fortune and most of his credit. What was worse to him, he was conscious that he had lost his nerve. Where should he turn? Unless luck turned or he could get help he would go down. He canvassed the various means of escape. Man after man had fallen away from him. Every scheme had failed.

He attributed it all to Norman—to Norman and Keith. Norman had ruined him in New York; Keith had blocked him and balked him in the South. But one resource remained to him. He would make one more supreme effort. Then, if he failed! He thought of a locked drawer in his desk, and a black pistol under the papers there. His cheek blanched at the thought, but his lips closed tight. He would not survive disgrace. His disgrace meant the known loss of his fortune. One thing he would do. Keith had escaped him, had succeeded, but Norman he could overthrow. Norman had been struck hard ; he would now complete his ruin. With this mental tonic he straightened up and walked rapidly down the street.

That evening Wickersham was closeted for some time with a man who had of late come into especial notice as a strong and merciless financier—Mr. Kestrel.

Mr. Kestrel received him at first with a coldness which might have repelled a less determined man. He had no delusions about Wickersham; but Wickersham knew this, and unfolded to him, with plausible frankness, a scheme which had much reason in it. He had at the same time played on the older man's foibles with great astuteness, and had awakened one or two of his dormant animosities. He knew that Mr. Kestrel had had a strong feeling against Norman for several years.

"You are one of the few men who do not have to fall down and worship the name of Wentworth," he said.

"Well, I rather think not," said Mr. Kestrel, with a glint in his eyes, as he recalled Norman Wentworth's scorn of him at the board-meeting years before, when Norman had defended Keith against him.

"—Or this new man, Keith, who is undertaking to teach New York finance?"

Mr. Kestrel gave a hard little laugh, which was more like a cough than an expression of mirth, but which meant that he was amused.

"Well, neither do I," said Wickersham. "To tell you frankly, I hate them both, though there is money, and big money, in this, as you can see for yourself from what I have said. This is my real reason for wanting you in it. If you jump in and hammer down those things, you will clean them out. I have the old patents to all the lands that Keith sold those people. They antedate the titles under which Rawson claims. If you can break up the deal now, we will go in and recover the lands from Rawson. Wentworth is so deep in that he'll never pull through, and his friend Keith has staked everything on this one toss."

Old Kestrel's parchment face was inscrutable as he gazed at Wickersham and declared that he did not know about that. He did not believe in having animosities in business

matters, as it marred one's judgment. But Wickersham knew
enough to be sure that the seed he had planted would bear
fruit, and that Kestrel would stake something on the chance.

In this he was not deceived. The next day Mr. Kestrel
acceded to his plan.

For some days after that there appeared in a certain
paper a series of attacks on various lines of property hold-
ings, that was characterized by other papers as a "strong
bearish movement." The same paper contained a vicious
article about the attempt to unload worthless coal-lands on
gullible Englishmen. Meantime Wickersham, foreseeing
failure, acted independently.

The attack might not have amounted to a great deal but
for one of those untimely accidents that sometimes overthrow all calculations. One of the keenest and oldest finan-
ciers in the city suddenly dropped dead, and a stampede
started on the Stock Exchange. It was stayed in a little
while, but meantime a number of men had been hard hit,
and among these was Norman Wentworth. The papers
next day announced the names of those who had suffered,
and much space was given in one of them to the decline of
the old firm of Wentworth & Son, whose history was almost
contemporary with that of New York.

By noon it was extensively rumored that Wentworth &
Son would close their doors. The firm which had lasted for
three generations, and whose name had been the synonym
for honor and for philanthropy, which had stood as the
type of the highest that can exist in commerce, would go
down. Men spoke of it with a regret which did them
honor—hard men who rarely expressed regret for the losses
of another.

It was rumored, too, that Wickersham & Company must
assign ; but this caused little surprise and less regret. Aaron
Wickersham had had friends, but his son had not succeeded
to them.

Keith, having determined to talk to Alice Lancaster
about Lois, was calling on the former a day or two after

her interview with Wickersham. She was still some-what disturbed over it, and showed it in her manner so clearly that Keith asked what was the trouble.

It was nothing very much, she said. Only she had broken finally with a friend she had known a long time, and such things upset her.

Keith was sympathetic, and suddenly, to his surprise, she broke down and began to cry. He had never seen her weep before since she sat, as a girl, in the pine-woods and he lent her his handkerchief to dry her tears. Something in the association gave him a feeling of unwonted tender-ness. She had not appeared to him so soft, so feminine, in a long time. He essayed to comfort her. He, too, had broken with an old friend, the friend of a lifetime, and he would never get over it.

"Mine was such a blow to me," she said, wiping her eyes; "such cruel things were said to me. I did not think any one but a woman would have said such biting things to a woman."

"It was Ferdy Wickersham, I know," said Keith, his eyes contracting; "but what on earth could he have said? What could he have dared to say to wound you so?"

"He said all the town was talking about me and Nor-man." She began to cry again. "Norman, dear old Nor-man, who has been more like a brother to me than any one I have ever known, and whom I would give the world to bring back happiness to."

"He is a scoundrel!" exclaimed Keith. "I have stood all—more than I ever expected to stand from any man living; but if he is attacking women"—he was speaking to himself rather than to her—"I will unmask him. He is not worth your notice," he said kindly, addressing her again. "Women have been his prey ever since I knew him, when he was but a young boy." Mrs. Lancaster dried her eyes.

"You refer to the story that he had married that poor girl and abandoned her?"

"Yes—partly that. That is the worst thing I know of him."

"But that is not true. However cruel he is, that accusation is unfounded. I know that myself."

"How do you know it?" asked Keith, in surprise.

"He told me the whole story: explained the thing to my satisfaction. It was a poor crazy girl who claimed that he married her; said Mr. Rimmon had performed the ceremony. She was crazy. I saw Mr. Rimmon's letter denying the whole thing."

"Do you know his handwriting?" inquired Keith, grimly.

"Whose?"

"Well, that of both of them?"

She nodded, and Keith, taking out his pocket-book, opened it and took therefrom a slip of paper. "Look at that. I got that a few days ago from the witness who was present."

"Why, what is this?" She sprang up in her excitement. "It is incredible!" she said slowly. "Why, he told me the story with the utmost circumstantiality."

"He lied to you," said Keith, grimly. "And Rimmon lied. That is their handwriting. I have had it examined by the best expert in New York City. I had not intended to use that against him, but only to clear the character of that poor young creature whom he deceived and then abandoned; but as he is defaming her here, and is at his old trade of trying to deceive women, it is time he was shown up in his true colors."

She gave a shudder of horror, and wiped her right hand with her left. "Oh, to think that he dared!" She wiped her hand on her handkerchief.

At that moment a servant brought in a card. As Mrs. Lancaster gazed at it, her eyes flashed and her lip curled.

"Say that Mrs. Lancaster begs to be excused."

"Yes, madam." The servant hesitated. "I think he heard you talking, madam."

"Say that Mrs. Lancaster begs to be excused," she said firmly.

467

The servant, with a bow, withdrew.

She handed the card to Keith. On it was the name of the Rev. William H. Rimmon.

Mr. Rimmon, as he stood in the hall, was in unusually good spirits, though slightly perturbed. He had determined to carry through a plan that he had long pondered over. He had decided to ask Mrs. Lancaster to become Mrs. Rimmon.

As Keith glanced toward the door, he caught Mr. Rimmon's eye. He was waiting on the threshold and rubbing his hands with eager expectancy. Just then the servant gave him the message. Keith saw his countenance fall and his face blanch. He turned, picked up his hat, and slipped out of the door, with a step that was almost a slink.

As Mr. Rimmon passed down the street he knew that he had reached a crisis in his life. He went to see Wickersham, but that gentleman was in no mood for condolences. Everything had gone against him. He was facing utter ruin. Rimmon's upbraiding angered him.

"By the way, you are the very man I wanted to see," he said grimly. "I want you to sign a note for that twenty thousand I lost by you when you insisted on my holding that stock."

Rimmon's jaw fell. "That you held for me? Sign a note! Twenty-six thousand!"

"Yes. Don't pretend innocence—not on me. Save that for the pulpit. I know you," said the other, with a chilling laugh.

"But you were to carry that. That was a part of our agreement. Why, twenty thousand would take everything I have."

"Don't play that on me," said Wickersham, coldly. "It won't work. You can make it up when you get your widow."

Rimmon groaned helplessly.

"Come; there is the note. Sign."

Rimmon began to expostulate, and finally refused point-blank to sign. Wickersham gazed at him with amusement.

"You sign that, or I will serve suit on you in a half-hour, and we will see how the Rev. Mr. Rimmon stands when my lawyers are through with him. You will believe in hell then, sure enough."

"You won't dare do it. Your marriage would come out. Mrs. Lancaster would—"

"She knows it," said Wickersham, calmly. And, as Rimmon looked sceptical, "I told her myself to spare you the trouble. Sign." He rose and touched a bell.

Rimmon, with a groan, signed the paper.

"You must have showed her my letter?"

"Of course, I did."

"But you promised me not to. I am ruined!"

"What have I to do with that? 'See thou to that,'" said Wickersham, with a bitter laugh.

Rimmon's face paled at the quotation. He, too, had betrayed his Lord.

"Now go." Wickersham pointed to the door.

Mr. Rimmon went home and tried to write a letter to Mrs. Lancaster, but he could not master his thoughts. That pen that usually flowed so glibly failed to obey him. He was in darkness. He saw himself dishonored, displaced. Wickersham was capable of anything. He did not know where to turn. He thought of his brother clergymen. He knew many good men who spent their lives helping others. But something deterred him from applying to them now. To some he had been indifferent, others he had known only socially. Yet others had withdrawn themselves from him more and more of late. He had attributed it to their envy or their folly. He suddenly thought of old Dr. Templeton. He had always ignored that old man as a sort of crack-brained creature who had not been able to keep up with the world, and had been left stranded, doing the work that properly belonged to the unsuccessful. Curiously enough, he was the one to whom the unhappy man now turned. Besides, he was a friend of Mrs. Lancaster.

A half-hour later the Rev. Mr. Rimmon was in Dr. Templeton's simple study, and was finding a singular sense of relief in pouring out his troubles to the old clergyman. He told him something of his unhappy situation—not all, it is true, but enough to enable the other to see how grave it was, as much from what he inferred as from what Rimmon explained. He even began to hope again. If the Doctor would undertake to straighten out the complications he might yet pull through. To his dismay, this phase of the matter did not appear to present itself to the old man's mind. It was the sin that he had committed that had touched him.

"Let us carry it where only we can find relief," he said. "Let us take it to the Throne of Grace, where we can lay all our burdens"; and before Rimmon knew it, he was on his knees, praying for him as if he had been a very outcast.

When the Rev. Mr. Rimmon came out of the shabby little study, though he had not gotten the relief he had sought, he, somehow, felt a little comforted, while at the same time he felt humble. He had one of those brief intervals of feeling that, perhaps, there was, after all, something that that old man had found which he had missed, and he determined to find it. But Mr. Rimmon had wandered far out of the way. He had had a glimpse of the pearl, but the price was great, and he had not been able to pay it all.

Wickersham discounted the note; but the amount was only a bagatelle to him : a bucket-shop had swallowed it within an hour. He had lost his instinct. It was only the love of gambling that remained.

Only one chance appeared to remain for him. He had made up with Louise Wentworth after a fashion. He must get hold of her in some way. He might obtain more money from her. The method he selected was a desperate one ; but he was a desperate man.

After long pondering, he sat down and wrote her a note, asking her "to meet some friends of his, a Count and Countess Torelli, at supper" next evening.

CHAPTER XXXII

THE RUN ON THE BANK

IT was the day after the events just recorded that Keith's deal was concluded. The attack on him and the attempt made by Wickersham and Kestrel to break up his deal had failed, and the deeds and money were passed.

Keith was on his way back to his office from his final interview with the representative of the syndicate that had bought the properties. He was conscious of a curious sensation, partly of exhilaration, partly of almost awe, as he walked through the crowded streets, where every one was bent on the same quest: gold. At last he had won. He was rich. He wondered, as he walked along, if any of the men he shouldered were as rich as he. Norman and Ferdy Wickersham recurred to him. Both had been much wealthier; but Wickersham, he knew, was in straits, and Norman was in some trouble. He was unfeignedly glad about Wickersham; but the recollection of Norman clouded his face.

It was with a pang that he recalled Norman's recent conduct to him—a pang that one who had always been his friend should have changed so; but that was the way of the world. This reflection, however, was not consoling.

He reached his office and seated himself at his desk, to take another look at his papers. Before he opened them he rose and locked the door, and opening a large envelope, spread the papers out on the desk before him.

He thought of his father. He must write and tell him of his success. Then he thought of his old home. He remembered his resolution to restore it and make it what it used to be. But how much he could do with the money it would take to fit up the old place in the manner he had contemplated! By investing it judiciously he could double it.

Suddenly there was a step outside and a knock at his door, followed by voices in the outer office. Keith rose, and putting his papers back in his pocket, opened the door. For a second he had a mingled sensation of pleasure and surprise. His father stood there, his bag clutched in his hand. He looked tired, and had aged some since Keith saw him last; but his face wore the old smile that always illumined it when it rested on his son.

Keith greeted him warmly and drew him inside. "I was just thinking of you, sir."

"You would not come to see me, so I have come to see you. I have heard from you so rarely that I was afraid you were sick." His eyes rested fondly on Gordon's face.

"No; I have been so busy; that is all. Well, sir, I have won." His eyes were sparkling.

The old gentleman's face lit up.

"You have? Found Phrony, have you? I am so glad. It will give old Rawson a new lease of life. I saw him after he got back. He has failed a good deal lately."

"No, sir. I have found her, too; but I mean I have won out at last."

"Ah, you have won her? I congratulate you. I hope she will make you happy."

Keith laughed.

"I don't mean that. I mean I have sold my lands at last. I closed this morning with the Englishmen, and received the money."

The General smiled.

"Ah, you have, have you? That's very good. I am glad for old Adam Rawson's sake."

472

"I was afraid he would die before the deeds passed," said Keith. "But see, here are the drafts to my order." He spread them out. "This one is my commission. And I have the same amount of common stock."

His father made no comment on this, but presently said : "You will have enough to restore the old place a little."

"How much would it cost to fix up the place as you think it ought to be fixed up?"

"Oh, some thousands of dollars. You see, the house is much out of repair, and the quarters ought really all to be rebuilt. Old Charlotte's house I have kept in repair, and Richard now sleeps in the house, as he has gotten so rheumatic. I should think five or six thousand dollars might do it."

"I can certainly spare that much," said Keith, laughing.

"How is Norman?" asked the General.

Keith was conscious of a feeling of discontent. His countenance fell.

"Why, I don't know. I don't see much of him these days."

"Ah! I want to go to see him."

"The fact is, we have—er—had—. There has been an unfortunate misunderstanding between us. No one regrets it more than I; but I think I can say it was not at all my fault, and I have done all and more than was required of me."

"Ah, I am very sorry for that. It's a pity—a pity!" said the old General. "What was it about?"

"Well, I don't care to talk about it, sir. But I can assure you, I was not in the least to blame. It was caused mainly, I believe, by that fellow, Wickersham."

"He's a scoundrel!" said the General, with sudden vehemence.

"He is, sir!"

"I will go and see Norman. I see by the papers he is in some trouble."

"I fear he is, sir. His bank has been declining."

"Perhaps you can help him?" His face lit up. "You remember, he once wrote you—a long time ago?"

"I remember; I have repaid that," said Keith, quickly. "He has treated me very badly." He gave a brief account of the trouble between them.

The old General leant back and looked at his son intently. His face was very grave and showed that he was reflecting deeply.

"Gordon," he said presently, "the Devil is standing very close to you. A real misunderstanding should always be cleared up. You must go to him."

"What do you mean, sir?" asked his son, in some confusion.

"You are at the parting of the ways. A gentleman cannot hesitate. Such a debt never can be paid by a gentleman," he said calmly. "You must help him, even if you cannot restore the old place. Elphinstone has gone for a debt before." He rose as if there was nothing more to be said. "Well, I will go and wait for you at your rooms." He walked out.

Keith sat and reflected. How different he was from his father! How different from what he had been years ago! Then he had had an affection for the old home and all that it represented. He had worked with the idea of winning it back some day. It had been an inspiration to him. But now it was wealth that he had begun to seek.

It came to him clearly how much he had changed. The process all lay before him. It had grown with his success, and had kept pace with it in an almost steady ratio since he had set success before him as a goal. He was angry with himself to find that he was thinking now of success merely as Wealth. Once he had thought of Honor and Achievement, even of Duty. He remembered when he had not hesitated to descend into what appeared the very jaws of death, because it seemed to him his duty. He wondered if he would do the same now.

He felt that this was a practical view which he was now taking of life. He was now a practical man; yes, practical like old Kestrel, said his better self. He felt that he was not as much of a gentleman as he used to be. He was further from his father; further from what Norman was. This again brought Norman to his mind. If the rumors which he had heard were true, Norman was now in a tight place.

As his father had said, perhaps he might be able to help him. But why should he do it? If Norman had helped him in the past, had he not already paid him back? And had not Norman treated him badly of late without the least cause—met his advances with a rebuff? No; he would show him that he was not to be treated so. He still had a small account in Norman's bank, which he had not drawn out because he had not wished to let Norman see that he thought enough of his coldness to make any change; but he would put his money now into old Creamer's bank. After looking at his drafts again, he unlocked his door and went out on the street.

There was more commotion on the street than he had seen in some days. Men were hurrying at a quicker pace than the rapid gait which was always noticeable in that thoroughfare. Groups occasionally formed and, after a word or two, dispersed. Newsboys were crying extras and announcing some important news in an unintelligible jargon. Messengers were dashing about, rushing in and out of the big buildings. Something unusual was evidently going on. As Keith, on his way to the bank of which Mr. Creamer was president, passed the mouth of the street in which Norman's office was situated, he looked down and saw quite a crowd assembled. The street was full. He passed on, however, and went into the big building, on the first floor of which Creamer's bank had its offices. He walked through to the rear of the office, to the door of Mr. Creamer's private office, and casually asked the nearest clerk for Mr. Creamer. The young man said he was engaged. Keith, however, walked up to the door, and was about to knock, when, at a word spoken by his informant, another clerk came hastily forward and said that Mr. Creamer was very busily engaged and could see no one.

"Well, he will see me," said Keith, feeling suddenly the courage that the possession of over a quarter of a million dollars gave, and he boldly knocked on the door, and, without waiting to be invited in, opened it.

Mr. Creamer was sitting at his desk, and two or three other men, one or two of whom Keith had seen before, were seated in front of him in close conference. They stared at the intruder.

"Mr. Keith." Mr. Creamer's tone conveyed not the least feeling, gave no idea either of welcome or surprise.

"Excuse me for interrupting you for a moment," said Keith. "I want to open an account here. I have a draft on London, which I should like to deposit and have you collect for me."

The effect was immediate; indeed, one might almost say magical. The atmosphere of the room as suddenly changed as if May should be dropped into the lap of December. The old banker's face relaxed. He touched a bell under the lid of his desk, and at the same moment pushed back his chair.

"Gentlemen, let me introduce my friend, Mr. Keith." He presented Keith in turn to each of his companions, who greeted him with that degree of mingled reserve and civility which is due to a man who has placed a paper capable of effecting such a marked change in the hands of the most self-contained banker in Bankers' Row.

A tap at the door announced an answer to the bell, and the next moment a clerk came in.

"Ask Mr. Penwell to come here," said Mr. Creamer. "Mr. Penwell is the head of our foreign department," he added in gracious explanation to Keith.

"Mr. Keith, gentlemen, is largely interested in some of those Southern mining properties that you have heard me speak of, and has just put through a very fine deal with an English syndicate."

The door opened, and a cool-looking, slender man of fifty-odd, with a thin gray face, thin gray hair very smoothly brushed, and keen gray eyes, entered. He was introduced to Mr. Keith. After Mr. Creamer had stated the purpose of Keith's visit and had placed the drafts in Mr. Penwell's hands, the latter stated, as an interesting item just off the ticker, that he understood Wentworth was in trouble. Some one had just come and said that there was a run on his bank.

"Those attacks on him in the newspapers must have hurt him considerably," observed one of the visitors.

"Yes, he has been a good deal hurt," said Mr. Creamer. "We are all right, Penwell?" He glanced at his subordinate.

Mr. Penwell nodded with deep satisfaction.

"So are we," said one of the visitors. "This is the end of Wentworth & Son. He will go down."

"He has been going down for some time. Wife too extravagant."

This appeared to be the general opinion. But Keith scarcely heard the speakers. He stood in a maze.

The announcement of Norman's trouble had come to him like a thunder-clap. And he was standing now as in a dream. Could it be possible that Norman was going to fail? And if he failed, would this be all it meant to these men who had known him always?

The vision of an old gentleman sitting in his home, which he had lost, came back to him across the years.

"That young man is a gentleman," he heard him say. "It takes a gentleman to write such a letter to a friend in misfortune. Write to him and say we will never forget his kindness." He heard the same old gentleman say, after years of poverty, "You must pay your debt though I give up Elphinstone."

Was he not now forgetting Norman's kindness? But was it not too late? Could he save him? Would he not simply be throwing away his money to offer it to him? Suddenly again, he seemed to hear his father's voice:

"The Devil is standing close behind you. You are at the parting of the ways. A gentleman cannot hesitate."

"Mr. Creamer," he said suddenly, "why don't Norman Wentworth's friends come to his rescue and help him out of his difficulties?"

The question might have come from the sky, it was so unexpected. It evidently caught the others unprepared with an answer. They simply smiled vaguely. Mr. Creamer said presently, rubbing his chin:

"Why, I don't suppose they know the extent of his difficulties."

"And I guess he has no collateral to offer?" said another.

"Collateral! No; everything he has is pledged."

"But I mean, why don't they lend him money without collateral, if necessary, to tide him over his trouble? He is a man of probity. He has lived here all his life. He must have many friends able to help him. They know that if he had time to realize on his properties he would probably pull through."

With one accord the other occupants of the room turned and looked at Keith.

"Did you say you had made a fortune in mining deals?" asked one of the gentlemen across the table, gazing at Keith through his gold-rimmed glasses with a wintry little smile.

"No, I did not. Whatever was said on that subject Mr. Creamer said."

"Oh! That's so. He did. Well, you are the sort of a man we want about here."

This remark was received with some amusement by the others; but Keith passed it by, and turned to Mr. Creamer.

"Mr. Creamer, how much money will you give me on this draft? This is mine. The other I wish to deposit here."

"Why, I don't know just what the exchange would be. What is the exchange on this, Penwell?"

"Will you cash this draft for me?" asked Keith.

"Certainly."

"Well, will you do me a further favor? It might make very little difference if I were to make a deposit in Norman's bank; but if you were to make such a deposit there, it would probably reassure people, and the run might be stopped. I have known of one or two instances."

Mr. Creamer agreed, and the result was a sort of reaction in Norman's favor, in sentiment if not in action. It was arranged that Keith should go and make a deposit, and that Mr. Creamer should send a man to make a further one and offer Wentworth aid.

When Gordon Keith reached the block on which stood Norman's bank, the street was already filled with a dense crowd, pushing, growling, complaining, swearing, threatening. It was evidently a serious affair, and Keith, trying to make his way through the mob, heard many things about Norman which he never could have believed it would have been possible to hear. The crowd was in an ugly mood, and was growing uglier. A number of policemen were trying to keep the people in line so that they could take their turn. Keith found it impossible to make his way to the front. His explanation that he wished to make a deposit was greeted with shouts of derision.

"Stand back there, young man. We've heard that before; you can't work that on us. We would all like to make deposits—somewhere else."

"Except them what's already made 'em," some one added, at which there was a laugh.

Keith applied to a policeman with hardly more success, until he opened the satchel he carried, and mentioned the name of the banker who was to follow him. On this the officer called another, and after a hurried word the two began to force their way through the crowd, with Keith between them. By dint of commanding, pushing, and explaining, they at length reached the entrance to the bank, and finally made their way, hot and perspiring, to the counter. A clerk was at work at every window counting out money as fast as checks were presented.

Just before Keith reached the counter, on glancing through an open door, he saw Norman sitting at his desk, white and grim. His burning eyes seemed deeper than ever. He glanced up, and Keith thought he caught his gaze on him, but he was not sure, for he looked away so quickly. The next moment he walked around inside the counter and spoke to a clerk, who opened a ledger and gave him a memorandum. Then he came forward and spoke to a teller at the receiving-window.

"Do you know that man with the two policemen? That is Mr. Gordon Keith. Here is his balance; pay it to him as soon as he reaches the window."

The teller, bending forward, gazed earnestly out of the small grated window over the heads of those nearest him. Keith met his gaze, and the teller nodded. Norman turned away without looking, and seated himself on a chair in the rear of the bank.

When Keith reached the window, the white-faced teller said immediately:

"Your balance, Mr. Keith, is so much; you have a check?" He extended his hand to take it.

"No," said Keith; "I have not come to draw out any money. I have come to make a deposit."

The teller was so much astonished that he simply ejaculated:

"Sir—?"

"I wish to make a deposit," said Keith, raising his voice a little, and speaking with great distinctness.

His voice had the quality of carrying, and a silence settled on the crowd,—one of those silences that sometimes fall, even on a mob, when the wholly unexpected happens,—so that every word that was spoken was heard distinctly.

"Ah—we are not taking deposits to-day," said the aston-ished teller, doubtfully.

Keith smiled.

"Well, I suppose there is no objection to doing so? I have an account in this bank, and I wish to add to it. I am not afraid of it."

The teller gazed at him in blank amazement; he evidently thought that Keith was a little mad. He opened his mouth as if to speak, but said nothing from sheer astonishment.

"I have confidence enough in this bank," pursued Keith, "to put my money here, and here I propose to put it, and I am not the only one; there will be others here in a little while."

"I shall—really, I shall have to ask Mr. Wentworth," faltered the clerk.

"Mr. Wentworth has nothing to do with it," said Keith, positively, and to close the discussion, he lifted his satchel through the window, and, turning it upside down, emptied before the astonished teller a pile of bills which made him gasp. "Enter that to my credit," said Keith.

"How much is it?"

The sum that Keith mentioned made him gasp yet more. It was up in the hundreds of thousands.

"There will be more here in a little while." He turned his head and glanced toward the door. "Ah, here comes some one now," he said, as he recognized one of the men whom he had recently left at the council board, who was then pushing his way forward, under the guidance of several policemen.

The amount deposited by the banker was much larger than Keith had expected, and a few well-timed words to those about him had a marked effect upon the depositors. He said their apprehension was simply absurd. They, of course, had the right to draw out their money, if they wished it, and they would get it, but he advised them to go home and wait to do so until the crowd dispersed. The bank was perfectly sound, and they could not break it un-less they could also break its friends.

A few of the struggling depositors dropped out of line, some of the others saying that, as they had waited so long, they guessed they would get their money now.

The advice given, perhaps, had an added effect, as at that moment a shriek arose from a woman near the door, who declared that her pocket had been picked of the money she had just drawn.

The arrival of the new depositors, and the spreading through the crowd of the information that they represented several of the strongest banks in the city, quieted the ap-prehensions of the depositors, and a considerable number of them abandoned the idea of drawing out their money and went off. Though many of them remained, it was evident that the dangerous run had subsided. A notice was posted on the front door of the bank that the bank would remain open until eight o'clock and would be open the following morning at eight, which had something to do with allay-ing the excitement of the depositors.

That afternoon Keith went back to the bank. Though depositors were still drawing out their money, the scene outside was very different from that which he had witnessed earlier in the day. Keith asked for Mr. Wentworth, and was shown to his room. When Keith entered, Norman was sitting at his desk figuring busily. Keith closed the door behind him and waited. The lines were deep on Norman's face; but the hunted look it had borne in the morning had passed away, and grim resolution had taken its place. When at length he glanced up, his already white face grew yet whiter. The next second a flush sprang to his cheeks; he pushed back his chair and rose, and, taking one step forward, stretched out his hand.

"Keith!"

Keith took his hand with a grip that drove the blood from the ends of Norman's fingers.

"Norman!"

Norman drew a chair close to his desk, and Keith sat down. Norman sank into his, looked down on the floor for a second, then, raising his eyes, looked full into Keith's eyes.

"Keith—?" His voice failed him; he glanced away, reached over, and took up a paper lying near, and the next instant leant forward, and folding his arms on the desk, dropped his head on them, shaken with emotion.

Keith rose from his chair, and bending over him, laid his hand on his head, as he might have done to a younger brother.

"Don't, Norman," he said helplessly; "it is all right." He moved his hand down Norman's arm with a touch as caressing as if he had been a little child, but all he said was: "Don't, Norman; it is all right."

Suddenly Norman sat up.

"It is all wrong!" he said bitterly. "I have been a fool. I had no right—. But I was mad! I have wrecked my life. But I was insane. I was deceived. I do not know even now how it happened. I ought to have known, but— I learned only just now. I can never explain. I ask your pardon humbly."

Keith leant forward and laid his hand upon him affectionately.

"There, there! You owe me no apology, and I ask no explanation; it was all a great mistake."

"Yes, and all my fault. She was not to blame; it was my folly. I drove her to—desperation."

"I want to ask just one thing. Was it Ferdy Wickersham who made you believe I had deceived you?" asked Keith, standing straight above him.

"In part—mainly. But I was mad." He drew his hand across his forehead, sat back in his chair, and, with eyes averted, sighed deeply. His thoughts were evidently far from Keith. Keith's eyes rested on him, and his face paled a little with growing resolution.

"One question, Norman. Pardon me for asking it. My

483

only reason is that I would give my life, a worthless life you once saved, to see you as you once were. I know more than you think I know. You love her still? I know you must."

Norman turned his eyes and let them rest on Keith's face. They were filled with anguish.

"Better than my life. I adore her."

Keith drew in his breath with a long sigh of relief and of content.

"Oh, I have no hope," Norman went on despairingly. "I gave her every right to doubt it. I killed her love. I do not blame her. It was all my fault. I know it now, when it is too late."

"It is not too late."

Norman shook his head, without even looking at Keith.

"Too late," he said, speaking to himself.

Keith rose to his feet.

"It is not too late," he declared, with a sudden ring in his voice; "she loves you."

Norman shook his head.

"She hates me; I deserve it."

"In her heart she adores you," said Keith, in a tone of conviction.

Norman turned away with a half-bitter laugh.

"You don't know."

"I do know, and you will know it, too. How long shall you be here?"

"I shall spend the night here," said Norman. "I must be ready for whatever may happen to-morrow morning.—I have not thanked you yet." He extended his hand to Keith. "You stemmed the tide for me to-day. I know what it must have cost you. I cannot regret it, and I know you never will; and I beg you to believe that, though I go down to-morrow, I shall never forget it, and if God spares me, I will repay you."

Keith's eyes rested on him calmly.

"You paid me long ago, Norman. I was paying a

debt to-day, or trying to pay one, in a small way. It was not I who made that deposit to-day, but a better man and a finer gentleman than I can ever hope to be—my father. It was he who inspired me to do that; he paid that debt."

From what Keith had heard, he felt that he was justified in going to see Mrs. Wentworth. Possibly, it was not too late; possibly, he might be able to do something to clear away the misapprehension under which she labored, and to make up the trouble between her and Norman. Norman still loved her dearly, and Keith believed that she cared for him. Lois Huntington always declared that she did, and she could not have been deceived.

That she had been foolish Keith knew; that she had been wicked he did not believe. She was self-willed, vain, extravagant; but deep under her cold exterior burned fires of which she had once or twice given him a glimpse; and he believed that her deepest feeling was ever for Norman.

When he reached Mrs. Wentworth's house he was fortunate enough to find her at home. He was shown into the drawing-room.

When Mrs. Wentworth entered the room, Keith was conscious of a change in her since he had seen her last. She, too, had heard the clangor of the evil tongues that had connected their names. She greeted him with cordial words, but her manner was constrained, and her expression was almost suspicious.

She changed, however, under Keith's imperturbable and unfeigned friendliness, and suddenly asked him if he had seen Norman. For the first time real interest spoke in her voice and shone in her face. Keith said he had seen him.

"I have come to see if I could not help you. Perhaps, I may be able to do something to set things right."

"No—it is too late. Things have gone too far. We have just drifted—drifted—!" She flung up her hands and tossed them apart with a gesture of despair. "Drifted!" she repeated. She put her handkerchief to her eyes.

Keith watched her in silence for a moment, and then rising, he seated himself beside her.

"Come—this is all wrong—all wrong!" He caught her by the wrist and firmly took her hand down from her eyes, much as an older brother might have done. "I want to talk to you. Perhaps, I can help you—I may have been sent here for the purpose—who knows? At least, I want to help you. Now tell me." He looked into her face with grave, kind eyes. "You do not care for Ferdy Wickersham? That would be impossible."

"No, of course not,—except as a friend,—and Norman liked another woman—your friend!" Her eyes flashed a sudden flame.

"Never! never!" repeated Keith, after a pause. "Norman is not that sort."

His absolute certainty daunted her.

"He did. I have reason to think—" she began. But Keith put her down.

"Never! I would stake my salvation on it."

"He is going to get a—try to get a divorce. He is willing to blacken my name."

"What! Never."

"But you do not know the reasons I have for saying so," she protested. "If I could tell you—"

"No, and I do not care. Doubt your own senses rather than believe that. Ferdy Wickersham is your authority for that."

"No, he is not—not my only authority. You are all so hard on Ferdy. He is a good friend of mine."

"He is not," asserted Keith. "He is your worst enemy—your very worst. He is incapable of being a friend."

"What have you against him?" she demanded. "I know you and he don't like each other, but—"

"Well, for one thing, he deceived a poor girl, and then abandoned her—and—"

"Perhaps, your information is incorrect? You know how easy it is to get up a slander, and such women are—

not to be believed. They always pretend that they have been deceived."

"She was not one of 'such women,' " said Keith, calmly. "She was a perfectly respectable woman, and the granddaughter of an old friend of mine."

"Well, perhaps, you may have been misinformed?"

"No; I have the evidence that Wickersham married her —and—"

"Oh, come now—that is absurd! Ferdy married! Why, Ferdy never cared enough for any one to marry her—unless she had money. He has paid attention to a rich woman, but— You must not strain my credulity too far. I really thought you had something to show against him. Of course, I know he is not a saint,—in fact, very far from it,—but he does not pretend to be. But, at least, he is not a hypocrite."

"He is a hypocrite and a scoundrel," declared Keith, firmly. "He is married, and his wife is living now. He abandoned her, and she is insane. I know her."

"You know her! Ferdy married!" She paused in wonder. His certainty carried conviction with it.

"I have his marriage certificate."

"You have?" A sort of amaze passed over her face.

He took out the paper and gave it to her. She gazed at it with staring eyes. "That is his hand." She rose with a blank face, and walked to the window; then, after a moment, came back and sat down. She had the expression of a person lost. "Tell me about it."

Keith told her. He also told her of Norman's losses.

Again that look of amazement crossed her face; her eyes became almost blank.

"Norman's fortune impaired! I cannot understand it— *he* told me— Oh, there must be some mistake!" she broke out vehemently. "You are deceiving me. No! I don't mean that, of course,—I know you would not,—but you have been deceived yourself." Her face was a sudden white.

Keith shook his head. "No!"

"Why, look here. He cannot be hard up. He has kept up my allowance and met every demand—almost every demand—I have made on him." She was grasping at straws.

"And Ferdy Wickersham has spent it in Wall Street."

"What! No, he has not! There, at least, you do him an injustice. What he has got from me he has invested securely. I have all the papers—at least, some of them."

"How has he invested it?"

"Partly in a mine called the 'Great Gun Mine,' in New Leeds. Partly in Colorado.—I can help Norman with it." Her face brightened as the thought came to her.

Keith shook his head.

"The Great Gun Mine is a fraud—at least, it is worthless, not worth five cents on the dollar of what has been put in it. It was flooded years ago. Wickersham has used it as a mask for his gambling operations in Wall Street, but has not put a dollar into it for years; and now he does not even own it. His creditors have it."

Her face had turned perfectly white.

A look, partly of pity for her, partly of scorn for Wickersham, crossed Keith's face. He rose and strode up and down the room in perplexity.

"He is a common thief," he said sternly—"beneath contempt!"

His conviction suddenly extended to her. When he looked at her, she showed in her face that she believed him. Her last prop had fallen. The calamity had made her quiet.

"What shall I do?" she asked hopelessly.

"You must tell Norman."

"Oh!"

"Make a clean breast of it."

"You do not know Norman! How can I? He would despise me so! You do not know how proud he is. He—!" Words failed her, and she stared at Keith helplessly.

"If I do not know Norman, I know no one on earth.

Go to him and tell him everything. It will be the happiest day of his life—your salvation and his."

"You think so?"

"I know it."

She relapsed into thought, and Keith waited.

"I was to see Fer—Mr. Wickersham to-night," she began presently. "He asked me to supper to meet some friends—the Count and Countess Torelli."

Keith smiled. A fine scorn came into his eyes.

"Where does he give the dinner? At what hour?"

She named the place—a fashionable restaurant up-town. The time was still several hours away.

"You must go to Norman."

She sat in deep reflection.

"It is your only chance—your only hope. Give me authority to act for you, and go to him. He needs you."

"If I thought he would forgive me?" she said in a low tone.

"He will. I have just come from him. Write me the authority and go at once."

A light appeared to dawn in her face. She rose suddenly.

"What shall I write?"

"Write simply that I have full authority to act for you—and that you have gone to Norman."

She walked into the next room, and seating herself at an escritoire, she wrote for a short time. When she handed the paper to Keith it contained just what he had requested: a simple statement to F. C. Wickersham that Mr. Keith had full authority to represent her and act for her as he deemed best.

"Will that do?" she asked.

"I think so," said Keith. "Now go. Norman is waiting."

CHAPTER XXXIII

RECONCILIATION

FOR some time after Keith left her Mrs. Wentworth sat absolutely motionless, her eyes half closed, her lips drawn tight, in deep reflection. Presently she changed her seat and ensconced herself in the corner of a divan, leaning her head on her hand; but her expression did not change. Her mind was evidently working in the same channel. A tumult raged within her breast, but her face was set sphinx-like, inscrutable. Just then there was a scurry up-stairs; a boy's voice was heard shouting:

"See here, what papa sent us."

There was an answering shout, and then an uproar of childish delight. A sudden change swept over her. Light appeared to break upon her. Something like courage came into her face, not unmingled with tenderness, softening it and dispelling the gloom which had clouded it. She rose suddenly and walked with a swift, decisive step out of the room and up the richly carpeted stairs. To a maid on the upper floor she said hurriedly: "Tell Fenderson to order the brougham—at once," and passed into her chamber.

Closing the door, she locked it. She opened a safe built in the wall; a package of letters fell out into the room. A spasm almost of loathing crossed her face. She picked up the letters and began to tear them up with almost violence, throwing the fragments into the grate as though they soiled her hands. Going back to the safe, she took out box after box of jewelry, opening them to glance in and see that the jewels were there. Yes, they were there : a pearl necklace ; bracelets which had been the wonder of her set, and which her pretended friend and admirer had once said were worth as much as her home. She put them all into a bag, together with several large envelopes containing papers.

Then she went to a dress-closet, and began to search through it, choosing, finally, a simple, dark street dress, by no means one of the newest. A gorgeous robe, which had been laid out for her to wear, she picked up and flung on the floor with sudden loathing. It was the gown she had intended to wear that night.

A tap at the door, and the maid's mild voice announced the carriage ; and a few minutes later Mrs. Wentworth descended the stairs.

"Tell Mademoiselle Clarisse that Mr. Wentworth will be here this evening to see the children."

"Yes, madam." The maid's quiet voice was too well trained to express the slightest surprise, but as soon as the outer door had closed on her mistress, and she had heard the carriage drive away, she rushed down to the lower storey to convey the astounding intelligence, and to gossip over it for half an hour before she deemed it necessary to give the message to the governess who had succeeded Lois when the latter went home.

It was just eight o'clock that evening when the carriage drove up to the door of Norman Wentworth's bank, and a lady enveloped in a long wrap, her dark veil pulled down over her face, sprang out and ran up the steps. The crowd had long ago dispersed, though now and then a few timid depositors still made their way into the bank, to be on the safe side.

The intervention of the banks and the loans they had made that afternoon had stayed the run and saved the bank from closing ; but Norman Wentworth knew that if he was not ruined, his bank had received a shock from which it would not recover in a long time, and his fortune was crippled, he feared, almost beyond repair. The tired clerks looked up as the lady entered the bank, and, with glances at the clock, muttered a few words to each other about her right to draw money after the closing-hour had passed. When, however, she walked past their windows and went straight to Mr. Wentworth's door, their interest increased.

Norman, with his books before him, was sitting back in his chair, his head leaning back and resting in his clasped hands, deep in thought upon the gloom of the present and the perplexities of the future, when there was a tap at the door.

With some impatience he called to the person to enter.

The door opened, and Norman could scarcely believe his senses. For a second he did not even sit forward. He did not stir ; he simply remained sitting back in his chair, his face turned to the door, his eyes resting on the figure before him in vague amazement. The next second, with a half-cry, his wife was on her knees beside him, her arms about him, her form shaken with sobs. He sat forward slowly, and his arm rested on her shoulders.

"There ! don't cry," he said slowly ; "it might be worse."

But all she said was :

"Oh, Norman ! Norman !"

He tried to raise her, with grave words to calm her ; but she resisted, and clung to him closer.

"It is not so bad ; it might be worse," he repeated.

She rose suddenly to her feet and flung back her veil.

"Can you forgive me ? I have come to beg your forgiveness on my knees. I have been mad—mad. I was deceived. No ! I will not say that—I was crazy—a fool ! But I loved you always, you only. You will forgive me ? Say you will."

"There, there ! Of course I will—I do. I have been to blame quite as much—more than you. I was a fool."

"Oh, no, no ! You shall not say that ; but you will believe that I loved you—you only—always ! You will believe this ? I was mad."

He raised her up gently, and with earnest words reassured her, blaming himself for his harshness and folly.

She suddenly opened her bag and emptied the contents out on his desk.

"There! I have brought you these."

Her husband gazed in silent astonishment.

"I don't understand."

"They are for you," she said — "for us. To pay *our* debts. To help you." She pulled off her glove and began to take off her diamond rings.

"They will not go a great way," said Norman, with a smile of indulgence.

"Well, as far as they will go they shall go. Do you think I will keep anything I have when you are in trouble —when your good name is at stake? The house—everything shall go. It is all my fault. I have been a wicked, silly fool; but I did not know—I ought to have known; but I did not. I do not see how I could have been so blind and selfish."

"Oh, don't blame yourself. I have not blamed you," said Norman, soothingly. "Of course, you did not know. How could you? Women are not expected to know about those things."

"Yes, they are," insisted Mrs. Wentworth. "If I had not been such a fool I might have seen. It is all plain to me now. Your harassment—my folly—it came to me like a stroke of lightning."

Norman's eyes were on her with a strange inquiring look in them.

"How did you hear?" he asked.

"Mr. Keith—he came to me and told me."

"I wish he had not done it. I mean, I did not want you troubled. You were not to blame. You were deceived."

"Oh, don't say that! I shall never cease to thank him. He tore the veil away, and I saw what a heartless, vain, silly fool I have been." Norman put his hand on her soothingly. "But I have never forgotten that I was your wife, nor ceased to love you," she went on vehemently.

"I believe it."

"I have come to confess everything to you—all my folly —all my extravagance—my insane folly. But what I said just now is true : I have never forgotten that I was your wife."

Norman, with his arm supporting her, reassured her with comforting words, and, sustained by his confidence, she told him of her folly in trusting Ferdy Wickersham : of her giving him her money—of everything.

"Can you forgive me?" she asked after her shamefaced recital.

"I will never think of that again," said Norman, "and if I do, it will be with gratitude that they have played their part in doing away with the one great sorrow of my life and bringing back the happiness of my youth, the one great blessing that life holds for me."

"I have come to take you home," she said ; " to ask you to come back, if you will but forgive me." She spoke humbly.

Norman's face gave answer even before he could master himself to speak. He stretched out his hand, and drew her to him. "I am at home now. Wherever you are is my home."

When Norman came out of his private office, there was such a change in him that the clerks who had remained at the bank thought that he must have received some great aid from the lady who had been closeted with him so long. He had a few brief words with the cashier, explaining that he would be back at the bank before eight o'clock in the morning, and saying good night, hurried to the door after Mrs. Wentworth. Handing her into the carriage, he ordered the coachman to drive home, and, springing in after her, he closed the door behind him, and they drove off.

Keith, meantime, had not been idle. After leaving Mrs. Wentworth, he drove straight to a detective agency. Fortunately the chief was in, and Keith was ushered into his private office immediately. He was a quiet-looking, stout man, with a gray moustache and keen dark eyes. He might have been a moderately successful merchant or official, but for the calmness of his manner and the low tones of his voice. Keith came immediately to the point.

"I have a piece of important work on hand this evening," he said, " of a private and delicate nature." The detective's look was acquiescent. "Could I get Dennison?"

"I think so."

Keith stated his case. At the mention of Wickersham's name a slight change—the very slightest—flickered across the detective's calm face. Keith could not tell whether it was mere surprise or whether it was gratification.

"Now you see precisely what I wish," he said, as he finished stating the case and unfolding his plan. "It may not be necessary for him even to appear, but I wish him to be on hand in case I should need his service. If Wickersham does not accede to my demand, I shall arrest him for the fraud I have mentioned. If he does accede, I wish Dennison to accompany him to the boat of the South American Line that sails to-morrow morning, and not leave him until the pilot comes off. I do not apprehend that he will refuse when he knows the hand that I hold."

"No, he will not. He knows what would happen if proceedings were started," said the detective. "Excuse me a moment." He walked out of the office, closing the door behind him, and a few minutes later returned with David Dennison.

"Mr. Keith, this is Mr. John Dimm. I have explained to him the nature of the service you require of him." He looked at Mr. Dimm, who simply nodded his acquiescence. " You will take your orders from Mr. Keith, should anything arise to change his plans, and act accordingly."

"I know him," said Keith, amused at the cool professional air with which his old friend greeted him in the presence of his principal.

Dave simply blinked; but his eyes had a fire in them.

It was arranged that Dennison should precede Keith to the place he had mentioned and order a supper there, while Keith should get the ticket at the steamship office and then follow him. So when Keith had completed his arrangements, he found Dennison at supper at a table near the ladies' entrance, a view of which he commanded in a mirror just before him. Mr. Dimm's manner had entirely changed. He was a man of the world and a host as he handed Keith to his seat.

"A supper for two has been ordered in private dining-room 21, for 9 : 45," he said in an undertone as the waiter moved off. "They do not know whether it is for a gentleman and a lady, or two gentlemen; but I suppose it is for a lady, as he has been here a number of times with ladies. If you are sure that the lady will not come, you might wait for him there. I will remain here until he comes, and follow him up, in case you need me."

Keith feared that the waiter might mention his presence.

"Oh, no; he knows us," said Dave, with a faint smile at the bare suggestion.

Mr. Dimm called the head-waiter and spoke to him in an undertone. The waiter himself showed Keith up to the room, where he found a table daintily set with two covers.

The champagne-cooler, filled with ice, was already on the floor beside the table. Keith looked at it grimly. The curtains of the window were down, and Keith walked over to see on what street the window looked. It was a deep embrasure. The shade was drawn down, and he raised it, to find that the window faced on a dead-wall. At the moment the door opened and he heard Wickersham's voice.

"No one has come yet?"

"No, sir, not as I knows of," stammered the waiter. "I have just come on."

"Where is Jacques, the man who usually waits on me?" demanded Wickersham, half angrily.

"Jacques est souffrant. Il est très malade."

496

Wickersham grunted. "Well, take this," he said, "and remember that if you serve me properly there will be a good deal more to follow."

The waiter thanked him profusely.

"Now, get down and be on the lookout, and when a lady comes and asks for 21, show her up immediately. If she asks who is here, tell her two gentlemen and a lady. You understand?"

The waiter bowed his assent and retired. Wickersham came in and closed the door behind him.

He had just thrown his coat on a chair, laid his hat on the mantelpiece, and was twirling his moustache at the mirror above it, when he caught sight in the mirror of Keith. Keith had stepped out behind him from the recess, and was standing by the table, quietly looking at him. He gave an exclamation and turned quickly.

"Hah! What is this? You here! What are you doing here? There is some mistake." He glanced at the door.

"No, there is no mistake," said Keith, advancing; "I am waiting for you."

"For me! Waiting for me?" he demanded, mystified.

"Yes. Did you not tell the waiter just now a gentleman was here? I confess you do not seem very pleased to see me."

"You have read my looks correctly," said Wickersham, who was beginning to recover himself, and with it his scornful manner. "You are the last person on earth I wish to see—ever. I do not know that I should weep if I never had that pleasure again."

Keith bowed.

"I think it probable. You may, hereafter, have even less cause for joy at meeting me."

"Impossible," said Wickersham.

Keith put his hand on a chair, and prepared to sit down, motioning Wickersham to take the other seat.

"The lady you are waiting for will not be here this evening," he said, "and it may be that our interview will be protracted."

Wickersham passed by the last words.

"What lady? Who says I am waiting for a lady?"

"You said so at the door just now. Besides, I say so."

"Oh! You were listening, were you?" he sneered.

"Yes; I heard it."

"How do you know she will not be here? What do you know about it?"

"I know that she will no more be here than the Countess Torelli will," said Keith. He was looking Wickersham full in the face and saw that the shot went home.

"What do you want?" demanded Wickersham. "Why are you here? Are you after money or a row?"

"I want you—I want you, first, to secure all of Mrs. Wentworth's money that you have had, or as much as you can."

Wickersham was so taken aback that his dark face turned almost white, but he recovered himself quickly.

"You are a madman, or some one has been deceiving you. You are the victim of a delusion."

Keith, with his eyes fastened on him, shook his head.

"Oh, no; I am not."

A look of perplexed innocence came over Wickersham's face.

"Yes, you are," he said, in an almost friendly tone. "You are the victim of some hallucination. I give you my word, I do not know even what you are talking about. I should say you were engaged in blackmail—" The expression in his eyes changed like a flash, but something in Keith's eyes, as they met his, caused him to add, "if I did not know that you were a man of character. I, too, am a man of character, Mr. Keith. I want you to know it." Keith's eyes remained calm and cold as steel. Wickersham faltered. "I am a man of means—of large means. I am worth—. My balance in bank this moment is—is more than you will ever be worth. Now I want to ask you why, in the name of Heaven, should I want anything to do with Mrs. Wentworth's money?"

"If you have such a balance in bank," said Keith, "it

will simplify my mission, for you will doubtless be glad to
return Mr. Wentworth's money that you have had from
Mrs. Wentworth. I happen to know that his money will
come in very conveniently for Norman just now."

"Oh, you come from Wentworth, do you?" demanded
Wickersham.

"No; from Mrs. Wentworth," returned Keith.

"Did she send you?" Wickersham shot at Keith a level
glance from under his half-closed lids.

"I offered to come. She knows I am here."

"What proof have I of that?"

"My statement."

"And suppose I do not please to accept your statement?"
Keith leant a little toward him over the table.

"You will accept it."

"He must hold a strong hand," thought Wickersham.
He shifted his ground suddenly. "What, in the name
of Heaven, are you driving at, Keith? What are you
after? Come to the point."

"I will," said Keith, rising. "Let us drop our masks;
they are not becoming to you, and I am not accustomed to
them. I have come for several things: one of them is Mrs.
Wentworth's money, which you got from her under false
pretences." He spoke slowly, and his eyes were looking in
the other's eyes.

Wickersham sprang to his feet.

"What do you mean, sir?" he demanded, with an oath.
"I have already told you—! I will let no man speak to me
in that way."

Keith did not stir. Wickersham paused to get his
breath.

"You would not dare to speak so if a lady's name were
not involved, and you did not know that I cannot act as I
would, for fear of compromising her."

An expression of contempt swept across Keith's face.

"Sit down," he said. "I will relieve your mind. Mrs.
Wentworth is quite ready to meet any disclosures that may

come. I have her power of attorney. She has gone to her husband and told him everything."

Wickersham's face whitened, and he could not repress the look of mingled astonishment and fear that stole into his eyes.

"Now, having given you that information," continued Keith, "I say that you stole Mrs. Wentworth's money, and I have come to recover it, if possible."

Wickersham rose to his feet. With a furious oath he sprang for his overcoat, and, snatching it up, began to feel for the pocket.

"I'll blow your brains out."

"No, you will not," said Keith, "and I advise you to make less noise. An officer is outside, and I have but to whistle to place you where nothing will help you. A warrant is out for your arrest, and I have the proof to convict you."

Wickersham, with his coat still held in one hand, and the other in the pocket, shot a glance at Keith. He was daunted by his coolness.

"You must think you hold a strong hand," he said. "But I have known them to fail."

Keith bowed.

"No doubt. This one will not fail. I have taken pains that it shall not, and I have other cards which I have not shown you. Sit down and listen to me, and you shall judge for yourself."

With a muttered oath, Wickersham walked back to his seat; but before he did so, he slipped quietly into his pocket a pistol which he took from his overcoat.

Quickly as the act was done, Keith saw it.

"Don't you think you had better put your pistol back?" he said quietly. "An officer is waiting just outside that door, a man that can neither be bullied nor bought. Perhaps, you will agree with me when I tell you that, though called Dimm, his real name is David Dennison. He has orders at the least disturbance to place you under arrest. Judge for yourself what chance you will have."

"What do you wish me to do?" asked Wickersham, sullenly.

"I wish you, first, to execute some papers which will secure to Norman Wentworth, as far as can possibly be done, the amount of money that you have gotten from Mrs. Wentworth under the pretence of investing it for her in mines. Mrs. Wentworth's name will not be mentioned in this instrument. The money was her husband's, and you knew it, and you knew it was impairing his estate to furnish it. Secondly, I require that you shall leave the country to-morrow morning. I have arranged for passage for you, on a steamer sailing before sunrise."

"Thank you," sneered Wickersham. "Really, you are very kind."

"Thirdly, you will sign a paper which contains only a few of the facts, but enough, perhaps, to prevent your returning to this country for some years to come."

Wickersham leant across the table and burst out laughing.

"And you really think I will do that? How old do you think I am? Why did you not bring me a milk-bottle and a rattle? You do my intellect a great deal of honor."

For answer Keith tapped twice on a glass with the back of a knife. The next second the door opened, and Dave Dennison entered, impassive, but calmly observant, and with a face set like rock.

At sight of him Wickersham's face whitened.

"One moment, Dave," said Keith; "wait outside a moment more."

Dennison bowed and closed the door. The latch clicked, but the knob did not settle back.

"I will give you one minute in which to decide," said Keith. He drew from his pocket and threw on the table two papers. "There are the papers." He took out his watch and waited.

Wickersham picked up the papers mechanically and glanced over them. His face settled. Gambler that he was with the fortunes of men and the reputations of women, he knew that he had lost. He tried one more card—it was a poor one.

"Why are you so hard on me?" he asked, with something like a whine—a faint whine—in his voice. "You, who I used to think—whom I have known from boyhood, you have always been so hard on me! What did I ever do to you that you should have hounded me so?"

Keith's face showed that the charge had reached him, but it failed of the effect that Wickersham had hoped for. His lip curled slightly.

"I am not hard on you; I am easy on you—but not for your sake," he added vehemently. "You have betrayed every trust reposed in you. You have deceived men and betrayed women. No vow has been sacred enough to restrain you; no tie strong enough to hold you. Affection, friendship, faith, have all been trampled under your feet. You have deliberately attempted to destroy the happiness of one of the best friends you have ever had; have betrayed his trust and tried to ruin his life. If I served you right I would place you beyond the power to injure any one, forever. The reason I do not is not on your account, but because I played with you when we were boys, and because I do not know how far my personal feeling might influence me in carrying out what I still recognize as mere justice." He closed his watch. "Your time is up. Do you agree?"

"I will sign the papers," said Wickersham, sullenly.

Keith drew out a pen and handed it to him. Wickersham signed the papers slowly and deliberately.

"When did you take to writing backhand?" asked Keith.

"I have done it for several years," declared Wickersham. "I had writer's cramp once."

The expression on Keith's face was very like a sneer, but he tried to suppress it.

"It will do," he said, as he folded the papers and took another envelope from his pocket. "This is your ticket

502

for the steamer for Buenos Ayres, which sails to-morrow morning at high tide. Dennison will go with you to a notary to acknowledge these papers, and then will show you aboard of her and will see that you remain aboard until the pilot leaves her. To-morrow a warrant will be put in the hands of an officer and an application will be made for a receiver for your property."

Wickersham leant back in his chair, with hate speaking from every line of his face.

"You will administer on my effects? I suppose you are also going to be administrator, *de bonis non*, of the lady in whose behalf you have exhibited such sudden interest?"

Keith's face paled and his nostrils dilated for a moment. He leant slightly forward and spoke slowly, his burning eyes fastened on Wickersham's face.

"Your statement would be equally infamous whether it were true or false. You know that it is a lie, and you know that I know it is a lie. I will let that suffice. I have nothing further to say to you." He tapped on the edge of the glass again, and Dennison walked in. "Dennison," he said, "Mr. Wickersham has agreed to my plans. He will go aboard the Buenos Ayres boat to-night. You will go with him to the office I spoke of, where he will acknowledge these papers; then you will accompany him to his home and get whatever clothes he may require, and you will not lose sight of him until you come off with the pilot."

Dennison bowed without a word; but his eyes snapped.

"If he makes any attempt to evade, or gives you any cause to think he is trying to evade, his agreement, you have your instructions."

Dennison bowed again, silently.

"I now leave you." Keith rose and inclined his head slightly toward Wickersham.

As he turned, Wickersham shot at him a Parthian arrow:

"I hope you understand, Mr. Keith, that the obligations I have signed are not the only obligations I recognize. I owe you a personal debt, and I mean to live to pay it. I *shall* pay it, somehow."

Keith turned and looked at him steadily.

"I understand perfectly. It is the only kind of debt, as far as I know, that you recognize. Your statement has added nothing to what I knew. It matters little what you do to me. I have, at least, saved two friends from you."

He walked out of the room and closed the door behind him.

As Wickersham pulled on his gloves, he glanced at Dave Dennison. But what he saw in his face deterred him from speaking. His eyes were like coals of fire.

"I am waiting," he said. "Hurry."

Wickersham walked out in silence.

The following afternoon, when Dave Dennison reported that he had left his charge on board the outgoing steamer, bound for a far South American port, Keith felt as if the atmosphere had in some sort cleared.

A few days later Phrony's worn spirit found rest. Keith, as he had already arranged, telegraphed Dr. Balsam of her death, and the Doctor went over and told Squire Rawson, at the same time, that she had been found and lost.

The next day Keith and Dave Dennison took back to the South all that remained of the poor creature who had left there a few years before in such high hopes.

One lady, closely veiled, attended the little service that old Dr. Templeton conducted in the chapel of the hospital where Phrony had passed away, before the body was taken South. Alice Lancaster had been faithful to the end in looking after her.

Phrony was buried in the Rawson lot in the little burying-ground at Ridgely, not far from the spot where lay the body of General Huntington. As Keith passed this grave he saw that flowers had been laid on it recently, but they had withered.

All the Ridge-neighborhood gathered to do honor to

Phrony and to testify their sympathy for her grandfather. It was an exhibition of feeling such as Keith had not seen since he left the country. The old man appeared stronger than he had seemed for some time. He took charge and gave directions in a clear and steady voice.

When the services were over and the last word had been said, he stepped forward and raised his hand.

"I've got her back," he said. "I've got her back where nobody can take her from me again. I was mighty harsh on her; but I've done forgive her long ago—and I hope she knows it now. I heard once that the man that took her away said he didn't marry her. But—" He paused for a moment, then went on: "He was a liar. I've got the proof.— But I want you all to witness that if I ever meet him, in this world or the next, the Lord do so to me, and more also! if I don't kill him!" He paused again, and his breathing was the only sound that was heard in the deathly stillness that had fallen on the listening crowd.

"—And if any man interferes and balks me in my right," he continued slowly, "I'll have his blood. Good-by. I thank you for her." He turned back to the grave and began to smooth the sides.

Keith's eyes fell on Dave Dennison, where he stood on the outer edge of the crowd. His face was sphinx-like; but his bosom heaved twice, and Keith knew that two men waited to meet Wickersham.

As the crowd melted away, whispering among themselves, Keith crossed over and laid a rose on General Huntington's grave.

CHAPTER XXXIV

THE CONSULTATION

KEITH had been making up his mind for some time to go to Brookford. New York had changed utterly for him since Lois left. The whole world seemed to have changed.

The day after he reached New York, Keith received a letter from Miss Brooke. She wrote that her niece was ill and had asked her to write and request him to see Mrs. Lancaster, who would explain something to him. She did not say what it was. She added that she wished she had never heard of New York. It was a cry of anguish.

Keith's heart sank like lead. For the first time in his life he had a presentiment. Lois Huntington would die, and he would never see her again. Despair took hold of him. Keith could stand it no longer. He went to Brookford.

The Lawns was one of those old-fashioned country places, a few miles outside of the town, such as our people of means used to have a few generations ago, before they had lost the landholding instinct of their English ancestors and gained the herding proclivity of modern life. The extensive yard and grounds were filled with shrubbery—lilacs, rose-bushes, and evergreens—and shaded by fine old trees, among which the birds were singing as Keith drove up the curving road, and over all was an air of quietude and peace which filled his heart with tenderness.

"This is the bower she came from," he thought to himself, gazing around. "Here is the country garden where the rose grew."

Miss Brooke was unfeignedly surprised to see Keith.

She greeted him most civilly. Lois had long since explained everything to her, and she made Keith a more than ample apology for her letter. "But you must admit," she said, "that your actions were very suspicious.—When a New York man is handing dancing-women to their carriages!" A gesture and nod completed the sentence.

"But I am not a New York man," said Keith.

"Oh, you are getting to be a very fair counterfeit," said the old lady, half grimly.

Lois was very ill. She had been under a great strain in New York, and had finally broken down.

Among other items of interest that Keith gleaned was that Dr. Locaman, the resident physician at Brookford, was a suitor of Lois. Keith asked leave to send for a friend who was a man of large experience and a capital doctor.

"Well, I should be glad to have him sent for. These men here are dividing her up into separate pieces, and meantime she is going down the hill every day. Send for any one who will treat her as a whole human being and get her well."

So Keith telegraphed that day for Dr. Balsam, saying that he wanted him badly, and would be under lasting obligations if he would come to Brookford at once.

Brookford! The name called up many associations to the old physician. It was from Brookford that that young girl with her brown eyes and dark hair had walked into his life so long ago. It was from Brookford that the decree had come that had doomed him to a life of loneliness and exile. A desire seized him to see the place. Abby Brooke had been living a few years before. She might be living now.

As the Doctor descended from the cars, he was met by Keith, who told him that the patient was the daughter of General Huntington—the little girl he had known so long ago.

"I thought, perhaps, it was your widow," said the Doctor.

A little dash of color stole into Keith's grave face, then flickered out.

"No." He changed the subject, and went on to say that the other physicians had arranged to meet him at the house. Then he gave him a little history of the case.

"You are very much interested in her?"

"I have known her a long time, you see. Yes. Her aunt is a friend of mine."

"He is in love with her," said the old man to himself. "She has cut the widow out."

As they entered the hall, Miss Abby came out of a room. She looked worn and ill.

"Ah!" said Keith. "Here she is." He turned to present the Doctor, but stopped with his lips half opened. The two stood fronting each other, their amazed eyes on each other's faces, as it were across the space of a whole generation.

"Theophilus!"

"Abby!"

This was all. The next moment they were shaking hands as if they had parted the week before instead of thirty-odd years ago. "I told you I would come if you ever needed me," said the Doctor. "I have come."

"And I never needed you more, and I have needed you often. It was good in you to come—for my little girl." Her voice suddenly broke, and she turned away, her handkerchief at her eyes.

The Doctor's expression settled into one of deep concern. "There—there. Don't distress yourself. We must reserve our powers. We may need them. Now, if you will show me to my room for a moment, I would like to get myself ready before going in to see your little girl."

Just as the Doctor reappeared, the other doctors came out of the sick-room, the local physician, a simple young man, following the city specialist with mingled pride and awe. The latter was a silent, self-reliant man with a keen eye, thin lips, and a dry, business manner. They were presented to the Doctor as Dr. Memberly and Dr. Locaman, and looked him over. There was a certain change of man-

508

ner in each of them : the younger man, after a glance, increased perceptibly his show of respect toward the city man ; the latter treated the Doctor with civility, but talked in an ex-cathedra way. He understood the case and had no question as to its treatment. As for Dr. Balsam, his manner was the same to both, and had not changed a particle. He said not a word except to ask questions as to symptoms and the treatment that had been followed. The Doctor's face changed during the recital, and when it was ended his expression was one of deep thoughtfulness.

The consultation ended, they all went into the sick-room, Dr. Memberly, the specialist, first, the young doctor next, and Dr. Balsam last. Dr. Memberly addressed the nurse, and Dr. Locaman followed him like his shadow, enforcing his words and copying insensibly his manner. Dr. Balsam walked over to the bedside, and leaning over, took the patient's thin, wan hand.

"My dear, I am Dr. Balsam. Do you remember me ? "

She glanced at him, at first languidly, then with more interest, and then, as recollection returned to her, with a faint smile.

"Now we must get well."

Again she smiled faintly.

The Doctor drew up a chair, and, without speaking further, began to stroke her hand, his eyes resting on her face.

One who had seen the old physician before he entered that house could scarcely have known him as the same man who sat by the bed holding the hand of the wan figure lying so placid before him. At a distance he appeared a plain countryman ; on nearer view his eyes and mouth and set chin gave him a look of unexpected determination. When he entered a sick-room he was like a king coming to his own. He took command and fought disease as an arch-enemy. So now.

Dr. Memberly came to the bedside and began to talk in a low, professional tone. Lois shut her eyes, but her fingers closed slightly on Dr. Balsam's hand.

"The medicine appears to have quieted her somewhat. I have directed the nurse to continue it," observed Dr. Memberly.

"Quite so. By all means continue it," assented Dr. Locaman. "She is decidedly quieter."

Dr. Balsam's head inclined just enough to show that he heard him, and he went on stroking her hand.

"Is there anything you would suggest further than has already been done?" inquired the city physician of Dr. Balsam.

"No. I think not."

"I must catch the 4:30 train," said the former to the younger man. "Doctor, will you drive me down to the station?"

"Yes, certainly. With pleasure."

"Doctor, you say you are going away to-night?" This from the city physician to Dr. Balsam.

"No, sir; I shall stay for a day or two." The fingers of the sleeper quite closed on his hand. "I have several old friends here. In fact, this little girl is one of them, and I want to get her up."

The look of the other changed, and he cleared his throat with a dry, metallic cough.

"You may rest satisfied that everything has been done for the patient that science can do," he said stiffly.

"I think so. We won't rest till we get the little girl up," said the older doctor. "Now we will take off our coats and work."

Once more the fingers of the sleeper almost clutched his.

When the door closed, Lois turned her head and opened her eyes, and when the wheels were heard driving away she looked at the Doctor with a wan little smile, which he answered with a twinkle.

"When did you come?" she asked faintly. It was the first sign of interest she had shown in anything for days.

"A young friend of mine, Gordon Keith, told me you

were sick, and asked me to come, and I have just arrived. He brought me up." He watched the change in her face.

"I am so much obliged to you. Where is he now?"

"He is here. Now we must get well," he said encouragingly. "And to do that we must get a little sleep."

"Very well. You are going to stay with me?"

"Yes."

"Thank you"; and she closed her eyes tranquilly and, after a little, fell into a doze.

When the Doctor came out of the sick-room he had done what the other physicians had not done and could not do. He had fathomed the case, and, understanding the cause, he was able to prescribe the cure.

"With the help of God we will get your little girl well," he said to Miss Abby.

"I begin to hope, and I had begun to despair," she said. "It was good of you to come."

"I am glad I came, and I will come whenever you want me, Abby," replied the old Doctor, simply.

From this time, as he promised, so he performed. He took off his coat, and using the means which the city specialist had suggested, he studied his patient's case and applied all his powers to the struggle.

The great city doctor recorded the case among his cures; but in his treatment he did not reckon the sleepless hours that that country doctor had sat by the patient's bedside, the unremitting struggle he had made, holding Death at bay, inspiring hope, and holding desperately every inch gained.

When the Doctor saw Keith he held out his hand to him. "I am glad you sent for me."

"How is she, Doctor? Will she get well?"

"I trust so. She has been under some strain. It is almost as if she had had a shock."

Keith's mind sprang back to that evening in the Park, and he cursed Wickersham in his heart.

"Possibly she has had some strain on her emotions?"

Keith did not know.

"I understand that there is a young man here who has been in love with her for some time, and her aunt thinks she returned the sentiment."

Keith did not know. But the Doctor's words were like a dagger in his heart.

Keith went back to work; but he seemed to himself to live in darkness. As soon as a gleam of light appeared, it was suddenly quenched. Love was not for him.

CHAPTER XXXV

THE MISTRESS OF THE LAWNS

STRANGE to say, the episode in which Keith had figured as the reliever of Norman Wentworth's embarrassment had a very different effect upon those among whom he had moved, from what he had expected. Keith's part in the transaction was well known.

His part, too, in the Wickersham matter was understood by his acquaintances. Wickersham had as good as absconded, some said; and there were many to tell how long they had prophesied this very thing, and how well they had known his villany. Mrs. Nailor was particularly vindictive. She had recently put some money in his mining scheme, and she could have hanged him. She did the next thing: she damned him. She even extended her rage to old Mrs. Wickersham, who, poor lady, had lost her home and everything she had in the world through Ferdy.

The Norman-Wentworths, who had moved out of the splendid residence that Mrs. Norman's extravagance had formerly demanded, into the old house on Washington Square, which was still occupied by old Mrs. Wentworth, were, if anything, drawn closer than ever to their real friends; but they were distinctly deposed from the position which Mrs. Wentworth had formerly occupied in the gay set, who to her had hitherto been New York. They were far happier than they had ever been. A new light had come into Norman's face, and a softness began to dawn in hers which Keith had never seen there before. Around them, too, began to gather friends whom Keith had never known of, who had the charm that breeding and kindness give, and opened his eyes to a life there of which he had hitherto hardly dreamed. Keith, however, to his surprise, when he was in New York, found himself more sought after by his former acquaintances than ever before. The cause was a simple one. He was believed to be very rich. He must have made a large fortune. The mystery in which it was involved but added to its magnitude. No man but one of immense wealth could have done what Keith did the day he stopped the run on Wentworth & Son. Any other supposition was incredible. Moreover, it was now plain that in a little while he would marry Mrs. Lancaster, and then he would be one of the wealthiest men in New York. He was undoubtedly a coming man. Men who, a short time ago, would not have wasted a moment's thought on him, now greeted him with cordiality and spoke of him with respect; women who, a year or two before, would not have seen him in a ball-room, now smiled to him on the street, invited him among their "best companies," and treated him with distinguished favor. Mrs. Nailor actually pursued him. Even Mr. Kestrel, pale, thin-lipped, and frosty as ever in appearance, thawed into something like cordiality when he met him, and held out an icy hand as with a wintry smile he congratulated him on his success.

"Well, we Yankees used to think we had the monopoly of business ability, but we shall have to admit that some of you young fellows at the South know your business. You have done what cost the Wickershams some millions. If you want any help at any time, come in and talk to me. We had a little difference once; but I don't let a little thing like that stand in the way with a friend."

Keith felt his jaws lock as he thought of the same man on the other side of a long table sneering at him.

"Thank you," said he. "My success has been greatly exaggerated. You'd better not count too much on it."

Keith knew that he was considered rich, and it disturbed

him. For the first time in his life he felt that he was sailing under false colors.

Often the fair face, handsome figure, and cordial, friendly air of Alice Lancaster came to him ; not so often, it is true, as another, a younger and gentler face, but still often enough. He admired her greatly. He trusted her. Why should he not try his fortune there, and be happy? Alice Lancaster was good enough for him. Yes, that was the trouble. She was far too good for him if he addressed her without loving her utterly. Other reasons, too, suggested themselves. He began to find himself fitting more and more into the city life. He had the chance possibly to become rich, richer than ever, and with it to secure a charming companion. Why should he not avail himself of it? Amid the glitter and gayety of his surroundings in the city, this temptation grew stronger and stronger. Miss Abby's sharp speech recurred to him. He was becoming "a fair counterfeit" of the men he had once despised. Then came a new form of temptation. What power this wealth would give him ! How much good he could accomplish with it !

When the temptation grew too overpowering he left his office and went down into the country. It always did him good to go there. To be there was like a plunge in a cool, limpid pool. He had been so long in the turmoil and strife of the struggle for success—for wealth ; had been so wholly surrounded by those who strove as he strove, tearing and trampling and rending those who were in their way, that he had almost lost sight of the life that lay outside of the dust and din of that arena. He had almost forgotten that life held other rewards than riches. He had forgotten the calm and tranquil region that stretched beyond the moil and anguish of the strife for gain.

Here his father walked with him again, calm, serene, and elevated, his thoughts high above all commercial matters, ranging the fields of lofty speculation with statesmen, philosophers, and poets, holding up to his gaze again lofty ideals; practising, without a thought of reward, the very gospel of universal gentleness and kindness.

There his mother, too, moved in spirit once more beside him with her angelic smile, breathing the purity of heaven. How far away it seemed from that world in which he had been living!—as far as they were from the worldlings who made it.

Curiously, when he was in New York he found himself under the allurement of Alice Lancaster. When he was in the country he found that he was in love with Lois Huntington.

It was this that mystified him and worried him. He believed—that is, he almost believed—that Alice Lancaster would marry him. His friends thought that she would. Several of them had told him so. Many of them acted on this belief. And this had something to do with his retirement.

As much as he liked Alice Lancaster, as clearly as he felt how but for one fact it would have suited that they should marry, one fact changed everything: he was not in love with her.

He was in love with a young girl who had never given him a thought except as a sort of hereditary friend. Turning from one door at which the light of happiness had shone, he had found himself caught at another from which a radiance shone that dimmed all other lights. Yet it was fast shut. At length he determined to cut the knot. He would put his fate to the test.

Two days after he formed this resolve he walked into the hotel at Brookford and registered. As he turned, he stood face to face with Mrs. Nailor. Mrs. Nailor of late had been all cordiality to him.

"Why, you dear boy, where did you come from?" she asked him in pleased surprise. "I thought you were stretched at Mrs. Wentworth's feet in the— Where has she been this summer?"

Keith's brow clouded. He remembered when Wicker-sham was her "dear boy."

"It is a position I am not in the habit of occupying—at least, toward ladies who have husbands to occupy it. You are thinking of some one else," he added coldly, wishing devoutly that Mrs. Nailor were in Halifax.

"Well, I am glad you have come here. You remember, our friendship began in the country? Yes? My husband had to go and get sick, and I got really frightened about him, and so we determined to come here, where we should be perfectly quiet. We got here last Saturday. There is not a man here."

"Isn't there?" asked Keith, wishing there were not a woman either. "How long are you going to stay?" he asked absently.

"Oh, perhaps a month. How long shall you be here?"

"Not very long," said Keith.

"I tell you who is here; that little governess of Mrs. Wentworth's she was so disagreeable to last winter. She has been very ill. I think it was the way she was treated in New York. She was in love with Ferdy Wickersham, you know? She lives here, in a lovely old place just outside of town, with her old aunt or cousin. I had no idea she had such a nice old home. We saw her yesterday. We met her on the street."

"I remember her; I shall go and see her," said Keith, recalling Mrs. Nailor's speech at Mrs. Wickersham's dinner, and Lois's revenge.

"I tell you what we will do. She invited us to call, and we will go together," said Mrs. Nailor.

Keith paused a moment in reflection, and then said casually:

"When are you going?"

"Oh, this afternoon."

"Very well; I will go."

Mrs. Nailor drove Keith out to The Lawns that afternoon.

In a little while Miss Huntington came in. Keith observed that she was dressed as she had been that evening at dinner, in white, but he did not dream that it was the result of thought. He did not know with what care every touch had been made to reproduce just what he had praised, or with what sparkling eyes she had surveyed the slim, dainty figure in the old cheval-glass. She greeted Mrs. Nailor civilly and Keith warmly.

"I am very glad to see you. What in the world brought you here to this out-of-the-way place?" she said, turning to the latter and giving him her cool, soft hand, and looking up at him with unfeigned pleasure, a softer and deeper glow coming into her cheek as she gazed into his eyes.

"A sudden fit of insanity," said Keith, taking in the sweet, girlish figure in his glance. "I wanted to see some roses that I knew bloomed in an old garden about here."

"He, perhaps, thought that, as Brookford is growing so fashionable now, he might find a mutual friend of ours here?" Mrs. Nailor said.

"As whom, for instance?" queried Keith, unwilling to commit himself.

"You know, Alice Lancaster has been talking of coming here? Now, don't pretend that you don't know. Whom does every one say you are—all in pursuit of?"

"I am sure I do not know," said Keith, calmly. "I suppose that you are referring to Mrs. Lancaster, but I happened to know that she was not here. No; I came to see Miss Huntington." His face wore an expression of amusement.

Mrs. Nailor made some smiling reply. She did not see the expression in Keith's eyes as they, for a second, caught Lois's glance.

Just then Miss Abigail came in. She had grown whiter since Keith had seen her last, and looked older. She greeted Mrs. Nailor graciously, and Keith cordially. Miss Lois, for some reason of her own, was plying Mrs. Nailor with questions, and Keith fell to talking with Miss Abigail, though his eyes were on Lois most of the time.

The old lady was watching her too, and the girl, under

the influence of the earnest gaze, glanced around and, catching her aunt's eye upon her, flashed her a little answering smile full of affection and tenderness, and then went on listening intently to Mrs. Nailor; though, had Keith read aright the color rising in her cheeks, he might have guessed that she was giving at least half her attention to his side of the room, where Miss Abigail was talking of her. Keith, however, was just then much interested in Miss Abigail's account of Dr. Locaman, who, it seemed, was more attentive to Lois than ever.

"I don't know what she will do," she said. "I suppose she will decide soon. It is an affair of long standing."

Keith's throat had grown dry.

"I had hoped that my cousin Norman might prove a protector for her; but his wife is not a good person. I was mad to let her go there. But she would go. She thought she could be of some service. But that woman is such a fool!"

"Oh, she is not a bad woman," interrupted Keith.

"I do not know how bad she is," said Miss Abigail. "She is a fool. No good woman would ever have allowed such an intimacy as she allowed to come between her and her husband; and none but a fool would have permitted a man to make her his dupe. She did not even have the excuse of a temptation; for she is as cold as a tombstone."

"I assure you that you are mistaken," defended Keith. "I know her, and I believe that she has far more depth than you give her credit for—"

"I give her credit for none," said Miss Abigail, decisively. "You men are all alike. You think a woman with a pretty face who does not talk much is deep, when she is only dull. On my word, I think it is almost worse to bring about such a scandal without cause than to give a real cause for it. In the latter case there is at least the time-worn excuse of woman's frailty."

Keith laughed.

"They are all so stupid," asserted Miss Abigail, fiercely. "They are giving up their privileges to be—

what? I blushed for my sex when I was there. They are beginning to mistake civility for servility. I found a plenty of old ladies tottering on the edge of the grave, like myself, and I found a number of ladies in the shops and in the churches; but in that set that you go with—! They all want to be 'women'; next thing they'll want to be like men. I sha'n't be surprised to see them come to wearing men's clothes and drinking whiskey and smoking tobacco—the little fools! As if they thought that a woman who has to curl her hair and spend a half-hour over her dress to look decent could ever be on a level with a man who can handle a trunk or drive a wagon or add up a column of figures, and can wash his face and hands and put on a clean collar and look like—a gentleman!"

"Oh, not so bad as that," said Keith.

"Yes; there is no limit to their folly. I know them. I am one myself."

"But you do not want to be a man?"

"No, not now. I am too old and dependent. But I'll let you into a secret. I am secretly envious of them. I'd like to be able to put them down under my heel and make them—squeal."

Mrs. Nailor turned and spoke to the old lady. She was evidently about to take her leave. Keith moved over, and for the first time addressed Miss Huntington.

"I want you to show me about these grounds," he said, speaking so that both ladies could hear him. He rose, and both walked out of the parlor. When Mrs. Nailor came out, Keith and his guide were nowhere to be found, so she had to wait; but a half-hour afterwards he and Miss Huntington came back from the stables.

As they drove out of the grounds they passed a good-looking young fellow just going in. Keith recognized Dr. Locaman.

"That is the young man who is so attentive to your young friend," said Mrs. Nailor; "Dr. Locaman. He saved her life and now is going to marry her."

It gave Keith a pang.

"I know him. He did not save her life. If anybody did that, it was an old country doctor, Dr. Balsam."

"That old man! I thought he was dead years ago."

"Well, he is not. He is very much alive."

A few evenings later Keith found Mrs. Lancaster in the hotel. He had just arrived from The Lawns when Mrs. Lancaster came down to dinner. Her greeting was perfect. Even Mrs. Nailor was mystified. She had never looked handsomer. Her black gown fitted perfectly her trim figure, and a single red rose, half-blown, caught in her bodice was her only ornament. She possessed the gift of simplicity. She was a beautiful walker, and as she moved slowly down the long dining-room as smoothly as a piece of perfect machinery, every eye was upon her. She knew that she was being generally observed, and the color deepened in her cheeks and added the charm of freshness to her beauty.

"By Jove! what a stunning woman!" exclaimed a man at a table near by to his wife.

"It is not difficult to be 'a stunning woman' in a Worth gown, my dear," she said sweetly. "May I trouble you for the Worcestershire?"

Keith's attitude toward Mrs. Lancaster puzzled even so old a veteran as Mrs. Nailor.

Mrs. Nailor was an adept in the art of inquisition. To know about her friends' affairs was one of the objects of her life, and it was not only the general facts that she insisted on knowing: she proposed to be acquainted with their deepest secrets and the smallest particulars. She knew Alice Lancaster's views, or believed she did; but she had never ventured to speak on the subject to Gordon Keith. In fact, she stood in awe of Keith, and now he had mystified her by his action. Finally, she could stand it no longer, and so next evening she opened fire on Keith. Having screwed her courage to the sticking-point, she attacked boldly. She caught him on the verandah, smoking alone, and watching him closely to catch the effect of her attack, said suddenly :

"I want to ask you a question : are you in love with Alice Lancaster?"

Keith turned slowly and looked at her, looked at her so long that she began to blush.

"Don't you think, if I am, I had better inform her first?" he said quietly.

Mrs. Nailor was staggered ; but she was in for it, and she had to fight her way through. "I was scared to death, my dear," she said when she repeated this part of the conversation, "for I never know just how he is going to take anything ; but he was so quiet, I went on."

"Well, yes, I think you had," she said ; "Alice can take care of herself ; but I tell you that you have no right to be carrying on with that sweet, innocent young girl here. You know what people say of you?"

"No ; I do not," said Keith. "I was not aware that I was of sufficient importance here for people to say anything, except perhaps a few persons who know me."

"They say you have come here to see Miss Huntington?"

"Do they?" asked Keith, so carelessly that Mrs. Nailor was just thinking that she must be mistaken, when he added : "Well, will you ask people if they ever heard what Andrew Jackson said to Mr. Buchanan once when he told him it was time to go and dress to receive Lady Wellesley?"

"What did he say?" asked Mrs. Nailor.

"He said he knew a man in Tennessee who had made a fortune by attending to his own business."

Having failed with Keith, Mrs. Nailor, the next afternoon, called on Miss Huntington. Lois was in, and her aunt was not well ; so Mrs. Nailor had a fair field for her research. She decided to test the young girl, and she selected the only mode which could have been successful with herself. She proposed a surprise. She spoke of Keith and noticed the increased interest with which the girl listened. This was promising.

"By the way," she said, "you know the report is that Mr. Keith has at last really surrendered?"

"Has he? I am so glad. If ever a man deserved happiness it is he. Who is it?"

The entire absence of self-consciousness in Lois's expression and voice surprised Mrs. Nailor.

"Mrs. Lancaster," she said, watching for the effect of her answer. "Of course, you know he has always been in love with her?"

The girl's expression of unfeigned admiration of Mrs. Lancaster gave Mrs. Nailor another surprise. She decided that she had been mistaken in suspecting her of caring for Keith.

"He has evidently not proposed yet. If she were a little older I should be certain of it," she said to herself as she drove away; "but these girls are so secretive one can never tell about them. Even I could not look as innocent as that to save my life if I were interested."

That evening Keith called at The Lawns. He did not take with him a placid spirit. Mrs. Nailor's shaft had gone home, and it rankled. He tried to assure himself that what people were thinking had nothing to do with him. But suppose Miss Abigail took this view of the matter? He determined to ascertain. One solution of the difficulty lay plain before him: he could go away. Another presented itself, but it was preposterous. Of all the women he knew Lois Huntington was the least affected by him in the way that flatters a man. She liked him, he knew; but if he could read women at all, and he thought he could, she liked him only as a friend, and had not a particle of sentiment about him. He was easy, then, as to the point Mrs. Nailor had raised; but had he the right to subject Lois to gossip? This was the main thing that troubled him. He was half angry with himself that it kept rising in his mind. He determined to find out what her aunt thought of it, and decided that he could let that direct his course. This salved his conscience. Once or twice the question dimly presented itself whether it were possible that Lois could care for him. He banished it resolutely.

When he reached The Lawns, he found that Miss Abigail was sick, so the virtuous plan he had formed fell through. He was trying to fancy himself sorry ; but when Lois came out on the verandah in a dainty blue gown which fell softly about her girlish figure, and seated herself with uncon- scious grace in the easy-chair he pushed up for her, he knew that he was glad to have her all to himself. They fell to talking about her aunt.

"I am dreadfully uneasy about her," the girl said. "Once or twice of late she has had something like fainting spells, and the last one was very alarming. You don't know what she has been to me." She looked up at him with a silent appeal for sympathy which made his heart beat. "She is the only mother I ever knew, and she is all I have in the world." Her voice faltered, and she turned away her head. A tear stole down her cheek and dropped in her lap. "I am so glad you like each other. I hear you are engaged," she said suddenly.

He was startled ; it chimed in so with the thought in his mind at the moment.

"No, I am not ; but I would like to be."

He came near saying a great deal more ; but the girl's eyes were fixed on him so innocently that he for a moment hesitated. He felt it would be folly, if not sacrilege, to go further.

Just then there was a step on the walk, and the young man Keith had seen, Dr. Locaman, came up the steps. He was a handsome man, stout, well dressed, and well satisfied.

Keith could have consigned him and all his class to a distant and torrid clime.

He came up the steps cheerily and began talking at once. He was so glad to see Keith, and had he heard lately from Dr. Balsam?—"such a fine type of the old country doctor," etc.

No, Keith said ; he had not heard lately. His manner

had stiffened at the young man's condescension, and he rose to go.

He said casually to Lois, as he shook hands, "How did you hear the piece of news you mentioned?"

"Mrs. Nailor told me. You must tell me all about it."

"I will sometime."

"I hope you will be very happy," she said earnestly; "you deserve to be." Her eyes were very soft.

"No, I do not," said Keith, almost angrily. "I am not at all what you suppose me to be."

"I will not allow you to say such things of yourself," she said, smiling. "I will not stand my friends being abused even by themselves."

Keith felt his courage waning. Her beauty, her sincerity, her tenderness, her innocence, her sweetness thrilled him. He turned back to her abruptly.

"I hope you will always think that of me," he said earnestly. "I promise to try to deserve it. Good-by."

"Good-by. Don't forget me." She held out her hand.

Keith took it and held it for a second.

"Never," he said, looking her straight in the eyes. "Good-by"; and with a muttered good-by to Dr. Locaman, who stood with wide-open eyes gazing at him, he turned and went down the steps.

"I don't like that man," said the young Doctor. This speech sealed his fate.

"Don't you? I do," said Lois, half dreamily. Her thoughts were far from the young physician at that moment; and when they returned to him, she knew that she would never marry him. A half-hour later, he knew it.

The next morning Lois received a note from Keith, saying he had left for his home.

When he bade Mrs. Lancaster good-by that evening, she looked as if she were really sorry that he was going. She walked with him down the verandah toward where his carriage awaited him, and Keith thought she had never looked sweeter.

He had never had a confidante,—at least, since he was a college boy,—and a little of the old feeling came to him. He lingered a little; but just then Mrs. Nailor came out of the door near him. For a moment Keith could almost have fancied he was back on the verandah at Gates's. Her mousing around had turned back the dial a dozen years.

Just what brought it about, perhaps, no one of the participants in the little drama could have told; but from this time the relations between the two ladies whom Keith left at the hotel that Summer night somehow changed. Not outwardly, for they still sat and talked together; but they were both conscious of a difference. They rather fenced with each other after that. Mrs. Nailor set it down to a simple cause. Mrs. Lancaster was in love with Gordon Keith, and he had not addressed her. Of this she was satisfied. Yet she was a little mystified. Mrs. Lancaster hardly defined the reason to herself. She simply shut up on the side toward Mrs. Nailor, and barred her out. A strange thing was that she and Miss Huntington became great friends. They took to riding together, walking together, and seeing a great deal of each other, the elder lady spending much of her time up at Miss Huntington's home, among the shrubbery and flowers of the old place. It was a mystification to Mrs. Nailor, who frankly confessed that she could only account for it on the ground that Mrs. Lancaster wanted to find out how far matters had gone between Keith and Miss Huntington. "That girl is a sly minx," she said. "These governesses learn to be deceptive. I would not have her in my house."

If there was a more dissatisfied mortal in the world than Gordon Keith that Autumn Keith did not know him. He worked hard, but it did not ease his mind. He tried retiring to his old home, as he had done in the Summer; but it was even worse than it had been then. Rumor came to him that Lois Huntington was engaged. It came through Mrs. Nailor, and he could not verify it; but, at least, she was lost to him. He cursed himself for a fool.

The picture of Mrs. Lancaster began to come to him oftener and oftener as she had appeared to him that night on the verandah—handsome, dignified, serene, sympathetic. Why should he not seek release by this way? He had always admired, liked her. He felt her sympathy; he recognized her charm; he appreciated her—yes, her advantage. Curse it! that was the trouble. If he were only in love with her! If she were not so manifestly advantageous, then he might think his feeling was more than friendship; for she was everything that he admired.

He was just in this frame of mind when a letter came from Rhodes, who had come home soon after Keith's visit to him. He had not been very well, and they had decided to take a yacht-cruise in Southern waters, and would he not come along? He could join them at either Hampton Roads or Savannah, and they were going to run over to the Bermudas.

Keith telegraphed that he would join them, and two days later turned his face to the South. Twenty-four hours afterwards he was stepping up the gangway and being welcomed by as gay a group as ever fluttered handkerchiefs to cheer a friend. Among them the first object that had caught his eye as he rowed out was the straight, lithe figure of Mrs. Lancaster. A man is always ready to think Providence interferes specially in his case, provided the interpretation accords with his own views, and this looked to Keith very much as if it were Providence. For one thing, it saved him the trouble of thinking further of a matter which, the more he thought of it, the more he was perplexed. She came forward with the others, and welcomed him with her old frank, cordial grasp of the hand and gracious air. When he was comfortably settled, he felt a distinct self-content that he had decided to come.

A yacht-cruise is dependent on three things: the yacht itself, the company on board, and the weather. Keith had no cause to complain of any of these.

The "Virginia Dare" was a beautiful boat, and the

weather was perfect—just the weather for a cruise in Southern waters. The company were all friends of Keith; and Keith found himself sailing in Summer seas, with Summer airs breathing about him. Keith was at his best. He was richly tanned by exposure, and as hard as a nail from work in the open air. Command of men had given him that calm assurance which is the mark of the captain. Ambition—ambition to be, not merely to possess—was once more calling to him with her inspiring voice, and as he hearkened his face grew more and more distinguished. Providence, indeed, or Grinnell Rhodes was working his way, and it seemed to him—he admitted it with a pang of contempt for himself at the admission—that Mrs. Lancaster was at least acquiescent in their hands. Morning after morning they sat together in the shadow of the sail, and evening after evening together watched the moon with an ever-rounder golden circle steal up the cloudless sky. Keith was pleased to find how much interested he was becoming. Each day he admired her more and more; and each day he found her sweeter than she had been before. Once or twice she spoke to him of Lois Huntington, but each time she mentioned her, Keith turned the subject. She said that they had expected to have her join them; but she could not leave her aunt.

"I hear she is engaged," said Keith.

"Yes, I heard that. I do not believe it. Whom did you hear it from?"

"Mrs. Nailor."

"So did I."

CHAPTER XXXVI

THE OLD IDEAL

ONE evening they sat on deck. Alice Lancaster had never appeared so sweet. It happened that Mrs. Rhodes had a headache and was down below, and Rhodes declared that he had some writing to do. So Mrs. Lancaster and Keith had the deck to themselves.

They had been sailing for weeks among emerald isles and through waters as blue as heaven. Even the "still-vex'd Bermoothes" had lent them their gentlest airs.

They had left the Indies and were now approaching the American shore. Their cruise was almost at an end, and possibly a little sadness had crept over them both. As she had learned more and more of his life and more and more of his character, she had found herself ready to give up everything for him if he only gave her what she craved. But one thing had made itself plain to Alice: Keith was not in love with her as she knew he could be in love. If he were in love, it was with an ideal. And her woman's intuition told her that she was not that ideal.

This evening she was unusually pensive. She had never looked lovelier or been more gracious and charming, and as Keith thought of the past and of the future,—the long past in which they had been friends, the long future in which he would live alone,—his thought took the form of resolve. Why should they not always be together? She knew that he liked her, so he had not much to do to go further. The moon was just above the horizon, making a broad golden pathway to them. The soft lapping of the waves against the boat seemed to be a lullaby suited to the peacefulness of the scene; and the lovely form before him, clad in soft raiment that set it off, the fair face and gentle voice, appeared to fill everything with graciousness. Keith had more than once, in the past few weeks, considered how he would bring the subject up, and what he would say if he ever addressed her. He did not, however, go about it in the way he had planned. It seemed to him to come up spontaneously. Under the spell of the Summer night they had drifted into talking of old times, and they both softened as their memory went back to their youth and their friendship that had begun among the Southern woods and had lasted so many years.

She had spoken of the influence his opinions had had with her.

"Do you know," he said presently, "I think you have exerted more influence on my life than any one else I ever knew after I grew up?"

She smiled, and her face was softer than usual.

"I should be very glad to think that, for I think there are few men who set out in life with such ideals as you had and afterwards realize them."

Keith thought of his father and of how steadily that old man had held to his ideals through everything. "I have not realized them," he said firmly. "I fear I have lost most of them. I set out in life with high ideals, which I got from my father; but, somehow, I seem to have changed them."

She shook her head, with a pleasant light in her eyes.

"I do not think you have. Do you remember what you said to me once about your ideal?"

He turned and faced her. There was an expression of such softness and such sweetness in her face that a kind of anticipatory happiness fell on him.

"Yes; and I have always been in love with that ideal," he said gravely.

She said gently: "Yes, I knew it."

"Did you?" asked Keith, in some surprise. "I scarcely knew it myself, though I believe I have been for some time."

"Yes?" she said. "I knew that too."

Keith bent over her and took both her hands in his. "I love and want love in return—more than I can ever tell you."

A change came over her face, and she drew in her breath suddenly, glanced at him for a second, and then looked away, her eyes resting at last on the distance where a ship lay, her sails hanging idly in the dim haze. It might have been a dream-ship. At Keith's words a picture came to her out of the past. A young man was seated on the ground, with a fresh-budding bush behind him. Spring was all about them. He was young and slender and sun-browned, with deep-burning eyes and close-drawn mouth, with the future before him; whatever befell, with the hope and the courage to conquer. He had conquered, as he then said he would to the young girl seated beside him.

"When I love," he was saying, "she must fill full the measure of my dreams. She must uplift me. She must have beauty and sweetness; she must choose the truth as that bird chooses the flowers. And to such an one I will give worship without end."

Years after, she had come across the phrase again in a poem. And at the words the same picture had come to her, and a sudden hunger for love, for such love,—the love she had missed in life,—had seized her. But it was then too late. She had taken in its place respect and companionship, a great establishment and social prominence.

For a moment her mother, sitting calm and calculating in the little room at Ridgely, foretelling her future and teaching, with commercial exactness, the advantages of such a union, flashed before her; and then once more for a moment came the heart-hunger for what she had missed.

Why should she not take the gift thus held out to her? She liked him and he liked her. She trusted him. It was the best chance of happiness she would ever have.

Besides, she could help him. He had powers, and she could give him the opportunity to develop them. Love would come. Who could tell? Perhaps, the other happiness might yet be hers. Why should she throw it away?

Would not life bring the old dream yet? Could it bring it? Here was this man whom she had known all her life, who filled almost the measure of her old dream, at her feet again. But was this love? Was this the "worship without end"? As her heart asked the question, and she lifted her eyes to his face, the answer came with it: No. He was too cool, too calm. This was but friendship and respect, that same "safe foundation" she had tried. This might do for some, but not for him. She had seen him, and she knew what he could feel. She had caught a glimpse of him that evening when Ferdy Wickersham was so attentive to the little Huntington girl. She had seen him that night in the theatre when the fire occurred. He was in love; but it was with Lois Huntington, and happiness might yet be his.

The next moment Alice's better nature reasserted itself. The picture of the young girl sitting with her serious face and her trustful eyes came back to her. Lois, moved by her sympathy and friendship, had given her a glimpse of her true heart, which she knew she would have died before she would have shown another. She had confided in her absolutely. She heard the tones of her voice:

"Why, Mrs. Lancaster, I dream of him. He seems to me so real, so true. For such a man I could—I could worship him!" Then came the sudden lifting of the veil; the straight, confiding, appealing glance, the opening of the soul, and the rush to her knees as she appealed for him.

It all passed through Mrs. Lancaster's mind as she looked far away over the slumbering sea, while Keith waited for her answer.

When she glanced up at Keith he was leaning over the rail, looking far away, his face calm and serious. What was he thinking of? Certainly not of her.

"No, you are not—not in love with me," she said firmly.

Keith started, and looked down on her with a changed expression.

She raised her hand with a gesture of protest, rose and stood beside him, facing him frankly.

"You are in love, but not with me."

Keith took her hand. She did not take it from him; indeed, she caught his hand with a firm clasp.

"Oh, no; you are not," she smiled. "I have had men in love with me—"

"You have had one, I know—" he began.

"Yes, once, a long time ago—and I know the difference. I told you once that I was not what you thought me."

"And I told you—" began Keith; but she did not pause.

"I am still less so now. I am not in the least what you think me—or you are not what I think you."

"You are just what I think you," began Keith. "You are the most charming woman in the world—you are my—" He hesitated as she looked straight into his eyes and shook her head.

"What? No, I am not. I am a worldly, world-worn woman. Oh, yes, I am," as dissent spoke in his face. "I know the world and am a part of it and depend upon it. Yes, I am. I am not so far gone that I cannot recognize and admire what is better, higher, and nobler than the world of which I speak; but I am bound to the wheel— Is not that the illustration you wrote me once? I thought then it was absurd. I know now how true it is."

"I do not think you are," declared Keith. "If you were, I would claim the right to release you—to save you for—yourself and—"

She shook her head.

"No, no. I have become accustomed to my Sybarite's couch of which you used to tell me. Would you be willing to give up all you have striven for and won—your life—the honors you have won and hope to win?"

"They are nothing—those I have won! Those I hope

to win, I would win for us both. You should help me. They would be for you, Alice." His eyes were deep in hers.

She fetched a long sigh.

"No, no; once, perhaps, I might have—but now it is too late. I chose my path and must follow it. You would not like to give up all you—hope for—and become like—some we know?"

"God forbid!"

"And I say, 'Amen.' And if you would, I would not be willing to have you do it. You are too much to me—I honor you too much," she corrected quickly, as she caught the expression in his face. "I could not let you sink into a—society man—like—some of those I sit next to and dance with and drive with and—enjoy and despise. Do I not know that if you loved me you would have convinced me of it in a moment? You have not convinced me. You are in love,—as you said just now,—but not with me. You are in love with Lois Huntington."

Keith almost staggered. It was so direct and so exactly what his thought had been just now. But he said:

"Oh, nonsense! Lois Huntington considers me old enough to be her grandfather. Why, she—she is engaged to or in love with Dr. Locaman."

"She is not," said Mrs. Lancaster, firmly, "and she never will be. If you go about it right she will marry you." She added calmly: "I hope she will, with all my heart."

"Marry me! Lois Huntington! Why—"

"She considers me her grandmother, perhaps; but not you her grandfather. She thinks you are much too young for me. She thinks you are the most wonderful and the best and most charming man in the world."

"Oh, nonsense!"

"I do not know where she got such an idea—unless you told her so yourself," she said, with a smile.

"I would like her to think it," said Keith, smiling; "but I have studiously avoided divulging myself in my real and fatal character."

"Then she must have got it from the only other person who knows you in your true character."

"And that is—?"

She looked into his eyes with so amused and so friendly a light in her own that Keith lifted her hand to his lips.

"I do not deserve such friendship."

"Yes, you do; you taught it to me."

He sat back in his chair, trying to think. But all he could think of was how immeasurably he was below both these women.

"Will you forgive me?" he said suddenly, almost miserably. He meant to say more, but she rose, and at the moment he heard a step behind him. He thought her hand touched his head for a second, and that he heard her answer, "Yes"; but he was not sure, for just then Mrs. Rhodes spoke to them, and they all three had to pretend that they thought nothing unusual had been going on.

They received their mail next day, and were all busy reading letters, when Mrs. Rhodes gave an exclamation of surprise.

"Oh, just hear this! Little Miss Huntington's old aunt is dead."

There was an exclamation from every one.

"Yes," she went on reading, with a faint little conventional tone of sympathy in her voice; "she died ten days ago—very suddenly, of heart-disease."

"Oh, poor little Lois! I am so sorry for her!" It was Alice Lancaster's voice.

But Keith did not hear any more. His heart was aching, and he was back among the shrubbery of The Lawns. All that he knew was that Rhodes and Mrs. Rhodes were expressing sympathy, and that Mrs. Lancaster, who had not said a word after the first exclamation, excused herself and left the saloon. Keith made up his mind promptly. He went up on deck. Mrs. Lancaster was sitting alone far aft in the shadow. Her back was toward him, and her hand was to her eyes. He went up to her. She did not look up; but Keith felt that she knew it was he.

"You must go to her," she said.

"Yes," said Keith. "I shall. I wish you would come."

"Oh, I wish I could! Poor little thing!" she sighed.

Two days after that Keith walked into the hotel at Brookford. The clerk recognized him as he appeared, and greeted him cordially. Something in Keith's look or manner, perhaps, recalled his former association with the family at The Lawns, for, as Keith signed his name, he said:

"Sad thing, that, up on the hill."

"What?" said Keith, absently.

"The old lady's death and the breaking up of the old place," he said.

"Oh!—yes, it is," said Keith; and then, thinking that he could learn if Miss Huntington were there without appearing to do so, except casually, he said:

"Who is there now?"

"There is not any one there at all, I believe."

Keith ordered a room, and a half-hour later went out.

Instead of taking a carriage, he walked. There had been a change in the weather. The snow covered everything, and the grounds looked wintry and deserted. The gate was unlocked, but had not been opened lately, and Keith had hard work to open it wide enough to let himself through. He tramped along through the snow, and turning the curve in the road, was in front of the house. It was shut up. Every shutter was closed, as well as the door, and a sudden chill struck him. Still he went on; climbed the wide, unswept steps, crossed the portico, and rang the bell, and finally knocked. The sound made him start. How lonesome it seemed! He knocked again, but no one came. Only the snowbirds on the portico stopped and looked at him curiously. Finally, he thought he heard some one in the snow. He turned as a man came around the house. It was the old coachman and factotum. He seemed glad enough to see Keith, and Keith was, at least, glad to see him.

"It's a bad business, it is, Mr. Kathe," he said sadly.

"Yes, it is, John. Where is Miss Huntington?"

"Gone, sir," said John, with surprise in his voice that Keith should not know.

"Gone where?"

"An' that no one knows," said John.

"What! What do you mean?"

"Just that, sir," said the old fellow. "She went away two days after the funeral, an' not a worrd of her since."

"But she's at some relative's?" said Keith, seeking information at the same time he gave it.

"No, sir; not a relative in the world she has, except Mr. Wentworth in New York, and she has not been there."

Keith learned, in the conversation which followed, that Miss Abigail had died very suddenly, and that two days after the funeral Miss Lois had had the house shut up, and taking only a small trunk, had left by train for New York. They had expected to hear from her, though she had said they would not do so for some time; and when no letter had come they had sent to New York, but had failed to find her. This all seemed natural enough. Lois was abundantly able to take care of herself, and, no doubt, desired for the present to be in some place of retirement. Keith decided, therefore, that he would simply go to the city and ascertain where she was. He thought of going to see Dr. Locaman, but something restrained him. The snow was deep, and he was anxious to find Lois; so he went straight down to the city that evening. The next day he discovered that it was not quite so easy to find one who wished to be lost. Norman knew nothing of her.

Norman and his wife were now living with old Mrs. Wentworth, and they had all invited her to come to them; but she had declined. Keith was much disturbed.

Lois, however, was nearer than Keith dreamed.

Her aunt's death had stricken Lois deeply. She could not bear to go to New York. It stood to her only for hardness and isolation.

Just then a letter came from Dr. Balsam. She must
come to him, he said. He was sick, or he would come for
her. An impulse seized her to go to him. She would
go back to the scenes of her childhood: the memories
of her father drew her; the memory also of her aunt in
some way urged her. Dr. Balsam appeared just then
nearer to her than any one else. She could help him. It
seemed a haven of refuge to her.

Twenty-four hours later the old Doctor was sitting in his
room. He looked worn and old and dispirited. The death
of an old friend had left a void in his life.

There was a light step outside and a rap at the door.

"It's the servant," thought the Doctor, and called somewhat gruffly, "Come in."

When the door opened it was not the servant. For a
moment the old man scarcely took in who it was. She
seemed to be almost a vision. He had never thought of
Lois in black. She was so like a girl he had known long,
long ago.

Then she ran forward, and as the old man rose to his feet
she threw her arms about his neck, and the world suddenly
changed for him—changed as much as if it had been new-
created.

From New York Keith went down to the old plantation
to see his father. The old gentleman was renewing his
youth among his books. He was much interested in Keith's
account of his yachting-trip. While there Keith got word
of important business which required his presence in New
Leeds immediately. Ferdy Wickersham had returned,
and had brought suit against his company, claiming title to
all the lands they had bought from Adam Rawson.

On his arrival at New Leeds, Keith learned that Wickersham had been there just long enough to institute his suit,
the papers in which had been already prepared before he
came. There was much excitement in the place. Wickersham had boasted that he had made a great deal of money
in South America.

"He claims now," said Keith's informant, Captain Turley, "that he owns all of Squire Rawson's lands. He says you knew it was all his when you sold it to them Englishmen, and that Mr. Rhodes, the president of the company, knew it was his, and he has been defrauded."

"Well, we will see about that," said Keith, grimly.

"That's what old Squire Rawson said. The old man came up as soon as he heard he was here; but Wickersham didn't stay but one night. He had lighted out."

"What did the squire come for?" inquired Keith, moved by his old friend's expression.

"He said he came to kill him. And he'd have done it. If Wickersham's got any friends they'd better keep him out of his way." His face testified his earnestness.

Keith had a curious feeling. Wickersham's return meant that he was desperate. In some way, too, Keith felt that Lois Huntington was concerned in his movements. He was glad to think that she was abroad.

But Lois was being drawn again into his life in a way that he little knew.

In the seclusion and quietude of Ridgely at that season, Lois soon felt as if she had reached, at last, a safe harbor. The care of the old Doctor gave her employment, and her mind, after a while, began to recover its healthy tone. She knew that the happiness of which she had once dreamed would never be hers; but she was sustained by the reflection that she had tried to do her duty: she had sacrificed herself for others. She spent her time trying to help those about her. She had made friends with Squire Rawson, and the old man found much comfort in talking to her of Phrony.

Sometimes, in the afternoon, when she was lonely, she climbed the hill and looked after the little plot in which lay the grave of her father. She remembered her mother but vaguely: as a beautiful vision, blurred by the years; but her father was clear in her memory. His smile, his cheeriness, his devotion to her remained with her. And the memory of him who had been her friend in her childhood came to her sometimes, saddening her, till she would arouse herself and by an effort banish him from her thoughts.

Often when she went up to the cemetery she would see others there : women in black, with a fresher sorrow than hers ; and sometimes the squire, who was beginning now to grow feeble and shaky with age, would be sitting on a bench among the shrubbery beside a grave on which he had placed flowers. The grave was Phrony's. Once he spoke to her of Wickersham. He had brought a suit against the old man, claiming that he had a title to all of the latter's property. The old fellow was greatly stirred up by it. He denounced him furiously.

"He has robbed me of her," he said. "Let him beware. If he ever comes across my path I shall kill him."

So the Winter passed, and Spring was beginning to come. Its harbingers, in their livery of red and green, were already showing on the hillsides. The redbud was burning on the Southern slopes ; the turf was springing, fresh and green ; dandelions were dappling the grass like golden coins sown by a prodigal ; violets were beginning to peep from the shelter of leaves caught along the fence-rows ; and some favored peach-trees were blushing into pink.

For some reason the season made Lois sad. Was it that it was Nature's season for mating ; the season for Youth to burst its restraining bonds and blossom into love? She tried to fight the feeling ; but it clung to her. Dr. Balsam, watching her with quickened eyes, grew graver, and prescribed a tonic. Once he had spoken to her of Keith, and she had told him that he was to marry Mrs. Lancaster. But the old man had made a discovery. And he never spoke to her of him again.

Lois, to her surprise and indignation, received one morning a letter from Wickersham asking her to make an appointment with him on a matter of mutual interest. He wished, he said, to make friends with old Mr. Rawson and she could help him. He mentioned Keith and casually spoke of his engagement. She took no notice of this letter; but one afternoon she was lonelier than usual, and she went up the hill to her father's grave. Adam Rawson's horse was tied to the fence, and across the lots she saw him among the rose-bushes at Phrony's grave. She sat down and gave herself up to reflection. Gradually the whole of her life in New York passed before her: its unhappiness; its promise of joy for a moment; and then the shutting of it out, as if the windows of her soul had been closed.

She heard the gate click, and presently heard a step behind her. As it approached she turned and faced Ferdy Wickersham. She seemed to be almost in a dream. He had aged somewhat, and his dark face had hardened. Otherwise he had not changed. He was still very handsome. She felt as if a chill blast had struck her. She caught his eye on her, and knew that he had recognized her. As he came up the path toward her, she rose and moved away; but he cut across to intercept her, and she heard him speak her name.

She took no notice, but walked on.

"Miss Huntington." He stepped in front of her.

Her head went up, and she looked him in the eyes with a scorn in hers that stung him. "Move, if you please."

His face flushed, then paled again.

"I heard you were here, and I have come to see you, to talk with you," he began. "I wish to be friends with you."

She waved him aside.

"Let me pass, if you please."

"Not until you have heard what I have to say. You have done me a great injustice; but I put that by. I have been robbed by persons you know, persons who are no friends of yours, whom I understand you have influence with, and you can help to right matters. It will be worth your while to do it."

She attempted to pass around him; but he stepped before her.

"You might as well listen; for I have come here to talk

541

to you, and I mean to do it. I can show you how important it is for you to aid me—to advise your friends to settle. Now, will you listen?"

"No." She looked him straight in the eyes.

"Oh, I guess you will," he sneered. "It concerns your friend, Mr. Keith, whom you thought so much of. Your friend Keith has placed himself in a very equivocal position. I will have him behind bars before I am done. Wait until I have shown that when he got all that money from the English people he knew that that land was mine, and that he had run the lines falsely on which he got the money."

"Let me pass," said Lois. With her head held high she started again to walk by him; but he seized her by the wrist.

"This is not Central Park. You shall hear me."

"Let me go, Mr. Wickersham," she said imperiously. But he held her firmly.

At that moment she heard an oath behind her, and a voice exclaimed:

"It is you, at last! And still troubling women!"

Wickersham's countenance suddenly changed. He released her wrist and fell back a step, his face blanching. The next second, as she turned quickly, old Adam Rawson's bulky figure was before her. He was hurrying toward her: the very apotheosis of wrath. His face was purple; his eyes blazed; his massive form was erect, and quivering with fury. His heavy stick was gripped in his left hand, and with the other he was drawing a pistol from his pocket.

"I have waited for you, you dog, and you have come at last!" he cried.

Wickersham, falling back before his advance, was trying, as Lois looked, to get out a pistol. His face was as white as death. Lois had no time for thought. It was simply instinct. Old Rawson's pistol was already levelled. With a cry she threw herself between them; but it was too late.

She was only conscious of a roar and blinding smoke in her eyes and of something like a hot iron at her side; then, as she sank down, of Squire Rawson's stepping over her. Her sacrifice was in vain, for the old man was not to be turned from his revenge. As he had sworn, so he performed. And the next moment Wickersham, with two bullets in his body, had paid to him his long-piled-up debt.

When Lois came to, she was in bed, and Dr. Balsam was leaning over her with a white, set face.

"I am all right," she said, with a faint smile. "Was he hurt?"

"Don't talk now," said the Doctor, quietly. "Thank God, you are not hurt much."

Keith was sitting in his office in New Leeds alone that afternoon. He had just received a telegram from Dave Dennison that Wickersham had left New York. Dennison had learned that he was going to Ridgely to try to make up with old Rawson. Just then the paper from Ridgely was brought in. Keith's eye fell on the head-lines of the first column, and he almost fell from his chair as he read the words:

DOUBLE TRAGEDY — FATAL SHOOTING

F. C. WICKERSHAM SHOOTS MISS LOIS HUNTINGTON AND IS KILLED BY SQUIRE RAWSON

The account of the shooting was in accordance with the heading, and was followed by the story of the Wickersham-Rawson trouble.

Keith snatched out his watch, and the next second was dashing down the street on his way to the station. A train was to start for the east in five minutes. He caught it as it ran out of the station, and swung himself up to the rear platform.

Curiously enough, in his confused thoughts of Lois Huntington and what she had meant to him was mingled the constant recollection of old Tim Gilsey and his lumbering stage running through the pass.

543

It was late in the evening when he reached Ridgely; but he hastened at once to Dr. Balsam's office. The moon was shining, and it brought back to him the evenings on the verandah at Gates's so long ago. But it seemed to him that it was Lois Huntington who had been there among the pillows; that it was Lois Huntington who had always been there in his memory. He wondered if she would be as she was then, as she lay dead. And once or twice he wondered if he could be losing his wits; then he gripped himself and cleared his mind.

In ten minutes he was in Dr. Balsam's office. The Doctor greeted him with more coldness than he had ever shown him. Keith felt his suspicion.

"Where is Lois—Miss Lois Huntington? Is she—?" He could not frame the question.

"She is doing very well."

Keith's heart gave a bound of hope. The blood surged back and forth in his veins. Life seemed to revive for him.

"Is she alive? Will she live?" he faltered.

"Yes. Who says she will not?" demanded the Doctor, testily.

"The paper—the despatch."

"No thanks to you that she does!" He faced Keith, and suddenly flamed out: "I want to tell you that I think you have acted like a damned rascal!"

Keith's jaw dropped, and he actually staggered with amazement. "What! What do you mean? I do not understand!"

"You are not a bit better than that dog that you turned her over to, who got his deserts yesterday."

"But I do not understand!" gasped Keith, white and hot.

"Then I will tell you. You led that innocent girl to believe that you were in love with her, and then when she was fool enough to believe you and let herself become— interested, you left her to run, like a little puppy, after a rich woman."

"Where did you hear this?" asked Keith, still amazed,

but recovering himself. "What have you heard? Who told you?"

"Not from her." He was blazing with wrath.

"No ; but from whom?"

"Never mind. From some one who knew the facts. It is the truth."

"But it is not the truth. I have been in love with Lois Huntington since I first met her."

"Then why in the name of heaven did you treat her so?"

"How? I did not tell her so because I heard she was in love with some one else—and engaged to him. God knows I have suffered enough over it. I would die for her." His expression left no room for doubt as to his sincerity.

The old man's face gradually relaxed, and presently something that was almost a smile came into his eyes. He held out his hand.

"I owe you an apology. You are a d—d fool!"

"Can I see her?" asked Keith.

"I don't know that you can see anything. But I could, if I were in your place. She is on the side verandah at my hospital—where Gates's tavern stood. She is not much hurt, though it was a close thing. The ball struck a button and glanced around. She is sitting up. I shall bring her home as soon as she can be moved."

Keith paused and reflected a moment, then held out his hand.

"Doctor, if I win her will you make our house your home?"

The old man's face softened, and he held out his hand again.

"You will have to come and see me sometimes."

Five minutes later Keith turned up the walk that led to the side verandah of the building that Dr. Balsam had put up for his sanatorium on the site of Gates's hotel. The moon was slowly sinking toward the western mountain-tops, flooding with soft light the valley below, and touching to silver the fleecy clouds that, shepherded by the gentle wind, wreathed the highest peaks beyond. How well Keith remembered it all : the old house with its long verandah ; the moonlight flooding it ; the white figure reclining there ; and the boy that talked of his ideal of loveliness and love. She was there now ; it seemed to him that she had been there always, and the rest was merely a dream. He walked up on the turf, but strode rapidly. He could not wait. As he mounted the steps, he took off his hat.

"Good evening." He spoke as if she must expect him.

She had not heard him before. She was reclining among pillows, and her face was turned toward the western sky. Her black dress gave him a pang. He had never thought of her in black, except as a little girl. And such she almost seemed to him now.

She turned toward him and gave a gasp.

"Mr. Keith !"

"Lois—I have come—" he began, and stopped.

She held out her hand and tried to sit up. Keith took her hand softly, as if it were a rose, and closing his firmly over it, fell on one knee beside her chair.

"Don't try to sit up," he said gently. "I went to Brookford as soon as I heard of it—" he began, and then placed his other hand on hers, covering it with his firm grasp.

"I thought you would," she said simply.

Keith lifted her hand and held it against his cheek. He was silent a moment. What should he say to her? Not only all other women, but all the rest of the world, had disappeared.

"I have come, and I shall not go away again until you go with me."

For answer she hid her face and began to cry softly. Keith knelt with her hand to his lips, murmuring his love.

"I am so glad you have come. I don't know what to do," she said presently.

"You do not have to know. I know. It is decided. I love you—I have always loved you. And no one shall ever

546

"Lois—I have come"—he began.

come between us. You are mine—mine only." He went on pouring out his soul to her.

"My old Doctor—?" she began presently, and looked up at him with eyes "like stars half-quenched in mists of silver dew."

"He agrees. We will make him live with us."

"Your father—?"

"Him, too. You shall be their daughter."

She gave him her hands.

"Well, on that condition."

The first person Keith sought to tell of his new happiness was his father. The old gentleman was sitting on the porch at Elphinstone in the sun, enjoying the physical sensation of warmth that means so much to extreme youth and extreme age. He held a copy of Virgil in his hand, but he was not reading; he was repeating passages of it by heart. They related to the quiet life. His son heard him saying softly:

> " 'O Fortunatos nimium, sua si bona norint,
>   Agricolas!' "

His mind was possibly far back in the past.

His placid face lit up with the smile that always shone there when his son appeared.

"Well, what's the news?" he asked. "I know it must be good."

"It is," smiled Keith. "I am engaged to be married."

The old gentleman's book fell to the floor.

"You don't say so! Ah, that's very good! Very good! I am glad of that; every young man ought to marry. There is no happiness like it in this world, whatever there may be in the next.

> 'Interea dulces pendent circum oscula nati.'

I will come and see you," he smiled.

"Come and see me!"

"But I am not very much at home in New York," he pursued rather wistfully; "it is too noisy for me. I am too old-fashioned for it."

"New York? But I'm not going to live in New York!" A slight shadow swept over the General's face.

"Well, you must live where she will be happiest," he said thoughtfully. "A gentleman owes that to his wife.—Do you think she will be willing to live elsewhere?"

"Who do you think it is, sir?"

"Mrs. Lancaster, isn't it?"

"Why, no; it is Lois Huntington. I am engaged to her. She has promised to marry me."

"To her!—to Lois Huntington?—my little girl!" The old gentleman rose to his feet, his face alight with absolute joy. "That is something like it! Where is she? When is it to be? I will come and live with you."

"Of course, you must. It is on that condition that she agrees to marry me," said Keith, smiling with new happiness at his pleasure.

"'In her tongue is the law of kindness,'" quoted the old gentleman. "God bless you both. 'Her price is far above rubies.'" And after a pause he added gently: "I hope your mother knows of this. I think she must: she seems so close to me to-day."